a moder...

Publishers Weekly on *A Passionate Hope*

"*A Passionate Hope* is a wonderful novel rich with historical detail about real people who suffer the heartache that comes from stepping out ahead of God, and the miracle of grace that comes when we cry out to Him."

Francine Rivers, bestselling author of *Redeeming Love*, on *A Passionate Hope*

"Smith's fresh retelling of the story of Ruth and Naomi portrays these strong biblical women in a thoughtful and reflective manner. Her impeccable research and richly detailed setting give readers a strong sense of life in ancient Israel."

Library Journal on *Redeeming Grace*

"Smith has brought the story to life in this richly descriptive and dramatic novel, enhancing it with colorful details about life in ancient Moab and Israel, including the political and religious climates of the time."

DISCARD

Booklist on *Redeeming Grace*

"This is both a well-drawn love story as well as the wistful imaginings of early Israel."

Publishers Weekly on *The Prophetess*

"Rahab's story is one of the most moving redemption accounts in Scripture. *The Crimson Cord* perfectly captures all the drama of the original, fleshing out the characters with care and thought, and following the biblical account every step of the way. Jill's thorough research and love for God's Word are both evident, and her storytelling skills kept me reading late into the night. A beautiful tale, beautifully told!"

Liz Curtis Higgs, *New York Times* bestselling author of *Mine Is the Night*, on *The Crimson Cord*

Books by Jill Eileen Smith

THE WIVES OF KING DAVID

Michal

Abigail

Bathsheba

WIVES OF THE PATRIARCHS

Sarai

Rebekah

Rachel

DAUGHTERS OF THE PROMISED LAND

The Crimson Cord

The Prophetess

Redeeming Grace

A Passionate Hope

The Heart of a King

When Life Doesn't Match Your Dreams

THE HEART OF A KING

THE LOVES OF SOLOMON

JILL EILEEN SMITH

Revell

a division of Baker Publishing Group
Grand Rapids, Michigan

© 2019 by Jill Eileen Smith

Published by Revell
a division of Baker Publishing Group
PO Box 6287, Grand Rapids, MI 49516-6287
www.revellbooks.com

Portions of this book previously published as ebooks under the titles *The Desert Princess* (2014), *The Shepherdess* (2015), *Daughter of the Nile* (2016), and *The Queen of Sheba* (2017)

Printed in the United States of America

Library of Congress Cataloging-in-Publication Data
Names: Smith, Jill Eileen, 1958– author.
Title: The heart of a king : the loves of Solomon / Jill Eileen Smith.
Description: Grand Rapids, MI : Revell, [2019]
Identifiers: LCCN 2018034596 | ISBN 9780800722401 (pbk. : alk. paper)
Subjects: | GSAFD: Christian fiction. | Bible fiction.
Classification: LCC PS3619.M58838 H43 2019 | DDC 813/.6—dc23
LC record available at https://lccn.loc.gov/2018034596

ISBN 978-0-8007-3620-0 (casebound)

This is a work of historical reconstruction; the appearance of certain historical figures is therefore inevitable. All other characters, however, are products of the author's imagination, and any resemblance to actual persons, living or dead, is coincidental.

Published in association with the Books & Such Literary Agency, 52 Mission Circle, Suite 122, PMB 170, Santa Rosa, CA 95409-7953.

19 20 21 22 23 24 25   7 6 5 4 3 2 1

To those who have tasted what is forbidden
only to find it meaningless.
May Solomon's wisdom and the love he
craved show you a better way.

Prelude

The Teacher looked at his scroll, light dancing in little ringlets over the words from the flickering candle at his side. Flickering like the breath of wind. One circlet encompassed the word he could not stop writing, could not pour enough emphasis into, though his stylus had scratched the repeated word clean through the parchment.

Meaningless. Meaningless. Meaningless.

Like chasing the wind. Everything was meaningless.

Everything.

A sigh escaped, a weighted thing within his chest. Memories flooded him, both good times and bad. *Yes, everything*, he insisted to his battered heart. No whisper of dawn brought him joy as in days of old. And though three times he had heard God's voice, that too carried no thrill, no fear, no awe.

What had become of the days when he taught his children that wisdom was priceless and a wife's value far above rubies? When had his search for wisdom as something hidden and precious become less than the gift it was?

Wisdom *had* been a great gift then. A gift given directly from the mouth of Almighty God. And he had used it well.

Until he hadn't. Until he doubted and tested and questioned and thought too highly of the gift. Until he let the gift displace the giver.

A fool says in his heart there is no God.

He'd never said that. But oh, how he had acted the part.

Sometimes foolishness is overconfidence in one's own wisdom. And pride had changed everything.

ONE

JERUSALEM, 975 BC

Solomon looked up from studying the temple model in the room his father had set aside for the miniature palatial structure. Footsteps stopped outside the room, and his ever-present guard opened the door. His mother breezed past the guard without a word and came to his side.

"The ambassador of Ammon has arrived," she said, placing a jeweled hand on his arm. "Shobi has brought his daughter with him."

"Naamah?" How long it had been since they had spoken. "Undoubtedly she is no longer a girl of ten."

"I believe it has been five years since they came to our aid in Mahanaim." Bathsheba touched his bearded chin. "Do you wish to speak with her or shall I keep her occupied? I did once promise her a tour of the city, but I sense she did not come just to see me."

Solomon caught the slight smile and twinkle in his mother's eyes. "Are you suggesting something, Ima?" He had been of marriageable age for over a year, but only one thing had occupied his thoughts since that day when his half brother had sent them running for their lives. His own coronation.

"Only that Naamah was an interesting girl, and you seemed to enjoy corresponding with her for a time." She searched his face. "I know she is a foreign princess, but Shobi has been a friend and ally of your father for years . . . and you are ready to seek a wife." She tilted her head, and he couldn't escape the knowing look in her eyes.

"I am more ready to have my father name me co-regent. You do understand that we are in danger, as is any wife I would take, until my right to rule is secure." His jaw tensed with the reminder. His mother knew the truth only too well.

She patted his arm. "I am trying, my son. But though your father promised me, he is young enough to live many more years and isn't ready to think about his heir."

"His older sons don't seem to mind thinking about it." He scowled and rubbed his chin, hating the way the uncertainty made him feel. "Would my father combine a coronation with a wedding? I would feel more at ease to even consider marriage if I knew you and my brothers were safe from Adonijah and my other half brothers."

Bathsheba's brows knit and she nodded. "I understand, my son. And I will continue to speak to your father as the opportunity allows. I'm not suggesting you marry Shobi's daughter, though of course it is something to consider. I'm simply asking if you would like to speak with her. I think that much can be arranged." She smiled again, and this time he returned the gesture.

"I would enjoy speaking with her, Ima." Images of the curious young girl of years past flitted through his mind's eye. Was the woman Naamah beautiful, as the girl had hinted she would be?

"Good," Bathsheba said, interrupting his thoughts. "I will invite her to tour with me and then you can meet me in the anteroom and take over. I will beg off my meeting with her until the evening meal."

"You would leave me alone with her?" He raised a brow.

"You will have the guards."

"Yes. Of course. Always the guards." He rubbed his beard.

"It is a fact of life for a prince . . . and a king." She touched his cheek. "You will never escape them, my son, so as always, we make the best of where God has placed us in life."

"If only God would prompt my father to name me co-regent . . ." He let the sentence dangle at his mother's look.

She backed slightly away from him. "I will bring Naamah soon. Be ready."

He nodded as she slipped from the room, knowing that his true wishes were yet again delayed. Something he should be used to by now, but he chafed at the thought just the same.

Naamah's camel turned at the bend in the road and carried her through the guarded gate to King David's palace. The sights, the beauty of the place, caused such a hitch in her breath it blocked even the sounds of her father ordering the camels to kneel. Sparkling-white stone pillars held the roof above a grand porch, and gleaming, golden lion's-head sculptures were mounted on either side of the great wide doors.

She blinked, trying to clear her thoughts and focus on what the guard was saying to her father, but she could not shake her dazed feeling. What splendor! The palace in Rabbah was nothing in comparison. The realization hit hard. She was no match for King David's son. She could not expect an alliance to be made on her behalf. She was the daughter of a reluctant ambassador and subject of this king, nothing more.

The sobering thought would not abate as she followed the guard to the anteroom several steps behind her father. When at last the guard left them to wait their turn to see the king, she sought her father's ear.

"I did not think the king quite so wealthy." She kept her voice low. "They had so little in Mahanaim, and even the stories you told . . ." Words failed her, and she gave him an imploring look. "I should not have come."

He gave her arm a reassuring pat. "Of course you should have come," he said in his soft, comforting tone. "King David came from humble means, my child. All of this wealth"—he waved a hand over the room rich with tapestries and colorful mosaic tiles in shades of blue and gold and gleaming white—"means little to this king. He is still a humble man, my daughter. You need not fear." His smile helped but a little to overcome her anxious thoughts.

"I will try, Abba." She held her tongue as another guard approached to usher them into the audience chamber.

A golden throne stood at the end of a long room, and tables and additional seats were placed beneath arched porticos on either side of the hall. Scribes and courtiers stood or sat in these areas, their gazes fixed, watching them. Heat crept up Naamah's neck, and she thanked the God of Solomon for the veil that hid her sudden embarrassment.

They stopped at a line of green and blue tiles before the

raised dais and bowed low, but not before she dared a glance in the king's direction. Another chair was to his right, and Solomon's mother sat upon it. She drew in a sharp breath. Bathsheba was more beautiful than she recalled. The woman smiled at her, and Naamah quickly lowered her gaze. Did this kind woman remember her?

But it was Solomon whose form she longed to set eyes upon, yet she had seen no sign of him. Where could he be? Her heart beat faster as thoughts tumbled inside her head. Abba was wrong. She should not have come.

"Shobi, my friend. It is so good to see you again." King David's voice was strong, and when she glanced up at him, she noted the genuine affection in his eyes. "Is this your little daughter?" The king's brow lifted and he offered an approving smile. "Though she is a child no longer."

Her father inclined his head in Naamah's direction. "Yes, my lord. This is my Naamah. She was anxious to see Jerusalem, and now that she is a woman grown, I thought the time was right."

King David glanced at his wife. "You remember Naamah, my love?"

Bathsheba's smile warmed her as it had the day they met in Mahanaim. "Yes, of course, my lord." She smiled at the king, then took Naamah's measure. "She has grown into a lovely woman." She turned her gaze to Naamah's father. "You must be quite proud of her."

"Quite proud," her father said, going on to assure them both that Naamah had exceeded his greatest plans for her, that she was well versed in all matters worthy of a princess of Ammon. The praise caused the heat to crawl up her neck and she hid her eyes from their perusal, studying the tiles at her feet instead, suffering the unpleasant feeling that she was on display.

"Naamah." Bathsheba spoke, jarring her attention from the tiles.

Naamah looked her way once more. "Yes, my queen?" Was she a queen? She suddenly realized that the guard had not instructed them on what to say or how to address the king or this obviously favored wife.

"While your father and the king discuss their business dealings, I would like to show you around the palace. Would you like that?"

She nodded. "Yes, my queen." Though she wished it was Solomon who had asked the question. Would they meet him in the halls? Should she ask after him?

"Very good," Bathsheba said, rising from her gilded chair. "Come with me." She descended the steps and walked toward a side door Naamah had not noticed before.

Naamah glanced at her father. At his quick nod, she knew she should not linger. She bowed low before King David once more, then stood and walked with graceful steps toward the door the queen had entered.

As she stepped into a smaller but more private antechamber, she stopped short. Bathsheba stood talking with someone that at first she did not recognize. By his resplendent robes she knew him to be royalty, but when he turned to look her way, she found it difficult to breathe. There was no mistaking the resemblance to his mother and father. And though she had not seen him in five years, she would never forget the intensity in those dark eyes or the twinkle that accompanied his approving smile.

He glanced at his mother, then strode to Naamah's side.

"Naamah?" He bowed at the waist, and she did the same, unsure at that moment what to do with her hands. She clasped them together to still her sudden nervousness.

"Solomon?" She smiled, though he could not see it behind the veil.

"What a pleasure to see you again," he said. "Father told me he expected your father to arrive today. I am glad you chose to accompany him this time. I had hoped you would come one day, and here you are."

His smile seemed to hold genuine kindness, though his words were probably said to be polite, because what else could he say to a young woman who begs her father to travel with his caravan?

She realized how shameless it must look for her to be here at all. What other ambassador would bring his daughter on such a trip? But she ignored the uneasiness that thought evoked. She was here now, and the man of her many dreams stood before her.

"Thank you, my lord," she said, glancing from him to her sandaled feet. "I am glad to be here."

He didn't respond immediately, causing her to look up. He exchanged a look with his mother, but she could not make sense of his guarded expression or their silent communication. When he returned his attention to her, he smiled. "My mother has allowed me the privilege of escorting you on a tour of the palace. That is, if you would like to join me?"

She studied him a moment, aware of the slight strain in the pull of his mouth and the fine lines hidden beneath the heavy dark bangs across his brow.

"I would enjoy that very much." She glanced at his mother. "I hope you will join us, my lady?"

Bathsheba stepped closer and shook her head. "I will look forward to meeting with you before the evening meal. If you don't mind, I have a few things I need to attend to first."

Naamah forced herself to remain calm and dignified as she had been taught, though she was suddenly unsure of herself. Five years had changed Solomon, but she could not tell if he was simply wary or worried. When he offered his arm, she gladly took it.

"Though my father has not yet declared it, I am his intended heir," he said, leaning close to her ear as he led her through the antechamber. "Unfortunately, his hesitance to say so publicly puts me and my mother at risk." He indicated the guard that followed at a discreet distance. "Thus the guards."

"It seems to me," she said, feeling that sense of understanding they had shared so briefly as children return to her now, "that you were in the same predicament when we met five years ago."

He leaned away to better look at her and chuckled. "So it would seem."

The hall led to a private door, which he opened without pause. "What is like vinegar to the teeth and smoke to the eyes?" he asked as they stepped into the grandeur of the king's gardens.

She squinted as she had that day when she was ten and he had first posed the riddle. "A sluggard," she said, laughing.

He laughed with her. "You remembered."

"It was not something I would easily forget."

He smiled and settled her on a bench beneath a large terebinth tree, then sat beside her. He fingered the veil at her temple, gently brushing his hand against her cheek. She

16

flushed hot, tingling even beneath the veil. "Five years ago, we did not have this between us. I enjoyed the ability to look on your face, to easily read your expressions."

She lowered her gaze, her senses heightened and attuned to his nearness. "I don't suppose I have to wear it the whole visit," she said, though she knew her maid, Inaya, would scold her for days to come if she removed it now.

He seemed to think on that as he used to do when they were young. At last he shook his head. "No. Keep it on." He smiled in that lazy way that must make every woman in Jerusalem love him. "You are temptation enough with it."

She did her best not to fidget with the belt at her waist.

"How was your trip from Ammon? I am sorry I have yet to visit your town."

"It was longer than I expected. At times I can still feel the camel beneath me."

He laughed, revealing straight white teeth. She caught the hint of mint on his breath. "I prefer the horse to the camel. They are such proud, powerful creatures."

"They are prettier than a camel, I daresay. And not as ornery." She clasped her hands to force her nerves to still. Being so close to him after all these years brought on a headier feeling than she had imagined. "Horses would not make the trip as easily, though," she said. "Some of the terrain we traveled was better suited to a camel, and the ride was slightly less bumpy than a horse could be."

"You are right, of course. But a horse is far better in battle. Any nation that would be great needs a strong military might. That means a great number of horses and chariots."

"You have put much thought into your future reign," she said, hoping he could hear the admiration in her voice.

He shrugged. "I am observant. And I have been sitting on my father's court most of my life. I would simply choose what is wise for the kingdom."

"You will make a fine king someday." In that moment, she realized that as king, he would not want to be saddled with a foreign wife. Would he?

Before she could pursue the thought, he changed the subject to other topics, to riddles and worship and the political intrigue he could not escape.

"May I ask you something?" she said when their conversation lapsed momentarily into silence. He seemed far away in that moment, and she yearned to know why.

He leaned into the bench, his gaze curious. "Ask whatever you like, Princess."

Her face flushed at the look in his eyes, but she determined not to allow herself to be flustered by disobedient emotions. "Why did you stop our correspondence? Not a single word came from you once I turned thirteen." She looked at her hands, suddenly embarrassed at her boldness. "Did I somehow offend you, my lord?"

Silence followed her question, and she feared that if she had not offended him before, she certainly had done so now. But a moment later he touched her arm. She looked up, meeting his gaze.

"It was not proper to continue to write to a princess of marriageable age. Not without declaring some kind of intentions." His voice showed little emotion, but as she held his gaze, it was he who finally looked away.

"I understand," she said at last, feeling the loss of something she had savored for too long. He did not want her. He had not spent the past five years pining for her as she

18

had for him. Suddenly she felt utterly foolish for coming to this place.

"Naamah," Solomon said, coaxing her chin up with the slightest pressure of his fingers.

She lifted her head, too aware of the moisture filling her eyes. What a fool she was!

"I'm glad you came," he said, his smile relaxed, as though trying to put her again at ease. "I have thought often of you in the past few years, but I have been caught up in finishing my father's plans for the temple model, the temple he wants me to build one day. And there is the constant worry that though he acts as if I am his heir, he will not name me so. The tension of waiting and the threat that is always there from my older brothers has been immense."

She touched his hand, losing herself in the vulnerability of his smile. "I'm sorry. I must sound like a petulant child. It is only that I missed hearing from you. There were so many questions I wanted to ask you—about Adonai."

He leaned back and studied her. "You have come to believe in Him." It was not a question. Could he read her faith in her eyes?

She nodded. "Molech no longer holds me captive. But I have often longed to hear more of Adonai from your lips."

He squeezed her hand and smiled. "I would have enjoyed such a conversation," he assured her.

Their words grew less awkward after that. The sun moved past the halfway point, and still they talked as though time had never separated them. Her stomach grumbled, and they both heard it. He laughed and she joined him.

"I think we have missed the midday meal," he said, standing. He offered his hand. "But I know where we can find some almonds and dates to still the hunger until the banquet this evening."

She allowed him to help her rise, grateful to move her limbs after sitting for so long. "And I suppose we should take that tour of the palace you promised me," she said, casting him a coy look. She glanced quickly at the guard, who stood watch near the door to the gardens.

Solomon laughed, and the musical ring to it melted her heart. She was in love with this man, as she had been since her youth. She just prayed that she would be able to convince her father that Solomon was in love with her in return.

TWO

The banquet hall shimmered from the glow of many oil lamps, throwing dappled light against the woven tapestries lining the wall. Solomon barely noticed the familiar setting, though his gaze took in the many occupants who stood as the trumpet blared, announcing each prince's arrival. He came fourth after Adonijah, Shephatiah, and Ithream. Chileab, Abigail's son, avoided court life and had left Jerusalem to take over his mother's estate in Carmel. But the two in line for the throne ahead of him seemed to favor Adonijah, whom Solomon disdained.

He moved to his seat nearest the king's right hand, though Adonijah sat on his father's left. Naamah's father, Shobi, had been given the seat of honor next to Solomon. By all accounts—and Solomon did not miss the scowl on Adonijah's handsome face—it looked to the world that Solomon was indeed the king's intended heir. Then why would his father not dispense with the waiting and name him co-regent?

He glanced at Adonijah, then faced the door where his

parents were announced and watched as his father seated his mother in the most honorable place among the women. Naamah stood near, waiting with the rest of the attendees for the king and queen to take their seats. He glanced at her, this foreign princess who had captured his imagination. She was attractive and engaging, but he felt a hesitance in his spirit when he considered his mother's suggestion. Form an alliance with Ammon through marriage to her? What of marriage for the sake of love—as his mother shared with his father?

He sat as servants came by with platters piled high with fowl and lamb and the choicest beef. He allowed his plate to be layered with meat and vegetables, and wine flowed throughout the meal like water from a rushing stream.

He leaned toward Shobi and smiled, lifting his golden cup to his lips. "It is always good to see you, Shobi. I trust your trip was uneventful?" he asked as the older man tore a piece of bread from a loaf.

Shobi met his gaze. "Thankfully, yes. Our entourage is large enough to scare off any bandits hiding in the hills. At least that is what I tell myself." He laughed, and Solomon thought the sound pleasing, like Naamah's.

"If you ever fear for your safety, you know you have only to ask and my father would send a contingent of military men to aid your protection." He knew Shobi would not take kindly to an overt offer of aid. Subject or not, a man had his pride.

"I will admit bringing Naamah caused me concern for her safety, though I knew we were well guarded. A father always feels more protective when a child is along." Shobi scooped a bit of lamb onto the bread and plopped it into his mouth.

Solomon nodded and turned his attention to his own plate. His hunger was not nearly strong enough to cause him to eat everything the servants had placed there. His stomach knotted with the sound of Adonijah's laughter and the sickeningly smooth way he spoke to the king. Was he trying to woo the man to name him heir in front of the entire assembly?

He glanced at his mother, but she was engaged in conversation with Naamah. He turned and offered his father a fresh loaf that sat on a silver platter between them, pulling the king's attention away from his brother.

"Have you and Shobi finished with the business that brought him here?" Solomon asked, angling his head the ambassador's way.

The king met Solomon's gaze and smiled, then looked beyond him to Shobi. "We have a few more meetings scheduled yet tomorrow, is that not right, my friend?"

Shobi lowered his head, then nodded. "Yes, my lord. I have lesser meetings yet tonight, and we will finish our business here tomorrow."

"You will stay on a few days to enjoy Jerusalem, I hope. You know you are always welcome." The king lifted his cup to Shobi.

Shobi did the same and the two drank in a moment of silence. "Thank you, my king. I am certain Naamah would enjoy a tour of the city and some time in your marketplace."

The king chuckled and Solomon with him. "Tell the merchants to go easy on the prices. They will see her royal clothing and try to get the most they can."

"Perhaps I will have to limit her spending before we start.

My Naamah is a good haggler though. I do not worry about her . . . much."

"Except as a father does about every daughter." A shadow crossed the king's face, and Solomon looked at him.

"You are thinking of Tamar," he said, his voice too low for others to hear.

His father gave a slight nod. "One never forgets the things they regret, my son, despite the passage of time."

If not for Tamar's defilement by Amnon, Solomon's oldest half brother, both Amnon and Absalom would still live. But deep down, Solomon knew the greater regret was his father's own adultery with his mother, despite the love they had come to have for each other.

He patted his father's arm, hoping the man was not having second thoughts about the promise he'd made to his mother. As his mind drifted to his hoped-for co-regency, he inwardly shook himself. He could not keep thinking like this. One look at Shobi and he forced himself to ask about Ammon and not think about the history that country had with his father and mother. Or about all that was wrong with his life at this moment.

—⁓—

Naamah retreated to her chamber that evening and lay upon the soft bed. Did Solomon love her as she loved him? The question still beat with the rhythm of her heart as she awoke with the predawn light the next morning. She rose quickly, determined to meet her father before he could run off to more meetings. She must know—what was to become of her?

She dressed and donned her veil without Inaya's help but

found her father still abed. His manservant allowed entrance into her father's chamber, and she sat in a wooden chair on the balcony overlooking Mount Moriah, the famed mountain where Solomon said that God stopped the very thing He had asked of Abraham—to offer his son Isaac on a stone altar. An anxious flutter filled her heart as she saw the scene in her mind's eye. But soon Molech's bronze arms replaced the vision and she shuddered at the thought. Belief in Solomon's God had stripped Molech of his power over her but had not erased the memories.

"King David tells me that his son will one day build a temple to Adonai on that mountain."

She turned at the sound of her father's voice and rose to kiss his cheeks. He had dressed in his day clothes and combed his hair, looking refreshed and more at peace than she had seen him in many days.

"You are awake at last," she said, smiling at him.

He rubbed a hand along his stubbled chin. The men of Ammon did not grow hair on their faces as the men of Israel did.

"And you are up very early, my daughter." He kissed her cheek as well, and they both sat at a small food-laden table along the balcony.

As her father studied her, she felt the prick of uncertainty and suddenly wondered if she was making a huge mistake. She swallowed her fear—and her pride—and held his gaze.

"I wanted to speak with you before you were whisked away from me again." She took a sip of grape juice, a distraction from her churning thoughts.

"It must be important to wake you before Inaya's third

25

attempt to get you to rise." He chuckled and she joined him, though she was certain it came out sounding false.

"It is. To me. Important, that is." She set the grape juice down and put a hand to her middle.

He lifted a brow and looked at her a moment, then chose a fresh fig from the tray and took a bite.

She drew in a steadying breath. If she didn't speak now, the chance might not come again. "I want you to give me to Solomon as his wife."

Her father held the half-eaten fig in his hand, then set it down and clasped his hands over hers. "This is a hard thing you ask, my daughter." He glanced beyond her as if seeing something in the distance, then again held her gaze. "How do you know Solomon wants you? What if his father refuses me?"

She suddenly realized the blow to her father's pride that such a refusal would mean. And yet she took comfort in her father's touch. He loved her. He would do as she asked, surely.

"He spent the day with me yesterday. We talked and laughed, and I think he would have kissed me if not for the veil." She had removed the veil in her father's presence and casually pointed to where it lay on the chair beside them. "I love him, Abba." She searched his face, hoping he could see the earnestness of her plea.

"Do you now?" He released her hands and looked toward the mountain. At last he spoke again. "And did he voice any desire to make you his bride?"

Disappointment curled in her middle, but she could not lie to her abba. "No," she said barely above a whisper. "But . . ." She stopped, seeking the right words.

Her abba faced her once more, and his sigh seemed weighted. "You are a beautiful young woman, Naamah. A princess fit for kings' palaces." He fingered the goblet of juice, still looking at her. "But you must know that if Solomon is to be king, he will take wives other than you for political gain. This is not ideal, and I do not wish such a life for you." He picked up the goblet but did not drink. Instead, he studied the contents as one reads a scroll.

"I love him, Abba. I have loved him since I was ten and never stopped."

"He is a Hebrew."

Her heart beat faster in that moment as she studied her abba's intense dark eyes, so loving. He was certain he knew what was best for her.

"He believes in Yahweh . . ." She pulled in a breath and slowly released it. "As do I." She waited, watching him for some sign of displeasure.

He glanced beyond her toward the sun-washed hills, his thoughts hidden from her as they often were when he grew reflective. At last he set the goblet on the table and took her hand in his.

"Your mother, peace be upon her soul, was Hebrew." He looked intently at her. "I never told you, but it is the truth."

She stared at him, her erratic pulse making her feel as though she had run a race and lost. "Why did you not tell me?"

He looked away again, and his face darkened as one ashamed of his silence. "I should have." He sighed deeply and stood, pacing the small balcony. At last he seemed to weary of his movement, his agitation gone, and settled in the seat beside her.

"Your mother had been a slave in Ammon—actually, the daughter of a slave in my father's house. When Hanun was deposed by King David and I was made acting ruler in his place, I freed your mother and married her."

Her heart beat to a strange yet familiar, joyous rhythm that she had this heritage, this link to Solomon's people. "You loved Ima." Her father only nodded. "As I love Solomon, Abba."

He searched her face as though trying to read her thoughts, and she knew her words had settled within him. She waited, silently praying to the Unseen One that her father would take her case before the king.

"You risk heartache, my daughter," he said at last, looking into her eyes, his own filled with uncertainty and remembered pain.

"All love risks such loss, Abba. Whether I lose Solomon as you lost Ima or I lose him to another wife along the way, it is a risk I must take."

He nodded, his bearing resigned. "I will see what I can do."

She jumped up and kissed his cheeks, laughing with joy. But as he left for a meeting with the king to discuss her fate, she decided that if God gave her Solomon, she would not lose him to any other woman. She would love him so completely that he would want no one but her.

THREE

Solomon walked the halls to one of his father's private meeting rooms and found Naamah's father already seated, speaking with the king. The presence of Ammon's ambassador didn't surprise him, but his father's request to see him in the same setting did. He glanced about the ornate room where the king had copies of the law read to him each morning, where he had written psalm after psalm on fine leather parchments now resting in stone niches or jars along the walls that reached from floor to ceiling.

The king sat on a plush chair at the head of a low, intricately carved wooden table. Shobi sat to his left. Solomon entered and bowed, kissing the king's signet ring.

"Solomon, my son," the king said, a smile in his eyes, "please join us." He pointed to his right where another seat waited. Solomon took it, his mind whirling, assessing.

"My son," his father said again, "Shobi has come to me seeking an alliance with us. He would like to offer his daughter Naamah to you in marriage."

Solomon held his father's gaze, not daring a glimpse at Shobi until his thoughts were under control. "A country makes alliances with kings, not princes, do they not?" Was his father willing to proclaim him heir apparent—even name him co-regent at last?

"In this you are correct, my son, but I do not need another wife, and Naamah would make a good wife to you. Especially as one day I fully expect you to be king in my place." His father's smile widened, and Solomon's heart lightened at his words.

"Does this mean a marriage and a coronation to become your co-regent might take place together?" It was a bold question to ask in front of Naamah's father, but he sensed that if he did not risk the question now, the opportunity might not come again. Could he marry Naamah without such a promise? What if he were never king? The fear of such a thing quickened his heartbeat again.

He glanced at Shobi and read understanding in his gaze, but before his father could respond the door opened again and Naamah was led into the room. Was he to have no real say in this then? The thought troubled him further. He liked Naamah well enough, but to wed her?

He stood at her entrance and watched as she approached, her gaze fixed on her father.

"Naamah," the king said, jolting Solomon's thoughts. "Please, my child, sit." He pointed to a cushioned chair beside her father. Her servant stayed near the door in the shadows, but Naamah moved to obey the king's word.

She approached the king and bowed before she did as he asked. "Thank you, my lord."

Solomon watched the exchange, saw his father's obvious pleasure in the moment. Somehow his father and Shobi had already come to an agreement without consulting him at all, leaving him to accept or reject Naamah in her very presence. His stomach tightened with a hint of anger, and he felt himself spiraling downward, control of his choices suddenly lost.

He looked at Naamah, a brief glance, and noted the way her limbs trembled as she sat beside her father. Was this her desire or her father's? He looked away quickly before she could meet his unsettled gaze and masked his emotions as the guard announced his mother's entrance. Had his mother convinced his father of this without consulting him too?

His mother moved and bowed before the king, who rose from his seat, took her hand, and kissed it. Solomon did not miss the look of affection they shared, something he wondered if he would ever feel toward any woman. He lifted his chin and kept his gaze above the heads of those around him as his father led his mother to her seat.

The king returned to his gilded chair, and Solomon sensed his father's gaze on him. He did not meet it.

"Your father has requested an alliance with my house," the king said to Naamah. "He has offered to give you to my son Solomon to wife. Is this agreeable to you, Naamah?"

Solomon allowed a glimpse in Naamah's direction. Clearly she had not expected to be asked such a question. Perhaps neither one of them had been consulted in this matter.

"Yes, my lord." Her answer seemed to indicate it pleased her.

King David shifted to look at his son. "Solomon, do you agree to spread your garment over Naamah, to take her as your wife?"

Solomon held his father's gaze for a lengthy moment. Love aside, his anger still brewing, this was not a question he could refuse. Better to do as asked and turn the situation to his advantage. He did like Naamah, after all. She was easy to talk with, and perhaps the alliance would bring about that longed-for coronation.

He looked her way and smiled, allowing his gaze to take her in, but his heart remained stubbornly uncertain. For a tense moment he waited, wanting to bargain for the condition of his coronation, but one glance at his mother stayed the words. "I agree, Father," he said without emotion.

Naamah watched him from that moment on as though he was the only person in the room, despite the conversation going on around them. Solomon caught some of the words between Shobi and his parents, but no mention of coronation accompanied the promise of marriage within a year. Why had he hesitated to insist on it? Frustration curled in his middle, but he continued to smile and mask his true feelings. The meeting soon ended with bread and salt and wine between them, and the atmosphere took on a less formal tone.

Solomon held back a sigh. Marriage without the solidarity of the kingdom firmly in his hands put Naamah at risk, just as it did his mother and brothers. Why couldn't his father see this? What was holding him back from naming Solomon co-regent, to dispel the rumors that Adonijah thought himself next in line for the throne?

The thoughts grew in strength, with this new marital twist adding to the burden he found already great enough to bear, but he moved to sit beside Naamah, to get his mind to focus on his new bride—anything but his strong-willed brother. It was better to speak words of love into the ear of a beautiful woman than to fear the future. Of course it was.

"I will admit, this comes as a surprise," he whispered close to Naamah's ear. Her face was still hidden beneath the veil, but he caught the longing in her dark eyes. She wanted this. Was not nearly as surprised as he was. He amended his tone. "A year is a long time to wait."

"I know," she said, the words barely audible. The voices of Shobi and his parents buzzed around them, making it difficult to talk freely.

He fingered the edge of her veil. "It is within my right now to kiss you," he said, smiling into her eyes. "But I think we will both enjoy it more if we wait."

Her look held disappointment, telling him that the girl was definitely besotted, perhaps even in love with him. "Yes. You are probably right." Her answer surprised him. She was better at keeping her emotions in check than he expected.

He took a date from a nearby tray and touched it to his lips, then held it out to her. Their fingers brushed as she took it from him, slipped it beneath the veil, and touched it to her lips in return. A delayed kiss. A promise of sweetness to come. It was the best he could do. He had too much to process to give this young woman what she surely deserved. They were friends of a sort, after all. Would he ever be able to feel anything beyond friendship, as she did for him?

"We dare not awaken love before it pleases," he said softly, hoping to appease her.

Her smile reached her eyes. "We dare not," she agreed. "Though I fear love has already opened both my heart and my mind."

He grew thoughtful. "I am glad. I feared it was only I who carried such feelings." He told himself it wasn't a lie, though a twinge of guilt accompanied the fact that love to her was not the same as it was to him in that moment. "Shall we?" He stood and moved a hand toward the door.

She went ahead of him as they left the room, escorted by a guard, to walk the gardens and halls of the palace. Solomon showed her views of the valleys and mountains and told her stories of his people and this place she did not yet know.

"I do not know why my father waits to name me his heir," he finally admitted to her, unable to keep the frustration at bay as they stood on the palace roof overlooking the Kidron Valley. "He has raised me to rule, and yet the people do not know it. Court gossip tells me that Adonijah expects to be named co-regent, and I fear he has the backing of some of my father's leaders."

"Perhaps your father will include your coronation with our wedding day. Surely there is still time for this?" She touched his arm, and instinctively his muscles tensed.

His gaze swept hers. For one heady moment he was tempted to lift the veil and kiss her the way her whole body was telling him to. But the footsteps of the guard caused them both to take a step away from each other.

"I will pray that Adonai gives you this blessing of coronation, Solomon." She leaned slightly closer. "But I would marry you whether you were a king or a poor man."

He looked at her again, trying to read her expression, wondering what her true thoughts were. At last he glanced at the moon. "I pray Adonai hears your prayers." He leaned closer. "If my father does not act soon, you may be a widow before you are a wife."

"Surely not!" Though the outburst held shock, her voice remained a whisper.

"You have always known of the danger surrounding me, Naamah. I would not lie to you about this now."

Her hand sought his and he squeezed her fingers. "We must trust Adonai that this will not be. Surely He will work all things out for your good."

Solomon nodded, his emotions still pensive, but at last he softened. He smiled with genuine warmth. "It is time I let you rest."

He bowed to her then, released her hand, and let the guard lead her away.

FOUR

974 BC

Solomon stood in his father's receiving chamber, trying to keep from tapping his foot. Anxiety caused his palms to sweat as he watched Naamah and her ten maids enter the room. His father and Shobi bent over a table that held the wedding ketubah and placed their seals on the final agreement, legally binding him to the Ammonite princess.

He straightened, feeling the weight of what he was about to do settle over him. He had imagined marriage so differently. But what had he really expected? To find a woman without his parents' help and have his heart bound to her in an instant? To carry her away from all of the demands of royal life and live hidden from the constant fear that he carried with him each day?

He was a prince, heir apparent to his father's throne. Of course he would marry a princess. But how was he to truly protect this young woman who looked up at him now with such love, such hope?

The priest spoke, and Solomon opened his brightly colored robe and draped a corner of it over her shoulder. His fingers glanced off her, and he felt a slight movement as though his touch had caused her to jump. She was as nervous as he. He smiled at her, trying to calm them both.

After the priest had given the prescribed words, his father stepped forward and blessed their union. "May you be fruitful and multiply," he said, his voice strong, his smile wide.

He held out a golden cup of wine. Solomon took it and shared it with Naamah, still feeling as though she loved him far more than he could love her in return. Was he a fraud to marry a woman and pretend to feel the same as she did? Was he a selfish brute to accept her when his heart was so torn between other matters that took his thoughts far from love?

Guilt filled him as he returned the cup to his father, the wine still tingling on his tongue. He listened with swirling emotions to his father's final blessing. He led Naamah to the dais, where they sat to receive well-wishers.

"I am sorry he did not choose this moment to also name you king," Naamah whispered.

"He sees no need to rush things." Solomon spoke in her ear, his arm grazing hers. He felt her lean closer, and the sweet smell of her perfume wafted to him, rousing his senses. Perhaps she would be a better distraction and companion than he first thought. She could help him to stop fretting about the future of the kingdom.

"Perhaps soon, though," she said, her tone hopeful.

Too many guests interrupted them after that, and the feasting lasted long into the night. Naamah seemed to eat little, and he felt her gaze on his every movement as he left her side to move about the room.

He glanced her way after speaking a word to her father and noticed a servant offer her another cup of wine. The drumbeat quickened in the background, and he felt his pulse increase with the telltale sound. He strode toward her from behind and touched her shoulder, bending low to her ear. "There is better wine in our tent, beloved. Come." He took her hand as he wrapped his other arm around her.

The bridal tent sat surrounded by palace rooms yet secluded in the central courtyard, and the music of the wedding feast grew muffled, distant. He lifted the flap and ushered her into the glow of soft lamps and the beauty of gold-laced white fabric over the canopied place where they would share their love.

Love. He could call it that, for wasn't the coming together of a man and wife love? His guilt lessened, and he turned her to face him. He slowly traced a line along her cheek, then undid the clasp that held the veil keeping her from him. His breath caught as the veil fell to the earth. "You are more lovely than I remembered." The words were soft, a caress. He bent his lips over hers, tasting of love's first kiss.

"How long I have wanted to hold you, Naamah!" The words were true. He lifted the crown from his head and removed his bejeweled robe, then helped her remove hers. He faced her again, and he could see the pulse throb in her neck. He leaned over her once more and kissed the very spot.

—⚏—

Solomon stood looking out of the large window in Naamah's chambers, watching the sun emerge from its nest. Two weeks had passed since she had worn a colorful bridal gown and ridden a jewel-bedecked camel, hidden beneath a tent-like covering, with fifty guards running before and behind.

He turned at the touch of her hand on his shoulder. "Let him kiss me with the kisses of his mouth—for your love is more delightful than wine," she whispered into his ear. "Pleasing is the fragrance of your perfumes; your name is like perfume poured out."

He turned to face her and clasped her warm fingers in his own, pulling her close. "How beautiful you are, my darling! Oh, how beautiful! Your eyes are doves." The poetry was some they had begun together that first week.

He bent low and kissed her with the passion he knew she expected. Passion that was easy to muster with a bride as alluring as Naamah. When their lips parted, she leaned close, nearly melting into him. The silence felt comfortable, like the warmth of a blanket, until at last she lifted her head from his shoulder.

"Take me to see the outer gardens today." She gave him one of her most alluring smiles. "I will ask one of the servants to pack food for us, and I will feed you beneath the almond trees." She stroked his beard and pulled his head closer to her lips.

"What a little temptress you are, my dove." He laughed at her slight pout as she entwined her arms about his neck.

"You know you want to," she fairly purred in his ear.

He kissed her again, slowly, thoroughly, letting himself memorize each sweet taste of her lips, wishing he could give in to her pleas. But he broke contact and settled her at arm's length from him. "I can't."

"Why not?"

He had sensed a hint of the spoiled and stubborn in her, but now he saw it more clearly in her disappointed gaze. He studied her, keeping his own expression masked, as he had learned to do so well in the past few years. Sharing his love was one thing. Sharing his heart, his plans, his dreams . . . he took far more caution there. Perhaps once he was king . . . But no. Even then he knew that he might not allow himself to trust his wife.

"My father has bid me to return to court. I have duties, my love. You know this." He touched her cheek, smiling to appease her, but she stepped closer and tried to coax him once again into her embrace.

He pushed her gently away and shook his head. "I can't," he said again. He turned then and donned the robe he had worn to her chambers, his mind churning. He should say something to make her realize that their wedding week was past, and he could no longer promise to spend every moment in her presence. He stopped once he reached the door. "I will return when I can." He smiled and winked at her, then walked slowly out the door.

—m—

Naamah stared after her husband, reeling. What had just happened? Solomon had been so attentive and they'd only been married a couple of weeks. How could he leave her so quickly and without warning?

Surely he would be back tonight. Surely he wasn't saying goodbye indefinitely, was he? She shook herself and moved across the room, then back toward the window, pacing, frustrated. Two weeks and barely enough time to get to know her husband. She wanted him to talk to her, open his heart to her, but the most he would do was tell her stories or engage her in romantic poetry.

She paused mid-stride and sank onto the couch. His mother knew him better than she did. Perhaps Bathsheba could be coaxed into giving her advice on how to keep his interest longer, daily. The thought spurred her up from her seat.

"Inaya!" She hurried to the chamber where her garments were kept and jars of makeup waited. Her servant appeared from a side room where she slept nearby. "You must dress me quickly. I am going to find the queen and find out what is going on with my husband."

Inaya had not tried to dissuade her, and within the hour Naamah found Solomon's mother in her sitting room, mending a garment for one of her children. As the guard allowed Naamah entrance, the queen rose gracefully and kissed her cheeks in greeting.

"Naamah, how good of you to come." Bathsheba motioned for her to sit on a cushioned seat opposite the one she had occupied.

She obeyed and waited as the queen gave instructions to a servant to bring them water from the spring and some of her famous date and honey cakes. At last she settled again across from Naamah and set her mending aside.

"I assume by your presence here that my son has finally left your side and returned to court?" The queen's eyes held sympathy.

Naamah nodded, trying to hold back sudden emotion. "I tried to coax him into staying, but he insisted he must go." The hurt in the admission stung, the feeling of failure acute.

Bathsheba's look grew thoughtful, her smile knowing and pensive. "It is hard to see the first weeks of marriage come to an end and life return to normal." She glanced at some point beyond Naamah, who wondered where her thoughts took her.

"I only wish," Naamah said, filling the sudden silence, "to be all that he needs. I want to share everything with him, and him with me."

Bathsheba looked into her eyes, but Naamah studied the soft folds of her robe, unable to hold the queen's gaze.

"You will never be all that he needs, dear girl," the queen said.

Naamah looked up, disturbed by the words.

"Only God can give us all that we need. Only He can feed the hungriest places in our soul." Bathsheba smiled again, and Naamah was touched by her serenity. "Do not try to force Solomon. Give him time, my daughter."

"It is just . . ." She could not finish and yet knew she must. "That is . . . I wish things were different for him. I wish he didn't have so many worries."

"I know." She patted the seat next to her, and Naamah reluctantly rose and sat on the edge. Bathsheba took hold of her hand as she imagined her mother might have done, though the memories of her dear face had long since faded from her mind's eye.

"If Solomon reigns as king as his father has intended, he will need you to be strong, to raise a son to rule after him. This is where you must place your focus and your love, my daughter." The queen coaxed Naamah to look at her. "This is how you will best show Solomon your love."

Naamah's hand moved of its own accord to the place

where a child might one day lie. A child of the love she and Solomon shared.

Did he share it?

She pondered the question and his mother's lack of solid answers that night as she lay alone in her bed for the first time since her marriage. Would Solomon call for her again? How soon would he take another wife, and worse, how would she bear it?

FIVE

Naamah woke the next morning feeling utterly bereft and endured a scolding from Inaya, which was simply her maid's vain attempt to pull her from sudden melancholy. She need not have bothered, for on the following day, another without sight of Solomon, she was not only missing him but had apparently come down with an awful stomach illness as well. All she had eaten the night before was deposited in a clay pot before dawn, and she curled back onto her bed and hid her head under the soft linen sheets. Inaya knocked softly and entered without receiving a response.

"Go away," Naamah muttered from beneath the folds of cloth.

"I will do no such thing," Inaya said in that tone meant to fix things to rights again. Inaya had been fixing her since Ima passed on, and though she spoke sharply to Naamah and she reproved Inaya in return, Naamah could not bear to be without her. "What is wrong with you, dear girl? Are you ill?"

Inaya made a disgusted sound a moment later, and Naamah knew she had found the clay pot with her stomach contents.

"Yes," she said, poking her head out slowly from her hidden cocoon.

Inaya ordered a servant to clean the room, then threw open the shutters, sprinkled crushed mint leaves into the oil that fed the lamps, and lit the flames. When she was satisfied the room was sufficiently cleansed, she came and touched Naamah's forehead. "You are not feverish."

"No." The queasy feeling seemed to have subsided, so she pressed a hand to her stomach and slowly sat up.

Inaya looked her over with her no-nonsense scrutiny. "You have not had your time since two weeks before your wedding."

She counted backward. They had been married only two weeks. "It should have come last week."

Inaya looked thoughtful. "You are never past your time."

Truth dawned, and she stood, nearly losing her balance in the process. "Do you think . . ." She sat down, her longing for Solomon stronger than ever now. "I must tell him."

Inaya placed a hand on her arm. "Not yet. Wait until we are sure."

Naamah stood again and walked to the window, which overlooked the family courtyard. Her rooms were on the highest floor of the palace, above Bathsheba's suite of rooms, which were closest to the king. Solomon's chambers were not far from hers on the other side of the hall. Inaya's advice was probably wise, but suddenly she did not want wisdom. She wanted Solomon, and she had news he would want to hear.

She whirled about, avoiding her nurse's gaze. "Help me

dress." Her heart beat faster as anticipation mounted. "If I hurry, I might catch him before he leaves for court."

Inaya gave a disapproving scowl, but she did not argue. Naamah did not wait for Inaya to put up her hair but simply draped a veil over her head.

A few moments later she appeared before the guard who stood watch at Solomon's door and begged him entrance. He merely nodded once, then slipped inside. She waited through the space of many breaths, to the point that she began to chastise herself for making such a grave error. It had been only two days since he had been to her chambers. Was she making herself a nuisance by not giving him more time?

She tapped her slippered foot on the mosaic tiles and nearly turned around and ran back to her rooms before Solomon could reject her, when the door opened and the guard beckoned her to enter.

"Naamah," Solomon said, smiling as he strode toward her. His hair was rumpled and he still wore his night tunic.

"I woke you." She should have waited until evening or at least until she was certain. "I'm sorry. I can come another time. It is not important."

He took her hand and kissed it. "Of course it is important, or you would not be here." He led her to an area of plush cushions and settled her beside him. She glanced around, realizing that he had never brought her to this room. Why had he waited to welcome her here?

She studied their intertwined fingers a moment, then looked at him. He watched her, his expression puzzled as though he were trying to unravel a riddle she had proposed to him.

"I am not completely certain, my lord," she said softly,

feeling heat rush to her cheeks, but she did not look away. She wanted to see the ever-changing facets of his handsome face and see how he took her news. "But I believe I am carrying your child."

His dark eyes grew wide, and he seemed to think over the matter for a moment. A smile lit his face, and he took both of her hands in his and squeezed her fingers. "Already? I did not think . . . that is . . ." He let out a breath. "A child!" He kissed her then and pulled her close, laughing. "My dear Naamah. A child of our love." He held her at arm's length. "Surely God will give us a son."

She laughed in relief at his reaction. "I thought it wrong to come here, to tell you so soon. When you did not return last night . . ." Or the night before, though she did not say it. "I thought you had grown tired of me."

He held her close again, and she could feel the beat of his heart against her ear. "Never think such a thing, my love." The words were soft, a caress.

She rested her head against him, glad now that she had come. He held her for several moments, and she wished time would stand still. When at last he stood and pulled her to her feet, she looked into his eyes. He smiled down at her and walked her to the door, promising to call for her soon.

A baby! She pressed a hand to her heart, barely daring to believe it. Her father would be pleased beyond measure!

She did not realize it immediately, or even halfway through the morning as she penned a letter to her father with the news. So caught up was she in the excitement of the moment that it did not occur to her until the servants came to dress her for the evening meal that Solomon had not invited her to stay with him this day or to return to him this night. And in that moment she sensed a slight shift in their relationship. He had said he would call for her.

She was not to visit him unannounced again.

—m—

Solomon walked the halls of the palace after a meeting with his father, trying to slow his pace. His hands curled in and out, frustration oozing from his shoulders to his hurried feet. They'd spent the afternoon going over plans for the temple—a good, productive day. But then Solomon left the room with the temple model and ran into his manservant, who carried news that in the months since his wedding Adonijah's following was growing in strength. Yet still his father waited to name an heir.

He drew in a breath, told himself to calm. Anger would accomplish nothing. He was at God's mercy and he knew it. *Please, sovereign Lord, if my father dies, my mother and brothers and wife and future child will be killed.* He cared not for himself, though he had no desire to lose his life, but he could not bear to see others suffer because the wrong son took the throne.

And his father had told his mother that he, Solomon, was that promised heir. He'd spent his life training for the position. Why then did his father hesitate? Though he was still young, no one knew the day of his death. What if something happened suddenly? Would Adonijah try to kill their father as Absalom once had?

The thoughts churned as he walked until he found himself at Naamah's door. He stopped short. This had not been his intent, and in truth, his rooms were not far from here, but a moment later, he knocked and she welcomed him into her arms.

"I've missed you," she said, kissing him boldly. Her smile eased some of the tension, and he realized that perhaps this was exactly where he needed to be. But he would not complain yet again about the lack of coronation. He needed a distraction, something to keep him from thinking of the kingdom at all.

"I went past the field of a sluggard today," he said, remembering his earlier ride through the fields outside of Jerusalem. He lounged close to her side among the pillows adorning a large couch.

"What did you see?" she asked, wrapping a hand around his arm.

"I saw a man who lacks judgment. Thorns had come up everywhere and the ground was covered with weeds. The stone wall was in ruins." He gave her a thoughtful look. "I applied my heart to what I observed and learned a lesson from what I saw."

"What did you learn?" Her eyes lit as though she loved hearing him teach her.

"I learned that a little sleep, a little slumber, a little folding of the hands to rest—and poverty will come on you like a bandit and scarcity like an armed man."

Their gazes locked a moment, and he could not stop the slightest clenching of his jaw, for he could not completely forget the irony of the foolish sluggard compared to the wasted moments that his father continued to let slip by.

"You are not a man who would ever face such scarcity, my husband, for you are too wise to be lazy." She took his hand, again easing some of his tension. He gave hers a gentle squeeze. "I like it when you share your thoughts with me."

He gazed down at her and traced a finger along her jaw.

"Thank you for listening." He looked beyond her, his mind drifting.

"I find the heart of my husband a deep well. One whose depths I long to scale, to know your every thought." She leaned closer to him and kissed his bearded cheek.

She drew him back as only she could. He pulled her onto his lap and kissed her. She relaxed into his embrace.

"As the heavens are high and the earth is deep, beloved, so the hearts of kings are unsearchable. Though I may not yet be king, I fear you wish to know more than I am able to tell. I don't fully understand myself. How can I share with you what I have yet to grasp?"

"Your mother seems to understand you," she said softly, stroking his cheek and coaxing his gaze toward hers.

He touched a finger to her lips. "Only God knows the heart, dear wife. My mother knows me even less than you do."

"Well, I am glad to know you at all!" She wrapped both arms around his neck and kissed him. "My lover is mine and I am his," she whispered in his ear.

The poem, so often shared, made him laugh. "Your lips are like a scarlet ribbon, my love," he said as he hovered a kiss just over her lips. "Your mouth is lovely." He had returned to the dance of their love, one he had nearly forgotten in his constant occupation with ruling. They spoke the words like a sacred song.

He rested beside her that night. But no sooner had he drifted into sleep than shouts in the outer halls shook them both awake.

"Stay here," Solomon ordered as he quickly dressed and left her rooms.

SIX

A shiver worked through Naamah, and her mind whirled with images of her past, of Ima, of a cousin lost to Molech, and of the ever-present worry of Solomon's own brothers. She wanted desperately to follow Solomon, to feel his reassurance beside her. But by his tone she knew he was not to be disobeyed.

Quaking, she wrapped the covers about her and crept to the door. If anything happened to Solomon . . . She placed a hand over the place where the babe grew in the secret place, her stomach twisting in a sickening knot. She had to protect him . . . or her. Footsteps rushed through the halls outside her door, and she heard distant shouts coming from both directions. Her nerves were near the snapping point when Inaya burst through the door.

"What happened?" She rushed to Inaya's side, pulled into her maid's strong embrace.

"The king is ill."

She stepped back and searched Inaya's worried gaze. Inaya

was her rock, her strength, but the fear in her eyes made Naamah's knees wobble once more.

She sank onto her bed, which still held Solomon's warmth. Had only a few moments passed? "Why hasn't Solomon come to tell me this?" In her condition, she needed him more than ever now.

"You should be asking me, 'How ill?' dear girl, not worrying about why your husband is not here. If the king dies without naming Solomon king, there will be more trouble than you have seen in your lifetime." Inaya paced the floor in front of her.

She had never seen her maid so agitated, wringing her hands, and suddenly Naamah was no longer weary but contrite. Inaya was right, and she was being childish. "What can we do?"

"Pray to Solomon's God to spare the king's life until Solomon's coronation. Your life and the life of your child depend on it."

She put a hand to her belly where the slight swell of a child had started to show. She had proudly shown Solomon just hours before, and he had held her close. "I had not thought of that." In all of her worry, the danger had always been for her husband and his mother. She had not seriously thought that the life of her child could also be a threat to Adonijah or any other of Solomon's older brothers.

"Well, it is time you did." Inaya stopped pacing and sank to her knees on a lambskin rug in front of the couch. She bowed low, and Naamah recognized her intent.

Naamah slipped from the bed and came to kneel beside her nurse, bowing low on the floor as well. She closed her eyes, her thoughts swirling, incoherent. She did not know how to pray for this! *Please, Unseen One, spare my husband.* The prayer became a mantra in her heart until she heard Inaya begging God to save the king's life. Fear still held its grip on her heart, but slowly, haltingly, her prayers included the king and Solomon's mother and the babe. She did not ask for herself. It seemed too selfish a prayer, but as the night wore on, she pleaded with Him to save the king's life until her husband was king and David could hold his grandson on his knees.

A knock on her door startled her, but she could not get up from kneeling fast enough to open it. A servant relieved her of the need, and she had just regained her bearings when Bathsheba's maid Tirzah approached her.

"What news do you bring?" She moved to coax her legs to cease their tingling.

"The king is quite ill, but they believe he will recover."

Naamah paused her pacing. "They are quite sure of this?" Relief filled her, and her head felt suddenly too light. The room moved, though she was standing still.

Tirzah, seeming to sense her wooziness, steadied her and guided her to her couch. "As sure as anyone can be about life and death, mistress."

A servant brought her water and she greedily drank. "This is good news. Thank you for telling me."

Tirzah smiled. "As always, mistress." She bid farewell, and Inaya helped Naamah to her bed, where she crawled beneath the covers to finally sleep. But the trauma of the night brought fitful dreams.

—m—

Solomon stood at the foot of his father's bed, looking down at his sleeping form. He'd seen improvement in the past few weeks, however slight. But even in sleep, the king's body involuntarily shivered. A sliver of fear worked through Solomon, raising his anxiety to even greater heights than it had been the past year. He drew in a breath of the heated air and moved from the room, quietly slipping into his mother's adjoining apartments.

"Solomon! How good of you to come." His mother rose from her seat and embraced him.

Solomon returned her embrace, clinging to her for a brief moment. There was something comforting in his mother's arms. She was the one person he had always known would defend and care for him no matter what befell them. "I'm worried, Ima." Solomon took the seat she offered while she sat opposite him. Tirzah hurried to supply them with watered wine and a simple platter of dates and nuts and cheese.

"He is much improved from his attack," she said, eyeing him closely. "But you are right. There is cause for concern. Who knows what is causing this malady that has made him shiver day and night? Even my body warmth does nothing to reach the deep chill within him." She took a drink, but their gazes held over the lip of the cup.

"Is he strong enough to rule? Can we convince him to name me co-regent before it is too late?" He wrung his hands, wishing he didn't feel so utterly helpless.

"The king's counselors have decided, with the king's permission, to send for a virgin to warm the king's bed. Perhaps that will help him." His mother gave him a resigned look. "It is not ideal, of course, as a new wife will have constant access to your father. She will be his nurse and warm his bed, but the king has assured me that the woman will remain a virgin.

She will be a wife in name only." She smoothed a wrinkle in her robe. "The king would appease his counselors."

"And how do they plan to choose a trustworthy and beautiful woman? Scour the entire land?" He leaned closer, elbows on his knees, and searched her gaze. "You know Adonijah could try to place a spy in my father's very rooms if he hears of this."

"Adonijah will not be the person to choose the girl, even if he discovers the need for her." His mother's look held a sense of serenity even as she clenched her jaw.

"Who will?" he asked, though he already knew the answer. The realization brought a small feeling of relief.

"They have already searched the kingdom and brought several candidates to Jerusalem. I will visit with each of them and choose the one best suited for the job." His mother gave him a reassuring look. "Trust me, my son, I will make sure Adonijah is nowhere near when I interview the girls, and I have learned over time that one must be both cautious and discerning." She folded her hands. "And I believe I know the type of woman who would please you when the time comes."

He leaned against the couch and allowed a slight smile. "I would enjoy the chance to meet her, or at least see the choices."

His mother looked at her cup a moment, then met his gaze, unflinching. "I think, my son, that your current pregnant wife would be very hurt if she ever learned that you were already considering choosing another bride." The rebuke stung, and Solomon straightened. "I know that one day it is inevitable that you as king will take more wives, but you know how palace servants talk. A meeting like this would get back to Naamah, and I simply do not think it wise."

Solomon nodded, feeling chastened but accepting the truth of his mother's words. She was right, of course. "When will this choice take place?"

"The girls should arrive in a few days. I will begin meeting with them after they have settled. The sooner the better for your father's sake. I only hope we find one who is gentle and caring, who can be all that your father needs." She sipped her wine and set the cup aside.

Solomon stood and she joined him. He took her hands in his. "As always, Ima, you are wise. And I am thinking of my future while you are thinking of my father's well-being. I must admit, I am ashamed to have thought only of my future and not his."

"You fear that he will pass into Sheol before you have been named king. I fear it too, my son." He saw the vulnerable look pass through her dark eyes. "I did not expect this to happen to him. Not now. He is too young."

Solomon kissed her cheek. "He may yet recover, Ima. We must not lose hope."

"No, we must not. Perhaps the new nurse will have healing powers to help him. Do not yet fret over the future, my son. When the time is right, God will make a way." She squeezed his hands and released them, then embraced him once more. "Thank you for stopping to see me."

He touched her cheek. "Always, Ima." Whatever would he do without her someday? She had always been his confidante. He needed her even more than he needed his father, even more than he needed Naamah, though he loved each in his own way.

"I will choose a good wife," she assured him as he headed to the door. "Never fear."

He looked back at her and smiled. "I won't." His heart felt lighter as he made his way to court. He would help preside over it with his older brothers, while they all wondered how long the king would be bound to his bed.

CHAPTER

SEVEN

The palace court loomed before the small caravan, dwarfing the camels in its size, stunning the women in its opulence. Abishag had not expected this. But then, she had never traveled any distance from home until now. And she had certainly never seen such wealth.

The camels lumbered beneath arched gates and came to rest on a tiled courtyard. Gleaming limestone steps led to a columned portico where wide double doors stood shut, and the face of a lion greeted each visitor from the carved wood above their heads. Abishag turned, taking in every facet of the outer palace, as her camel dutifully knelt on the command of one of the men. She was barely aware of his hand offered for her dismount and did not realize her mouth gaped open until Mica, one of the other girls, touched her shoulder and whispered the knowledge in her ear. She clamped it shut.

"It is not anything like I imagined," she whispered, seeing Mica's own expression held the awe she felt.

Mica nodded. "The gossips did not tell the whole tale."

They never did. But she did not say so. Instead, she followed the woman in charge of their care around the back of the palace to a door that she said led to the women's quarters.

"You will be given rooms here and beauty treatments for seven days," she said once they were all settled within the compound. "At the end of the week, the queen will visit the group of you, and those she picks will receive a second interview. It would be in your best interest to try to please her." She spun on her heel after that, and another group of female servants ushered them to separate rooms.

The space she was given was bigger than the chamber she'd shared with her younger nieces back home, but it felt odd and strangely discomforting to be so alone. "Am I not to share the room with another?" she asked as a young girl laid fresh linens on a low table and poured water from a pitcher into a golden goblet.

The girl handed the goblet to Abishag. "No, my lady. Each candidate has a place of her own. I am afraid it is small compared to the normal rooms of the king's concubines, but most of you will not be staying." She turned then and looked the room over, as if making sure she had not forgotten anything. "Are there any more questions you have for me?" she asked, facing Abishag again. She smiled, showing slightly crooked teeth. She was pretty in an odd sort of way, though she was too young to know what beauty her life might hold.

"No. No more questions." Abishag grasped the water goblet between both hands, feeling the coolness of the water seep from the metal to her fingers. She nearly saw her reflection in the shining gold but did not let her gaze linger. She had plenty of questions, if the truth was known, but she watched the maid leave without voicing them. The girl had answered most of them when she said, "Most of you will not be staying."

—⁂—

The week passed so quickly, Abishag had to stop several times a day to remind herself of her surroundings. Mornings were spent eating specially made foods and plenty of fresh water and fruit, then they would take baths in a mixture of goat's milk and honey. Even their hair and faces were treated with milk and oils from the olive trees and the more rare oil from the coconut palm.

By week's end they stood before a eunuch named Kato, the man in charge of the king's harem. He looked them over as though they were sheep to be sold at market, even forcing them to smile wide so he could inspect their teeth. Abishag found the whole thing ridiculous and nearly choked on a laugh when he drew close enough to smell her breath.

She did not expect him to ask her to follow him. When he did, she stole a glance at Mica, whose look said, "Didn't I tell you?" Nissa, another girl from the area near Shunem, followed Kato, and two more Abishag did not recognize. Mica was not chosen, much to Abishag's sadness.

"You will wait here for the queen," Kato said after he had ushered them down a long hall and into a room large enough to hold a small feast. There were no couches or chairs to sit on, but one glance around the room showed a variety of tapestries and painted objects, as though this was a small treasury. She would learn much later that it was merely an antechamber to the audience hall.

"Are you nervous?" Nissa asked after they had waited longer than they expected to.

Abishag nodded. "I suspect we are all wondering what awaits us in the unknown." She could tell by the way Nissa held her arms that she could barely keep from shivering in fear. Abishag did not want her to think she didn't understand, but she truly did not feel as though her life were about to end. She was more interested in studying the painted urns and woven patterns in the tapestries. Such skill to create such beauty! Oh for the time and ability to learn these skills. She had spent too many days in the fields or tending to the needs and whims of her sisters-in-law to learn the ways of artists. But her heart did not miss the song that seemed to move among the objects, from the paintings on the walls to the wooden stringed instruments standing on display.

The door opened, catching her by surprise, but as she turned at the hush of the girls' voices, she saw that they were no longer to be kept waiting. The queen, dressed in royal garments with a thin golden circlet about her thick dark hair, swept into the room with gentle grace.

The girls quickly bowed before her, faces to the tiles, and Abishag suddenly realized her mistake when she was the only one still standing, staring at the queen's beauty. She sank to her knees and followed the example of the others, but not before catching the hint of a smile on the queen's beautiful but aging face.

"Rise, all of you," the queen said, her voice commanding yet carrying a slight lilt.

Abishag rose slowly, keeping time with the others, and clasped her hands in front of her. She could not keep her gaze from searching the queen's, though she told herself she would surely be the first one sent away if she did not remember all she had been so quickly taught.

"One of you will be chosen today, and as soon as your father or brother can be summoned, you will enter the private chambers of my husband to become his wife." Her kind eyes did not match the tight lines that suddenly appeared around her mouth. She looked from one to the other, and when her gaze rested on Abishag's, she gave a slight nod.

So there was to be no second interview. The king's need for this wife—one of them—must be great for the queen to act in such haste. The thought troubled Abishag.

"Does this please you?" The queen's question startled her, but she could smile and nod vigorously as Nissa did when the queen met her gaze. It would please her to serve the king. But it did not please her to wed a man old enough to be her father.

Bathsheba asked several more questions and seemed to find great interest in their reactions as she silently studied them, then one by one she took the girls to a side room and spoke to them privately. Abishag waited while the others completed their interview and then left by the door in which they had come.

At last Abishag and the queen were alone.

"It seems there is no reason to pull you aside to the smaller room, Abishag." The queen's voice had softened, and her tone once again carried the lilt of music, matching that of Abishag's heart. She liked her immediately and offered a true smile.

"I am curious about you, Abishag," she said, crossing her arms in front of her. "You are not like the others."

Abishag found a sudden need to look at her feet for a lengthy breath, then lifted her gaze once more to meet the queen's. "I suppose that has been true all of my life, my queen. I wonder, though, why the king needs another wife when he has you?"

The queen smiled despite Abishag's audacity.

She, on the other hand, covered her mouth, aghast at the words she had allowed to slip past. "I'm sorry," she hastened to add. "I had no right to speak such words."

"On the contrary, my girl. This is precisely why I like you. I could sense honesty in you the moment I walked into the room and you forgot to bow." She chuckled, but Abishag would not allow herself to do the same, though her heart fluttered at the comment.

"Forgive me, my queen. This is all so new to me." She swept her arm in an arc to encompass the room, though she knew the queen understood she meant the palace, the wealth, and all of Jerusalem.

"And much more will become new in days to come." She extended a hand to grasp Abishag's and briefly squeezed it. "The king does not need another wife so much as he needs a nurse. He is ill, Abishag. And nothing I do or his servants can do will warm him as he once held warmth. In his rooms, braziers glow day and night, and I admit, my body cannot stand the added heat at this time of my life."

Abishag nodded, though she did not fully understand. Her sister-in-law Batya had blown hot and cold from time to time. Perhaps that was what the queen meant.

"So what exactly would I do as his nurse?" She felt the need to ask something, though she was not sure this question was the right one.

The queen touched her chin with a delicate ringed hand as though contemplating her answer. "Whatever he needs, I suppose. Most of all, you will lie beside him as he sleeps and try to draw his ardor. Make him desire you, Abishag, that he might feel warmth once more."

Heat crept up Abishag's cheeks at the words. How was she to court his desire? Not even her closest sister-in-law, Kelila, had spoken to her of the ways of men. She had learned what little she knew from watching the rams and ewes mate. But she did not share her ignorance. Somehow she hoped the king would tell her.

"Does the king . . . that is, can the king do the things he once did?" She meant walk and talk and go about his kingly duties, but by Bathsheba's look, she must have assumed a different train of thought.

The queen's smile was sad. "The king is not as he once was, Abishag. I do not know how many more days God will choose to give him. It may be that you will remain a wife, yet not a wife." She studied her ringed fingers, and Abishag sensed the subject a painful one. "But rest assured, you will be well provided for all of your days."

The queen bid her farewell then, until the morrow, and Abishag returned to her chambers, where maids waited to whisk her off to yet another beauty treatment. She did not stop to consider the queen's words or the intent behind them until sleep eluded her and the song faded from her heart.

EIGHT

One night a few weeks after Abishag's addition to the royal family, the king was again conspicuously absent from the evening's banquet. Afterward, Solomon offered Naamah his arm and guided her along the halls that led to his father's rooms.

"Is something wrong, my lord?" she asked as they passed the king's gardens and stopped at one of the doors with the lion's-head symbol.

Solomon looked down, smiled, and shook his dark head. "Nothing is wrong, my love. I wanted to pay my father a visit and thought you would like to come."

She smiled her pleasure and gave him a slight bow. "I am honored, my husband." She gently squeezed his arm where her hand rested.

He ushered her past the guard and into the opulent quarters of the king. The heat from several braziers hit like a wave, and it took a moment for her body to adjust to the change from the temperatures in the cooler halls. Lamps flickered in golden sconces along the walls, and the king sat huddled in blankets before one of the fires. Bathsheba sat beside him. One glance around the room showed no sign of the new wife.

She let out a breath, relieved though slightly disappointed, wanting to meet this future rival, Abishag.

"My son." The king's voice did not hold the strength or stability it once did. Many thick blankets covered him from head to foot, and yet he shivered.

Solomon knelt at the king's side and placed a hand on his father's knee. "How are you this evening, Abba?" She loved the closeness Solomon shared with his father and prayed in that moment that her child would share the same relationship.

"All is well, my son." King David smiled at Solomon, then seemed to notice her for the first time. "Is this our Naamah?" He lifted a veined hand from beneath the blankets, and she hurried forward to take it in her own. How cold it felt! She did not reveal her shock at how quickly his health had taken a turn. Was it not only a few months past that he had been so strong?

"I am here, my lord. I pray for you daily, that your health will return to you."

He smiled at that and squeezed her fingers before releasing his hold and drawing his hand back beneath the covers. Movement from the shadows caught her attention as she stood, and she noticed a beautiful young woman emerge from wherever she had been hiding. The woman placed another blanket over the king's back, then stood above him and gently kneaded his shoulders.

Solomon took Naamah's elbow and led her to a couch near his mother while he took a chair closer to his father.

"Introductions are in order, my son," Bathsheba said. She glanced between them and inclined her head to Abishag.

Solomon pulled his gaze from watching the young woman. "Of course, Ima." He looked at Naamah, his eyes twinkling. "Naamah, this is Abishag, my father's newest wife."

Abishag looked up at the mention of her name and offered a genuine smile.

"A pleasure to meet you," Naamah managed to say. She narrowed her eyes, taking in every facet of the girl's beauty, finding her own wanting. She firmed her lips into a thin line, forcing back the sudden jealousy that rose like a coiling snake within her, wanting to strike out at this woman who was a wife yet not a wife. King David's wife. Not Solomon's, she reminded herself, wishing she was sitting close enough to take Solomon's arm possessively in hers.

"A pleasure to meet you as well, mistress." Abishag's voice fairly floated like the graceful movement of an eagle's wings. She smiled as she continued to massage the king's shoulders.

Naamah did not want to watch the girl but was struck by her simple beauty. As the night waned, her laughter filled the room with greater warmth than the braziers, and Naamah could not help but like her. She did not want to like her. Not when she saw the way her husband laughed with her and seemed freely at ease in her presence. His gaze moved as often to her as it did to Naamah, perhaps more so. She was already losing him to a woman that was not even his!

The thought churned unstoppably on their walk to her rooms after they bid the king and queen good night. Barely able to contain jealous tears, she wondered if Solomon even noticed her mood. Surely he would leave her chambers and go quickly to his own, but in a surprising instant he followed her inside and scooped her into his arms, laughing.

He settled her among the bed cushions. "What did you think of Abishag?" he asked, his voice light, almost jubilant.

She looked away, unable to hold his intent gaze. "She makes a fine nurse for your father. She is gentle and kind. Her laughter is enjoyable."

He cupped Naamah's chin and coaxed her gaze upward. He bent low, his face close enough for her to catch the minty scent of his breath. "I'm glad you like her. She will serve my father well." His kiss held familiar longing, but she struggled to return it. He lifted a brow, searching her face. "What troubles you, beloved?"

She scooted backward against the wooden frame of the bed. Her lower lip trembled despite the silent admonishment she gave herself not to cry. A tear slipped down her cheek, betraying her.

Solomon's expression softened, and he caught the tear with his thumb. "Tell me," he said gently. He placed one hand over the babe and with the other drew her close. "Is this about Abishag?"

She nodded against him. "Is she to be your new wife?"

His chest lifted in a sigh, and for a moment he did not speak. At last he held her slightly away so their gazes touched. "Probably."

She swallowed hard, fighting the anger that rose at his nonchalance. "Your father has not yet named you king."

His jaw tightened, but his look never wavered. He stroked

her cheek. "Naamah, a king's power is measured by the size of his harem. Marriage alliances with foreign nations are better than war. I would be unwise if I did not make such choices." He paused. "My marriage to you, while out of love, was also such an alliance."

His words made sense yet stung at the same time. "I will lose you to a harem." She lifted both hands to cup his cheeks and touched her nose to his. "I want what your mother and father have. Do not make me fight for you, my husband."

His smile took in every facet of her face, and she sensed the slightest flutter from the babe beneath his hand. Wonder filled her that she felt such movement at all. Perhaps it was only her heightened awareness of his nearness. He held such power over her!

"My mother and father have been through much hardship and struggle to achieve the love they share. I pray we never face such hardship." He cupped her cheek and traced a finger along her jaw. "I love you, Naamah," he said, kissing her. His fingers moved from her middle to sift the strands of her hair. "Never doubt that."

She nodded, wishing she could promise what he wanted, but the words would not come. Instead, she returned his kiss, giving in to his desire. She would use whatever feminine charm she possessed to please him.

But he was right about war and the power of kings. She had seen enough as her father's daughter to know that truth. His words filled her with nagging doubts for their future. If she could find a way to change it, she would.

—✺—

Solomon left Naamah's rooms before dawn, choosing to allow her to sleep. Her words had caught him off guard the night before, and he'd done the only thing he could think to do. He'd reassured her of his love. As he'd done many times since their marriage. As he'd done now to appease the guilt he felt over his attraction to Abishag.

He couldn't deny his feelings for his father's nurse. *Wife.* Yes, wife. But his mother had picked well, both of them knowing the girl would likely remain a virgin until she passed into Solomon's hands. He shook himself. Abishag belonged to his father, not him. Yet it didn't stop Solomon from feeling a connection to her. Abishag shared his love of artistry and beauty and song. Naamah attempted to join the dance with him, but he always felt as though their connection was on an intellectual level more than an artistic one.

But her jealousy was real. And justified. He *had* paid too much attention to Abishag in Naamah's presence and laughed a little too freely in response to the girl's musical, lilting laughter. A smile begged to emerge at the memory as he walked the halls to his rooms, but he refused to allow it. He must get hold of his emotions and keep Naamah satisfied. Especially while she carried his child. The last thing he needed was for her to fall into despair before the babe was born. Something could happen to the child, or perhaps Naamah would not live through childbirth. He would never forgive himself if he caused her undue pain.

Someday she would have to accept other wives, which he was certain she understood. To think she could keep him to herself once he ruled as king was unthinkable and unwise.

He entered his rooms and sank onto a couch as servants

rushed to bring him food and drink to break the fast with a morning meal. He wasn't nearly as hungry as he usually was. But as he thought on the issue that would not let him rest, he decided that he was right about wives and the power they brought to kings. In time, Naamah would learn to accept that fact.

NINE

The sound of the door creaking caught Abishag's attention. No one allowed it to linger open for long lest the cool air from the outer hall suck the heat from the king's chambers. She glanced up, and her heart gave the slightest kick at the sight of Solomon in his princely garb. He was alone, without his wife Naamah.

Her whole body grew warm as he strode into the room, and she knew it was not from the fire in the brazier. She tucked the blanket more securely about the king's shoulders and added a piece of wood to the already blazing fire. Still the king shivered, despite her attempts to warm him.

"How are you today, Father?" Solomon knelt on the plush wool rug beneath his father's wrapped feet and kissed the hem of his robe, as careful as she had been not to disturb the piles of blankets surrounding the king.

"I am well, my son. Better now that you have come." King David extended his shaking ringed hand for Solomon to hold and briefly squeeze. Solomon did not kiss the king's ring as she had seen Adonijah and David's other sons do. But then Solomon seemed to hold a special bond with his father. The king smiled even as he pulled his hand beneath the covers once more.

"Are you up to discussing the plans for the temple?" Solomon asked. It was then that she noticed the scroll he had tucked securely into his belt. He pulled it from its hold and held it up for the king to see.

David nodded. "I would like nothing better."

Abishag hurried to bring a small table to set between them so Solomon could spread the parchment before the king, then moved to stand along the wall to listen.

She learned much in these times and found herself privy to information even some of the king's own advisors did not know. She was the only wife who did not leave the king's side unless Bathsheba came to stay with him. Even then, she often bid Abishag remain. They were a strange family—the king and queen, Solomon and his wife, together with her, though she told herself she was not really part of this relation. The marriage was simply a formality to allow her to serve the king in such a personal way. He was neither her father nor her husband in the real sense, and Solomon was neither her brother nor her husband. She felt driven and tossed in an aimless sea. Especially when Adonijah came to sit among them.

"I wondered about gathering more of the precious stones and wood and metals we will need to build this palatial structure, Father. Are you strong enough to call the elders together to request their participation?"

She studied Solomon as she pondered his question. She barely heard the king's response but knew it would be no different today than every other day that Solomon had asked. What Solomon really wanted to say had more to do with his coronation than gathering funds for the temple. For without the power, all the gold in Jerusalem would not allow him the means to command that such a temple be built.

She shook herself from her wayward thoughts as she noticed Solomon motion her to join them. He inclined his head toward his father, whose head now bobbed forward in sleep. The king often fell into unexpected naps, even when talking with his favorite son.

She hurried to place another pillow to cradle the king's head, tucked the blanket more securely about him, and backed slowly away. Solomon stood and bid her walk him to the door.

"How are you today?" he asked once they were out of the king's hearing.

"I am well, thank you." She smiled, hoping he did not notice the way her cheeks flamed at his nearness. "And you?"

His shoulders sagged then, surprising her. "He does not see how ill he is." He glanced toward the center of the room where the king snored softly. "If he does not name an heir soon, there will be war over the right to wear the crown."

His words chilled her, despite the heated room. "Adonijah?" She need say no more.

He nodded. "I have heard rumors," he whispered. "I fear my older brother is gaining quite the following, not unlike Absalom."

She had heard the tales of Absalom's treachery. And Adonijah was the next in line who cared to claim David's crown. "What will you do?"

He looked beyond her, and his chest lifted in a deep sigh.

"I don't know. I had hoped . . ." His voice trailed off a moment until he looked at her once more. "When I married Naamah, I had hoped my father would also name me coregent with him. But he saw no need to rush things, in spite of my mother's suggestions. Then he became ill."

"And now the chill drains his energy so that he thinks of little else." She touched his arm in comfort before realizing what she had done and quickly removed her hand.

His smile unnerved her. "You know him well."

She studied her feet. "Only a little."

His fingers lifted her chin, causing her pulse to jump. "You have a good heart, Abishag." He released his grip. "If I brought you parchment and ink, would you set down the words to your songs?" He knew she had created songs for his father, as his father had done himself since his youth.

"I fear I do not know how to write. It is a skill the women of my village had no need to learn."

"But as the wife of a king, there is much you should now know," he said. "I will send the parchment, along with a tutor. Whatever skill you wish to master, you may do so when my father sleeps."

His kindness unnerved her. "Thank you, my lord." She bowed at the waist. She had never been given any training for the sheer pleasure of learning. "There is so much I long to understand." She laughed softly and he joined her.

"This is why I like you," he said, bending closer to her ear. "You long for the things I long for. If only I had the time to seek them."

He didn't say the rest, what she knew was true. Until he was named king, he was not free to do as he pleased. He spent his waking moments learning all he could about the kingdom and how to manage it, while he spent his nights praying he would be the one allowed to do so.

—◦◦◦—

The weeks came and went in continual sameness. Solomon, true to his word, sent parchment and a tutor, and King David delighted in watching her learn in between his intermittent naps. Music filled the king's chambers as the king taught her to play some of the instruments he had fashioned, and she thrilled to feel the joy of song bringing more warmth to his body than the fire or the woolen coverings.

One evening as she played a song she had created for the king and queen, the guard entered, asking permission for Adonijah to join them. Solomon always strode past the guards and needed no introduction, which she discerned did not go unnoticed by his brothers or those who would gossip throughout the palace. Abishag was secretly glad Solomon enjoyed this pleasure.

She was not at all happy to greet Adonijah.

Her fingers stilled on the strings of the lyre and the words died on her lips as Adonijah stepped into the room.

"Please, do not stop on account of me," he said, his smile confident and the look in his eyes too focused on her.

She looked away and glanced at her husband the king, suddenly relieved to have that connection to him. Adonijah could not touch her as long as King David lived. In that moment, she prayed he would live forever.

Adonijah knelt at his father's side and kissed the signet ring on the king's extended hand. He merely nodded politely at Bathsheba, and Abishag saw his lips twitch in the slightest tightening of his jaw.

"You look well tonight, Father." Adonijah took the seat opposite David and Bathsheba, closest to Abishag.

"As do you, my son. To what do I owe the honor of this visit?"

She knew the real question had more to do with what the king could do for his son. Everyone came seeking something from the king, even in his weakened state.

"I had heard you were feeling better, that you are moving forward with plans to build the temple, so I wanted to come to offer my assistance." Adonijah's smile seemed genuine, but Abishag did not trust him.

"I have no plans to build the temple. Adonai has only allowed me to assist in the design and preparation. This has not changed." The king's frown troubled her. Had someone fed Adonijah false information, or was this son trying to use the king's favorite subject to learn things he should not know?

She silently slipped from her seat. There would be no more music in Adonijah's presence.

Adonijah laughed, the sound jarring. "I see I am mistaken then. It is your heir who will build the temple to our God." It wasn't a question, and the king did not respond to it. "Forgive me, Father. I listened to false information. If there is anything I can do to help you gather the materials you need, if you should want me to call the elders together to bring their treasures to the king's storehouses, you have only to ask."

Abishag's heart beat double time as she set the lyre in the leather casing and took it to the shelf where it normally rested. Solomon discussed this so often with his father that she could not imagine the words coming out of anyone else's mouth. Yet this was clearly not Solomon sitting before his father now. Surely the king would not give in to Adonijah's request.

She slipped farther into the shadows of the room, her hands clasped, wishing she had reason to leave and yet glad to be privy to this conversation. Perhaps there was some way she could warn Solomon.

"Thank you for your offer, my son." King David's words drew her wayward thoughts into focus. "I am sure there will be time enough for what you suggest."

She studied Adonijah's reaction, saw the clenching of his hands, but a moment later he relaxed them, smiled, and stood. "Very well then. I only came for a moment to see how you are faring. I am glad to see you are doing much better than the rumors foretold."

"Thank you for taking the time to come, my son."

Adonijah bowed before the king once more, then turned and walked from the chambers without a backward glance. Once he was out of sight and the door was securely shut, she moved closer to the king and queen.

"Can I get you anything, my lord?" she asked, kneeling at his side.

He touched her shoulder. "A blanket. Several. And add some wood to the fire." She touched his arm, surprised at the coolness of his skin. Somehow he had shown himself strong in the presence of the son who wanted to wear his crown. But he was not strong.

She hurried to do his bidding.

TEN

Despite Abishag's concerns over the king's frailty, his slow improvement surprised her. He was still not well enough to return to court or to preside over official matters other than a few daily conversations with his advisors, but he allowed her to use less wood in the brazier, and he took fewer naps during the waking hours.

One morning she had arisen early to use the palace mikvah before returning to the king. It felt good to be purified, clean once more before Adonai. Since she could not stray from the palace walls, she could not visit the tabernacle where the ark rested. Her worship came in song and dance, and in recent weeks she had taken to sketching the trees and flowers in the garden on scraps of clay. Someday she hoped Bathsheba would teach her to use the mosaics and turn the tiled walkway of the king's gardens into more than simple stone.

But all thoughts of such pursuits fled her mind when she nearly bumped into Adonijah in the king's halls as she passed near the audience chamber. His presence here should not have jolted her as it did. The king's sons and courtiers met daily in the chamber to judge some of the lesser cases the king could not, though the more difficult ones were still brought to him through his advisors. She knew that Solomon took turns with his brothers, but none had taken over as co-regent. It would not be fitting without the king's approval.

"Abishag. I did not expect to see you here." Adonijah's voice was smooth, like the oil of the olive at its first pressing. "How lovely you look, my queen."

His queen? She was not a queen in any sense. But clearly Adonijah thought her worthy of the title. "Thank you, my lord." She ducked her head and turned to go to the king's chambers by another route. But Adonijah stayed her with a hand to her shoulder. His touch felt like the scorching of fire. She jerked, stepping away from him.

He held up a hand in apology. "Forgive me, Abishag. I have no business detaining you." He paused, but his intense gaze held her captive. "I wonder, though, if you might consider doing something for me."

Wariness crept up her spine. "That depends, of course, on what you are asking of me, my lord." She clasped her hands together, determined to still the sudden trembling that had overtaken her.

He tilted his head and lifted a brow, studying her. "You are as beautiful as they say." The statement seemed to come out of nowhere. He had seen her in the king's presence enough times to know what she looked like.

She held her peace, waiting, anxious.

Adonijah glanced around as if fearing they would be overheard. "I wonder if you might convince the king to allow me more authority to judge the people in his absence.

There is much work to be done, and many in the city are worried that the kingdom is falling into chaos while my father fights his illness. My brother Solomon already takes on many of the cases here in the palace courts, but there are other places to judge, at the city gates or in some of the cities of refuge."

"I do not see what this has to do with me, my lord." Though she saw too clearly what he did not say. "I am merely the king's nurse. I do not engage in matters of the kingdom."

"Perhaps not," he said, leaning close. "But you have the king's ear. You can convince my father to name his heir, or at the very least to appoint us to act with greater power in his place."

She could not imagine why Adonijah thought she would agree with him or act on his behalf. He was older than her oldest brother and held no appeal whatsoever. Besides, she did not like his arrogance. But he did not know her heart yearned for Solomon, even more than it once did for the love of her youth.

"If my father names me king," he said softly, leaning closer still, "I would gladly take you as my wife."

She nearly felt his breath on her cheek and instinctively took a step back. "I belong to King David, my lord. And I must hurry back to him."

"King David will not live forever." Adonijah almost seemed pleased with that thought.

"Nevertheless, let us hope his days are long on the earth." She turned then and fled down the corridor, hoping he did not follow. Her heart thumped with the speed of many horses but was no match for her running feet. She did not stop until she reached the king's chambers and slipped inside, her breath heaving. Thanks be to Adonai, the king was still sleeping.

⸺◊⸺

The following day on Abishag's return from the palace cooking rooms, Rani, one of the servants, stopped her in the halls. "Have you heard the news?"

She had met Rani once or twice and was told the girl would one day become her own servant. But Abishag had no need of a servant when it was she who served the king. She shook her head. "What news?" Rani's expression set her heart to racing.

"Nathan the prophet is here. He just entered the queen's apartments." Her excited tone and wide eyes said this was important, but Abishag could not imagine why.

"Is this unusual?" She hated to appear the novice that she was, but she had only heard of the prophet through tales of long ago, before she was born.

"Nathan the prophet rarely brings good news," Rani whispered.

Abishag gave in to the tiniest frown. "Tell me what else you have heard." The gossips would have spread many a rumor by now. Surely this girl had listened to them.

Rani glanced behind and beyond her, then leaned in close to share her secret. "There are rumors in the city that Adonijah has declared himself king and our lord doesn't know it."

Abishag sucked in a breath. How quickly Adonijah had acted when only yesterday he spoke as though such a thing were a long way off. As if he needed her help! The liar!

The prophet must be here to warn Bathsheba and Solomon.

She thanked Rani with a nod and ran all the way back to the king's rooms. She greeted the guard with furrowed brow. "Is anyone with him?" she whispered for his ears alone.

The man shook his head. "No, mistress. He is still abed, as you left him."

Her heartbeat slowed its anxious racing. "Good." She brushed past him into the chambers and hurried to the king's side, her mind telling her to confirm the guard's words, and found King David exactly as she had left him.

He opened his eyes and smiled at her approach. "You are back."

"Yes, my lord. How are you feeling today?" He seemed frail yet slightly stronger than yesterday.

"Tired of this bed," he said with a soft chuckle. "Perhaps you can help me to the couch. I need to stretch these old limbs."

"Of course," she said, glancing quickly around for his thickest robe. She snatched it from the peg where she had placed it the night before, then gently pulled the covers back and took his arm. He wrapped a thin arm around her, and together they managed to get him to his feet.

"Age seems to have caught up with me, Abishag." He straightened, and she saw the slightest wince cross his still handsome features, as though something pained him.

"Do you hurt, my lord?" The physician had left her enough of the willow bark to give the king as he needed it, to ease the aches of whatever malady had overtaken him.

Oh how she wished he were well again. She wondered what life would have been like for him if he had not succumbed to this illness. She did not consider until later that she would not have met the king if he were well. She would still be living in her small village in her brother's house, forgotten and treated as a servant.

"No. No pain," he said, drawing her thoughts to him again. She glanced at him, assessing him. If he did not speak truth, it was only because he was weary of sleeping. The willow bark made him sleep day and night.

"That is good." She settled him onto his couch and tucked thick blankets around him.

His chest lifted in a deep sigh. "Thank you." He smiled at her but said nothing more.

She stepped into the adjoining chamber to heat some spiced wine over a small brazier and returned with a cup and placed it in the king's hands. He nodded at her and took a sip.

"Are you comfortable, my lord?"

He seemed not to hear her at first, his gaze taking her in, then growing distant.

"My lord?"

"What? Oh yes, I am quite snug in all of these blankets. Thank you."

She looked up at the sound of the king's side door opening, the one that led to his gardens and Bathsheba's chambers. The king's personal guard, Benaiah son of Jehoiada, entered.

"My lord, the lady Bathsheba would speak a word with you."

"Send her in then," the king said, straightening. He lifted the goblet to Abishag, and she hurried to take it from him.

Bathsheba entered quickly with a smile that did not reach her eyes. Abishag watched the king assess her, and a silent communication passed between them, as if the king could read her thoughts. She bowed, touching her forehead to the lion's skin that covered the tile floor at his feet.

"What is your wish?" he asked.

She rose with a grace Abishag had often admired and stretched her hands in supplication toward him. The lines along her mouth and brow increased. She drew in a shallow breath, and Abishag knew that her need was urgent.

"My lord," she said softly, her tone respectful, "you swore by Adonai Eloheikhem, the Lord your God, to your maidservant, saying, 'Assuredly Solomon your son shall reign after me, and he shall sit on my throne.' But now Adonijah has become king, and my lord the king, you do not know about it."

Abishag's pulse quickened, and she watched the king's eyes widen then narrow slightly, as though he struggled to accept the queen's words. But she knew it was true. She glimpsed an older man, his hair hanging long as the Nazirites wore it, standing beyond Bathsheba near the door. He was nearly hidden by Benaiah's broad bulk.

"He has sacrificed oxen and fattened cattle and sheep in abundance," Bathsheba continued, "and has invited the sons of the king, Abiathar the priest, and Joab. But he has not invited Solomon your servant. My lord the king, the eyes of all Israel are on you, to learn from you who will sit on the throne after you. Otherwise as soon as my lord the king is laid to rest with his fathers, Solomon and I will be treated as criminals."

Her words fell like a heavy pall in the room, and Abishag's own heart fell with them. A sick feeling settled within her, and she saw again the look in Adonijah's eyes as he had leaned too close and spoken to her just yesterday. Her heart beat heavy with dread. She should have warned the king or Solomon of what she suspected. And yet, she'd had no real proof. A simple virgin nurse-wife did not accuse a prince of treason without evidence. And now it stood, glaring before them.

The king straightened, and one of the blankets slipped from his shoulders. She moved slowly forward to tuck it in behind him again, but he waved her off, extending a hand to Bathsheba instead. Their fingers clasped, but before the king could speak a word, Benaiah stepped into the room, closer to the king. Their hands parted, and Bathsheba moved into the shadows, out of the king's line of vision. She glanced at Abishag once, but her gaze quickly focused again on the king.

Benaiah entered the space where Bathsheba had stood and bowed low. "My lord," he said, "Nathan the prophet is here."

CHAPTER

ELEVEN

Naamah's pregnancy was in its fifth month, and she had begun to feel movement on a regular basis. One bright afternoon when a nap beckoned her, Inaya burst into the room unannounced. She rushed to Naamah's side.

"Are you sleeping?" Inaya touched her shoulder.

Naamah turned to face her. "That was my intent." She sat up slowly, not wishing to pull herself from the edge of slumber. "What has happened?" Inaya's expression said the news was not good.

"Adonijah has declared himself king, and King David is unaware of it!" She lowered her voice, and Naamah knew her maid feared the other servants and even the birds outside the window might hear and spread the news.

Naamah sat straighter, alarm rushing through her. "What can we do?"

Inaya looked at her a moment, then seemed to notice her state of undress and hurried to her chest and searched her garments. She pulled one of the better jeweled robes from its place and held it open for her. Naamah stood and quickly tied the belt, then slipped into her sandals.

"We will go to the queen's rooms and see what is to become of us." She turned, fully expecting Naamah to follow. "Come."

Naamah fell into step with her maid, but they said little as they passed guards pacing the halls, took the stairs to the floor below, and moved silently to the queen's rooms.

"She is with the king and Nathan the prophet," the guard told them at the door.

"We will wait inside for her then," Naamah said with more authority than she knew was hers to wield.

The guard seemed to consider her request for a moment, then nodded and allowed them entrance. Tirzah greeted them with a concerned look.

"Is it true?" Naamah asked, grasping Tirzah's outstretched hands.

"I am afraid it is." Tirzah hugged her close, then led her to a couch. How like Inaya she was in body and spirit! "Nathan the prophet came to tell my mistress the news. Benaiah, the captain of the king's guard, and Zadok the priest are all with my mistress in the king's chambers."

"They are good men," Naamah said, daring to hope good news would come of this.

"Yes. And they favor Solomon. Joab and Abiathar have followed Adonijah."

—⁓—

Solomon paced outside his father's chambers, worrying the guards who stood at every entrance. Word had reached him through one of Benaiah's men of Adonijah's treachery.

He cursed under his breath. Not only Adonijah but Joab, his father's trusted captain, and Abiathar the priest who had been with the king since before he wore the crown, had betrayed the king's wishes. How could they do such a thing, when they *knew* that he was his father's choice? Even Nathan had predicted it at his birth.

He paused before the doors with lions carved into them, the entrance to his father's chambers. Normally he would walk in without question, but now he hesitated. Nathan, Zadok, Benaiah, and his mother must be the ones to convince his father. Nothing Solomon had ever tried in the past had worked, and he dare not risk saying the wrong thing to him now. Surely his youth was a factor that had kept his father from acting. Despite his years of training, surely there was a reason why his father continually delayed.

The door creaked as it opened a crack, and the three men slipped out and closed it quickly, obviously to keep the heat in. They stopped short at the sight of him.

"Good, you are exactly who we wanted to see," Nathan said, bowing slightly. "Come. We must dress you quickly in the king's robes." He ushered Solomon to his father's dressing rooms, where a variety of robes were kept away from the heat that might damage them in his father's chambers. In the distance, he heard Zadok command a guard to hurry to the tabernacle for anointing oil, while Benaiah sent another to get the king's mule from the stables.

"What is happening?" Solomon asked.

Nathan spoke to the servant in charge of the king's apparel and waited while the man returned with the royal robe and crown. "Isn't it obvious, my son?" Nathan patted his arm. "Your father has declared that we are to take you, riding on his own mule, to the Gihon spring and anoint you king there."

"And when Adonijah and Joab hear of it?" A hint of fear threatened his sense of relief that his father had finally chosen to act.

"The Lord is on our side, Solomon." Nathan met his gaze, unflinching. "God has loved you since your birth. He told your father you would build the temple he wanted to build. Nothing Adonijah does can stop the will of our God."

Solomon allowed the servant to help him remove his princely robe and slip into the king's garment and crouched as the man placed the crown on his head. Jewels from his father's storeroom were brought and placed on his arms in addition to the ones he wore as prince.

A knock on the door made them turn to see Bathsheba enter, smiling. She stepped closer to Solomon and held out his father's signet ring.

"I can't accept this." Solomon took a step back. "The king is still the king, Ima. I am simply co-regent. We will have a ring made for me while my father still lives."

His mother shook her head and stepped closer, taking Solomon's right hand. "Your father gave this to me to give to you. He desires you to have it now." She placed it on his index finger, then bent to kiss it. She smiled up at him, tears in her eyes.

"We best hurry and get our new king to the Gihon," Nathan said, interrupting the moment.

Solomon straightened. The next few hours would change everything, both for the kingdom and for him and his father's family. There was no time to waste lest Adonijah and Joab gain so great a following that his father's wishes were for naught.

TWELVE

Naamah sat waiting with both Inaya and Tirzah, wishing her hands had something to occupy them, when at last the door to Bathsheba's gardens opened and the queen entered.

"Tirzah, you must come with me!" She glanced about, seeming to see Naamah for the first time. "Naamah! Just the person I hoped to see. Come, both of you. Solomon is on his way even now with Benaiah, Zadok, and Nathan to the Gihon to be anointed king over Israel!"

Her smile melted Naamah's fear, and she jumped up to follow her. Inaya and Tirzah hurried close behind.

———〰〰———

Things moved quickly after Bathsheba left the king, carrying his signet ring for Solomon. Abishag's heart skipped several beats as she imagined the coming hours, the tension she knew would fill the city until Solomon sat securely on his father's throne.

Please, Adonai, protect Solomon. How often she had imagined a future day when she would pass into his court to become one of his wives. But now . . . Adonijah's face floated in her mind's eye, his proud face laughing down at her as though he had already won. What use was this meeting of the few leaders who remained? Adonijah had Joab, whose military might filled the tales around campfires. And the king was so old.

Shouts were heard in the halls outside, and jubilant cries floated away on hurried footsteps. Abishag poured the king another cup of spiced wine, then sat on the edge of his couch and looked into his shining eyes.

"Your son will soon be king," she said softly, smiling at him.

"My son Solomon," he said, as though he needed to remind her of his intentions.

"Yes. Solomon." She patted his hand and tucked the blanket closer to his neck. She kissed his cheek then, something she had never done before. "This is a good day."

He nodded and sipped his wine, smiling. He looked long at her, and she wondered what thoughts went through his mind.

"Your son Solomon will make a good king, my lord. His name will be as great as yours." She did not know why she said it, but she was certain it would be true in time.

"He will build the temple to Yahweh. His name will far surpass mine," the king said. He handed her the empty goblet. "I have lived to see a son sit on my throne." He closed his eyes for a moment, and she thought he would sleep, but he surprised her by throwing off the covers and rising.

He walked to the window and opened the shutters. She could see his thin shoulders shake with the sudden cold.

She clutched a soft woolen blanket and carried it to him, draping his back.

"You will be a great asset to Solomon one day, Abishag." He pulled the blanket closed at the neck and nodded his thanks. "When I no longer have need of you."

She followed his gaze to look down on the outer court-yard, where crowds were gathering and the king's own mule waited. Solomon emerged from the palace dressed in royal finery and climbed atop the mule. Her heart picked up its pace at the sight of him. Nathan the prophet, Zadok the priest, Benaiah, and the Kerethites and Pelethites, merce-nary soldiers loyal to King David, led the mule and Solomon toward the Gihon spring. She caught sight of Bathsheba and Solomon's wife Naamah in the group of men and women closely following.

"They will return soon, and Solomon will surely come to visit you, my lord. Perhaps you will feel well enough to greet him as he enters the throne room?" She touched the king's arm. His frail strength seemed to suddenly need her support. She moved her hand beneath his elbow. His arm came around her, and she pressed close, hoping to instill in him greater warmth. The sun's bright rays came through the open window, kissing their faces.

The king drew in a breath and slowly released it. "I have missed the sun on my cheeks." His grip tightened ever so slightly as the crowd moved through the palace gates. He kissed the top of her head. "I would like to see him crowned."

She nodded, truly hoping to help give him what he so desired. But his strength ebbed quickly as they stood there and the last of the crowd disappeared from sight. She closed the shutters and helped him back to his bed, tucking him in.

―≋―

Guards surrounded Solomon and his men as the cheers of the people erupted. Runners went before and behind Solomon along the path he rode on the king's own mule to the Gihon spring. As he knelt at the water's edge, Naamah felt a surge of pride rush through her. Water from the spring was sprinkled over him before the oil of anointing ran down his head and into his beard.

The trumpet sounded, and her voice rose with the crowd as Solomon mounted the mule once more for the ride back to the palace.

"Long live King Solomon!" The ground shook with the noise.

Solomon laughed and smiled and waved to the people as he rode slowly between them. Flutists took up a festive song, and as she hurried to keep up with him, she caught his gaze. His wink felt like an intimate touch. He stopped the mule and ordered mules brought for his mother and for her, elevating their status in the eyes of all.

Life would be different now as Solomon moved from prince to king. And when the crowds disappeared, he would still belong to her, and she to him. His only wife and the mother of his child. She lifted her chin and kept pace with his mother all the way back to the palace.

―≋―

Solomon stood at the threshold to his father's audience chamber—now *his* audience chamber—and waited for the trumpeters to announce his entrance. Crowds filled the room, and excited servants and courtiers took their places

94

along the walls. Solomon drew in a breath, silently telling his racing heart to still. His mother and wife stood to the right, closest to the throne. He glanced his mother's way, thankful for her presence. How long would he have her guidance? She was much younger than his father and in good health. Surely they had many years left together.

The trumpeters sounded and everyone in the room bowed low. He walked through the arched door and climbed the grand steps to the royal throne. He took the scepter and tapped the floor twice. Everyone rose slowly, facing his direction.

He spotted Nathan, Zadok, and Benaiah standing to his left in the place of petition. "Come," he said, nodding to Benaiah.

The man bowed and stepped closer.

"What have you heard?" Despite the uproar of the people on the ride back to the palace, Solomon sensed trouble still brewed where Adonijah and Joab had conspired against him.

"My lord, it is said that Adonijah fears you, for he has laid hold of the horns of the altar, saying, 'Let King Solomon swear to me first that he will not put his servant to death with the sword.'"

Solomon's grip tightened on the scepter, his knuckles whitening. Adonijah would remain a bane to him, as would Joab. He could not be too careful.

After a quick glance at his mother, he looked hard at Benaiah. "If he will show himself a worthy man, not one of his hairs shall fall to the earth, but if wickedness is found in him, he shall die." He forced his hand to release its tight grip. "Tell him to come down from the altar and bring him to me."

"Yes, my lord." Benaiah bowed and backed from Solomon's presence, hurrying to do his bidding.

The room came alive the moment Benaiah left, with each of his father's courtiers and advisors and his brothers and half brothers stepping forward to pay him homage. They would celebrate later with a great feast, but for now, Solomon greeted each one and thanked them for their service to his father. He exacted promises from his half brothers to pledge allegiance to him.

After the last of his kin had stepped aside to allow the advisors his attention, he glanced again at his mother and glimpsed Naamah leaning close, speaking to her. He must elevate his mother's status and have another throne built for her to sit beside him when she chose to enter these chambers.

He pushed the thoughts aside, caught up in the moment, and suddenly wished his father were also sitting at his right, sharing this joy, this rule. But word had come to him through Abishag that the king was rejoicing comfortably in his bed and would be glad to see him when he could get away. She did not say that his father was simply too frail to be here at this, his finest hour. If only . . . But it would do no good to regret the past or wish for things that could not be changed.

He glanced up from speaking to an advisor at the sound of a commotion near the door to the chamber. The people parted and allowed Benaiah entrance, Adonijah in his strong grip.

Adonijah looked visibly shaken. He fell to his knees and bowed low before the steps of the throne. "May my lord King Solomon live forever," he said, his voice raspy as though he had been forcing back emotion for too long. "I am your humble servant."

Solomon stared at his prostrate form for many breaths. This man would cause him trouble. Of that he had no doubt, but he was his half brother, after all. And this was a day to celebrate, not destroy.

Solomon cleared his throat and tapped the floor with the scepter. "Go to your house," he said.

Adonijah rose slowly, bowing several more times as he backed from the chamber. Solomon released a breath. If only this was the last time he would have to deal with jealous brothers. But he knew that to think so was to delude himself.

CHAPTER
THIRTEEN

973 BC

The pains came upon Naamah, a sharp knife to her back, as the sun was just beginning its descent toward the west. She paced her chambers while Inaya fretted, and the palace midwife was quickly summoned. They needn't have come so soon, as the babe fought his birth throughout the night.

Sweat trickled over every area of her skin, and weariness dogged her with the aching need to sleep when at last her son decided to make his appearance, in perfect time with the crest of dawn. Bathsheba appeared in her rooms toward the last and dispatched a guard to tell Solomon the moment their son gave his first lusty cry.

"He is beautiful, Naamah." Bathsheba was the first to hold her son after the midwife cleaned him and swaddled his small limbs. She kissed his forehead and gazed lovingly into his eyes. "He looks a little like Solomon did at his birth, but I daresay he favors you." She handed him to Naamah, who directed his mewling mouth to her breast. His pull was strong, and Bathsheba laughed at the sight. "How well I remember!"

Naamah blinked, startled by the surge of love and emotion she felt for this child, her son. She closed her eyes as he nursed and would have slept but for the commotion in the halls.

Solomon entered her rooms without fanfare and stood near the door separating the sleeping chambers from the sitting room. His smile widened as she gently released her son's hold and held him so Solomon could see.

Bathsheba came and took him from her, leaving her arms aching, bereft. How quickly the child had molded to her! Solomon looked momentarily awkward as he reached for the child, and she feared that he might not keep his hold on the boy. But he soon warmed to his new role and settled their son more closely to his heart. At last he looked at her and smiled.

"He is Rehoboam," he said with the authority she had come to expect from him now that he reigned as co-regent king. "'He builds up the people.' A good name for a future king."

"Rehoboam," she said softly, liking the name. She smiled, and Solomon looked from their son to her.

"Thank you," he said. His voice had lost its strong edge, and he kissed the boy's forehead and handed him back to Bathsheba, who returned him to Naamah.

She breathed in the scent of her son and held him against her cheek. Greater love than she had ever known filled her, and she knew in that moment that even her love for Solomon could not replace what she felt for her son. She barely noticed when Solomon turned and left her rooms.

Eight days later, Solomon followed his father, who leaned on Abishag's arm, and Zadok to a side room in the palace, where Zadok would perform the circumcision on his first-born son.

The flint knife rested on a cloth beside a golden bowl in the center of the room. The women were already present—his mother and Naamah, holding Rehoboam—along with courtiers and Solomon's brothers.

Zadok walked slowly toward Naamah and held out his hands for the boy. Solomon straightened, glanced briefly at Naamah, then focused on his son. The act was swift, the boy's cries pitiful, and Solomon sensed Naamah's angst and desire to rush to his side and pull the boy into her arms.

Zadok placed olive oil and cloths over the wound and wrapped the boy in a soft white blanket, then held him for all to see. "Blessed be the Lord our God, who has sanctified us by His precepts and given us circumcision." He stepped over to Solomon and placed the boy in his arms.

Solomon looked into the child's crying eyes and said, "Who has sanctified us by His precepts and has granted us to introduce our child into the covenant of Abraham our father." He looked from the boy to his own father, who smiled. Pride filled Solomon's heart, and he bent to kiss his son's forehead. "His name is Rehoboam," he said, holding him high. Though he had already declared it to Naamah and his mother, now his name was official.

He looked at Zadok. The priest dipped his head and addressed the group. "This rite of circumcision was given to our people as a sign of the Abrahamic covenant. God spoke to Abraham and said, 'This is my covenant, which you shall keep between me and you, and your seed after you.'"

The priest finished with a prayer. Solomon took the squirming child to Naamah and saw the relieved look in her eyes the moment she could comfort her son. Their gazes held for the slightest moment, and he wondered if her past had come back to trouble her as she watched the scene. Circumcision was nothing like the sacrifices of infants she had experienced in Ammon.

Rehoboam would never suffer such a fate.

"We invite you to join us this evening for a meal in the dining hall to celebrate the future heir to the throne." King David spoke to the crowd, his voice stronger than Solomon had heard it in recent weeks.

He glanced at his father and smiled. "Yes, come. Let us celebrate this child and the promise he holds for the future." Solomon waved a hand over the room. After nods and quick bows from those present, the ceremony ended, and Solomon returned to court while Abishag and his mother escorted the king to his rooms and Naamah slipped away to tend to their son.

Solomon walked behind the guards and trumpeters but caught one last glimpse of his father, upheld by both women as he attempted to walk with his head held high. A deep ache settled within Solomon. *How long will we have him, Adonai?* He wasn't ready to rule without his father's wisdom. But he knew the circumcision ceremony had taken a toll, and he wondered if his father would have the strength to even attend the evening's banquet.

The thought sobered him as the trumpets announced his entrance to the audience chamber and he took his seat upon his father's throne. He needed wisdom. He needed his father's guidance. As he listened to the people come before him with their needs, he said a silent prayer for help because he knew he could not do this on his own.

—♒—

Later that evening after the meal, Naamah sat with Rehoboam in her chambers, quietly rocking him to sleep. She looked up as the outer door opened. Her personal guard appeared, bowed, and stepped aside to allow her husband entrance.

"My lord," she said, attempting to rise.

He stayed her with his hand and took the seat opposite her.

"How are you, my love? I have spoken little to you since Rehoboam's birth, and of course, there was no time to speak at the banquet." He settled himself as though he intended to stay for a time, though she knew he could not share her bed for many days until her purification.

She lifted Rehoboam from her shoulder, his limp body telling her he was sleeping. "Would you like to hold him?"

At his nod, she tucked the blanket better around the boy and placed him in Solomon's arms. The look on her husband's face was one of wonder, a reminder of the Solomon of her youth, her only love.

They sat in silence many moments while Solomon traced a line along their son's jaw and brushed the soft dark hair, so like his own, from his temples.

"How are you, my husband?" she asked after Solomon at last handed Rehoboam to Inaya. She settled him in a cradle of soft linens in the next room, close enough so that Naamah could hear his cries.

He leaned into the cushions and stretched both legs out

in front of him, crossing them at the ankles. "I was sorry my father was not well enough to attend the banquet." Worry lines appeared along his brow. "I am grateful he could attend the circumcision, but I fear . . ." He looked into her eyes. "I fear he grows weaker, and while I spend the mornings passing judgment on those who seek it and the afternoons with him going over plans for the temple, I wonder. There is still much to be gathered to have enough gold and silver and cedar and more to build the structure. I'm not ready to do this without him, Naamah." His eyes held the swiftest hint of pain, but a moment later, he blinked and the old sense of adventure, of life, sparked within them as he spoke. "The building will be palatial, Naamah, bigger than my father's palace."

She shook herself, trying to understand how he could switch so quickly from worry over his father to the excitement of the plans he had shared with the king since childhood. She tried to envision things as he described them. "Can you show me the plans?" She longed to know more, especially as she watched the way his delight in the telling drew him out of his melancholy.

His look grew thoughtful. "I think that could be arranged."

"Where does he keep the model?"

"Near his bedchamber. Do you want to see it now?"

She glanced in the direction of her sleeping son, hating the thought of leaving him. But one look into Solomon's eyes told her that she could not put aside his wishes—not if she hoped to continue to hold his heart.

"Yes," she said, rising from her chair. "Let me change to a better robe." At his nod, she hurried from the room and quickly changed.

He was standing over Rehoboam's cradle, looking down at him with a proud smile, when she pronounced herself ready. He lifted his gaze to hers and took her hand in his.

They walked the corridors and came to a room near King David's bedchamber. A guard allowed them entrance, and a servant lit the lamps in the four corners. A table stood along one wall, and on it sat the most intricate, beautiful creation of buildings she had ever seen.

"There are two courts," Solomon said, pointing to an inner and outer area that surrounded a lengthy building. "And two pillars, Boaz on the north and Jachin to the south, stand in the temple portico, at the entrance to the temple on the east. The *Hekhal*, the first chamber, or Holy Place, is where the bread of the presence rests, where the seven-pronged lamp burns before the Lord from evening until morning, and where the altar of incense stands before the curtain that separates this place from"—he pointed to the furthest inner room—"the *Kodesh Hakodashim*, the Most Holy Place. This is where the Ark of the Covenant, the most sacred symbol of our God, will find its final resting place."

She leaned closer, amazed at the detail. "You have even carved the walls with cherubim, palm trees, and open flowers and overlaid the cedar with gold." She looked up. "I would not have expected such accuracy in a mere model."

He smiled. "My father was not allowed to build this temple, but God did allow him to know its design. Since I was a boy of ten, my father has shared the drawings and plans with me. We built this together."

She straightened and came alongside him, wrapped her arms around his neck, and looked into his eyes. "You have done amazing work, my love. I cannot wait to see this completed and standing on that mountain."

He placed a gentle kiss on her lips, then leaned back. "I too look forward to that day. My father has called an assembly of the elders to come to Jerusalem next month to bring gifts to give in its building. Assuming he still has the strength to attend such a meeting." He stroked a finger along her temple, his look thoughtful again. "I want you to be there with my mother and our son."

She clung to him, hoping her desire was evident in her embrace. "I am honored, my husband. I would not miss it!"

The assembly was one of the grandest festivals she had ever witnessed. Men from every tribe gathered to bring gifts for the building of the temple and to pay tribute to King David and King Solomon. But it was the sight of those great men bowing low before the Lord and the kings that caused a lump in Naamah's throat. How blessed she was to see this!

The following day rivaled her wedding day, and she watched in awe to see the exuberance and joy throughout the palace and all of Jerusalem. A thousand bulls, a thousand rams, and a thousand male lambs, together with drink offerings and other sacrifices, were offered in abundance at the place where the temple would stand, while male singers, Levites whom King David had set apart, sang praise songs to Adonai.

Solomon knelt at the head of the company before Zadok, and her heart swelled with deep respect and pride as the priest poured the anointing oil over Solomon's head for the second time.

"Long live King Solomon! May your reign be greater than your father David's!" Shouts from the crowd filled the city until the ground shook, as though the earth itself rejoiced in that moment.

Rehoboam startled and gave a vigorous cry as she held him close against her chest, his cries drowned out by the joy surrounding them. She patted his back and cooed softly in his ear as she walked with Solomon's mother and the other women of King David's court toward the throne room.

She handed Rehoboam to Inaya as they were ushered to seats nearest the throne, and as she turned to watch the trumpeters and flag bearers, she felt a soft touch on her arm. She looked beside her and found herself wrapped in the warmth of Bathsheba's smile.

"This is a great day for him," Naamah said, and she did not miss the look in her mother-in-law's eyes that carried more memories than she could share. "At last they have accepted him."

Bathsheba nodded. "As they should."

The crowd in the hall grew silent a moment later as Solomon swept into the room with regal grace, head held high, his father's glittering crown on his head. He reached the steps and paused, nodding in deference to his mother and father, who sat to the right and left of King David's gilded throne. How glad she was that the king had remained strong enough for this day, quenching Solomon's fears.

She waited, wondering if Solomon would acknowledge her as well, and felt a pang of disappointment when he took his seat without a single glance her way. Was this how it would be from now on?

The thought worried her as she watched King David stand

and give his scepter to his son. Solomon embraced his father, and she thought not for the first time how blessed her husband was to be so favored by his father. Would Rehoboam fare the same?

As King David took his seat again with Solomon's aid, the entrance to the throne room filled with his officers and mighty men, and she noticed with relief King David's sons, Solomon's half brothers, leading the way. They walked the long hall and came to bow at Solomon's feet, pledging their submission to the new king.

Even Adonijah.

As this former rival bowed before her husband, she noticed the slightest clenching of Solomon's jaw, the slightest straightening of his spine. His grip whitened on the scepter, but as Adonijah rose, Solomon simply nodded to each of these brothers who had turned against him six months before. Now they were promising to obey Solomon. She shuddered to think what Solomon would do if they broke that promise.

FOURTEEN

*L*ife did not change as much as Abishag expected it would once Solomon wore the crown as co-regent with his father. Adonijah no longer visited the palace, and some said he had left Jerusalem entirely. She actually saw more of Solomon in the king's chambers than in earlier days, for Solomon seemed eager to learn all he could from his father while the king still had breath. The whole assembly of Israel had gathered, bringing gifts to help pay for the construction of the temple Solomon would one day build. All seemed well, and she fell into the dangerous position of thinking things would remain as they were.

One late afternoon, after she had applied a poultice of pepper flakes and olive oil to the king's back to coax greater warmth into him, a treatment she had learned from talking to some of the palace servants, she was pleased to see the king awaken from a nap with a smile on his lips.

"Good afternoon to you, Abishag," he said, his voice unwavering. She felt a measure of pride that her treatment might have been the cause.

"Did you sleep well, my lord?" She helped him to stand, and they moved to a sitting area, where a tray of nutmeats and dates and fresh fruit awaited them. She poured the king a golden goblet of goat's milk and sat beside him, grateful for the light in his eyes.

"I feel refreshed, Abishag." He sipped the milk but did not touch the food. Lately he had given up wine in favor of fresh milk but took little else, even when the palace cooks coaxed him with their finest dishes.

"Will you not try some of the grapes? They are fresh from the vines in the gardens." She searched his lined face, longing to restore deeper color to his cheeks and perhaps add a bit of thickness to his bones. She was not sure when it happened, but she had grown to deeply love the king. Not in the way of wife to husband, but as daughter to father. He treated her with such unequaled kindness.

He looked at her, his brows slowly knitting to a frown. "I am sorry, Abishag. I fear I have no hunger left, nor appetite to enjoy the tastes I once knew." He smiled, but his eyes were distant, as though seeing into a place she could not go.

She nodded, surprised at the emotion his admission revealed to her heart. She sensed his implication, and she did not like it.

"My days left with you are few, my dear girl." His words coaxed her to meet his gaze. He lifted his hand to hers and clasped cold fingers over her much warmer ones. "Soon it will be my time to go the way of all the earth." He said the words with acceptance and gentleness, as if he knew how much she would miss him.

"I'm not ready," she said, her voice breaking on a sob she desperately tried to hold back.

He squeezed her fingers. "No one is ever ready to let go of one they love." Their gazes met, and she sensed he did love her. He cupped her cheek, brushed a stray tear with his thumb. "Adonai will give you strength when the time comes."

She swallowed and nodded. "I will miss you." She knew she would miss him more than anyone since Ima. "Sheol has stolen too many of those I love."

He seemed to consider her words but said nothing for the space of many moments. "It is the way of all," he said at last, and she wondered where his memories took him.

He removed his hand from hers and sipped the milk once more, then set the goblet on a small table that still held a tray too full of food. He drew in a breath that barely lifted his chest. A soft cough followed. She jumped up and stroked his back, but the cough did not linger. She settled him among the cushions in his sitting room, and Bathsheba visited for a short time. But he tired quickly after she left.

"I want you to summon Solomon and a scribe," the king said once she had pulled the covers over him again in his bed. His breathing had grown slightly labored, sending alarm through her. She relaxed only a little when she heard his soft snores.

She tiptoed from his bedchamber and sent a guard to summon Solomon, then took a rare moment to sink onto the king's plush couch, awaiting his son's arrival. She did not have long to wait, as the door opened soon after and Solomon swept past the guard, the scribe on his heels, closing the door behind him.

Solomon approached her and angled his head toward his father's chambers. "He sleeps?"

She nodded. "It's very strange."

The scribe moved away from them and set up his tools in a corner of the king's chamber, while Solomon quirked a brow and came to sit across from her, completely at ease in his surroundings. "Explain 'very strange' to me. For I would think that everything about your home here seems strange to you."

His gentle smile warmed her. Solomon made her feel something far different than she had ever felt before.

"This place is not as strange as it once was," she said, offering him a smile of friendship. Could he see the longing in her gaze? She quickly lowered it lest she give her heart away before love beckoned it. She had no certainty that he would take her as a true wife once his father passed into Sheol.

"What puzzles you then?" He clearly wanted her answer, as he wanted answers to all things he did not understand. Solomon was inquisitive above any man or woman she had ever known. She wondered often if his mind allowed him to rest at night.

"Your father," she whispered, tossing a glance over her shoulder toward David's chambers. "He told me he will not be with us much longer." She glanced beyond him, aware of the moisture in her eyes. "And after Bathsheba's visit, his breathing became slightly labored."

Solomon ran a hand along his neatly trimmed beard, the fading sunlight coming in along the slatted window catching the stones in his father's signet ring, illuminating the carved lion's head. He turned it around his finger, studying it. After a lengthy silence he looked at her. "It has been over two years, nearly three since he was afflicted," he said softly. "The time is coming for great loss." He clasped his hands in front of him. "And much change."

111

She was not ready for what Solomon implied.

"Surely there is still time." She said it to make it so. She said it not because she feared becoming Solomon's wife or concubine but because she feared losing David. Her friend.

"Perhaps." But his voice lacked conviction.

A stirring from the bedchamber roused them both from their stupor of sadness. Solomon rose first, and she quickly followed. He allowed her to see to the king's needs before entering the room. When she had him propped on several pillows, Solomon came to kneel at his father's side.

"Solomon. My son."

"I am here, Father." Solomon kissed the king's hand, something he rarely did, then secured it between his own.

David drew in a breath and released it, slowly meeting Solomon's gaze. The look of love that passed between them sent an aching longing to her middle. But she pushed the longing away and moved to the foot of the bed.

"My son," David said again, holding fast to Solomon's dark gaze. "I am about to go the way of all the earth."

Her throat grew thick with unshed tears. *No, please. The kingdom needs you. I need you.* She stuck a fist to her mouth to stifle the unwanted cries.

"So be strong," the king said, his eyes alight with force though his body obviously lacked the strength to rise, "act like a man, and observe what the Lord your God requires. Walk in obedience to him, and keep his decrees and commands, his laws and regulations, as written in the Law of Moses. Do this so that you may prosper in all you do and wherever you go and that the Lord may keep his promise to me: 'If your descendants watch how they live, and if they walk faithfully before me with all their heart and soul, you will never fail to have a successor on the throne of Israel.'"

Solomon bowed his head in an act of acknowledgment. The Solomon she knew, what little she did know of him, would do all in his power to follow exactly what his father had requested. She had no doubt he would always honor Adonai and that Adonai would surely bless him. But as she watched the exchange between father and son, feeling terribly like an intruder, she could not stop the silent tears wetting her cheeks. She made no move to swipe them away.

"Now you yourself know what Joab son of Zeruiah did to me," King David continued, drawing her attention to him once more, "what he did to the two commanders of Israel's armies, Abner son of Ner and Amasa son of Jether. He killed them, shedding their blood in peacetime as if in battle, and with that blood he stained the belt around his waist and the sandals on his feet. Deal with him according to your wisdom, but do not let his gray head go down to the grave in peace."

The words troubled her, not for the judgment they would exact but for the fear Joab instilled in her. He had taken Adonijah's side. He could still be a formidable foe to Solomon.

"But show kindness to the sons of Barzillai of Gilead," the king continued, "and let them be among those who eat at your table. They stood by me when I fled from your brother Absalom."

Solomon's face softened at this, and she saw the light of reflection in his gaze. She was too young to remember much of Absalom's treachery, but Solomon had lived through it. No doubt he knew this man of whom his father spoke.

"And remember, you have with you Shimei son of Gera,

the Benjamite from Bahurim, who called down bitter curses on me the day I went to Mahanaim." David's tone hardened ever so slightly at the mention of this man's name.

She searched her mind for what the court gossips had said of him but came up empty. A Benjamite, however, was likely related to King Saul, Michal's father—David's enemy. Had Shimei been as mean to the king as her own sister-in-law Batya had been to her?

"When he came down to meet me at the Jordan, I swore to him by the Lord: 'I will not put you to death by the sword.' But now, do not consider him innocent. You are a man of wisdom; you will know what to do to him. Bring his gray head down to the grave in blood."

He paused a moment, leaned back, and closed his eyes. She thought perhaps his words were spent and he would sleep once more, but he rallied when Solomon stood as if to leave.

"There is more I would say to you, my son."

Solomon sat on the edge of the king's bed, again taking his hand. "I am here, Father. Speak whatever is on your mind."

"These are the last words you are to record for me. These are my final words."

A lump formed in the pit of Abishag's stomach, and fresh tears stung her eyes. He could not possibly be so near death as to give his final words this soon. He had seemed so well, so strong, this very morning! Did he know something in his spirit she could not see? She leaned against the bedpost and listened, her breath coming shallow for the fear that seemed ready to steal it from her.

The king glanced at the scribe. "Are you ready to record these words?"

"Yes, my lord," the man replied. He lifted his reed pen as if to show the king he was indeed taking down every word.

David seemed satisfied and looked to Solomon once more. "The inspired utterance of David son of Jesse, the utterance of the man exalted by the Most High, the man anointed by the God of Jacob, the hero of Israel's songs."

She knew this to be the introduction to tell future generations who had authored these words.

"The Spirit of the Lord spoke through me; his word was on my tongue." Pure silence followed, as if even the birds outside the window had stopped to listen. "The God of Israel spoke, the Rock of Israel said to me: 'When one rules over people in righteousness, when he rules in the fear of God, he is like the light of morning at sunrise on a cloudless morning, like the brightness after rain that brings grass from the earth.' If my house were not right with God," he said, his words dropping in pitch, "surely he would not have made with me an everlasting covenant, arranged and secured in every part; surely he would not bring to fruition my salvation and grant me my every desire." A sigh lifted his chest, and for the first time she heard the labor with which he spoke. He closed his eyes, and she waited. Was this the end of his utterance?

Solomon glanced from his father to her but looked back as David spoke.

"But evil men are all to be cast aside like thorns, which are not gathered with the hand. Whoever touches thorns uses a tool of iron or the shaft of a spear; they are burned up where they lie."

He stopped abruptly, drew in a long slow breath, and sighed. Solomon nodded to the scribe, who quietly picked up his tools and left the room. She struggled to make sense of all King David had said, but apparently Solomon understood. She had gotten caught up in the king's description—*light of morning at sunrise on a cloudless morning, like the brightness after rain that brings grass from the earth*—easily recalling such days in her youth when she frolicked among the vineyards or with the goats. Her soul missed those times, and when she heard his last comments they did not make sense to her.

But just as suddenly as the king had urged them to listen to him, his words seemed used and drained like water released from the mikvah. He closed his eyes and sank deeper into the pillows, his breath coming shallower, labored, his hand still held in Solomon's. She moved slowly closer.

"Would you like me to do anything for you, my lord?" she whispered in Solomon's ear.

He glanced her way. "Call for my mother," he said, and she knew in that moment that Solomon understood what King David had been trying to tell her only moments ago. He was truly about to go the way of all the earth, and Solomon wanted to share the moment with his mother, King David's beloved.

She hurried from his side to Bathsheba's apartments, tears blinding her every step of the way.

CHAPTER

FIFTEEN

The breeze lifted the curtains from the window in Naa-mah's sitting room, and birdsong came from the trees in the courtyard below. An urgent knock sounded on the outer door. Her breath came faster as Inaya hurried to her side.

"Is it King David?" The king had not been well in recent days, and by her stricken look she already knew the answer.

She nodded. "He gave his final words to Solomon last night, and word has it that he just now slipped into Sheol."

Naamah set her stitching aside and folded her idle hands in her lap, staring at the small calluses the needlework had caused. Solomon had not come to her last night or told her about his father's final words.

"Where is Solomon?" She could think of nothing else to ask and suddenly wished he were the one standing beside her to give her this news and hold her close to his heart. Though he had not taken another wife since his coronation, his visits to her were few. And when they visited his father's chambers together, she did not miss the looks that passed between him and Abishag. She could not stop the jealousy that crowded her heart during those times.

"He is with his mother, making arrangements for the burial." Inaya came to her and sat at her side, her own callused hand taking hold of Naamah's.

Rehoboam left his blocks and crawled onto her lap, and she buried her face in his soft hair, grateful for the chubby arms that came around her neck. Of course Solomon would be with his mother. Solomon confided often in her. Though she loved her mother-in-law, she did not love the woman's hold over her husband. He shared so little of himself with Naamah these days, yet Bathsheba seemed to know more about his goings-on than she did.

"What shall we do?" She felt the need to do something but had no idea what.

"Wait," Inaya said, stroking Rehoboam's soft curls. "They will send word when it is time for the procession to the tomb."

Solomon had built a grand tomb for his father, a project that had taken nearly two years to complete. And now it was ready as the king's final resting place. She hugged Rehoboam close as she pondered that thought.

Word spread quickly through the palace and the city of Jerusalem. By that afternoon before the sun had set, the mourners stood behind King David's bier, ready for the trek through the streets to the grand building Solomon had erected for his father's burial. Bathsheba stood directly behind the bier with Solomon to her right. Abishag followed Bathsheba, and Solomon's wife Naamah came some distance behind them.

Loud cries erupted in the streets, weeping and gnashing

of teeth, as they slowly wound their way through a crowd of onlookers. Tears blurred Abishag's vision, and her headscarf blocked the view of the weeping women along the path. What would become of her now? King David had become her life, his daily care her only routine. In her mind's eye she still heard the remnants of the songs he had taught to her.

The Lord is my shepherd, I shall not be in want . . . Even though I walk through the valley of the shadow of death, I will fear no evil . . .

Had he feared the shadow as he passed through from this life? If he had, she'd seen no flicker of such a thing in his eyes. She swiped at her own eyes as fresh tears fell once more. Zadok spoke words she did not listen to. She felt the press of the people around her. One glance to her left revealed King David's other sons, Adonijah among them. He caught her eye. She did not like the look he gave her and swiftly turned her attention back to the priest.

She sidled closer to Bathsheba once King David's body rested in this lovingly carved tomb, relieved when she was not sent away. Bathsheba's smile, though sad, welcomed her, and she drew Abishag into her arms like she would a young daughter.

"My dear Abishag," she whispered as they began the long walk back to the palace. "Tonight you will stay with me." She slipped her hand in Abishag's and squeezed. "Tomorrow is time enough to move you to the women's quarters."

Abishag nodded, overcome with the sudden realization that a single day had completely changed her life—again. No longer would she live in the king's quarters, caring for his needs. No longer would she be privy to private conversations between the king and his advisors or his family. His family was no longer her family. She was simply one of many who now belonged to Solomon.

That thought brought less comfort than she had long hoped.

—⁂—

The night was one of sleepless sorrow as Abishag listened to the soft weeping of Bathsheba in her chambers and her maid Tirzah in her own smaller quarters near the queen. She tossed on one of the beds once used by Bathsheba's younger sons, all of whom had moved on to rooms of their own. Though the palace had become home to her, Bathsheba's chambers were foreign. She missed the king's warmth, what little he possessed, next to her. She missed the spacious bed, the sound of his voice, his smile.

Tears wet the pillow beneath her head, but she could not sob as Bathsheba did. She had lost a companion. She had not lost her heart's true love. She was not sure she could even define such a feeling.

That thought troubled her, and she rose from the bed, shivering as her bare feet dangled over the side and touched the tiled floor. She padded softly from the room, past the other bedchambers and sitting room, and entered the gardens that had adjoined King David's and Bathsheba's rooms.

Moonlight cast a dappled glow over the inlaid stones, the only light with the torches unlit, and a soft breeze tickled the curls at her neck. She had forgotten her robe and wished for it now as she made her way to a stone bench in the center of the foliage, watched over by spreading trees. The colorful flowers, so bright in daylight, lay in shadow now, much like her heart. She pulled her knees to her chest, tucking her feet beneath her tunic. How bare she felt without her robe and scarf, but there was no one here to see her. She rested her chin on her knees and sighed, allowing the regrets of the day, the bitterness of life, to seep from her.

Here in the garden she could find her song once more if she but searched for it. It lingered in the branches where the birds had mimicked David's psalms. And if she closed her eyes, she knew she would catch some of the tunes floating with the breeze.

She felt herself swaying to the silent tune, *The Lord is my shepherd* . . . Yes, her shepherd. He would not leave her alone in this place, just as he had not left her alone in her brother's misguided household. Surely David had understood God better than most. Surely Adonai had a plan for her yet.

She startled at the hushed thump of footsteps on the stones. A guard coming to make his rounds? But who would care to explore the gardens by night? Would they not risk coming upon Bathsheba, angering the queen mother?

She sat straight and hugged her arms to her chest, fearing exposure. A quick glance around showed no place to hide. She was too big to burrow her way into the bushes and had no desire to scratch her skin among the briars and thorns. Perhaps if she stood she could slip past whoever was approaching. But the footsteps grew louder, and she found her limbs would not obey the command to flee.

"Abishag?" In the shadows she might have mistaken him for another, but she could never forget the sound of his voice.

"My lord Solomon." This time she slipped easily to her knees and bowed at his feet. What was he doing here? But of course, these rooms were his now, and he had always been at home among them.

His fingers skimmed the top of her head with the lightest touch. Then before she could think or speak, he took her hand and pulled her into his arms. His grip was strong, needy, and she responded in kind. How long she had dreamed of this moment, this freedom to be held so securely.

His lips trailed a line from her forehead to her neck until her pulse could barely keep up with the startled intake of her breath. Heat filled her face at his familiar way with her, and she nearly lost herself when his lips covered hers.

"Abishag." His words were a whisper. "How long I have wanted you." He lifted her in his arms and swung her around as if they were lovers in an exotic dance. "How beautiful you are, my sister, my bride."

Had he said the words or merely breathed them against her ear?

"Am I your bride, my lord?" She clung to his arms as her words caught hold of him, and he slowly lowered her to the ground. He studied her and seemed to notice for the first time her state of undress.

He took a step back. "Yes," he said softly, touching her cheek. "You are part of the king's inheritance."

She glanced at her bare feet. She was only a prize to be gained, nothing more. "Should we not wait until the period of mourning is past then?" What would his father have thought if Solomon took her so soon? And yet . . . there was comfort in his kiss, and she sensed the living needed such comfort, whether it was proper or not.

He stroked her face, his touch unimaginably tender. "My dove," he whispered, leaning close. "You are my dove hiding in the clefts of the rock, in the hiding places on the mountainside."

She glanced at his own shadowed face, barely illumined by the moon, her heart stirred with his words.

"Show me your face, my dove, let me hear your voice; for your voice is sweet, and your face is lovely."

She could not disobey the pull of his earnest plea. She lifted her face to his and let him kiss her once more. But the kiss was gentle, chaste even, as he held himself back.

"Until the day breaks and the shadows flee," she said, drawing close to his ear, "turn, my beloved, and be like a gazelle or like a young stag on the rugged hills."

His ringed fingers grasped her shoulders, sending tingling warmth through her. Even in the moonlight she could not miss the longing in his eyes, the fire that he would put out for her sake, for propriety's sake. For to take her now before the proper time of mourning would bring scorn on him and his rule.

Perhaps that was the true motive for his self-control, even more than any imagined concern for her purity. But as he kissed her head in parting and turned to leave the gardens that were fully his—she was the usurper here—she did not allow herself to ponder how many reasons he had considered in this decision. Or that she was a bride of political gain. She chose instead to recall his sweetened words. *My dove.* And with the memory, she closed her eyes and almost dreamed that she had wings.

SIXTEEN

Solomon walked the length of the roof near the parapet, his gaze trailing now and then to the home where his mother once lived. How often he had heard the story of his father's lust and the taking of his mother when her husband was away fighting the king's battle. If not for the sin, he would not be here. But if not for the sin, his parents would not have suffered so many devastating losses.

He glanced heavenward. *Did You turn something heinous into something good?* Surely his parents had eventually found love, despite their sinful beginning. And God had blessed them in naming him king in his father's place.

Oh Abba, how will I rule without you? He was still young—nearly ten years younger than his father had been when he took the throne from King Saul. His father had been tested far more than he had and weathered life's trials in a way Solomon could only imagine.

I need wisdom. Hadn't his father called him a wise man?

But his father had no idea of the turmoil and uncertainty that flowed through Solomon's veins.

I am not ready. I was not ready to lose you, Abba. He blinked back the swift surprise of emotion and looked away from the brightly lit sky to focus on the city that lay in quiet darkness. His people needed him to be strong. He still had too many enemies to let his guard drop. He especially did not trust Adonijah. His fists curled at the thought of this usurping brother. He did not want bloodshed, but in that moment he realized that his rule might need bloodshed to be fully established. *Please, Lord, let it not be so.*

He shook the thoughts aside, knowing the prayer was one that went against his father's last wishes for Joab and Shimei. He would do what he must, regardless of the queasy feeling war and bloodshed brought. Kings didn't shy away from such things. And yet . . .

Hadn't God made him a king of peace? He paced to the other end of the roof, tired of looking on the city and his mother's former home. Tired of imagining what could have been, how he might never have been born. It did no good to try to rewrite what was already past. What could never change. The very idea was futile.

He came to the stairs where a guard stood watching him. For a fleeting moment he glanced at the women's quarters. Abishag would live there soon unless he took her to wife. Then he could set her up in different apartments, as he had Naamah. The thought quickened his pulse, but still he hesitated. The week of mourning may have passed, but his heart had not yet healed. He did not wish to take Abishag out of sorrow. No. Theirs should be a union of joy and song and of love at last fulfilled and true. She had already wed a man for the purpose of healing and forestalling the sorrow of all Israel. He could not put her through such a purpose again.

Love for Abishag could wait. Besides, he was not sure whether he wanted her for herself or for her beauty and the political strength she brought to his kingdom. She already belonged to him regardless. Waiting would make love grow, and his heart needed to heal more than it needed another wife.

He descended the stairs, wishing he believed his own conclusions.

—⁂—

The week of mourning came and went, and Abishag fully expected Bathsheba to send her to the women's quarters as she had promised. Perhaps she didn't because she took comfort in Abishag's presence. The queen had said she reminded her of the king, and she could not bear to part with her.

Solomon, on the other hand, seemed in no hurry now to take her as his wife. Though he glimpsed her now and then in his mother's chambers, they did not speak of their stolen moment in the king's garden, or the kisses that still haunted her dreams and warmed her to the depth of her soul.

My heart longs for you, my soul yearns for you in a dry and weary land where there is no water . . . Her mind sang the words as she worked alongside Bathsheba and Naamah, placing colorful tiles into a mosaic that would one day be set among the tiles of the queen's apartments. Her cheeks burned as Naamah glanced at her. The words had been King David's for Adonai, and here she had put Solomon in Adonai's rightful place. Could Naamah read her thoughts?

But Naamah's attention turned to Bathsheba as her hands

suddenly stilled on the tiles. "There is something I have wanted to tell you, my queen."

Bathsheba looked up and smiled at her daughter-in-law. She turned her head to the side as if trying to solve a riddle, one brow raised. "Tell me," she said, though by the gleam in her eyes Abishag sensed she had already guessed the news.

Naamah placed a hand on her middle. "I only just told Solomon last evening." She paused, and Abishag suspected the dramatics were for her benefit. She ignored the jealous thumping of her heart. Solomon had spent time with his wife. His first wife. His only wife. Why should he have any thought or need of another?

"I felt the child quicken yesterday." Naamah's words should not have jolted her, as she had heard some time ago that the woman carried Solomon's second child.

"I am happy for you," Abishag said without thinking, and Bathsheba clapped her hands and laughed with joy.

"Another son! I am sure of it," Bathsheba said, smiling. "But I would not mind a granddaughter, if God so desires." She bore a dreamy expression for the briefest moment, and Abishag wondered if she wished she had borne a girl. But as quickly as the expression came it left, replaced by a soft shadow. She leaned close to pat first Naamah's knee then Abishag's. "I have two wonderful girls to love right here." The words felt right and awkward at the same time, but the queen seemed to pay their discomfort no mind.

Abishag picked up her tiles once more and with graceful fingers fitted the stones in the pattern she had begun. But she felt Naamah's stare amid the once peaceful camaraderie. Naamah did not like having the queen consider Abishag a daughter. For to do so meant she also considered her a wife to her son. And Naamah most obviously had no desire to share him.

—⁓—

Several months passed, and Abishag found herself spending more and more time in the court of women, away from the queen. It was possible that Bathsheba had grown used to her in one sense, but in another she had also probably wanted to please Naamah, who often brought Rehoboam to visit his grandmother. She felt like an intruder during those times and often made excuses to roam the palace halls or hide in her rooms, strumming the instruments the king had given her. With the coins Solomon had allotted to her, she had taken Rani with a palace guard and gone to market, where she delighted in bargaining for fine threads to weave into the softest garments the king's coins could buy. With the threads she learned to create intricate designs such as Abigail had stitched on the first royal garments for the king.

But these things could not keep her heart from aching in the dead of night, nor give her a reason for being. To what end did she work? To what purpose did she craft garments and songs and learn to inscribe her words on clay tablets as the scribes had taught her when the king still lived? Without the king, what good did she bring?

Was she truly Solomon's wife? If so, why had he not come for her? Would there be a wedding in the real sense, or would he just take her to his bed like a common concubine? Had he forgotten her existence in the months since his father's death? She chafed under the strain of waiting, wondering.

From all accounts, Naamah seemed pleased with their current arrangements. She remained Solomon's one and only wife, while Abishag was no different than the few aging concubines left as widows when King David died.

She confided some of these thoughts one day to Rani as they walked through the spacious halls of the women's court, halls that rang hollow with the emptiness of loss. Few women lived here now, as most of King David's wives had died before him, and the ten concubines Absalom had claimed lived in a separate house outside the palace walls. Adonijah's mother, Haggith, and the older wives of David also lived in separate quarters with their children.

"Does Solomon call for any of them?" She inclined her head toward the apartments that still housed some of the younger concubines, then glanced at Rani as they entered a room near the mikvah used for the monthly purification rites.

"No, my lady," Rani said, her large pale eyes showing wide in her round face, as though the question had startled her. "While I suppose he is entitled to them, it seems like breaking the law, I think."

"Which law?" Moses had given so many of them. The law had not often been read in her brother's home, and she had never been to the tabernacle to hear it read until she came to Jerusalem.

"'Do not have sexual relations with your father's wife; that would dishonor your father,'" Rani quoted as though she had heard it often.

"But King Solomon's father is dead. Does the law apply the same then?" It was the habit of kings of the east to inherit the harems of the previous king. King David had taken King Saul's wives into his harem. But Saul was not David's father, only his father-in-law. And as far as she knew, King David had treated the women as widows.

"A king's wealth is measured by his women." Rani motioned for her to sit on a bench while she proceeded to bathe her feet and soften them with scented oils. "But that doesn't mean he sleeps with all of them."

She pondered this thought as she studied the slight girl. "You are so young, yet you know so much already."

"I was sold into service as a child," she said. "I am older than I seem." She took the towel from her waist and dried Abishag's feet, then tied her sandals in place. "I also tune my ear to listen."

"You are wise," Abishag said. Solomon would not take his father's wives if it meant breaking the Law of Moses. He cared too much about pleasing Adonai and about not repeating the sins of his father. He would not take a woman in adultery, nor would he take a forbidden woman. He would take only those he could rightfully marry.

The problem she faced now was a question she did not want to consider. Could Solomon rightfully marry her?

—◦〰◦—

Abishag slept fitfully that night, dreaming of her vineyards, of the sheep pens and the way the sky looked when the stars hung low and the moon cleared a path bright enough to outshine the fire in the pit. *Like an apple tree among the trees of the forest is my beloved among the young men*, she sang in her dreams. *I delight to sit in his shade, and his fruit is sweet to my taste.*

She awoke with a start. *Solomon.* Her heart yearned like one denied. *Wherefore, beloved?* The word once rang with a village boy's name, but no longer. Her heart beat for Solomon.

She rose from her bed in the women's quarters and wrapped a heavy robe about her, but she did not venture from her rooms. She sat instead on a couch and gazed into the courtyard through an open window. Night breezes lifted the curtains and whispered her name on the air. She listened for the night song, but the music did not meet her here, could not displace the heavy weight of the unfulfilled dream.

She did not realize she slept again until Rani woke her the following morning. "Mistress Abishag." She gently shook her shoulder. "You must dress at once and come."

Alarm shot through her at Rani's tone, and she jumped up, nearly losing her balance.

Rani's hand steadied her. "Do not fear. I did not mean to startle you, only to urge you to hurry."

She followed Rani into the bedchamber and allowed the girl to dress her. "Tell me what you have heard."

"There is news that Adonijah has entered the palace and is headed to Bathsheba's chambers to seek an audience with her," Rani said in a rush. "The queen's maid Tirzah said you must come."

Dread grew like a wild thing within her as Rani covered her hair with a headscarf and tied her sandals, tasks she seemed unable to perform herself. Adonijah. His visit here could do no good.

I would gladly take you as my wife . . . You are as beautiful as they say. Adonijah's words that long-ago day crowded out all other thoughts. What possible reason could he have to seek an audience with Bathsheba?

Her stomach sickened, though she forced herself to follow Rani's steady feet, fairly running toward the queen's chambers. She could not imagine why Bathsheba would want her present at Adonijah's visit. Unless . . . did she know something, even arrange something Abishag did not know? Was this Naamah's doing?

Impossible. Solomon's women would have nothing to do with Adonijah, considering the man was Solomon's rival. Her sense of dread heightened, her pulse erratic. Fear she could not name took hold, but she told herself to calm. She had no reason to work her emotions into panic.

She smoothed her hands on her hastily donned robe and released a long-held breath as they approached the guard at the queen's door.

Tirzah met her. "Good. You are here." She motioned her into the chamber she had used during those few weeks after King David's death.

"What is going on?" Abishag asked once Tirzah had closed them in the room. Bathsheba was nowhere to be seen, though she did hear movement coming from her bedchamber.

"The guard at the gate is keeping Adonijah waiting for an audience with my lady," Tirzah said, looking her over as though she were her charge. She straightened Abishag's headscarf and tsked her tongue at her disheveled hair. "Oh, child, you need not have rushed without completing your morning tasks."

Abishag's hands shook as she removed the scarf. "I can brush my hair here." She moved to the basket that still held the things she had used in this room, but Rani snatched the comb up before she could proceed, obviously anticipating her nervous mood. "You still have not explained the need for my presence," she said as she sank onto a bench and allowed Rani to dress her hair and reposition her headscarf.

"I only know that Adonijah wishes to speak to the queen, and your name was mentioned as the reason," Tirzah said.

Abishag's heartbeat quickened again as her mind flashed to the vision of Adonijah at his father's funeral, looking at her with that too-possessive gaze. She felt nearly faint when Bathsheba swept into the room, graceful and confident. Perhaps many men thought the queen weak, especially considering the way they said she had given herself to King David while she was still wed to Uriah the Hittite, but Abishag had seen much strength in her during the years of David's illness. Especially during the moments when she stood in defense of her son, begging the king to spare them both. She knew her mission and she knew her husband. She got what she wanted.

Abishag suddenly wondered what she wanted now.

"Thank you for coming, Abishag." Bathsheba's smile and gratitude both surprised and warmed her.

Abishag bowed low, then rose at the queen's touch. "I am always willing to serve you, my queen."

"Come," she said, leading her into the sitting room. How Abishag missed their time together in these chambers. "I want you to sit to the side, near the window, when Adonijah arrives. Just behind the curtain." She touched Abishag's arm. "Don't let him see you. Stay hidden as you so often did in the king's chambers."

Abishag raised a brow, then slowly nodded.

"I have a feeling I know what he wants," Bathsheba confided at her look. "I want you to be here as witness against him."

Abishag carried a similar feeling, but she did not have the certainty Bathsheba seemed to possess that all would be well. Still, she could not doubt her. She moved to the place assigned her.

Bathsheba took a seat among the plush cushions in the sitting room. "Tell the guard to let him in," she said to Tirzah.

Abishag leaned away from peeking out from behind her cover and tried to slow her breathing lest her nervous tension give her away. The moments seemed to pass in slow motion, until at last the guard announced Adonijah's presence.

Bathsheba's confident voice floated to her. "Do you come peacefully?"

"Yes, peacefully." From his arrogant tone, Abishag could nearly see the look he always gave her and felt her face heat at the thought. "I have something to say to you," he added, bringing a flutter of worry to Abishag's middle.

"You may say it." Bathsheba's voice held an edge.

Adonijah cleared his throat, but there was no waver in his tone. "As you know," he said clearly, "the kingdom was mine. All Israel looked to me as their king. But things changed, and the kingdom has gone to my brother, for it has come to him from the Lord. Now I have one request to make of you. Do not refuse me."

It was magnanimous of him to give credit to Adonai, but no words he uttered could mask his insincerity. Abishag clenched her hands, holding back the sudden urge to lash out at him. Bathsheba was speaking, and she forced herself to be the witness she had asked of her.

"You may make the request," she said.

Abishag heard the sound of shifting in a seat, of feet scraping the tiles, and she imagined Adonijah's sudden discomfort. "Please ask King Solomon . . ." He paused. "He will not refuse you—to give me Abishag the Shunammite as my wife."

Abishag's breath hitched. Didn't she know it? She gripped the edges of the chair and leaned even farther from the curtain, longing to disappear into the wall or, better yet, flee through the open window. Had he heard her swift intake of breath? Heat moved from her face to her limbs, and anger slowly replaced her shock. The audacity! He spoke treasonous words. She had belonged to King David and now to his heir, Solomon. Surely Bathsheba would not give in to such a ludicrous request! But her insides melted as she heard the queen mother say, "Very well. I will speak to the king for you."

Adonijah thanked her, but Abishag barely heard his retreating footsteps past the roaring in her ears. Bathsheba could not do this. Could she? Was this to protect Naamah, to keep Abishag from Solomon? She would live as King David's widow forever before she would consent to marry Adonijah!

Did she have a right to refuse, especially if Solomon agreed to the match?

She could not move, fearing she might faint. But a moment later, the curtain parted and Bathsheba knelt at her side. "Did you hear?"

She barely nodded. Words stuck in her throat.

"I will go at once and seek an audience with Solomon," she said.

Tears filled Abishag's eyes. She could not stop them.

Bathsheba pulled her into her embrace. "Do not fear, my dear girl. Adonijah has given us exactly what we need to secure Solomon's reign." She stood and patted her arm. "Do you want to come with me to the audience chamber? You may wait in the antechamber and listen."

Abishag slowly nodded as Bathsheba's words penetrated her racing, anxious thoughts. She was not seeking an audience with Solomon on Adonijah's behalf.

She was seeking an audience on Solomon's behalf.

Adonijah's request would soon cost him dearly.

CHAPTER

SEVENTEEN

The loss of King David had brought subtle changes to the palace, and Naamah's fears that Abishag would quickly replace her slowly dissipated. Months passed, and the time of her confinement came upon her. After a long night of intense struggle, she birthed a girl. Solomon briefly stopped in her chambers to hold the child on his knees, but he did not name her as he had Rehoboam. So Naamah named her Hephzibah, "my delight is in her."

One day when Hephzibah was three months old, she dared to hope that Solomon had ceased to think that a king's power was determined by the size of his harem, for she remained his only queen. As she quietly nursed Hephzibah, marveling at the perfection of her features, Inaya entered her chambers. Her brows knit in that telltale frown.

"What happened?" Naamah held Hephzibah closer.

"Adonijah has been to visit Bathsheba." She drew in a breath, but her pale eyes were alight with the thrill of gossip.

"He has asked her to go to Solomon and request Abishag's hand in marriage."

Naamah forced her racing heart to still lest she disturb Hephzibah, who was so close to sleeping. The child still woke often in the night to nurse, and Naamah did not have the energy to keep her awake just now.

"What does this mean?" How perfect for her it would be if Solomon gave the woman into Adonijah's care. And yet . . . "Solomon will see this as a threat." At Inaya's nod, her hopes quickly faded.

"Adonijah is risking his life," Inaya said.

"Will Bathsheba speak to Solomon on Adonijah's behalf? He will listen to her. It may be that Adonijah's request will be answered because it comes through Solomon's mother." But surely her wise mother-in-law would see Adonijah's request as the threat it was.

"It is said that the queen mother is on her way to the audience chamber even now. Adonijah's request will be laid before Solomon today."

"Within the hour, no doubt." She covered her breast as Hephzibah's mouth went slack and sleep claimed her. Naamah rose and settled her in the cradle Rehoboam had once occupied. She returned to Inaya. "Go to the audience chamber and find out what you can. Then come and tell me everything."

She wanted desperately to be the one to do the listening but decided now was not the time to appear at court. Not the way she was dressed, and there was no time to fix her hair or freshen herself.

Inaya hurried from the room to do her bidding while Naamah paced her rooms, wondering which way Solomon's judgment would go and who would be the one to suffer with the change.

—∿∿—

Tension pulsed in the very air as Abishag walked with the queen—she with purpose, Abishag with dread—through the nearly silent halls. Guards flanked them before and behind. Lamps set in niches in the walls caught the rubies draping Bathsheba's neck and glittering from her bejeweled robe. Confidence emanated from her. Abishag did not share her feelings.

Bathsheba left her in the side antechamber closest to the throne where she would be able to clearly hear her conversation with King Solomon, then continued on with her retinue of protectors to the main chamber doors and allowed them to announce her presence.

As Bathsheba neared the raised throne, King Solomon stood. Silence descended upon the court, and her heart beat with a mixture of awe and fear. Here in this place, Solomon did not look at all like the lover in the garden or the favorite son at his father's side. Power seeped from the throne, from the many guards standing watch, swords at the ready. The brilliant colors and jewels set along the steps leading to the raised dais and the insets in the lion's-head carvings of the throne spoke wealth and authority. Perhaps King David had once carried the same aura of power, but she had not seen it. She had seen only a weak and frail companion, one who seemed unaware of the kingdom around him.

A twinge of sorrow pricked her heart at the thought of her king. She had not expected to miss him as much as she did, but his loss had changed her. She no longer felt the joy she once did, and Rani did not make nearly so interesting a companion, a friend.

She stood still, struck by a thought she had not pondered until this moment. She missed the friendship King David had offered her. Abishag, a poor young girl from Shunem. And yet the king of all Israel had considered her his friend, even went so far as to confide in her.

Tears blurred her vision as she watched in awe and some disbelief while King Solomon descended his throne to meet his mother and bow down to her. Every courtier and guard in the chamber followed the king's example and also bowed in Bathsheba's direction. Though they could not easily see her, Abishag fell to her knees as Solomon had done.

Solomon took his mother's hand and led her up the steps, called for a throne to be brought for her at his right hand, and returned to his seat.

"What brings me the pleasure of your visit, Ima?" Solomon said softly. Abishag did not miss the endearment he seemed unashamed to say even in such a public setting. He smiled at Bathsheba, and Abishag caught a hint of the man she had come to know, not simply the king who now reigned here. If not for his mother, he would not be king at all, she reminded herself. She had protected him then, and she was protecting him still.

"I have one small request to make of you," Bathsheba said. "Do not refuse me."

Abishag could see the glint of fire in the queen's gaze. Solomon seemed to notice as well, for he paused a moment.

"Make it, my mother. I will not refuse you."

A slight frown rested between Bathsheba's brows, but she

quickly covered it with a smile. "Let Abishag the Shunammite be given in marriage to your brother Adonijah."

The previous silence could not compare to the awkward
heaviness, the absence of breath, that lingered in the chambers now. The heaviness also weighted Abishag's heart and
held her frozen to the place where she stood. But the mood
abruptly transformed with Solomon's sudden roar, a lion
loosed from his cage.

"Why do you request Abishag the Shunammite for Adonijah? You might as well request the kingdom for him—after
all, he is my older brother. Yes, for him and for Abiathar the
priest and Joab son of Zeruiah!"

Abishag leaned closer to the opening in the antechamber, her heart beating as though in tune with a war drum.
Solomon's knuckles whitened on the arms of the chair, but
as he met his mother's gaze, a look of understanding swept
over him, even peace. He drew in a breath and straightened,
suddenly releasing his heavy grip on the chair.

His mother gave him the slightest nod, as though his response was exactly what she'd expected. Then he turned to
address the crowded hall of courtiers and guards, his expression hardening. "May God deal with me, be it ever so se-
verely," he said, his voice carrying its full weight of authority,
"if Adonijah does not pay with his life for this request! And
now, as surely as the Lord lives—He who has established me
securely on the throne of my father David and has founded
a dynasty for me as He promised—Adonijah shall be put to
death today!"

Abishag's stomach turned over, and she felt as though her
thoughts moved through thick mud. Truly, Solomon was not
a man to be trifled with but a king to be feared and obeyed.

She leaned into the wall for support as the king summoned the chief guard, Benaiah, and said, "Go and strike down Adonijah."

She told herself to breathe as Benaiah offered a short bow, turned on his heel, and marched out of the chamber. King Solomon stood and helped his mother to her feet, and together they left the room.

———~m~———

The news reached Naamah long before Inaya returned to her rooms, as she could no longer bear to stay cooped up in her chambers. By the time she arrived at the audience hall, it was abuzz with chatter, and Solomon had retreated to his private quarters. His mother was also no longer in sight, and Naamah feared she had wasted too much precious time dressing.

Inaya met her in the halls as she headed back toward the stairs. "You must come with me, child." Her nurse touched her arm as she spoke, and her round face bore a frown. She had not called Naamah *child* since she had borne Rehoboam.

She followed her toward the king's gardens and walked partway down the path toward some overhanging vines. "What did you hear?"

Inaya bid her sit on the stone bench beneath the vines, but Naamah refused. "Just tell me." She knew she would not like her words.

"Solomon has ordered Benaiah to execute Adonijah for requesting Abishag as his wife!" She glanced about and lowered her voice. "I would not be the least surprised to discover that his mother made the request knowing that it would give Solomon the excuse he needed to rid himself of that man.

For all of his sincere words of allegiance to Solomon, I did not trust him."

Naamah looked beyond Inaya to the beauty that was once King David's royal gardens, now her husband's. One day Solomon would build bigger gardens and a larger palace. Solomon loved beauty, and he would do all in his power to create more than this.

Abishag's image floated before her thoughts, her virgin beauty a reminder of what was fading in her own. "What is to become of Abishag then?" Though she already knew.

Inaya shook her head. "I do not know, my lady." Her sudden use of the more respectful term made Naamah straighten and look deeply into her nurse's eyes. She spoke truth. "The king retreated to his chambers immediately after the judgment."

Naamah stood a moment in indecision. Solomon rarely summoned her to his chambers. Would he come to hers now?

Doubt sailed through her, but she straightened her spine and met Inaya's gaze. "I must go to him. I must know what he will do."

Inaya nodded. "You must do as you think best, mistress."

She gathered her robe about her, trying to ward off an inner chill that she suddenly could not shake. "Wait for me in my rooms," she said as she walked off alone. What would she say to her husband if he took Abishag now to be his wife? She could feel the longings of her youth, the determination to be all he needed, slipping like water through her clenched fingers.

A thousand thoughts filled her head, and she sorted through them, accepting some and discarding others as she walked. When she reached the rooms that once belonged to

Solomon's father, she paused. Her heart pounded with the beat of too many drums as she asked the guard for entrance. She smoothed sweaty palms on her robe and drew in a deep though labored breath. She felt as though she had run the length of Jerusalem, but she had only walked a few halls. Would he see her?

The door opened moments later, and Solomon met her just inside the door. She sank to her knees.

"My lord king," she said, her voice shaking. She discreetly cleared her throat as he bid her rise.

"Naamah, my love. Come. Sit." He guided her to a new gilded couch that she quickly realized was only one part of the changes he had made to transform this room into his own. The air was cooler, the extra braziers no longer needed to warm the old king. "What can I do for you today?" His smile seemed relaxed, and he leaned back on the couch beside her, his posture that of one who is at peace.

She glanced at him, emboldened by his bright smile. When he took her hand in his and squeezed, she wanted to promise him anything. Anything to keep her in his favor and him in hers.

She intertwined their fingers. "I have heard of Adonijah's request . . . and your judgment." She watched the lines along his brow draw slightly together, but then he took in a breath and relaxed again.

"His actions amounted to treason. To request a king's wife is to request the kingdom."

She nodded. She knew this. "We will breathe easier knowing he is no longer a threat to you or to Rehoboam." The subtle reminder that she had borne his heir brought a curious tilt to his head. "I was wondering," she said, straightening and holding the intensity of his gaze, "what is now to become of Abishag?"

He looked at her for a long, silent moment, his expression sobering. He leaned closer, lifted the veil over her shoulder, and traced a hand along her jaw. "I will wed her at week's end," he said, his tone so matter-of-fact and emotionless that she blinked, leaning back to better look into his eyes. He shrugged, fingering a strand of her hair. "If I don't take her to wife, another of my brothers could try to take her. I would rather not have to see all of them put to death on her account."

He leaned forward and kissed her cheek, his breath soft against her face. He was planning to take another wife, and yet here he sat wooing her, Naamah.

"Do you love her?" She recalled the laughter he'd shared with Abishag the first night she had met her.

Solomon leaned slightly away, his dark, mysterious eyes taking her in with a look she couldn't quite read. "I love you, Naamah. You are my first wife, mother of my heir." He leaned closer again and kissed her as he had the first time, the night of their wedding. "How beautiful you are, my darling! Oh, how beautiful! Your eyes are doves." His kiss deepened, and she wrapped her arms about him, clinging to him. "Your lips drip sweetness as the honeycomb, my bride; milk and honey are under your tongue," he said when at last he pulled back and cupped her face in his hands. "You have stolen my heart, my sister, my bride." He drew her to him and rested her head against his chest. "You have stolen my heart."

He held her then, and time seemed insignificant as they talked and laughed and he coaxed her to the cushions of his bed and encased her in his love.

When she left a few hours later to return to her chambers, she realized he had never answered her question about loving Abishag. But he had done more for her than he could have with any answer. He had reassured her of his love for her, and she knew that as Bathsheba had been to King David, she would not be set aside but favored. She would not allow herself to ever be forgotten.

EIGHTEEN

A week passed and Solomon forgot his promise to quickly marry Abishag in light of pressing business. The palace became a flurry of activity, people coming to him from all areas of Israel seeking judgment—judgment he had often sought his father's advice to give. The enormity of it all, the aloneness he felt, settled in on him, and he knew it was time to slip away, to sacrifice and pray. Instead of a wedding by week's end, Solomon led his entourage to Gibeon to sacrifice to Adonai.

While the daily sacrifices his father had set up in Jerusalem were sufficient to keep the law, Gibeon allowed him to sacrifice lavishly, for there was more space for the animals and for the priests to do the work. The smoke rising from the altar smelled sweet, as he hoped it also did to Adonai.

He always felt closer to God at Gibeon, but he wasn't sure why when the ark rested in Jerusalem. It was as if he sensed God's nearness, though he had seen no angel as some of his ancestors had in years past, heard no voice as Abraham had.

He watched the sacrifices from the sidelines, sometimes kneeling, sometimes head bowed, sometimes walking and praying in silence, the ever-present guards following. The many priests took the entire day to sacrifice a thousand bulls, but somehow Solomon wondered if it was enough. How could he ever repay Adonai for all He had already given to him? Allowing him to become king in his father's place was a blessing he had wanted but always wondered if he would ever receive. Now it weighed heavily on his shoulders, and he longed to hear from the God his father loved, the God he loved, to better learn how to rule this vast kingdom.

Please, Lord, have mercy. Surely God would listen. Yet still he waited.

Night fell as the last of the bulls spilled their blood on Yahweh's altar. A thousand seemed so minimal compared to the size of his household, his courtiers, his officers, and the workers in his kingdom. But the gift, the offering, had not been meant for them. Not really.

He knelt again, the dirt and stones pressing into his palms, and felt the weight of his failures, his sins, that the offerings represented. Was his gift given in the right spirit? Should he have inspected each animal himself, placed his hands on their heads, allowed his sin to transfer to them in complete repentance?

Guilt tugged at him that he had not done so, had not done enough despite the love he had come to feel for the Almighty One. Did his love stem from a true heart? Had he loved only because God had blessed or because God was God? Abishag had broached the question with him in the past few years. They had tried to capture the understanding of Him in their poetry and songs, but somehow the feelings were never enough.

Oh, to see Him face-to-face. To hear Him speak as a man speaks with a friend. But few had ever encountered an angel, let alone the Almighty.

Solomon rose slowly, letting the thoughts move through him, looking heavenward as the last wisps of smoke wafted upward. *I hope I have pleased You.* But it was doubtful he would ever know.

The sun dipped to its final resting place below the horizon, and Solomon slipped into his tent alone while his guards stood watch at the door. Cushions lined the floor and he rested his head among them, still pondering the great questions of love and worship and wishing again that he had tangible proof of God's presence. Hadn't he always been the inquisitive type? Were his questions and doubts a sign of disbelief? *May it never be!*

Of course he believed. He just wished he could climb a ladder to heaven like the one Jacob had seen in his dream. Or somehow hear like Abraham, who had been told to count the stars, for so would his descendants be. Descendants Solomon now ruled.

Sleep came as his thoughts twisted and turned.

Solomon.

He turned over, too weary to rise.

Solomon.

He sat up. Looked about the tent, absent of people. No one stood at the door or had poked their head inside. He lay down again, but this time the words were clear through a dream-filled haze.

Ask what I shall give you.

Brightness like a great light surrounded the words, and Solomon knew in an instant that the voice was not of this world. *Adonai?* Had God heard his silent longings?

Solomon swallowed hard and whispered lest he somehow be overheard. "O Lord, You have shown great and steadfast love to Your servant David my father, because he walked before You in faithfulness, in righteousness, and in uprightness of heart toward You. And You have kept for him this great and steadfast love and have given him a son to sit on his throne this day." He drew in a breath and hurried on. "And now, O Lord my God, You have made Your servant king in place of David my father, although I am but a little child. I do not know how to go out or come in. And Your servant is in the midst of Your people whom You have chosen, a great people, too many to be numbered or counted."

He paused again, afraid he was rambling, but sensed that the Presence was still with him. "Therefore, give Your servant an understanding mind to govern Your people, that I may discern between good and evil, for who is able to govern Your great people?"

He relaxed, relieved. He had released the longing of his heart.

The voice, deep like thunder yet quiet as a whisper, responded, "Because you have asked this, and have not asked for yourself long life or riches or the life of your enemies, but have asked for yourself understanding to discern what is right, behold, I now do according to your word. I give you a wise and discerning mind, so that none like you has been before you and none like you shall arise after you. I give you also what you have not asked, both riches and honor, so that no other king shall compare with you all your days. And if you will walk in My ways, keeping My statutes and My commandments, as your father David walked, then I will lengthen your days."

The words ended abruptly even as Solomon's heart cried out, *Yes, I will obey You.* And suddenly he awoke, blinking sharply at the darkness. A dream. And yet real. God had spoken to him in a dream as He had to Jacob those many years ago.

As morning dawned, Solomon stood already dressed beside his mule and commanded his men to lead the way back to Jerusalem. Gibeon was not enough. After such an amazing gift, there was only one place Solomon could think to go. To the tent his father had built. To stand before the Ark of the Covenant of the Lord, where he would sacrifice peace offerings for himself and all of his servants.

—⟶

Later that day as he continued to ponder the amazing words of Adonai, he allowed his servants to dress him in kingly garb and made his way to the audience chamber. Elihoreph, one of his secretaries, met him in the anteroom before the servants announced his presence to those waiting.

"My lord," Elihoreph said, bowing low then quickly rising. "There is news from Egypt."

Solomon crossed his arms and studied the man. "In my short time away, news comes all the way from Egypt?"

Elihoreph bobbed his head. "Yes, my lord. And most fascinating it is."

At that moment, Elihoreph's brother Ahijah, another secretary, approached.

"Ahijah, what is this of which your brother speaks?" Solomon raised a brow, his curiosity heightened.

"It seems that Egypt has conquered Gezer, and their pharaoh, Siamun the Great, wanted to be sure you knew of it."

Solomon met Ahijah's gaze, and Elihoreph gave a confirming nod. "Gezer is one of the cities the Lord God had promised to Israel, a city meant to be captured during Joshua's day, but neither Joshua nor my own father David was able to penetrate its walls. Obviously Pharaoh Siamun was determined to infiltrate territory that did not belong to him, flexing his might. But to what end?"

"I don't know, my lord. The messenger did not stay long, but it seems clear that Egypt wants you to know that they are close by, watching your kingdom."

"And no doubt are up to no good." The thought troubled him. His was a kingdom of peace, not war. "I have great interest in gaining this stronghold of Canaan, to expand Israel's territory to where our God intended it. But I will not go to war with Egypt." He rubbed his chin, wondering for a moment if he should call for Zabud, his priest and friend, for counsel.

A sigh escaped. He did not want to deal with Egypt right now or their veiled threats, if that's what this was.

"Surely there can be a peaceful solution to this situation," Ahijah said. "Your counselors agreed that Egypt is not nearly as powerful as it once was. Perhaps this pharaoh sent you the news as a bargaining piece, to make sure there is no war between your kingdoms."

Solomon glanced beyond his secretaries to the audience chamber where people awaited his judgment. "Send my regards and congratulations to Pharaoh Siamun. Tell him that he has accomplished a great feat and that someday I would enjoy hearing him tell of it." He walked toward the door as the last trumpet blared, then glanced back at his secretaries. "It appears we shall be closer neighbors with Egypt than we expected. Let us see whether this pharaoh seeks diplomacy or is looking to expand his kingdom."

Someday he would find a way to remove Gezer from Egypt's grasp, but it would take time, years perhaps, to decide how to do just that.

CHAPTER

NINETEEN

EGYPT

"There is nothing to do," Siti complained to her maid Akila. Two weeks had passed since their trip to Bubastis for the festival of Bastet and the burial of her favorite cat, Lapis. She dipped her right foot into the wading pool of her mother's inner court, listless and bored. Her kitten, Abdukar, slept peacefully beneath the shade of a low-hanging palm not far from her, while her maid tossed lotus petals onto the blue-green water. "Why are the days following a festival always so lifeless and mundane?" She flicked water upward with her toes, then pulled her leg beneath her and stood. "I am going to the garden sanctuary." She scooped Abdukar into her arms, and Akila hurried after her.

"Would you not rather go to the marketplace, my lady?" Siti allowed Akila to speak her mind with her, and the girl never missed an opportunity to do so.

"Why ask me such a thing, Akila? I want to observe the birds and the flowers and trees. The marketplace is noisy and dusty this time of day." She lifted her chin and straightened, looking at her maid through a slanted gaze.

Akila bowed her head, as she always did when she attempted to appease. "There is also excitement and exotic wares at the market. Perhaps you will hear a musician singing love songs. Would that not be more enjoyable than watching the winds rustle the leaves on the trees?"

Siti stopped, which caused Abdukar to wriggle out of her hold and hop down to saunter back to his sunning place. She shrugged. He had grown by half again as much in the past two weeks, and she knew the day was fast approaching when he would no longer sit so easily upon her lap.

She faced Akila. "Very well. To market we will go. But I must change my attire. I do not want the sun to further darken my skin, nor do I wish to be noticed. Come, help me." They would go with guards, which could not be helped, but she did not have to wear her best jewels or a costume that would set her apart.

They hurried to her chambers where Akila helped her dress, then strode through the harem, down a winding path of palace halls, and out the back way, guards on either side.

"They say Egypt has captured a great city in Canaan, my lady. Have you heard the details?" Akila spoke quietly as they walked, while Siti glanced about at area homes for signs of women working in courtyards or travelers gawking at the Great Pharaoh's grand buildings. Thebes was a popular stop for those moving from one country to another. Foreigners often made the journey just to admire the work of their great land.

"I have not," she admitted, leaning close to Akila's ear. "My mother has said nothing of this, though I have overheard my brothers talk of sending some soldiers outside our borders." In truth, she cared little for battles or war games, which seemed to spark life into the eyes of her brothers and male cousins.

Akila nodded, and they grew silent as they drew closer to the wide marketplace not far from the wharf, where craftsmen and fishermen and gardeners plied their wares. Traders from as far north as Damascus, down through King Solomon's Israel, and as far south as Nubia came to trade here on a regular basis. Sometimes rare spices and silks from Asia could be found, and her mother's maids were quick to pounce on such delicacies or rare objects.

"They say the city they captured is called Gezer," Akila said as they stood beneath the awning of a basket weaver. "A stronghold that withstood the onslaught of both Joshua and King David of Israel."

She had heard tales of Gezer. An impenetrable fortress. Her heart skipped a beat, pride swelling for her country. "And yet Egypt's might has conquered it." She touched several fabrics of multicolored weave dyed with rich colors. "Exquisite," she said to no one in particular, softly enough that the proprietor did not hear her words. She turned to one of her guards and nodded, pointing at the object, then turned her back on the booth and walked with Akila to another. The guard would have the fabrics in her rooms by nightfall.

"They say the soldiers are returning by week's end with more plunder than one town should ever hold." Excitement lit Akila's round face, and Siti smiled, her own heart feeling lighter than it had since Lapis's untimely death.

"There will be jewels and foreign robes," Siti said, stopping at a booth where an old, toothless woman strung bright beads on thin strands of gold.

"Undoubtedly, my lady. And so many birds—geese, ducks, pigeons, cranes, quail—the palace is sure to feast for weeks to come."

Siti nearly laughed at Akila's tone, for her maid dearly loved to eat, and whenever there was meat in abundance to please the men, the cooks always added extra honeyed confections to satisfy the pharaoh's wives—more sweets than the women of the harem could desire all year.

"I am sure the men will find plenty of ways to celebrate." She spoke absently as her mind drifted to how all of these distracting celebrations would affect her mother's plans for her sister's wedding. She should have been grateful, for at least that meant they could put off any suggestion of her marriage to Nakhti or any of her other cousins for at least a year or two. Perhaps by then Nakhti would have matured and outgrown his temper.

But she had her doubts.

A commotion near the wharf drew their attention, and her guards closed in, ready to protect her with their lives. "What is it?" she asked one of them, trying to see past his broad shoulder. "Have the soldiers returned so soon?"

Shouts increased in the distance.

"The first group to return, my lady," the guard said, his voice tense. He gently turned her back toward the palace. "Men like that can be . . . unrestrained." He guided both of them away from the market, moving quickly up the road back to the protection of the harem walls. The guards did not allow their movements to slow until they were inside the locked gates. But the ruckus outside only grew in intensity.

Men were celebrating and drinking, though it was not yet high noon.

She looked at Akila and motioned for her to follow as she made her way toward the great hall of her father. "I want to watch," she whispered, climbing the steps to an anteroom that looked down from her mother's balcony.

"Shouldn't we tell your mother and sister so they can join us?" Akila always worried about pleasing her mother, which annoyed Siti more than she cared to admit.

"The guards will tell them soon enough." They reached the balcony just as the first wave of military men entered the cavernous audience chamber. She glanced toward the throne where her father sat decked out in full regal attire, holding the crook and flail crisscrossed over his chest.

She recognized the general who bowed at her father's feet. He was one of the men always in council with her father.

"We have captured Gezer as we set out to do, my lord," the general said, his voice ringing in the silent hall.

"Very good," the Great Pharaoh said, though his mouth held its firm line. "And did you make the capture known?"

"Yes, my lord. Messengers were sent to Jerusalem that very hour. King Solomon now knows that Egypt is right at his side." The general remained with one knee bent on the floor, but he held her father's gaze.

Siti's heart fluttered at the mention of King Solomon. He was a young king by all accounts, with a handful of wives. The queen mother, Bathsheba, was known throughout the land as a shrewd but loving mother. It was said that she had conspired to remove Solomon's rival half brother from any chance of power once King David entered the underworld. Siti had respected the woman from the moment she'd heard the tale.

"There are rumors, my lord," the general continued, "that your message hit its mark, though nothing is yet sure."

"So it is possible King Solomon will travel to Egypt." It wasn't a question, for her father rarely asked questions, merely stated things that were to be answered regardless.

"Yes, my lord. Though the king himself was away offering sacrifices at Gibeon, the messenger spoke to some of the servants of highest rank. Israel had been promised Gezer by their god many years ago under their leader Joshua, but they were never able to capture it. King Solomon is a wise man, my lord. He will see this as an opportunity to do business with you."

"Do business?" she whispered to Akila. "What business could my father want with Israel?"

"If the man himself will come, we will welcome him," her father said, catching her attention once more. "They say his father was a great man. I would like to meet the son."

She turned away then as the talk turned to details of the war strategy, how they killed the lords of Gezer—which was far too gruesome for her ears—and what her father planned to do with the large amount of spoils they had acquired.

She descended the steps from the balcony, nearly bumping into her mother.

"Siti, what are you doing here?" Her questions always held that tone of accusation, as though Siti had nothing better to do but to sit in her apartments and stitch patterns on cloth or swim in the lotus pool.

She met her mother's gaze, quickly deciding to give her the one thing she would want to know above all the rest. "The men have captured a city in Canaan, and they say King Solomon might come to Egypt." She fled down the steps before her mother could think to respond, Akila quick on her heels. She ignored the distant calls of her name on her mother's lips.

"You really should have given her more than that," Akila said once they had safely arrived back in her rooms and Abdukar rested in her lap. Akila pulled the sandals from her feet and dipped each foot in soothing scented water.

"She will find out all she needs to know from my father or his menservants. She will know far more than I do by nightfall." She eased her back against the soft cushions and closed her eyes. Her mother delighted in gaining knowledge, whereas all Siti wanted to do now was imagine what was to come.

Solomon. Such a peaceful name. What was he like? How old was he? Did he have two wives or twenty? Reports were always so inaccurate.

"Do you think I will be allowed to meet him?" She met Akila's gaze as her maid wrapped one foot in a lotus-scented towel.

"Why would you not? You are Pharaoh's daughter." Akila rubbed the water droplets gently from Siti's feet and placed doeskin slippers on each one.

"My father has many daughters."

"And they will all likely be allowed to at least glimpse the foreign king. Even if it is only from the balcony, I am sure you will see him." Akila's tone was meant to soothe, but Siti's heartbeat quickened.

"I do not want to simply glimpse him," she realized with such certainty it startled her. "I want to speak with him." Her stomach did a little flip at the thought.

"You will likely hear him speak with your father from a

distance." Akila lifted the water trough and carried it to the pool, where she dumped the contents in.

"Well, if there is a way to meet him, I will find it," Siti said, holding Abdukar close and squinting at Akila. "And you will help me."

Akila lifted a brow at that, but she did not argue. Akila knew her well and seemed to enjoy her bouts of defiance almost as much as Siti did, despite her desire to please Siti's mother.

TWENTY

JERUSALEM

Abishag's mood slipped into melancholy as the months continued on after King David's death, a mood she had not experienced to any great length since her mother had passed into Sheol. But now . . . now she questioned everything.

Why did the sun shine so brightly when she longed for clouds to blot its warmth? Why did the food carry such a bitter taste? Why was the water in the mikvah not warm?

The bitter gossips of her youth filled her thoughts. She was becoming just like them!

But she could not stop herself. While she lay on her bed, her heart turned heavenward. *Why did You make me? Why allow me the enjoyment of knowing King David's kindness only to be the cause of Adonijah's death?*

Still Solomon kept his distance. She was as invisible as she had been in her brother's household, though at least there the sheep had kept her company, and even her sister-in-law Batya's scolding acknowledged her existence.

She searched her heart for some sin, some law she must have broken to cause her life such loss, such indifference from those living around her. Naamah had succeeded in keeping Solomon to herself. Bathsheba had not called for her since Adonijah's death.

She retreated to the women's quarters with Rani as her only companion. But the girl seemed to tire of her silence, and as the days passed, Abishag grew more listless.

"Perhaps you should play one of King David's songs, mistress," Rani said one day in her continual attempt to cheer her. "Or we could work on the tiles together. There is much you could teach me and so much I want to learn."

She said the words for Abishag's sake more than her own, as she knew Rani preferred to visit the cooking rooms and talk to the other servants more than she cared to spend time with her mistress in her current state. How self-absorbed she had become!

"I liked your songs," Rani said, still coaxing.

Abishag forced a smile.

"Perhaps a walk on the roof would revive you," she suggested when Abishag shook her head at Rani's first comments. "You cannot stay within these rooms forever, mistress. You are always welcome to eat at Bathsheba's table in the women's banquet hall. Let me fix your finest robes and you can join them tonight."

Perhaps she spoke wisdom. Abishag's self-proclaimed isolation had only fed her feelings of abandonment. But she did not have to allow herself to remain here. She was secluded by choice.

"All right," she said with a slight nod.

"The king will surely notice you."

Rani's assurances brought the slightest hint of hope to her heart. But a moment later she realized her error. "The king will not see me, my friend. I will be eating with the women."

But his mother would notice, and Naamah would notice, and the one with the greater influence over Solomon would decide whether she was worth remembering.

—⁓—

The banquet that night did indeed revive Abishag's spirits. Bathsheba hosted foreign wives of dignitaries, and Naamah was clearly the first wife among the women of the court whom Solomon had inherited from his father. Abishag sat among this group and tried to talk about trivial matters with one of the younger concubines. The girl seemed pleasant enough, and the flutists and harpists and later the dancing jugglers lightened the burden on her heart.

But she noticed the slightest frown fringe Naamah's brows. Memories surfaced of the princess's visits to King David's rooms on Solomon's arm, and she suddenly understood the woman's struggle. Solomon had paid Abishag undue attention during some of those moments. Surely Naamah had noticed. For the first time since her attraction to Solomon, she imagined how she would feel in Naamah's place.

Servants distracted her as they milled about, carrying golden platters filled with cups of spiced wine and sweet pastries. She nodded and smiled at something the woman next to her said, but she did not really hear her, for she could not shake the memories or the jealousy that still moved across the room between Naamah and her.

Suddenly the room seemed too warm, the friendships too forced. She could not stay and abide the hurt she had surely caused Solomon's wife. Her very being here posed a threat, and the only escape was to retreat to her chambers and hope somehow to convince Solomon to let her return to Shunem. If he was willing to compensate her enough, she could live on her own, tending the sheep and goats, and return to the fields she loved. She would not need a man to love her. She had the beauty of creation to feed and comfort her soul. In those places, she knew Adonai loved her. She needed no one else.

She abruptly stood, not seeing the large servant behind her, and nearly collided with him. "Forgive me!" she said, stepping away from his teetering tray. She breathed a relieved sigh when he righted the tray and none of the wine spilled.

"Think nothing of it, my lady. I should have been more aware."

Of course he would say such a thing. A servant would never think to put the blame on a master, even one as insignificant as she. "No, no," she said, wanting to ease the irritation that surely lay behind his broad smile. "I should have looked before I stood." She nodded to the man and ducked behind her seat, then straightened and walked gracefully toward the banquet hall doors.

No one stopped her exit, to her great relief. Bathsheba had been engaged in conversation with the ambassador's wife from Egypt, a visit no one had expected, given Egypt's disdain for the Israelites. But this particular pharaoh appeared to be impressed with Solomon's rise to power and seemed to want to keep peace between the two nations.

Abishag drew in a breath, suddenly longing for something other than these stone halls. She made her way through the labyrinth of palace twists and turns until she came to the stairs leading to the roof that overlooked all of Jerusalem.

She had brought the king here on the good days when the chill did not seep deep into his bones.

Lights shone from the houses below her, and moonlight added to the glow of tall sconces that lit the corners of the parapet. Night breezes brought a refreshing chill to her heated skin, heat that came from the fresh knowledge of what she must do. Her heart did not want to follow where her path clearly led.

She moved to the edge of the parapet and took in the brilliance of Jerusalem's evening glow. Her breathing slowed and peace followed. It was good to be free of Naamah's presence. Leaving this place was the right thing to do. If Solomon would allow it.

She pressed both hands against the stone rail and lifted her gaze to the stars, little dots of sparkling jewels. A half moon tilted like she imagined a ship at sea would. She had never seen one, only heard Solomon speak of them when conversing with his father.

Oh Solomon. How will I let go of my love for you?

"They are beautiful, are they not?"

She startled and turned so quickly she nearly lost her balance. His hand steadied her.

"My lord?" She slipped quickly to her knees and bowed low. "May you live forever, my king."

Silence followed her remark, but she heard him clear his throat as though her actions surprised him. He bent to grasp her hand and pulled her to her feet and into his arms. "I did not follow you here to be treated as your monarch." He tipped her chin up. His lips grazed hers.

"You followed me here?" She had not heard his footfalls, nor noticed anyone in the halls or on the steps behind her.

"Does that seem so impossible? A servant told me you had come. When my mother sent word that you had joined her banquet and that you were the loveliest woman in the room . . ." His voice trailed off, and his boyish smile caused a flip in her middle. "I had you followed."

She could find no words to respond to such a thing, so she simply nodded. He touched her nose and stroked his fingers along her cheek. "I am sorry I have neglected you." He paused and glanced away a moment. "I feared you might harbor ill feelings toward me . . . because of Adonijah." He looked at her then, his gaze searching.

"You did what you had to do with Adonijah." She tried not to remember the last words she had heard fall from Adonijah's lips and the arrogant way he had said them as he requested her hand in marriage.

Solomon did not speak. She searched his face, caught the fleeting look of vulnerability. "Had you hoped to marry him?" he asked at last.

"No," she said quickly. "I was quite relieved *not* to marry him."

He placed his fingers on the pulse at her throat. She swallowed, knowing he could feel the very beating of her heart. "I have missed you," she said softly. "Have missed the music we played in your father's rooms." She lowered her gaze, sensing his desire.

He drew her closer. "I want you, Abishag." His kiss tasted minty, and she felt the steady thrumming of his heart against hers.

She returned his kiss, feeling as though she needed to grasp this moment lest it never come again. His kiss deepened, and she felt herself falling into a place of no returning.

It was Solomon who gently broke his hold and held her at arm's length. "I want you, but not this way. I could legally take you as a concubine, my love, but I want you as my wife."

Her heart lifted with his pronouncement, but she placed a gentle hand on his chest. "And what of Naamah?"

His brow furrowed as though he did not understand.

"Do not think me foolish, my lord. I only worry because I know that Naamah does not want me in your life. I have known it from the beginning."

He stroked her cheek, his smile warm. "Do not fear Naamah. She knows I will take other wives. She has always known it, though she does not like it." His dark eyes glanced off hers as if remembering. "She thought in marrying me she could remain my first and only wife. But that is not possible when you marry a king. Surely you know this?" He seemed suddenly concerned with her opinion, and she recognized how easily women could sway him. He did not want to hurt them. But he wanted them to accept his choices without a fuss.

"I do not mind being second of many, my lord." She touched his beard and smiled. "It is enough to know you want me."

Joy lit his eyes then, and all thoughts of her request to return to Shunem vanished. "At week's end we will have a wedding such as you have never seen." He cupped her quivering chin, and she could not keep her eyes from filling with joyous tears.

He kissed her again but did not linger. "We must not awaken love until it is ready," he said, and she knew he tasted the joy of poetry in his words.

"No, we mustn't." She smiled. "A week? Not a few days?"

He chuckled at her anxious longing. "A week will cause the joy to be worth the wait. Before you know it you will be tired of me and wishing we had waited even longer." His arms around her told her that his words were not possible. Her soul had found its song again in the beat of his heart.

"I will never grow tired of you, my lord. I am yours all the days of my life."

TWENTY-ONE

A whirlwind of activity followed Solomon's pronouncement to Abishag. Bathsheba called her daily to her chambers, while maids frantically worked to sew an elaborate wedding robe, complete with embroidered sleeves and hem. The headscarf rivaled any she had seen the queen wear, and the jewels Solomon bestowed on her glistened like those in his crown.

Naamah was strangely absent from most of these preparations, but one afternoon as Abishag took a break to walk in the central courtyard where female servants worked at the spindle and distaff or sat at large looms placed beneath overhanging awnings, Naamah found her there.

Abishag stiffened at her approach, though she remembered to bow. "My lady." She rose and offered a conciliatory smile.

Naamah did not return it. "Abishag." She nodded once, though she could not hide the rigidity of her jaw. When she crossed her arms, Abishag braced herself for an onslaught of bitter words, which Batya had been so fond of using throughout Abishag's years in her brother's household.

Abishag waited, taking a step back from Solomon's first wife. "How can I help you?" She had often diffused anger by offering help. Perhaps the question would soften Naamah as well.

But her gaze seemed to harden as she scrutinized Abishag in silence. At last she spoke. "My son is Solomon's heir. Do not forget that."

Abishag drew in a breath. Was that the cause of her fear? "I am happy for you, mistress. How blessed you are to have borne his first son." She smiled, hoping to dispel the tension.

"I am also the first wife. Do not forget that either." She lifted her chin with not even the hint of a smile on her lips.

Abishag studied Naamah for a lengthy moment, searching her heart for understanding. Naamah's anger was simply a mask for her fear of losing Solomon to another. But she had not thought far enough to realize that Abishag would not be Solomon's last.

"You have nothing to fear from me, Naamah." She spoke softly, kindly. "I know Solomon loves you and the children you have given him. You are the first, as you will remain. I am second and insignificant in comparison." She extended a hand in supplication, hoping the woman would relax and unwind her crossed arms. "Solomon will take more wives after me. How many, I do not know, but I do understand that I will not be his last."

Naamah bristled at that comment, and Abishag feared she had said too much. But slowly, cautiously, Naamah lowered her arms and let her shoulders fall in a sense of defeat. "I have always known it." Her admission surprised Abishag.

"I have never wanted nor liked it, but I have known it deep in my heart."

Compassion filled Abishag, and she wondered how it must have felt to be given your heart's desire only to know you would lose it someday. She had never been given her own desire to lose. Until now.

"Our lives often do not turn out the way we expect," she said, taking a small step closer to her rival. "I would not be here if I had been given what I longed for, what life was meant to be."

Naamah met her gaze at that, as though she suddenly realized that Abishag too had a story of becoming, of being in this place. Naamah's story, as Abishag had heard Bathsheba tell it, was one of desire and choice.

Her own was not.

"Was there a man you had hoped to marry in your village?" Naamah asked as they turned to walk back toward the palace halls. The late afternoon shadows had fallen, and Abishag knew Naamah's children would have need of her soon and the servants would call them both to the banquet halls to dine.

"There was a boy I once thought I could love," she admitted. "But he married my niece soon after my brother signed the ketubah that wed me to the king."

Naamah seemed to ponder that a moment. "Do you miss your life in your village?"

Abishag shook her head. "No more than you miss your life in Ammon." They were near the turns in the hall that led in different directions—Naamah's to her rooms on the second floor, Abishag's to the court of women—and turned to face each other. "I choose to find the music of Adonai wherever

172

He has placed me," Abishag said, holding the princess's gaze. "I would like us to be friends."

Naamah blinked at that final word but did not bristle as Abishag had expected she might. "I will think on it," she said. And as they parted, Naamah cast a small smile her way.

TWENTY-TWO

Abishag awoke early the day of her wedding to Solomon, though she wondered if she had slept at all. Nerves heightened, she sensed rather than heard music in every word, every footfall, even in the chatter and quarrels of servants.

Her maids, especially Rani, hovered over her, subjecting her to one more goat's-milk-and-honey treatment, smoothing her skin, and plaiting her hair, pulling it into an elaborate style with the traditional seven combs for Solomon to remove.

Breads and pastries carried sweet scents from the cooking rooms, and a multitude of servants spread palm fronds, lit scented sconces, and filled basket upon basket with spiced nuts and fruits. Meats of every kind overpowered her senses. Even in her secluded rooms, she could hear the hurried footfalls and nearly taste the food by the enticing aromas. Solomon had clearly spared no expense on her behalf.

"It is time, my lady," Rani said once the last bit of kohl

adorned her eyes and the veil rested securely, covering all but her eyelashes. Her pulse quickened at the thought of seeing Solomon dressed in his wedding finery. What would he say when he saw her thus?

"I am ready." She allowed Rani to take her elbow and guide her through the halls. Guards surrounded them before and behind, and her heart beat to the pounding of their girded feet.

"Are you nervous?" Rani asked when they finally stopped in the anteroom outside the king's columned audience chamber.

Abishag stepped closer to the side door and pulled it slightly ajar. Her breath hitched at the brilliant beauty of this transformed place. "Now I am."

Rani stood on tiptoe behind her and peered into the room. She drew in a breath. "I have never seen such a thing."

"He spared nothing," Abishag said, finding it suddenly hard to breathe. How was it he could pour so much gold into transforming his chambers just for her? She was not even an official bride. Just an inheritance from his father. Unworthiness crept over her, and she felt heat fill her face. She looked about for a place to sit.

Rani seemed to notice, for she gripped Abishag's arm and guided her to a bench. "Are you all right, mistress?" She placed a cool hand on Abishag's forehead, careful not to mar the makeup she had so recently applied. "Let me fetch you some water." She nodded, and Rani hurried over to a guard to demand her request. Abishag smiled at her maid's boldness.

The water did revive her, and as she rested, her breathing grew normal. She allowed her mind to listen to the sounds going on around her. Somewhere in the distance a harpist tuned his instrument, and an ensemble of musicians played a few notes, waiting to announce her presence.

She closed her eyes, taking it all in. *Thank You, Adonai.* She could not imagine beginning her marriage without gratitude for all God had allowed in her life. She may not have chosen the path, but surely the Lord had directed her steps.

Trumpets blared moments later, announcing the king's arrival into the audience hall. Rani jumped up and down at her side like a giddy child, and she chuckled at the girl's obvious delight. "Calm down, Rani, or you will have me dancing before it is time."

"But you are about to marry the king!" Rani seemed completely taken with Solomon, and Abishag couldn't help but smile. He *was* the most handsome of men in all Israel, and she sensed that every woman who saw him loved him on sight.

"You forget that I already married one king," she said, steering the conversation away from Rani's obvious obsession with Solomon.

She sobered. "Yes, of course. But not like this." She brightened again and laughed.

"Hush now. They will hear you." Abishag did not mean to sound so stern, but she knew her tone was aimed more at her own racing heart than Rani's exuberance.

They waited an eternity for Solomon to make his way to his dais, and even longer for the singers to proclaim her beauty to the king in song. Female singers sang as she at last followed Rani to the entrance of the audience chamber and began the long descent toward the king's dais.

"Where has your beloved gone, most beautiful of women?" The singers' words carried the song, high-pitched and melodic, to her ears. "Which way did your beloved turn, that we may look for him with you?"

Abishag lifted her chin, her gaze first on the women, then on Solomon, who held her look so securely she lost all sense of fear. "My beloved has gone down to his garden, to the beds of spices, to browse in the gardens and to gather lilies," she said. "I am my beloved's and my beloved is mine. He browses among the lilies."

The words had been crafted between them during the week preceding this joyous day. She had feared that she would not remember her part, but Solomon's smile brought the words back with a rush of intense feeling. Her cheeks fairly burned as she spoke, knowing their hidden meaning, intimated between them as they had penned the words. But her emotions heightened even further as he uttered his lines while her feet drew her ever closer to him.

"You are beautiful, my darling, as lovely as Jerusalem, as majestic as troops with banners."

She looked at him through the hooded veil, holding that intense gaze of his.

"Turn your eyes from me—they overwhelm me," he said, his voice like that of an earnest lover. "Your hair is like a flock of goats descending from Gilead. Your teeth are like a flock of sheep coming up from the washing. Each has its twin—not one of them is missing. Your temples behind your veil are like the halves of a pomegranate. Sixty queens there may be, and eighty concubines, and virgins beyond number, but my dove, my perfect one, is unique, the only daughter of her mother, the favorite of the one who bore her. The young women saw her and called her blessed. The queens and concubines praised her."

He paused as her feet came to rest at the steps to his throne. Their gazes held, and for a heady moment she put aside the references to the queens and concubines he had mentioned, thankful that at least for now they were not true of him. One day they would be, she told herself in some rational corner of her mind. But not today. She would not allow the fear of the future to mar the beauty of this moment.

"Who is this that appears like the dawn?" the women continued as she gazed on her beloved, loving him despite every flaw others might have seen in him, even those she saw in him. "Fair as the moon, bright as the sun, majestic as the stars in procession."

"You who dwell in the gardens with friends in attendance," Solomon concluded, "let me hear your voice!"

The crowd looked to Abishag, the silence broken only by the music of a lone harp. She longed to glimpse the musician but instead closed her eyes to catch the timing of her final words. She opened her mouth to sing.

"Come away, my beloved." She extended a hand toward Solomon, and he met her on the steps. "And be like a gazelle or like a young stag on the spice-laden mountains."

The harp ceased, and Solomon pulled her to the top step to stand beneath a golden-edged canopy, where Zadok the priest stood in all his priestly finery to bless their union. She felt the pressure of Solomon's gentle touch on her elbow and blushed when he lifted the corner of his garment to rest it upon her shoulder.

"I am my beloved's," Solomon said after the last words of blessing were spoken.

"And he is mine," she said.

Solomon had chosen a different course to end their wedding festivities. Rather than taking her to the normal wedding tent in the palace courtyard, Solomon excused them both from the feast, which would last seven days, and guided her to his personal chambers. She did not realize then what a privilege he had bestowed on her. She did not think Naamah appreciated the treatment she received, but to her credit she appeared to do her best to put it behind them. They remained at a truce of distant friendship, one that Abishag suspected could grow closer once Solomon sought more wives.

But for now, she looked about his spacious and opulent chambers, stunned by the beauty and yet simplicity of the furnishings. Where gold and tapestries had adorned the audience hall, very little lined the walls in his chambers. Piles of plush cushions created a comfortable seating area, and a raised bed with heavy curtains took up the sleeping room.

He guided her there without pausing, and she noticed that servants had lit golden lamps set in niches in the walls. A single table sat to the side, where a small, carved cedar chest rested. She glanced at it with a curious look, but he simply tipped her chin to gaze into her eyes, turning her away from the trappings of his room.

"How beautiful you are, my dove," he whispered, his voice more earnest than it had been during the public ceremony. He lifted the clasp that held her veil in place and carefully laid it aside. One by one the combs Rani had wound through her hair came undone until her waist-length tresses fell like a covering around her. The unbinding of hair was a sacred symbol to her people, one that bound her to him in a way nothing else quite could.

He touched the strands as though they were silken gold, then slowly tucked a few behind one ear. His lips sought the place at her ear that he had exposed, then trailed along her chin, stopping at her lips. Her breath came faster with each touch of his lips against her skin.

"I belong to my beloved and his desire is for me," she said, boldly returning his kiss.

He laughed, a delightful sound, and she discovered how quickly all the finery of preparation could be undone in one passionate moment. Solomon wasted no time drawing her into his arms and leading her to the place where they could complete their love.

She did not hear the song of her youth or the desire of her past in his kiss, for a new song now filled her. A song of completeness and belonging, of knowing she was loved.

A song she would long remember.

Interlude

The Teacher looked through the window facing Mount Moriah, where the temple he had built to Adonai gleamed in the sunlight. His heart beat with a strange rhythm. So much had been given to him. A kingdom that extended to every place God had promised Israel. A throne firmly established and wisdom that had grown with each passing day.

He had not expected wisdom to need growth or testing for it to flourish. Surprises had come to him as he studied the creatures that crawled along the path and watched the great variety of birds nestled in the trees. He understood them—their structure, the way they were able to take flight, how they breathed whether in water or on land. Every day seemed to provide a new adventure in understanding.

He had not realized the weight of wisdom, nor the responsibility that came with such a gift. He had not seen that the pleasure of God rested heavily upon mere men. Had he known then . . . He shook the thought away. Despite the consequences, he knew his response to God's question would not have changed. For love sought understanding. He just did not reason through the cost of both.

TWENTY-THREE

Solomon walked beside his officer Adoniram, who was in charge of forced labor, as they inspected the area where cut and dressed stones prepared at the quarry were already being set in place to lay the foundation for the temple to Adonai. Thousands of men moved about the top of Mount Moriah, working in unison under 3,300 chief officers who made sure the men carried out the work.

"As you can see, my lord, the stones are nearly all in place where the inner sanctuary will be, and the men will work out from there as you requested."

"Good. Our God must be first, at the center of the temple and in the way we build it." Solomon looked over the area, his mind churning with possibilities. The stone would secure the foundation, but he would overlay it with cedar and overlay the cedar with gold. No expense was too costly. The work must be worthy of so great a King as Israel's God.

"Yes, my lord." Adoniram nodded and pointed to the next

phase of the foundation, but Solomon's mind had already wandered to the enormity of the structure, picturing what it would finally be like. As he had done when he helped his father build the model. To stand before such a grand temple would cause men and women of all nations to bow before the Creator. His heart lifted at the thought.

He turned as Adoniram faced west and caught sight of Ahishar, his palace official, hurrying toward him. The man bowed low, but Solomon bid him quickly rise.

"My lord, there is an incident in the audience hall. I told them it could wait, but I'm afraid the people are growing restless, as the two women will not stop shouting at one another." Ahishar wiped his brow and drew a breath as though he had run the entire distance.

"Two women, you say." Solomon stroked his beard, fighting an amused smile. "They aren't threatening to kill each other, are they?" What on earth could they possibly have done that needed their king's attention?

"They are prostitutes, my lord, and I fear it involves a child." Ahishar gave him a pleading look. "The officials are unable to answer their dilemma, and I fear you are the only one who can solve the issue."

Solomon straightened, fully intrigued now. "Take me to them then." He gave Adoniram a parting glance, followed Ahishar to his waiting mule, and rode to his father's palace with his fifty guards before and behind.

A crowd had gathered in front of the audience hall, so Solomon's guards led him to a back entrance. He dismounted and entered the cool halls, stopping only long enough to check his reflection in the gold etchings beside the door, then climbed the steps to his throne.

The crowd grew quiet at the trumpet blast and awaited his nod to bring the women before him.

"What is it you seek?" He spoke to the woman holding a newborn child.

"Oh, my lord," the woman said, slipping to her knees, "this woman and I live in the same house, and I gave birth to a child while she was in the house. Then on the third day after I gave birth, this woman also gave birth. There was no one else with us in the house. This woman's son died in the night, because she lay on him. And she arose at midnight and took my son from beside me while your servant slept, and laid him at her breast, and laid her dead son at my breast. When I rose in the morning to nurse my child, he was dead. But when I looked at him closely in the morning, he was not the child that I had borne."

"No!" The other woman's voice held a shrill tone, and Solomon noted that she did not bow. "The living child is mine, and the dead child is yours."

"No, the dead child is yours, and the living child is mine."

Solomon looked from one woman to the other, his gaze resting on the child. At last he spoke. "The one says, 'This is my son that is alive, and your son is dead,' and the other says, 'No, your son is dead, and my son is the living one.'"

Silence followed his remark as he continued to study both women. "Bring me a sword," he said at last.

Benaiah, the captain of his guard, stepped forward and unsheathed his sword, holding it out before him.

"Divide the living child in two, and give half to the one and half to the other."

A pall fell over the stunned crowd. Benaiah stepped closer to take the child from the kneeling woman.

"Oh, my lord," she said, tears streaming down her face, "give her the living child, and by no means put him to death."

But the other prostitute quickly responded, "He shall be neither mine nor yours. Divide him."

"Give the living child to the first woman. Don't kill him," Solomon said. "She is his mother." He stood then and descended the steps, leaving the hall without a backward glance.

Solomon spent the night alone in his chambers, pondering the strange visit of the prostitutes. Would he have known how to judge such a situation before Adonai promised to grant him wisdom? The thought to cut the child in half had come to him in an instant, and yet in that same instant he knew he would never be forced to hurt the child.

He walked to the window and opened it wide, allowing the night breeze to fill the room. Moonlight bathed the courtyard below, though few but his guards moved about at this hour. He should sleep or call one of his wives, but neither seemed appealing.

He moved away from the window to a small chest where he kept his writings. Perhaps if he crafted a new song or proverb, he could release this restless energy. His ringed fingers smoothed the richly carved cedar. Hiram, king of Tyre, had sent the chest to him after his father's death, as part of a bevy of gifts to recognize his place as king. Solomon lifted the lid, peering into the dark interior. He felt about for the blank scroll, but his hand rested instead on a folded piece of parchment.

His mother's gift to him when he first wore his father's crown.

He lifted it from the stack, forgoing the empty scrolls, and carried it to his couch where a lamp sat on a low table. How long it had been since he had read the words, though he had fairly memorized them back then. Still, something drew him back, and he carefully unfolded the parchment to read.

Listen, my son! Listen, son of my womb! Listen, my son, the answer to my prayers! Do not spend your strength on women, your vigor on those who ruin kings.

He paused in scanning the remaining words, returning again to these few. She was right, of course. The wrong woman could ruin a king. His thoughts traveled backward. His father had married eight wives and taken many more concubines, and the only one who may have ruined his reign was Solomon's own mother.

Guilt filled him with that thought. True or not, he did not fault her. His father alone was to blame in what happened. Though God had forgiven him, trouble had followed him the rest of his days, causing Solomon to promise himself that he would never take a woman who could not belong to him. He would not take another man's wife. And he would never awaken love before its time.

So why would his mother write such words to him? She knew his promise to marry rather than commit adultery. Did she fear he would commit adultery? A king's power rested in the size and strength of his harem, according to the kings of the east, so how could he not marry many women?

He folded the letter without reading the rest and set it on the cushion beside him. *He must not take many wives, or his heart will be led astray.* How many times had the priests or scribes read those words in his hearing? Words of the law directed to kings. And yet his father had assured the priests that his wives would never lead his heart astray. Though he sinned, his father had stayed true to Adonai all the days of his life.

Why should Ima think I would be any different?

He stood, knocking the letter to the rug, and walked the length of his room. Guards stood at attention as he opened the door and passed into the halls, one following discreetly behind him. He strode to the stairs that led to the roof of the palace and paced. The breeze wafted his night tunic away from his body. He should have robed himself. But his mind whirled with frustration and urgency and a sense of something missing.

The truth was, he liked women. God help him, he would rather marry to form an alliance with foreign nations than go to battle against them. And wasn't his kingdom supposed to be one of peace? Wasn't this precisely why Adonai had not allowed his father to build the temple—because he had been a man of war?

He ran both hands through his hair and gazed heavenward. *I would keep Your law, O God of my fathers, but how then am I to secure peace without war? And how do I stop this constant desire to build my kingdom, my harem, and Israel's dwellings, palaces, cities, defenses?*

Stars gazed down on him, but he heard no voice from heaven as he had that day at Gibeon. Did God's silence mean that Solomon had His approval? And yet . . . he sensed neither approval nor disapproval. Perhaps because he already had the words written and given to kings. Was he to act only on what had been written, nothing more?

He walked to the parapet and looked out at the dark and silent Mount Moriah where work on the temple had already begun. But years of work still awaited, and there were so many projects he longed to complete. So many places he wanted to see. So many things he needed to understand, to study.

"There is not enough time in a life," he said softly, though no one could hear. But there was time enough to pursue some of his dreams. And despite what his mother thought, no wife of his would be his downfall or his ruin. He would simply use the wisdom God had given and choose wisely.

CHAPTER
TWENTY-FOUR

Months passed, with no more serious talk of King Solomon or any possible visit of his to Thebes. Siti should have known such a thing would not happen. Men had the habit of speculating what they hoped would occur, while women simply worked to make it so. But there was nothing they could do to make a foreign king come to visit her father. King Solomon would have needed a very good reason to do so.

"What tunic should I wear to the banquet tonight?" She stood before a large array of white bejeweled gowns and different matching feathered headdresses and tapped her chin. Akila lifted one after another, but nothing seemed right. "I don't want to outshine Salama. This is her day."

Her mother had finally arranged for the ceremony that would link her sister to Hamadi from this day forward. The wedding would be a much grander affair, one for which new gowns would be made. But tonight she had insisted she needed nothing new, and her mother had for once not argued.

"You always look nice in this one," Akila said, picking her favorite pleated white tunic held up by one strap just above the breast, over which she would wear a sheer white robe. "If we dressed it with this wig, it will not look at all like you normally wear it."

A small golden goblet sat atop the chin-length curled black wig, which would hold the pleasing ox tallow and myrrh, a combination used by every woman in high society. The perfume masked the odor of too many people dancing and sweating in the crowded room.

She nodded at Akila, accepting her choices, and moved to the dressing table. She would arrange her hair to accept the wig and feathered headdress, draw deep lines of kohl above and beneath her eyes, ochre her cheeks and lips, and paint henna patterns on her hands. Soon she would be transformed into the princess she was but did not always care to be.

Akila's work took several hours, but too soon they were ushered into the long banquet hall, which shone like glittering stars in the night sky, making the room nearly as bright as day. Her mother had not had time to convince her father to build a new place to house this festivity or even the coming nuptials. But she had been allowed to spare no expense on everything else, and it showed.

Siti drew in a breath of the sweetened air and walked toward the place where her sister would soon sit. Servants lifted heavy palm fronds to move the heated air, which drew in the breeze coming off the Nile. Palace guards stood as a formidable wall about the open room, ever vigilant to protect the royal family. She took her seat near her sister's dais with Akila standing behind her, but they did not speak once the trumpets sounded and Hamadi's entrance was announced. Her sister followed, then her mother, and at last the Great Pharaoh.

Salama took her seat beneath a thick curtain, Hamadi at her side. Siti watched the quiet looks that passed between them. Sometimes her sister spoke frustrated words against this half brother/husband, but Siti could tell by her sister's smile that she cared for him. It was a necessary union, but at least one where they could live the lives they chose separately and sometimes together. Her sister would likely see little of him once they were finally wed.

She pondered that thought as the ceremony ended and the banquet ensued. Perhaps she held thoughts that were too fanciful, but she had always imagined a marriage of love over political convenience. She did not wish to be any man's bride to secure some alliance that money could purchase. She wanted what the exotic poems spoke of when the poets stood in the streets and sang or performed their art for the upper classes at banquets such as this.

"How beautiful you are, my sister, my bride." Hamadi quoted the famous poem to Salama more than once while he sat near her.

Did he mean what he said? The words were expected. Siti doubted his sincerity. She sipped from the cup of wine and took a honeyed fig from the silver tray as it passed.

Her mother sidled over and sat on the bench beside her. "You will be next, Siti," she said, smiling, her voice light with too much wine. The softest scent of the sweet myrrh wafted from her mother's wig, mingling with Siti's own.

"There is no rush, Mother," she said, tasting the fig with her tongue. "Let Salama have her year. I have plenty of time."

"Nakhti has asked after you again."

Her words caused Siti's stomach to recoil. She placed the treat on the table at her side.

"He is most insistent." Her mother faced her, turning Siti's chin in her manicured hand. "Tell me your thoughts on this, my daughter, for I must give him an answer or take his request to your father."

Siti gently pulled her chin out of her mother's grasp and lifted the silver goblet to her lips, moving slightly away from her as she did so. "I do not wish to marry Nakhti. He is arrogant and spoiled. His temper flares at every whim."

Her mother shrugged one sleeveless shoulder. "All men are arrogant and spoiled, my child. His temper will cool once he is wed."

She raised a brow and curled her lip, disbelieving. "Marriage does not cool the temper of any man I have seen. Either a man is good and kind or he is not. Nakhti is not, and I do not wish to be the one to teach him what he should have learned at his mother's knee."

Her mother stared at her for the longest moment, and Siti was certain she would give a blistering retort defending her father or brothers or men in general, but she said nothing. She looked toward the center of the room where the dancers were showing off their latest moves, swaying around a fancy juggler.

"Do you have another man in mind that you wish to marry? I have seen none other come to seek you out. Or is there some secret lover of which I am not aware? I cannot put off Nakhti if I do not have another one who wishes to wed you." She paused, and Siti sensed she was working her way into a long-winded speech. "If you are hoping to find a man who resembles all of those poems you hear, you will wait until Osiris calls you to the underworld. Those men do not exist."

Siti stared at her sister and Hamadi, catching a glimpse of the joy in their eyes, and she watched the dancers pose in erotic ways to entice the audience to think thoughts of love. In the background the singers expressed words of such beauty that her heart stirred with a longing she could not define.

If those kinds of men did not exist, then did love exist at all? And if not for love, then marriage truly was simply an aligning of two people with similar goals, to secure the future for the next generation.

The thought troubled her, and she had the sudden desire to leave the room and her mother and her future in this place. If marriage meant living in this harem or any harem with the boredom of sameness—no adventure, no bliss as the poets imagined—then she would never marry.

"I have no one in mind," she said dully, wishing her mother would leave her to her silent misery. "But I do not want to marry one of my cousins, nor my half brothers." She stared at the smoky, perfumed room. Black soot clung to white-washed walls from tall sconces set in niches, and suddenly the scents of smoke and sweat and myrrh were not pleasing to her senses. She stood. "Give me time, Mother. There is no need to decide tonight."

Her mother did not move as she stepped past her, but Siti did not miss her parting words. "If that is the case, you would be better off to marry a foreigner than a commoner, for there is no one else who matches you in rank."

She tossed a look over her shoulder. "Bring me King Solomon," she said flippantly, not meaning a word of it. "Make an alliance with him, and I will marry your foreigner."

She walked away, blushing at her own brashness, especially after she had just concluded that she wanted to marry for love, not political gain. And how foolish of her to make such a declaration at a banquet for her sister, where any of the wives of Pharaoh could hear.

Akila took her arm once they cleared the room and walked her back to her chambers.

"My tongue is going to get me into serious trouble someday," Siti said.

Akila did not disagree.

TWENTY-FIVE

TWO YEARS LATER

"My lord king," Ahijah said one afternoon, "as you requested, the reports have come in of Egypt's use of Gezer since its capture."

Solomon faced his secretary and nodded. "And?"

"And they have done little with the city, my lord. The place lies in ruins, though Egyptian guards protect it. There is some evidence that they are rebuilding the wall, but charred remains can still be seen within the city."

Solomon glanced at his courtiers, who lined his audience hall, then faced Ahijah once more. "Curious." He stroked his beard even as his mind whirled with a thousand thoughts. Why would this pharaoh capture a city and let it lie dormant for two years?

"One would think, my lord, that the Egyptians would want to make a stronger presence known among us, if they were truly interested in showing their might." Zabud, his priest, had stepped beside Ahijah, joining the conversation.

Several more advisors circled the area near his throne, as often happened when such news arrived.

"Perhaps they did not capture Gezer to show their might," Solomon said, moving his gaze from one advisor to the next. "Perhaps they had a different reason to make their victory known to me."

Ahijah twisted the stylus he carried with him, his expression confused. "What else could they possibly want?"

"My attention." Solomon knew he spoke truth, for there could be no other explanation that made sense. "I think," he said, again looking at each man, "that it is time I paid the pharaoh a visit."

"You're going to Egypt?" Zabud's tone carried disapproval. "Kings are warned not to return to Egypt. The law forbids it, my lord."

"The law states that the king must not cause the people to return to Egypt in order to acquire many horses," Solomon said. "I have no intention of causing the people to return that way again. My retinue will accompany me, and I do not plan to stay. Only to find out why Pharaoh Siamun has captured Gezer and done nothing with it."

Zabud's frown did not leave. "While your thoughts may seem wise, you put yourself at risk, my lord. The law seems quite clear."

Solomon smiled. Zabud read the law to him every month and the two had become friends, but sometimes even confidants could grow annoying. "My friend," he said, his tone conciliatory, "I do believe you have a point, but I also believe the spirit of the law is what matters here. I have no intention of breaking it. This is simply a diplomatic visit."

He looked at his advisors once more and saw no other

looks of disapproval. Good. Because no matter what Zabud suggested, he *was* going to Egypt. Gezer should belong to Israel, and Solomon had every intention of finding a way to get it under his control.

—⁓—

Solomon met his mother in the garden that separated their rooms the day before his trip to Egypt. She sat among the almond trees on the bench where he had found Abishag years ago. She smiled at his approach.

"Ima," he said, bowing to her. He took her hand and kissed it.

"My son." She stood and pulled him to her, her embrace warm, calming. "How good of you to come."

"I could not refuse you," he said, taking the seat beside her on the bench. "I would not leave for such a lengthy time without saying goodbye."

"So you are truly going to Egypt." She said it matter-of-factly, but her expression told him she was troubled.

He slowly nodded. "Pharaoh Siamun has captured Gezer, which by God's decree belongs to Israel, Ima. I must go to find a way to secure it back into our borders." She knew this. They had discussed it more than once, but he sensed there was more on her mind than acquiring one lone city. "Why does this really trouble you, Ima?" He took her hand and held it between both of his.

She looked into his eyes, silent, searching. At last she spoke. "You are not going there for the purpose of gaining horses or wives?"

Only he must not acquire many horses for himself . . .

"I know the law, Ima. It does not forbid accepting *some*

197

horses from Egypt or marrying one of their princesses, should the need arise. For peace."

"Peace. Yes." She held his gaze until he grew uncomfortable under her scrutiny.

"I am doing nothing wrong, Ima." Why did he feel as though he must defend himself? Going to Egypt to secure Gezer was a worthy goal. The Almighty had not forbidden such a thing.

"I understand, my son. I only want to see you walk in the path of truth, to obey our God as your father did. And be careful not to let beautiful women entice you." She cupped his face.

He squeezed her hand. "You do not need to worry about me, Ima. I love Adonai, my father's God, and I am not going to let horses or wealth or women cause my heart to turn away from Him. You can be sure of that."

She smiled then and leaned closer to kiss his cheek. "Nevertheless, I will never stop praying for you, my son."

She rose and left him. He watched her return to her rooms, wondering if she knew something about him that even he could not see.

TWENTY-SIX

Though Siti's father's men had captured the stalwart city of Gezer two years earlier and made the news known far and wide, the desired effect—to entice a visit from the king of Israel—had taken far longer than the Great Pharaoh expected. But at last the day came when King Solomon, in full regal splendor, graced their fair city with his presence.

"How long do you think he will stay?" Siti stood on the roof beneath a great wide awning of her father's palace, gazing toward the gleaming tents of Solomon shining like jewels against Ra's disappearing glow. "His entourage fills the entire plain along the Nile's banks."

"I suspect he will stay until he acquires what he came for," Akila answered at her side. She leaned against the parapet, her face upturned to catch the last rays of the sun.

"And what is that, exactly?" Rumors had abounded, but unless Solomon hoped to gain Gezer from her father without some type of trade, she saw no reason for his visit.

"I don't know, my lady." Akila faced her, her smile too

knowing. "Do you not find him fascinating though? It is as if he understands every creature on earth."

Solomon had spoken of many beasts and birds and reptiles during open discussions at court. Siti and her mother and sister had not missed a single moment of those meetings, and not a courtier or scribe in the audience chamber spoke, nor barely breathed, so rapt was the attention Solomon commanded. Her heart fluttered as it had done too often at the mere thought of the man.

"He is very wise," she said absently, wishing at that moment for an audience with him all to herself. "Do you think he brought any of his wives with him?" The tents were large, his retinue like the deluge of the Nile, but she had not seen any women of royal Hebrew heritage in conference with her mother.

"I would not know, my lady." Akila looked out toward the plains where the sun now sank beyond the horizon to die its death until it was reborn at another dawn.

"What help are you to me then?" she said, knowing how cross she sounded. "What good is it if you do not pay attention to the gossips?" She had gotten no closer to King Solomon than the balcony in the audience chamber. Perhaps at the banquet her father intended to host in a few weeks she could find a way to get a closer glimpse of him.

"I pay attention, my lady, but there is little to tell. King Solomon keeps to himself. They say he is cautious, and I daresay that his wisdom makes him careful, would you not agree? Even a servant who is wise can understand the need for caution. Kings have many enemies, even among those who are close to them."

"They say he made sure those enemies were removed from

existence when he first came to power. Even his own brother was not spared." She shuddered to think it, though the practice was not an uncommon one.

"Even so, no king is ever truly free of enemies, my lady." Akila faced her again.

She nodded, saying nothing. Her father had food tasters and wine tasters and tasters for the tasters before he would allow a single piece of food to pass his lips. Though everyone said he was a god, the very son of Ra, she knew her father was mortal and Osiris could snatch his soul from him, as he could from any of them at any given moment. The devourer was not to be trusted, nor men when they did his bidding.

"Well, I do wish my father would get to the point of why he wanted this visit." She moved toward the stairs to return to her rooms. "If a foreign king comes so far, even at my father's invitation, surely there is no need to drag out the purpose."

They passed guards who met them at the base of the stairs, but none followed them down the short hallway to her chambers. She entered and sank onto a cushioned couch, weary with wondering. "I want to meet him, Akila. Truly meet him." She lifted one foot to allow Akila to remove her sandals. "Do you think we can devise a way?"

Her maid worked in silence for several moments, her jaw moving as though she were testing and discarding words. "Would it be seemly for a princess to seek out a king, my lady? Would it not put the relations between your father and this king in jeopardy?"

She studied her hennaed foot a moment and wiggled her toes, now happily freed from the constraints of sandals. She stood abruptly and walked the length of the room, enjoying the cool feel of the painted floor. But after pacing the room several times, she sank back onto the cushions, defeated. "You are right, of course. I cannot just walk across the palace compound, cross the plains, and enter his tents uninvited. Not even a servant would be so bold without a cause."

Akila brought her a goblet of wine to ease her pouting, and she drank gladly. There must be a way to at least speak with this foreign king, who seemed to understand their language without a single hint of stumbling. But as she stared through her window into the moonlit night, she could think of nothing, no way to breach court etiquette or even sneak away as a commoner to glimpse what her heart desired. And in truth, she was not even sure her heart wanted such a thing. She wasn't sure whether she wanted to actually meet him or to know whether her flippant words about marrying him had been worth speaking.

Two days later, after deciding that her desire to meet King Solomon was not worth troubling herself over, Siti took a walk with Akila in the central garden encased inside Pharaoh's grand courtyard. The day was pleasant enough, though with summer upon them, she wished the wig she was forced to wear was at the bottom of the Nile. For all the sheer linen of their clothing to keep them cool, Egyptians did not seem to realize that the wigs they fashioned canceled out their efforts. But beauty mattered more than comfort, and she resigned herself to do her part.

The breeze lifted her spirits, bringing with it the scent of lotus blossoms floating on the wide pool that took up the center of the garden. Bastet's shrine stood tall at the end of the walkway, just past the pool. She had not been to her shrine in far too long. Abdukar had replaced her need of the goddess, she told herself, trying to allay her guilt. She praised the cat often enough and thanked Bastet for Abdukar's protection over her. But she should have paid her priests to place an offering before the goddess's statue on her behalf, to show her faithfulness.

They rounded the curve in the path at the end of the pool, whose blue tiles sparkled like lapis lazuli, and when she looked up, her heart nearly stopped beating. There, not far from Bastet's shrine, in all his royal splendor, sat King Solomon. He was not alone, of course, but spoke to her father's vizier, which she found curious. Would not a king speak only to another king? But her father would not arrange such a meeting in the gardens. He would hold them in his royal chambers.

She drew in a breath and glanced quickly at Akila, whose wide eyes told her she had noticed the king as well. She should move closer, let him catch a glimpse of her. But no. She dare not interrupt such a meeting. Better to honor Bastet with a prayer and move on.

She walked toward the base of the tall cat statue and slowly knelt before her image. She would have stayed longer, fully intending to pray to her, but she found that the words would not form in her thoughts. All she could think of in that moment was King Solomon. She stood, frustrated with herself, and stepped closer to Akila.

"It is no use," she said. "I cannot think as I should." Was there not some way to gain King Solomon's attention? Her back was to him and her father's vizier, but at Akila's wide-eyed look, she slowly turned.

"You are Pharaoh's daughter, are you not?" His accent was distinctly Hebrew, though the words were perfect Egyptian.

She stared, her heart pounding. Had her longing to speak to him spread to his ears? She had not spoken the request, nor even prayed it. And yet there he stood.

She bowed, willing her anxiety to ease. "And you are King Solomon," she said, surprised that her voice did not quake as her insides did.

"It appears we are both rather observant." His smile, lazy and yet holding that hint of power that kings carried no matter where they seemed to be, nearly stole her breath. "But I fear I am at a disadvantage, as I do not know your name."

"Siti," she said too quickly. "Younger daughter of Siamun, the Great Pharaoh, and the Great Royal Wife. You would have met my sister's husband, Hamadi, crown prince of Egypt."

Solomon tilted his head in such a way that his gaze fully captured hers. "You are the unmarried daughter of Pharaoh?"

She nodded, unable to speak at the sudden spark of interest in his gaze.

"It is my pleasure to meet you, Siti." He bowed slightly, and she did the same. He stood close enough for her to smell the heady scent of his spikenard.

"And mine as well," she said past a dry throat. She discreetly cleared it and offered him a slight smile. "I have listened to you speak in my father's chambers. Your depth of knowledge is impressive."

He seemed almost embarrassed at the praise but recovered quickly and lifted his head. "Any wisdom I have comes from our great God, the Creator of all things. I take no credit for it myself." He glanced beyond her at the statue of Bastet. "Is this the god you worship?"

She nodded and swallowed, trying to form some suitable reply. "Yes. Bastet is a great protector of women and children. She is the god I chose when I was but a small child."

"And why did you choose her?" He seemed genuinely interested in her answer, and his smile put her at ease.

She shrugged. "Perhaps because I love cats. Lapis, my favorite, kept me company in my crib and chased away the devourer, who surely wanted to snatch my soul at times when I grew ill. Bastet restored me to health, and I have worshiped her ever since." She almost winced at the slight lie and silently begged Bastet's forgiveness, for she had not worshiped her as a faithful follower should.

"And how do you know Bastet was the one who saved you? Perhaps the Creator spared your soul." His question was not spoken in the typical mocking tone that she heard so often from her brothers, who preferred other gods.

She looked at him, daring to meet his interested gaze. "You truly want to know?"

"Of course. Why ask a question if you do not wish to know the answer?"

"Some questions are spoken rhetorically, with no response needed. And some statements are meant to be questions, as my father is so fond of using them—requiring an answer though they seem not to need one." She released a long-held breath, relieved that her heart had managed to slow to a semi-normal rhythm.

"Your answer shows great wisdom, Daughter of Pharaoh," he said, bowing toward her again. "But to answer your question, yes, I truly want to know why you worship a stone image of an animal. Is not the enjoyment of the animal that walks the earth enough? Why not worship the one who created the beast in the first place?"

His question made her pause. How to answer without offending Bastet? "You pose a dilemma for me, oh king. Which god do you wish me to offend? My patron goddess or your creator?"

He studied her, and she found her heart beating faster again. Never in her life had she enjoyed such stimulating conversation with a man. Oh Amun, may it last forever!

"I think my question is one you must ponder and decide for yourself, Princess. But as you think on the wisdom of your answer, ask yourself which god holds the greater power. The one made or the one who makes things? I think you will find your answer there." He took a step back from her then, and she knew their conversation was at an end.

"I will think on it," she said quickly, already feeling the loss of his presence.

"I would like to see you again, Siti," he said softly. Her given name on his tongue set her heart aflame. "Would another meeting please you?"

She nodded, too dumbstruck to speak.

"Good. Expect it then." He turned and strode away with his guards, who only now seemed to materialize from the hedges that surrounded them. They had been watching him, watching them, the entire time.

She took Akila's arm, gripping it for strength as she was not sure her own legs would carry her, and went back in the direction from which they had come.

TWENTY-SEVEN

Weeks passed with a flurry of activity surrounding King Solomon's visit. Most of the time the near chaos was simply anxious servants fluttering about like overactive bees, flighty, darting here and there, all hurriedly planning a grand celebration Siti's father intended for King Solomon's final week in Egypt.

Siti had tried not to pout overmuch during the time just past, when her father took King Solomon for a grand tour of his stables, giving the Hebrew king horses and chariots as gifts, then surprising them all when he declared they would make a visit to the Valley of Kings. The Great Pharaoh had decided to show King Solomon the work slaves had done and continued to do on his tomb. She shivered at the very thought. She did not like the Valley of Kings, though she knew as royalty, she would someday have a small burial spot near her father.

She did not like to think about such things, despite her people's concerns with the afterlife and the planning of their final destination through the underworld. The devourer would surely destroy her at the scales where hearts are weighed in the balance, for she knew her heart was far from pure and truthful. Bastet forgive her, but she feared she would fail utterly against the Feather of Truth when that day approached.

She shuddered, pushing the thoughts aside as she strode with Akila through the palace halls, hoping for a glimpse of the banquet's grandeur, though she would see it in all its splendor this evening.

"Shouldn't we be heading to the heated baths, my lady?" Akila asked, her brows tucked in a most thorough frown. "There is barely time to complete all the beauty treatments before the banquet begins."

She was hinting at the late start they had gotten due to Siti's oversleeping. But she had lain awake many nights pondering Solomon's unnerving question about his creator and her Bastet. Their differences of faith would surely stop her father from ever considering an alliance, though rumors still set her heart astir.

She leaned close to Akila's ear. "Has there been any news?"

Akila shook her head. She knew her meaning, as they had discussed the possibility since the moment Siti's mother came striding into her rooms the week before.

"Have you bewitched your father with some strange magic?" Her mother sank onto her cushions, her expression clearly troubled. "He is talking nonsense, and just tonight he suggested we make a marriage alliance with this foreign king!" She skewered Siti with her pointed look. "Of course, the moment he said so, I had to discover what he meant. He thought to give the daughter of a lesser wife to King Solomon as a gesture of goodwill. But how could I allow such a thing after you practically prophesied to me that you would marry the man?"

Siti stared at her, bewildered. Prophesied? She had merely tossed a barb to get her mother to stop trying to wed her to Nakhti. "I did no such thing, Mother. I never planned to marry out of Egypt."

Her mother's look said her future had already been sealed. "You know very well that you have no desire whatsoever to marry a cousin or brother, a man of right standing in this land. You have given me no choice, Siti. I cannot allow the daughter of a lesser wife to wed such a king . . ." Her voice trailed off, and Siti realized that even her mother had been captivated by Solomon's wisdom, his allure.

"What are you saying?" Siti's voice trembled, and she could not stop her hands from shaking.

Her mother stood slowly, queenly, and crossed her arms like one passing judgment. "If I have my way, you will marry King Solomon. Your father will offer you to him as part of their agreement. Do not disappoint me." She whirled about and slipped out of her rooms as gracefully as she had appeared, leaving Siti stunned.

Even now, as she and Akila peered into the banquet hall that could soon become the place where Solomon accepted her hand in marriage, she could not quite wrap her mind around her mother's words. Things had moved so quickly. Despite Solomon's lengthy visit, he had spent so much time with her father that even his desire that they meet again had not yet come to pass. And soon he would leave them.

Would she be going with him? She could not possibly be ready in a week's time!

"Come, my lady," Akila said. "We must get you ready. In case."

Yes. In case. She followed like an obedient slave, wondering just what awaited her at day's end.

The afternoon waned, but the feverish activities of the servants did not. Akila had barely finished tracing elongated lines of kohl along her eyes when one of her father's servants knocked on her door. Akila dropped her tools and hurried to answer. Siti walked into the sitting area and allowed the woman to bow at her feet.

"The king instructs you to come," the servant said. "At once." She cast her an apologetic look. "I am sorry, mistress, that you did not have more notice."

Siti's heart quickened at the reasoning behind this summons. Her father never sought an audience with her alone. Always her mother accompanied her. "Akila," she commanded with greater fierceness than usual, "bring my best gown at once."

She dismissed the servant to wait in the hall while she followed Akila into her dressing chamber. "Whatever could he want of me?" Her palms grew sweaty with the sudden, fearful thought. "What if my mother's prediction is true?" She grabbed Akila's shoulders, forcing the girl to look her way.

"Perhaps your father wishes to hear your feelings on the matter, my lady." Akila touched Siti's hand. "Your father may not wish to give you to a foreign king without your consent."

She released her hold and accepted her maid's ministrations as she fitted the white garment over her shoulders and placed a golden collar about her neck. Fine jeweled bracelets were snapped into place along both arms, and the final piece, her best blue-black wig pleated with jewels, was placed over her bound hair. It had been nearly a year since she had allowed the shearers to shave her head to make a better fit for the wigs. She loathed the wigs, and in the quiet of her apartments she gave herself the luxury of letting down her hair, which had already reached her shoulders. Done well, her own hair was beautiful, but palace tradition—nay, Egyptian tradition—would not allow her to go against protocol. So she hid her guilty pleasure.

"You look like a goddess, my lady," Akila said when at last her handiwork was completed. She held up a bronze mirror to show what she could see far better than Siti could in the dim reflection.

She turned this way and that, barely recognizing herself. "Your work is well done, Akila. Now come with me, lest I quail at this request and find myself running in the opposite direction." Her maid was the only person with whom she could be so honest.

They followed her father's servant down many corridors, past bored guards and rushing servants, and Siti could already smell incense mingled with the heady scents of roasting fowl and baking bread. They climbed many steps to the king's apartments on the floors above the palace chambers, until at last they stopped before two great doors with the sign of the cobra staring down at them. She shivered. The cobra always made her feel small, despite the fact that she was Pharaoh's daughter.

Guards allowed them entrance, and she moved into the king's private quarters, a place she had never been before. Her heart thumped to the beat of a thousand drums as the servant led her to a balcony that overlooked the bustling court below. Her father stood there, watching. She bowed low as he turned.

"May the Great Pharaoh, son of Ra, live forever in good health." Her voice sounded small in her ears.

He left the balcony and motioned to a low table with cushioned chairs circling it. He sat comfortably and indicated she do the same. He glanced about the room, then met her gaze. "You have not been here until now."

"No, my lord. It is a great pleasure to be invited." Her mind whirled with the reason for this visit, and she wished Akila had not had to wait in the hall outside.

"You must be wondering why I asked you to come." He spoke in his usual unquestioning way, his fingers slowly drumming the great arm of his chair. "And I will not keep you wondering."

She nodded, wishing her heart would still.

"I have been in conference for weeks now with the king of Israel. But of course you know this."

She nodded again. "It has been a great honor to experience his visit." She clasped her hands in her lap, wishing Abdukar was there so she could stroke his soft fur to calm her nerves.

"I have made several agreements with him." Her father studied her as if he was unsure how much to tell a lowly daughter. "I have given him horses and chariots and the town of Gezer as a wedding gift." He let the words sink deep.

"A wedding gift?" she said at last. But by his look she did not need him to say the rest.

"I am giving him one of my daughters to be his wife. It is an alliance that must be sealed with royal trust." He took a date rolled in honey and crushed almonds from a tray on the table, one she only now noticed. "If you will agree, I intend that daughter to be you."

She had a choice in the matter? But of course she did not. "You would send me away from Egypt?" Suddenly the thought frightened her, despite her interest in this foreign king who worshiped a strange god. "To live in a land of one god? A god I do not know?" Her heart beat faster with each question, and she sensed her father's tension. He did not want to be faced with such things. He thought only of the political alliance her marriage to Solomon would bring.

"Solomon is powerful," her father said at last. He looked away briefly, and she knew what he did not say. Egypt could not match Israel's power. Though they had conquered Gezer two years before, they were not the nation they once were when the greatest pharaohs ruled the land. When Israel was captive to Egypt.

"You need him as your ally."

He met her gaze then, but his nod was brief. "I would like this to be a positive arrangement for you." His granite face softened, and this time his smile held a tinge of sadness. "I have always favored your mother . . . and her children." It was the closest her father had ever come to expressing love.

"Thank you." She swallowed. Solomon intrigued her, but the thought of a purely political marriage grated so harshly she nearly bit her tongue. All the exotic love poetry in the world would be wasted on a marriage of such alliance. For Solomon would surely marry other wives, no doubt already had, and could not possibly love them all—not the way she envisioned love. A knot settled in the pit of her stomach.

"What can I give you to make this transaction, for that is what it is, easier for you to bear?"

She heard the uncertainty—was it uncertainty?—in her father's voice. A sound she had never thought to hear. And she realized that though she could not refuse, she did hold some small amount of power in this situation. She could request things, people to come with her . . . Her mind trailed off in a thousand directions at once.

"I don't want to live in a harem," she blurted, startled by her own audacity. "I want a palace of my own." She squared her shoulders and sat straighter, hands clasped so tight her nails dug into her palms. "I want my maid to accompany me—several maids, in fact—and I will not give up my cat or the worship of Bastet. Solomon must agree to this." Would Solomon agree to a foreign wife and a foreign god in his kingdom?

Her father, the Great Pharaoh, looked at her strangely for the longest moment, but at last he sat tall and clapped his hands. Servants appeared from the shadows. "Send word to King Solomon to meet me in my personal antechamber." He looked back at her. "You shall have your wish before the banquet begins." He leaned close and touched her chin. "By nightfall, you shall be Solomon's wife, and every wish you could desire will be yours."

He took her hand, and she was surprised to find it nearly as moist as her own. Could her father be as nervous as she about this upcoming alliance? But they did not speak of it. She merely allowed him to help her to her feet, astonished when he bent to kiss her cheek. She boldly kissed his in return, rather than bend over his hand to kiss his signet ring. She knew she would never get this chance again, and after this night, she would never behold his face thus.

"I will miss you, my lord king," she said softly in his ear.

"You are the greatest of kings. And I will not let Solomon forget it."

He stroked her cheek, but he did not smile. "Be strong. Be true to Egypt and to your husband."

She pondered his words as she and Akila walked back to her chambers, wondering why he put Egypt first, above her loyalty to Solomon. But she knew the reason. This was indeed an alliance of nations. Her presence in Solomon's capital would be a constant reminder of that fact.

CHAPTER
TWENTY-EIGHT

The lights flickered in the antechamber of Pharaoh's audience chamber. Solomon entered, surprised to see the king of Egypt waiting for him, but he hid his emotion with a slight nod and benign expression.

"Greetings, my lord," Pharaoh Siamun said, rising from a cushioned dais to motion Solomon to a similar chair beside him. A courtesy to a visiting monarch, though the room was not one where Solomon would have conducted such meetings.

He sat as the pharaoh did and crossed his hands in his lap. "Thank you, my lord. It is an honor to meet with you here." Solomon noted the pharaoh's guards standing near, while Solomon's own guards stood on the opposite side of the room. Even kings could not fully trust one another.

"The pleasure is mine, King Solomon. But let us not waste words with pleasantries as the banquet is so soon in coming." Pharaoh Siamun placed both hands on his knees, which were covered by his white tunic. "We are in agreement that you will wed my daughter Siti this night."

Solomon nodded. They had made the arrangements days ago, but it was obvious that the pharaoh had something more on his mind. "Yes, of course, my lord. And you promised to give Israel the city of Gezer as a wedding gift."

Pharaoh inclined his head in agreement. "This arrangement has not changed." He paused. "But I have spoken with my daughter, and it seems she has some requests of her own. Some things she wants as part of the alliance."

Solomon lifted a brow at this surprising turn of events. Daughters rarely made demands in such an alliance, but it was obvious this king was willing to indulge the young woman. "And they are?"

"She wants a palace of her own, not a room in a harem. I fear she has grown weary of harem life, my lord, and wants to rule her own house." Pharaoh Siamun gave a slight shrug as though the request was nothing. "And she wants to bring her maids with her, and her cat, and her god Bastet."

Solomon leaned against the wall, the words a bigger blow than he chose to reveal. He studied this king even as the reminders of Zabud reading to him filled his ears. *You are not to return to Egypt . . . You shall have no other gods before Me.* How could he allow a wife to bring a foreign god into Israel, especially into Jerusalem, without angering Adonai?

"You pose a dilemma for me, oh king, for our God does not allow us to worship any other gods but Him." Dare he remind this man of the way Israel's God had defeated the gods of Egypt when He delivered Israel from slavery in Egypt hundreds of years ago? *We are not supposed to return there.*

"I understand this is not an easy decision, but it is the one thing I promised my daughter since I am sending her away from all she knows." Pharaoh's eyes narrowed the slightest as their gazes met. "Of course, if you would rather not make the alliance, I am sure I can make good use of Gezer."

Solomon caught the veiled threat, however small it might have been. Gezer was the one weakness in this alliance because Solomon had determined to gain it. "I can build a palace for your daughter, my lord, though it will have to be outside the walls of Jerusalem if she is to keep a shrine to . . . Bastet." He caught himself before he said, "her cat." The whole idea of a cat carved of stone to which homage was paid seemed as ridiculous to him as a river flowing uphill or a goat giving birth to an ox. The latter two were impossible and the first made no sense, for how could a stone see or hear or speak as he had heard God speak?

"As long as she is not far from you and well protected, that will be agreeable." Pharaoh Siamun stood then, and Solomon did the same. "I expect then that tonight's banquet will end simply, without the fanfare of a normal wedding, as you have indicated you wish to leave within the week."

"Siti may come with me to my tents once we have signed the documents," Solomon said, reminding the king they had yet to do so.

"Which we will do now," he said, glancing at one of his guards. "Bring my scribe and recorder with the scrolls." He looked at Solomon. "I have prepared copies for us both, to ensure that we are not in disagreement in the future."

"A wise choice, my lord." Solomon bowed in deference to his soon-to-be father-in-law.

The scribe and recorder appeared within moments, as though they had been standing outside of the chamber with parchments and stylus in hand. Solomon read the script, noting that the king had already added Siti's requirements, which told him that this had never been a bargain but an expected acceptance. If he had said no, he would lose Gezer.

He could not lose Gezer.

But later that evening as he followed the king to the banquet hall where Siti would await him, he wondered if Yahweh would be pleased with his placating solution.

—⁓—

Ra had already begun his journey to the underworld by the time Siti's father's banquet was in mid-course. She sat in the midst of it beneath a white canopy, singled out as her sister had been during her wedding feast. Yet this was not a wedding feast as she had imagined it would be. The dais she sat upon and the gown she wore had been hastily chosen, for her father had made it clear that by nightfall she would be wed to Solomon. Not a week or two from now, with time enough to have new garments made. Tonight.

She kneaded the fine linen she wore beneath the sheer robe, wishing instead to sink her fingers into Abdukar's soft fur. She should have insisted her cat accompany her here, but the noise of the banquet would have sent him fleeing. Akila's presence at her back was strength enough, she told herself. But as she watched King Solomon dine with her father, she wondered. Quiet conversation appeared to move between them, but if there had been any trouble with negotiations of her nuptial requests, neither man exhibited any tension now.

Would Solomon keep the bargains he had made? How soon would a palace be built that she could call her own? She half argued with herself that she should have insisted she would not move to Jerusalem until the palace was completed, but such a building project could take years, and she knew deep down that her father could not afford to wait to make this alliance.

And King Solomon did not strike her as a terribly patient man.

She worried her lower lip at that thought, forcing her mind not to jump too far ahead to the evening's final hours. The hour when Solomon would lead her to his gleaming tents across the plains on the edge of the Nile. How long would they wait to leave Egypt?

"Are you nervous, my lady?" Akila bent forward and whispered the words, but Siti still heard them above the din.

She nodded. "Yes. A little." She glanced at the grand platform where Pharaoh's tables spread out like the Nile itself, surrounded by courtiers, his taste testers standing at attention just behind him. "King Solomon looks relaxed. And pleased." She leaned back and turned her head to look at her maid. "My father's arrangements must have been to his liking."

"I suspect you will be to his liking, my lady." She smiled at Siti with that look she always gave when trying to convince her she was beautiful.

Compared to Salama, she never thought so.

"I guess I will find out soon enough." Siti turned then, suddenly not interested in discussions with her maid or anyone else. She wanted to walk gracefully from this place and back to her rooms, throw off the accursed wig, and hold Abdukar in her arms. But she did not follow her desires or instincts.

The hours passed, though she could not complain that the entertainment bored her. The worst part was that Solomon did not join her on the dais. He remained near her father the entire evening. To anyone watching, she must have looked like a wilting lotus blossom on a pedestal, for all the interest paid to her. But then, she recalled, this was a banquet, not a true wedding feast. The king's gift to a foreigner. Such a thing had never been done in Egypt, and her father had decided at the last to keep the wedding a simple, quiet affair. She was to sit as her sister had done, but there would be no exchange of vows or promises between them. Her father had already sealed those vows for her.

A touch on her shoulder made her jump. "It is time, my lady," Akila said, taking her arm, helping her to finally stand. Her legs were stiff from sitting so long. How strange she felt to be following Akila and ten other maids out of the room, as though fleeing the hunter's snare.

But they were not fleeing anything. Night air assaulted her as they moved from her father's grand palace to a waiting litter in the outer courtyard. Palm trees lined the walkway, and slaves held the gilded litter aloft. One helped her enter and made sure she was securely settled among the cushions.

"I will be right behind you, my lady." Akila's words drifted away as the slaves lifted her chair and began a quick trot over the smooth stones of the court, through the long, winding street, onto the King's Highway. The clop of horses' hooves and chariot wheels came at a distance behind them, and she leaned over to lift the edge of the curtain. She looked back, and the image took her breath. Her father's palace shone like glittering starlight amid a night so black it seemed almost starless in comparison. Her home.

And yet her home no longer, she told herself not for the first time that evening. She faced forward again, her heart pounding as though it had forgotten its normal rhythm. The litter stopped too soon before the bright white tents she had seen so often across the plains, the flags of King Solomon flying like banners above them.

A slave helped her alight, and Akila seemed to appear instantly at her shoulder. Her maid gripped her arm, and Siti feared she might have stumbled if Akila had not been there, though she lifted her chin high as they passed Hebrew servants and tents with more strange markings on them. Her maids surrounded her, and she walked as one of the dead, for that was how she felt in this strange place. They came to the center of camp where stood the largest tent of them all.

Guards dressed in foreign clothing flanked each side of the tent's opening, long, gleaming golden spears tilted at an angle in their hands. They bowed their heads when they saw Siti and stepped aside, allowing her maids to escort her in.

A Hebrew servant met her just inside the door. "You must be the princess," she said in barely understandable Egyptian.

Siti nodded. "Yes." Wasn't it rather obvious? What else would she be doing here?

"You will come with me. The king has prepared chambers for you." She turned without another word.

Siti looked at Akila, who simply shrugged, and realized there was nothing to do but follow. Was this how it was going to be then? She would follow foreign servants to foreign places, eat foreign food, and sleep with a foreign man who had barely spoken to her in the months he had been in Egypt?

Suddenly she did not want to be here. She glanced at Akila and knew her maid could read the fright in her eyes, for she took her hand and silently squeezed. Of course, she could not leave despite her uncertainties. This fate was one, by Bastet's great name, she had agreed to.

What a fool she had been. Even Nakhti seemed a better choice at this moment, though he would have known nothing of the love she craved. Would Solomon understand her need? Would he care for her as the love poems said he should?

Her thoughts drifted away as she entered the room the servant led her to—simply a partition of the king's elaborate tent, but it did not lack for anything she could want, except perhaps solid walls. The servant left them, and her maids quickly stripped her of her wig and wedding garments. Akila combed her hair until it fell softly over her shoulders. A soft linen robe had been left for her use, and she slipped her arms through it, tying a knot in the belt.

Male voices sounded too soon, and her heart nearly leapt from within her. "He's come," she hissed in Akila's ear. "Whatever shall I do?" She gripped her maid's hand so tight she winced.

"Whatever he asks of you, my lady," she whispered back, gently tugging her hand free of Siti's grasp. "I must go now." She laid the comb on a low table and quickly backed from the room, leaving Siti completely alone.

She breathed in and out, telling herself to calm. Solomon's voice came to her clearly now, speaking something in Hebrew to his guards. And then quiet fell upon the tent. No footfalls of servants, no quiet laughter. No music or drums in the distance to mask her fear.

A shadow fell across the opening to her partitioned room. She looked up from where she had been sitting and quickly stood, then fell to her face before him. "My lord king, may you live forever," she said, thinking it an odd thing to say to a husband. But even her mother addressed her father thus in public places.

He stepped into the room, and the space seemed to wrap itself around him, around them. "Siti." He bent low and touched her shoulder, reaching for her curled fingers. "Come." He pulled her up.

She looked into his face, finding it hard to breathe.

He touched her cheek with gentle fingers. "I like you much better without the wig." His smile was that of a man who is completely at ease with himself and his surroundings. A man who fears nothing.

She self-consciously touched the edges of her hair. "I never did like our wigs," she admitted, half smiling.

He laughed. "Good! You will have no need of them in Jerusalem."

The comment seemed to assume she would not mind the change as permanent, but she suddenly felt a stirring to cling to all things Egyptian. "And yet, we must not forget that I am Egyptian, my lord. Egyptians wear wigs."

He looked at her curiously but offered her a conciliatory nod. "No one will forget that fact, my princess. And if the wig pleases you, I have no objection." He took her hand, and she was shocked at how cold her fingers were next to his. "But not in my presence."

He pulled her down beside him on a soft couch and extended an arm behind her back. It was then she noticed a platter of sweets and a sweating jug of wine sitting there for their use. He took a date and touched it to his lips, then held it out to her. "Are you pleased with our agreement, Siti? Will you be able to leave Egypt with me?"

She took the date between her fingers and looked at it, not

sure what was expected of her. "I have agreed, my lord. I will do as I have said." She looked at him, holding the date aloft.

He chuckled. "It's a kiss between us. Taste it." He smiled, and it felt as though he had touched her.

She placed the date against her lips.

"Now take a bite of it and feed me the rest."

She did as he requested. They chewed in silence, but even before the last swallow, he was leaning close, his breath fanning her face. This time his lips hovered over hers, and she tasted the lingering sweetness of the date.

His fingers traced her cheek. A shiver worked through her.

"You are beautiful, Siti, daughter of Pharaoh." The words were soft, like the wind. "How beautiful you are, my sister, my bride."

Her heart quickened. "You speak Egyptian poetry?"

His lips moved closer. "I write Egyptian poetry, my love." He bent lower, his kiss gentle, tantalizing. But he pulled back too soon, leaving her bereft of the heady feeling. "We must not awaken love until it pleases."

She touched his bearded cheek, so strange compared to the clean-shaven men she had known all her life. "You toy with me." Was this not to be their wedding night?

He leaned back, his gaze intent, searching. "Nay, I do not."

She followed his lead, leaning away from him. "Am I not your wife? What love is there to awaken?"

He traced the oval of her face, resting his palm against her cheek. "Siti, I do not yet know you. You do not know me. I can make love to you, but I cannot truly love you until I know you."

She stared at him, dumbstruck. "I cannot go with you if we are not wed."

He lifted his chin, his look confident. "We are wed, I assure you."

"But . . ." Was she to be a wife but no wife at all?

He leaned closer to her again and took her hand in his. He turned it face up and kissed it, one finger at a time, until she thought she would melt from the gentle pressure of his lips against her skin. He was holding back so utterly that she wanted to flail her arms at him and demand he hold her close and fulfill what she had heard in all the love poems she had fairly memorized since her youth.

But he released her hand and stood, pulling her up with him. His arms came around her slowly, as though she were a lotus blossom that might crush under too much weight.

"Siti, I am a king with several wives. I have loved many women in my short term as king, but only two did I truly know before we wed. Your father told me that you did not want a political marriage, and I agreed. Although you are the one he has chosen to seal our bargain, I do not wish for our marriage to be only an alliance of political means." He paused, touched her nose, then lifted her chin to better look into her eyes. "You wish to marry for love, do you not?"

His gaze held her so intently that she could only nod.

"Then that is what I want too." He cupped her cheek again and gently kissed her, a tender kiss that held so much promise she wanted to weep. "Which is why we will wait until love awakens," he said, releasing her.

He strode from her chambers, leaving her alone and wanting.

CHAPTER

TWENTY-NINE

A day and a night passed, and Siti found herself spending nearly every moment in Solomon's presence. Apparently her resistant lover was not quite so interested in letting love lie fallow, for he sat with her at the morning meal, walked with her through the length and breadth of his camp, and spoke to her of Israel. When he spoke of Jerusalem and the temple he had been commissioned to build, his eyes shone like fire.

"So this god of yours is like our gods," she said, watching him closely. "We build temples for each one and there are many, but you build one temple, for you only have one god." He looked at her strangely for the longest moment, and she hurried on. "We had a pharaoh once who tried to make us believe in one god, Aten, claiming him the only god, but his efforts did not last. Even he has become more myth to us than history—that is, I am not even sure that pharaoh ever existed." Perhaps Solomon's god was like Aten?

Her husband seemed to ponder her words as they stood

on the bank of the Nile not far from the activity of Thebes's main wharf. Solomon's guards surrounded them, though they stayed far enough away that Siti had the sense they were alone.

"Our God does not need a temple in which to live, Siti." He took her hand as he spoke, his voice earnest, his gaze fervent, as though he intended to make her believe the way he did in one impassioned argument. He motioned to the skies. "Our God made the heavens. He made the ground upon which we stand." He looked out over the river's vast expanse. "He made the waters you worship, the sun you call deity." He leaned close, his breath against her ear. "He made us, my love."

Her breath felt shallow at his nearness. "Then why, if he does not need a place to live, do you build a temple for him?" She wanted to ask about the palace her father had requested for her use, but the timing did not seem right.

He kissed her fingers and walked with her along the bank, up an incline, and back toward his encampment. Ra slowly drifted toward the west, and the blaze of gold he left upon the water surrounded them like a cloak.

"My father longed to build this temple, but our God would not allow him the privilege. So the task has come to me." His words held a shadow of sadness, and she wondered if the feeling was for his father's loss or his own.

"And you promised your father." She understood such promises.

He nodded. "My God chose me to build it." He faced her. They stood almost at the edge of the first of his tents, and he clasped their hands, intertwining their fingers. "Our God does not need a place to live, Siti, but we need a place to find Him. He already established our laws and all the articles for sacrifice, the priesthood, and the Ark of the Covenant, which houses our most sacred relics. The temple simply gives us a place to bring them all together and to learn to worship our God in the majestic way He deserves."

She watched the lean curve of his mouth as he spoke and could not hold back a smile. "You are deeply devoted to your god, my lord."

The intensity softened, and a smile tugged those intriguing lips. "I suppose that is true. He has spoken to me. How can one hear such a voice and not love Him?" He looked away as though despite all his wisdom, it was a question he could not grasp.

"He spoke to you?" Her heart beat faster with this new revelation, and she realized in that moment that this new husband of hers wanted her to understand his heart before he took her to his bed. Suddenly she felt herself wanting to promise him anything. Even belief in his god.

He nodded even as his arms came around her. She rested her head against his chest, surprised at his outward display of affection. They were not even hidden within the privacy of his tent! But as she listened to the rapid beating of his heart, she knew this moment held something sacred between them. The voice of his god was powerful indeed, and its effect had not left him since.

"How long ago?" she whispered, longing to hear more. "When did you hear him speak?"

Solomon did not answer immediately, but after several heartbeats he drew in a slow breath and released his hold on her. "Two years ago, when I was sacrificing to Him at Gibeon. He offered to give me anything I wanted. It was mine for the asking."

She gasped. She had never heard of a god granting such a wide-ranging request. "Anything?"

"Anything."

She swallowed. "What did you ask of him?"

He paused, his gaze turned now to the west where Ra's rays dipped quickly below the horizon. "Wisdom," he said so softly she almost missed the word.

"Wisdom." She marveled. Most men would have asked for long life or riches or rescue from their enemies. "He gave it to you then." He was the wisest man in the entire known world, his fame spreading with each passing day. All the result of a request he'd made of his god?

"Yes." He took her hand again and walked her through his camp to his tent, where torches and lamps lit the rooms almost as though it was day.

He called for a servant to fill wine cups and bring trays of food to refresh them, and they continued to talk long into the night. He told her of his childhood, how his parents met, how two of his brothers had threatened his life and died for the effort, and about his mother, whom Siti had admired from a distance.

And this time, when he escorted her to her chambers, he did not walk away. He spoke words from her favorite Egyptian poem against her ear and led her into the inner places of her room, their love awakened.

———— ᴍ ————

"Must we leave so soon?" Siti asked Solomon the following morning as she dangled a lazy foot over the side of the bed.

He stood opposite her, wrapping himself in his robe,

something she was quite certain his servants normally did for him. But they were still alone, and he probably did not wish to come across one of the female slaves in naught but his skin.

"I have not had the proper time to gather all the things I will need in your great city."

She didn't exactly pout, for though she sensed Solomon had shared much with her in the past few days, she had not returned the favor. She had told him of her family, her favorite cats, her love of Egypt and beauty, but she had not allowed him to see the spoiled side of her that Akila knew so well.

He leaned over her and planted a kiss on her forehead. She wrapped both arms about his neck and pulled him down to her, tempting him with a full kiss instead. He drew away, laughing.

This time she did allow a small pout. "You mock me."

"Never," he said, but his voice still carried a hint of mirth.

"I amuse you then."

He smiled. "Perhaps." He straightened and took a step back.

She scrambled from the bed and latched onto him, desperate to keep him near, for she knew once he left, he would not be back so quickly as he had been these past few days.

His arms came around her. "Siti. We cannot stay. I have been in Egypt for two months. I have a kingdom to run, and though messengers have traveled daily between my kingdom and here, it has been long enough." He kissed her but then easily disentangled her arms from about him. "Now get dressed and meet me in my visiting chambers. You will tell my servants exactly what you need them to gather, and they will do it."

She lifted a brow but laughed all the same. "Then you do not wish to be away from me?" She snatched her robe from the ground and slipped into it, but he gently gripped her shoulders and held her at arm's length.

"I do not wish you away from me. But dress as a princess, not a sleepy bride." He touched her nose and turned away from her. "Be in my chambers before the sun moves above the palm trees."

She ignored the fact that he did not address the sun as Ra, though she silently apologized to the sun god for her husband's lack. She was not sure she could ever get used to his devotion to only one god. What did one do with all the rest then? What of Bastet?

Akila hurried to her side once Solomon left, and she spoke to her maid of her concerns. "I have yet to ask him of my desire to build a shrine to Bastet in my new palace." She tilted her head, accepting Akila's work of painting her eyes and cheeks and lips. "What if he says no?"

Akila frowned, leaned back to inspect her work, and declared her ready. "I don't know, my lady," she added as she tied a golden sash about Siti's waist. "Was this not part of your agreement?"

She perked up at the reminder. "Of course. My father would have told him that I required this when he sealed the contract."

Akila patted her shoulder. "There now. Then you have nothing to fear. Just remember to tell the servants to gather the shrine from your rooms before we leave."

She walked with new purpose to Solomon's chambers a few moments later, pleased when she saw him smile at her entrance. He motioned her to sit and summoned several

Hebrews and a handful of Egyptian slaves to stand at attention and make a list of her requirements.

When she mentioned they must bring Abdukar to her and gather her shrine to Bastet, she glanced Solomon's way. He met her gaze, and for a moment she wondered, would he let her do this? As king and as her husband, he could refuse, despite any prior agreement. But the moment passed, and the servant asked if there was anything else. Solomon remained silent.

THIRTY

Solomon rode atop a covered camel surrounded by thick linen curtains to keep out the dust. One hundred Egyptian horses and chariots moved ahead of him, and the rest of his entourage, along with his new bride, came behind. The trip to Egypt had been productive, and Solomon could not help but smile at the results. He had captured Gezer without sending a single man to war, and gained much more besides. There was something to be said for diplomacy, and peace without war cost much less in the lives of his men.

How many kingdoms would require such diplomacy in the future? Yet who could compete with Israel, especially now that he had obtained Gezer? Expanding his borders didn't seem necessary, as his father had already gained the allegiance of peoples in lands ranging from Dan to Beersheba.

He closed his eyes to the dip and sway of the camel, weary of the journey. Jerusalem was still half a day away, and he felt his pulse quicken at the thought of introducing Siti to his mother, his advisors, his wives.

It was his mother's acceptance he longed for most. She had warned him throughout his life not to take too many wives. And now he had several foreigners sharing that title, though at least Naamah had embraced Israel's God. What would his mother say when she saw that he had allowed Siti to bring her cat goddess to Israel?

Guilt gnawed at him despite the many times he had justified his actions to himself. What choice did he have? If he'd refused Pharaoh Siamun this request, the man might have revoked the wedding and thus gone back on his word to grant him Gezer. But did Siti have to bring that blasted idol with her? The cat he could accept. But why the statue? It meant nothing. Had no power. But she believed it did, and he knew convincing her otherwise was not going to happen easily.

It's just a carving in stone, he reminded himself not for the first time. No gods of the nations surrounding him had power. Hadn't Yahweh Himself shown Israel that He alone was God when He defeated the many gods of Egypt, including this one that Siti worshiped? But neither he nor Siti had been alive then to see that power, and even though Israel remembered it yearly during the Passover, the people were quick to forget. Especially when the Canaanites living nearby had physical objects to show them what a god looked like.

He needed to get the temple built quickly. He could not allow his people to be led astray by the gods of Ammon, Moab, Edom, and many other nations around them. And now Egypt. For surely he could not keep Siti from hiding her god forever. Could he?

You are the king. You can command what you wish.

He could tell her that she could not set up a shrine to Bastet in Jerusalem. It would desecrate the memory of his father. She would understand that. They could keep the statue outside of Jerusalem in a safe place under guard. Near one of the towers.

He smiled at the thought. Yes. Siti would accept that, for Egyptians valued the dead and the memory of the dead. She would certainly understand his devotion to his father, King David.

But as they neared Jerusalem, his thoughts turned a different direction. Would his father be pleased to know that his beloved son had married an Egyptian wife and allowed her to bring her false god into Yahweh's kingdom?

Guilt nudged him again, accompanied by a souring stomach. Despite all of his wisdom, he could not seem to keep himself from wishing he could undo everything he had just done.

—⁂—

They arrived in Jerusalem before the sun set with an almost holy orange glow over the western horizon. The town greeted them with wild fanfare, and Solomon felt a sense of homecoming and gratitude that they had missed him. He descended his kneeling camel, welcomed with hearty cheers and low bows from his advisors and courtiers. Even his wives and young children looked down from the balcony of the palace, and his mother met him when he entered the cool halls. Siti and her maids followed some distance behind him, but on his command they were ushered to rooms in the women's quarters until he could decide where Siti should stay while he planned her palace.

"You are back at last, my son," Bathsheba said, accepting his kiss on both cheeks. She responded with a warm embrace.

"We have missed you. The kingdom has not been the same in your absence."

"But there have been no threats to my rule?"

She smiled. "No. None of your brothers dared usurp your authority, even in your absence. And your advisors, particularly Benaiah and Zabud, have kept control of things."

"I expected nothing less." Solomon walked with her toward his rooms. He wanted to simply bathe, change clothes, and crawl into bed.

"I see you have brought several Egyptian women back with you." His mother's comment held a gentle tone, but Solomon stiffened, half afraid of her censure. "One looks like a princess."

"Yes—Siti. She is the daughter of Pharaoh Siamun. We married in Egypt, and the pharaoh gave me Gezer as a wedding gift." He glanced at her, then looked away.

She touched his arm. "So Gezer is at last in Israel's hands." Her words made him turn to look at her. "And this Siti, is she pleasing to you?"

Solomon studied her a moment as they at last stopped at the door to his rooms. "Yes and yes. Marrying Siti was the only way to gain Gezer, but I also find her most acceptable."

"And she is a follower of Adonai?" She would, of course, ask him such a thing, for Naamah had embraced Yahweh long before they wed.

He paused. "No. She worships their cat goddess, Bastet. She no doubt will build a shrine to her once I build her a palace outside of Jerusalem."

Bathsheba held his gaze, and he wondered what thoughts went through her mind. But he knew. She did not approve, nor would she approve of any more foreign wives, should he take them. "But you will not allow her to worship this god in Jerusalem," she said.

"No. Not in my father's palace, nor mine." He shifted from foot to foot.

Bathsheba drew a breath and smiled. "Well then, perhaps in time Siti will come to know our God as you do. You will have to introduce me to her soon."

Solomon's tense shoulders relaxed. "It will be my pleasure, Ima."

THIRTY-ONE

Siti awoke with a start to the sound of soft purring in her ear. She opened one eye and closed it again, then pulled Abdukar closer into her arms lest he awaken Solomon, who still slumbered peacefully beside her. It was a rare occurrence to have the king at her side in these past two years since coming to Jerusalem. A rarity she did all in her power to keep.

Solomon stirred, and she lay still, trying to hold a wiggling cat to no avail. Her cat, betraying little beast, favored her husband, and before she could stop him, he sidled up against Solomon's back as though he belonged there.

Fully awake now, she rolled onto her side, studying these two "men" who filled her heart and her daily thoughts. Solomon had taken more wives since their arrival to what had once been King David's palace. Building projects abounded throughout the city, the central focus being that of the temple, where stones from quarries and heavy timber of cedar and cypress from the king of Tyre were dragged up the side of the mount and set in place with as little marring as possible. And still the temple looked as though it had barely begun.

Siti's palace outside of Jerusalem—for that is where Solomon insisted they would build it—had yet to have a single foundation stone laid. Her brow furrowed too often of late, and she feared she was going to have unseemly lines across her forehead if she did not stop fretting. But living in the cramped quarters of King David's palace was wearing on her, and she chafed at this forced need to wait while Solomon built other structures and married women from other foreign lands.

He stirred again, and she straightened, smiling down at him when he rolled onto his back and pulled Abdukar into his arms. The cat settled on his chest, and Solomon's other arm came around her, drawing her close.

"This little beast should have his own room," he said, his voice still heavy with sleep.

"And so he shall when your wife has her own palace." She kissed his cheek lest he find her comment annoying.

A chuckle came from deep within him. "Ah, my little Egyptian minx." He pulled her closer and kissed the top of her head. "You will have your palace. Did you never notice how long it took to build something while you lived in Egypt?" He rose on one elbow to look at her.

She shrugged, giving him a playful pat. "I was young in Egypt. I didn't trouble myself about such things."

"And you are young here," he said, winding a strand of her hair around his finger. Abdukar took that moment to pounce on a piece that fell over the side of his hand. Solomon gently dragged the cat aside. "Kings in your land spend their whole lives building burial places. I promise it will not take your whole life to build you a home." He kissed her and set her cat between them. "But now that I am awake, I must go."

He rose quickly as he always did, and she with him. He faced her as he tied his robe. "Come to the temple mount with me today. Then, after I inspect the progress, we will choose a spot to start your palace."

She squealed and wrapped both arms tightly around his neck. "Truly?" She jumped up and down like a youth, but for once she did not care to be the polite Egyptian princess.

His laughter was like the sound of music to her ears. "Truly." He set her aside then, and the moment he walked through her doors, she called for Akila. Ra had barely crested the ridge.

—◈—

Before Ra stood halfway to the midpoint of the sky, she received a message from the king telling her that their plans had changed. She looked at Akila once the messenger left her rooms. "Why do I keep hoping?" She sank onto a chair, and Abdukar hopped onto her lap. "He is always breaking his promises to me. What excuse will he give me this time?"

She stood abruptly, shoving Abdukar to the floor. He arched his back as if in a huff, sauntered to the window ledge, and jumped up to watch the courtyard below.

"He must have a good reason." Akila moved behind her to straighten the pillows she had dislodged, but her restless legs would not sit again.

"I am going to find him and make him tell me." She was already dressed and ready for their meeting, but she glanced in the glass to make sure she looked her best.

Akila hurried after her as she strode through the palace

halls. Yet it was not Solomon whom she ended up finding but his mother. She nearly bumped into the queen mother as she entered the court of women, where Bathsheba had just come from the apartment of Abishag.

Siti bowed at her approach.

"Siti. How good it is to see you." Solomon's mother had a way about her that always made Siti feel at ease. Suddenly she realized that this woman could help her more with her frustration than Solomon himself, for he always ended up staying away until her irritation passed, and she usually found it impossible to gain an audience with him uninvited.

"Thank you, my queen. May I have a moment with you?" She had learned enough of the Hebrew language in these two years to be able to converse with others besides Solomon. She glanced around, unsure where to suggest they go, as she did not want this conversation heard in a harem full of Solomon's wives.

"Of course," Bathsheba said, smiling. Were those new lines along her brow? "Come to my apartments. I will have Tirzah bring us cool refreshments." She moved ahead of Siti, her gowns rustling with the faintest swish. Her apartments were closest to Solomon's.

Bathsheba's maid hurried to attend their needs, though she noticed the woman seemed to move slowly, a testament to her age. Siti looked sharply at her mother-in-law. When she first met her two years before, she had shown youth and strength in her bearing, in her gaze. Now she sank slowly to the cushions as if the action required more effort than it should.

"Siti," she said as she took the seat opposite hers and

accepted a cool goblet of mint water from her maid, "what can I do for you, dear girl?"

She swallowed, surprised that the endearment touched her as it did. How did this woman manage to make Solomon's many women feel as though they were the only one who mattered? Yet that was how she felt in that moment.

"I wonder if you can tell me why the king seems to always find a reason not to take me to see the building of the temple to your god. Nor has he kept his promise to my father to build a palace for me, where I can worship my goddess, Bastet, without angering your Yahweh." She watched Bathsheba's brow furrow the slightest bit, and she clasped jeweled hands in her lap.

Bathsheba sipped from her cup before she spoke. Siti waited, watching her.

"I do not understand why Solomon has offered to take you to the building site of our temple, Siti, but I suspect his reason for not doing so is because you are not of our heritage or our faith." She met Siti's gaze. "And I suspect that because the temple is such a palatial structure, he simply has not had time to divert resources or energy to your palace until the house of our God is completed."

Siti forced herself not to curl her lower lip into a pout. She was not a child, after all, but a wife of two years. "Are not the workmen of other nations? I daresay they don't all believe in your god, my queen. Does the king fear I will somehow defile the place?" She could not keep the tinge of anger from seeping into her tone.

Bathsheba shook her head. "No, no, my child. But perhaps he thinks you will not appreciate it for what it is. You are not a slave who is merely fulfilling a job. You are the king's wife. I suspect he resists showing you because he fears you disdain our faith."

Her words sank deep, though Siti did not think she meant them to wound. But it was clear that Solomon's mother was privy to far more of his thoughts than she, probably more so than any wife, foreign or Hebrew, in the kingdom.

"I do not disdain your faith, my queen," she said slowly. "I will admit . . ." She paused, meeting Bathsheba's gaze. "I have often wondered if Solomon disdains mine. Perhaps this is a contention between us that will never be resolved." She looked away, more frustrated than she had been before she sought out Solomon's mother. Did he disdain her worship of Bastet?

"I trust you will be patient with him, Siti," Bathsheba said, drawing her thoughts back to the conversation. "His father, King David, detailed elaborate plans for the temple, and so much needs yet to be done. Besides the stone and the cedar and gold, there are utensils of bronze that he has commissioned. Then there are the carvings, and everything must be done with perfection to his father's, and our God's, specifications."

"But such a project will take years." She hated the whiny quality that had seeped into her voice. "And then he wants to build his own palace, and so many more buildings and fortifications of cities, that it will take thousands of men and more time." She sat straighter, setting her jaw. "He owes me a palace. It was part of his agreement with my father, part of why my father allowed him to wed me." She left out the part about the city of Gezer that had probably mattered more to Solomon than she did. To admit such a thing—that a city that had eluded capture for so long should be more important than a wife—carried the edge of pain, like a knife pricking more than skin deep.

"Would it help if I speak to him?"

She looked up at that, surprised by her offer. "Would it change his plans?" Despite his mother's power, she wondered just how much that power could be wielded.

Bathsheba lifted one shoulder in a slight shrug. "I am not the one to decide these things, my daughter, but I have had a little influence over him now and then." She ran a finger along the rim of her golden goblet. "And if he made a promise, he should keep it. I see no reason why he could not set men to begin work on your home." She looked at Siti curiously, probably to see if such a thing would please her. Did it trouble the queen that such a promise had been made to no other wife? Not even Naamah, mother of Solomon's heir, would live in a palace all her own. But Naamah had not come to him offering him Gezer. And Egypt was a greater power than Ammon.

"If you can persuade him, I would be in your debt," Siti said, warming to the thought. While she would have preferred to have Solomon's ear more exclusively, it made sense to hold the good opinion of his mother.

"I will see then what can be done." Bathsheba looked for a moment as though she would stand, then settled back again among the cushions. "May I ask you to consider one thing, Siti?"

She nodded. "Anything, my queen."

"Allow one of our scribes to read to you from the book of our law. Learn the ways of our God. You might find the knowledge you gain there will help you understand my son better, and perhaps you might close that gap between the two of you." She lifted her cup to her lips but did not drink. "My son cares for you, Siti. I see it in his smile when you walk into a room. Learn to understand his faith and you will better learn to know him."

The faintest uneasy flutter filled Siti at her words. She was not so sure she wanted to hear the words of a strange god, one that Solomon considered so much better than her beloved Bastet. But she nodded to appease. "Perhaps it would also help if you could convince Solomon to try to understand my goddess as well, my lady."

The queen's eyes widened at her boldness, but she felt a bit of that old rebelliousness fill her spirit. She was not the one who should give up everything for Solomon. She had already given up so much, including that accursed wig that set her apart as Egyptian. She even dressed in the manner of the Hebrews much of the time.

"I suppose you have a point," Bathsheba said at last. "Though, forgive me, Siti, but my son already possesses a great knowledge of all the foreign gods of other nations."

Of course he did. She was referring to the wisdom his god had given him. And still he disdained Bastet. Didn't he?

She pondered the thought as she and Akila made their way back to her apartments later that afternoon. It troubled her that she could not answer her own question, for she did not know Solomon nearly as well as she should after two years of marriage. But she would find out. She would ask him the next time he came to her. And she would convince him to give her a place to worship Bastet, for he did not allow it here in his father's palace.

She would move out of this city to a place of her own. Sooner than he wanted, even if it meant she must send word to her father to act on her behalf if Bathsheba could not convince her son.

In the meantime, she would listen to their law. She would listen, and she would find out why Solomon placed it in such high esteem, making his god greater than hers. And perchance she would find a way to convince him that he was wrong.

THIRTY-TWO

Only he must not acquire many horses for himself or cause the people to return to Egypt in order to acquire many horses, since the Lord has said to you, 'You shall never return that way again.' And he shall not acquire many wives for himself, lest his heart turn away, nor shall he acquire for himself excessive silver and gold." The scribe had droned on for too long reading from this tired parchment, but when he read these words, Siti sat up, not nearly as bored as she had been.

"What did you say?" she interrupted.

The man raised his aged head and lifted a thick white brow.

"Please read that part again."

He nodded, seemingly pleased.

She listened with a sharply attuned ear. Solomon had not obeyed this at all. She glanced at her reflection in the glass and stood, dismissing the man, though he extracted a promise from her to come again later in the week. She was too distracted to argue with him. Why had King Solomon disobeyed such commands when in everything else he seemed so devoted to his god?

It had taken months of listening to the do's and don'ts of many insignificant laws before the scribe had come to this one—months that had shown no change in Solomon. She had seen little of him during that time, and though Bathsheba assured her that she had spoken to him, he had yet to find time to speak of Bastet or take her to choose the right land for her palace.

"Something has riled you, my princess. Were you disturbed by the words the scribe read today?" Akila entered from a side room where she had discreetly waited during the reading.

Siti looked at her maid, her mind whirling. "Only that I am more confused than I was before he came." She touched her chin, then glanced at her reflection again. "Akila, I want you to make me up in all my Egyptian finery. It is time I had an audience with Solomon, whether he wants it or not."

An hour later, she strode into Solomon's audience chamber and knelt at the edges of wide blue tiles that circled the area before his gilded throne. Six white, gleaming steps, each with a single golden statue of a lion guarding the edges, stretched from where she knelt to where he sat in royal splendor.

"Siti."

She lifted her head, and he beckoned her with one hand. She started forward, bowing one knee on each step, until she stood before him.

"What are you doing here like this?" His voice was low, allowing only his ever-present guards to hear. He looked her up and down, and she saw his lips twitch as though he intended to hide a smile. "You have come to bewitch me, my love."

"I have come to speak with you, my lord," she said softly. "My husband has been absent too often of late." She offered him her most beguiling smile and swayed her hips just enough to remind him of the many dances she had performed for him.

"Your husband needs to remedy that then," he said, his smile broader now. He extended a hand to her, and she bent to kiss his signet ring, but he clasped her fingers, preventing her attempt. "Go to the antechamber." He inclined his head to the right. "Wait for me there."

"Will I be forced to wait long, my lord? I fear my husband too often loses track of time." She held his gaze, narrowing her own.

He chuckled. "You toy with me, my love. A king has many obligations." He glanced toward the side where a long line of men of Israel stood waiting for judgment. She had waltzed right past them.

"Send them home until tomorrow," she said, squeezing his hand. "Surely a king has power to do as he pleases."

He tilted his head, flicking his gaze toward the priests and scribes and hundreds of courtiers who also sat at court, waiting to hear the lesser cases or present their own issues before him. "Siti," he said, his voice soft, almost vulnerable, "tell me you did not come simply to remind me of the things I have not yet done."

Guilt pricked her heart, and with it frustration that he

could so easily read her thoughts. "I came because I have missed you, my lord. I came because I have questions that only you can answer."

He gave a slight nod. "Very well. You shall have your answers." He released her hand and clapped. A servant appeared—his court recorder. "Send the people away, Jehoshaphat. I am finished for today."

He stood, taking her hand again, and walked them out a side door, down the corridors to his private chambers, not hers. Her heart beat fast as she recognized the lion's head carved into the door, a door she had not walked through during her entire stay in Jerusalem. A guard opened it for them, and Solomon drew her into the large sitting area. He set her carefully on a cushioned chair, then removed his royal robe and crown and sank carelessly onto a couch near her. She noted that he did not choose to sit her beside him. Why?

She cast the worry aside. She had gotten him this far. There was no going back now.

"All right, my love, tell me what it is you seek, other than the palace I promised to build for you. I may not have told you, but I have had architects drawing plans for it for the past few months. We should be ready to show you designs within the next few weeks." He folded his hands, his gaze taking in her full appearance.

She swallowed. "Why did you not tell me? I would have liked a say in the plans."

One dark brow lifted. "And so you shall, my love. These are simply preliminary. Later I will take you to the place where I think it best to build." He studied her, his look more intense than she had ever seen it. "But that is not the only reason you came to me dressed like we were back in Egypt."

She lowered her lashes lest the flash of irritation be visible to this man who seemed to be reading her thoughts. "I have been listening to your scribe read the law of your god to me. I would like to understand why the king of Israel, who is so faithful to his god in building his temple, is not faithful to the law regarding kings."

His mouth thinned with the slightest tightening of his jaw. "If you are speaking of the law regarding horses, gold, and wives . . . yes, I am aware of it."

"Then why do you break it?"

"I do not break it."

She stared at him. "You have done all the things the law says not to do in abundance, my lord. How is that not breaking it?"

"The horses were gifts, and since we wed, I have fed Egypt's coffers by allowing my men to continue to purchase them from your father. It was part of our agreement when I married you." He stroked his beard. "As for the gold, I never asked for gold or silver from my God, yet every foreign king who pays me homage or simply visits comes bearing great gifts. My wealth has not been sought, Siti. It is a gift from my God."

"I suppose the many wives are gifts from him too?" She couldn't deny the kick of jealousy she felt when she thought of the women continually pouring into his harem. A harem she did not want to share—ever.

"That law was written with good purpose—lest a king's many wives turn his heart away from his God." He gave her a slight smile. "That is not going to happen to me, Siti. These are political arrangements. I am wholly devoted to Yahweh, and I will not allow any woman to turn my heart away. Wisdom has taught me that would be indeed foolish."

"So these laws do not apply to you." She did not want to believe he thought so, but she wanted to hear him say it.

"Of course the laws apply to me. But I have not broken them of my own accord or for the wrong reasons. Why does this trouble you, my love? Surely you pulled me from court for more than this."

Was he mocking her? Suddenly all her reasons to see him seemed simple and futile. "I want to set up a shrine to Bastet," she said, lifting her chin with a slight show of defiance. "You have denied me these past two years, yet you are free to worship your god however you please. If I had a house of my own, I could have already made a place for her. Instead, her image remains hidden in a basket, out of sight, even outside the city gates. What if your guards look away and someone steals her? Her image is of great value and should be guarded in the king's house. Better, her shrine should be in a room near my own. Yet you do not allow it." She had never complained when he refused her initially, but she was weary of his changing moods, his changing plans, and her feelings of homesickness that made her long for the familiar, for Bastet.

He studied her for too long, and she began to regret her outburst. But the words were said, and she could do nothing but wait for an answer.

"I cannot allow you to place an idol in my father's house." He looked away. "My father was faithful to our God, and it would be a dishonor to his memory."

Her heart twisted at his expression at the mention of his father. "I would not wish to dishonor your father, my lord, but you dishonor my goddess by hiding her away."

"If your goddess had power, Siti, she would have risen

up and forced her way into this place. She would not have allowed herself to remain hidden." He leaned forward. "Do you not see? She is not powerful. Only Yahweh has such power. And He has kept her hidden."

She was not sure why anger bubbled so swiftly to the surface, but his flippant answer, his assumption that only his god was worthy or powerful, sent a wave of bitterness through her. "Egypt is powerful, and we have been around much longer than Israel," she said, wishing the words did not sound like barbs that she flung across the room. "Egypt's gods have proven their power over and over again. Does not Ra rise from the dead every dawn? Does not the Nile inundate our land to cause it to be the richest soil on earth? Did we not capture Gezer when your country could not?" She stood, restless. "How dare you suggest that my gods are less than yours." She walked to his window, shaking.

Silence fell like a pall in the room, and she felt as though her marriage had been dealt a death blow. Silence lingered until at last Solomon spoke.

"Years ago," he said softly, causing her to turn to face him again, "my people were slaves in Egypt. And Yahweh turned the day to darkness, vanquishing Ra. He turned the Nile to blood, cutting off your life force. And He took the life of every firstborn in Egypt, even the firstborn of Pharaoh, to show that only He gives life. Men are not gods, Siti. Stone images are not gods. The true God is one not made with human hands, nor is He like us. We are made to be like Him."

She stared at him, searching every facet of his face. His gaze did not hold the anger she felt. "So you disdain the gods of Egypt."

He shook his head. "I just do not believe they are gods

at all. They are merely objects made by men." He extended his ringed hand to her, and she reluctantly walked closer and took it.

Why did she allow him to move her? But there was comfort in his touch.

"I wish you shared my faith."

His honest desire startled her. "Yet you married me knowing I did not."

He nodded. "I have married many women knowing they do not. And I do not say this to each one of them. But I wish it true of you." He touched her cheek, moving the long strands from the wig aside, gently brushing his thumb beneath her lashes.

She slanted her gaze away from him, though she could not deny the kick in her heart that his touch evoked. He would woo her. It was his way. She did not know why she allowed it when her own honor was at stake.

"I care deeply for you, Siti," he said. "But you must understand, I cannot risk the anger of my God by putting other gods before Him. The first commandment He gave to our ancestor Moses was, 'You shall have no other gods before Me.' If I allow a foreign god into my house, I will be breaking a far worse command than the ones you accuse me of breaking." His words, spoken with that soothing tone of his, did manage to calm her. But they did not convince her.

"I do not understand your god, Solomon. Bastet, I understand. She is graceful and remote, yet she is fiercely protective of those who follow her. Abdukar is a constant reminder of her greatness, and I do her a disservice by ignoring her needs." How to make him see? "Does not your god require sacrifices? Well, Bastet has needs too. You slaughter animals to feed the hunger of your god, and when I bring a plate of food to Bastet or a cat dies and its mummy is placed in Bastet's temple, I do the same." She searched his gaze, but he was clearly not convinced.

He leaned away from her. "It is not the same."

"How then is it different? Surely the wisest man in all the earth can answer me that." She watched him wince at this latest barb and felt the familiar guilt prick her heart again. But if she did not stand up for Bastet, who would? Did she not owe Bastet for giving her the desire of her heart? The goddess had kept her from marrying Nakhti, had given her a husband who shared her love of poetry and dance and beauty and more. Could it be that her palace was so long in the making because of her neglect of her goddess?

"You are right," he said, his tone resigned. "The wisest man in all the earth should be able to answer your question. I have tried to, Siti. We have had this discussion many times."

Had they? She recalled their first meeting when he questioned her about Bastet. He had been planting ideas in her to abandon Bastet from the day she met him.

"But the one difference between Yahweh and the gods of Egypt, my love, comes down to a person's choice. You were taught to believe Egypt's gods were real, that each one performed certain tasks, that each one must be worshiped, cared for, or appeased." He took her hand in his. "Whereas I was taught about Yahweh from my birth. I was told the tales of Yahweh's power over the gods of Egypt and Canaan and how He called my ancestor Abraham out of Mesopotamia, away from the gods they worshiped, to follow Him alone. Nations think our forefathers invented a new religion, that their belief in only one God was something new. But it wasn't, Siti. From the beginning, there was one Creator. Only time and distance from Him have allowed people to put other gods in His rightful place."

He pulled her closer, and though she still inwardly balked at his words, she allowed him to wrap both arms about her. She leaned against his chest, listening.

"All nations feel as you do, my love. There is similarity in all the gods of other lands. Some worship the sun, others the moon. But all their gods are fashioned in created things or in the likeness of men. Our God is spirit. He is knowable and yet unknowable. He reveals Himself in what He has made, and yet no one can see His face and live. He is mercy and justice. His voice is thunder and whisper. His power is endless." He paused and looked away from her, and she wondered if he would say more.

At last he turned to face her. "We only understand Him by faith, Siti. I can explain many things about Him to you, but I cannot make you believe them. I'm sorry, my love. I'm afraid even the wisest man on earth does not truly grasp the nature of my God."

She looked at their twined hands for the longest time, his words stirring her, warring against all that she knew. "So your answer remains no." He would not allow her to build a shrine for Bastet. She looked into his dark eyes, saw the hint of sorrow there, and felt sorry that she had caused it.

"Not as long as you live in Jerusalem under my roof." He squeezed her hand, then pulled her to stand. "Would you care to see the place where I think we should build your palace?"

"Right now?" The change of subject was the best she could expect of him, for she knew now that she could not force her way with him. Not until she resided in her own palace, away from his god, whose very mention made her shudder.

He laughed, seemingly unaware of her inner battle. "Yes, now." He grabbed the robe he had so quickly discarded and called his servants. "Call for my driver and the royal chariot."

Guards surrounded them as they walked toward the courtyard and mounted the gilded chariot, pulled by perfectly matched Egyptian stallions, for a ride she would never forget.

THIRTY-THREE

Night flickered in glittering gems across the blackest sky Solomon had ever seen. Not a cloud marred the horizon, and the moon shone large, like a giant eye gazing down, ever seeing. He gazed at the constellations, the Bear, Orion, and Pleiades, and wondered at the way God had used even the stars to show the complexity of the universe. Why create Pleiades to look as though the seven major stars were chained together? Or show Orion belted for a hunt?

The thought stirred him. Who could match the greatness of his God? Yet for all of the magnificence around him, he could not convince Siti or his other foreign wives to see the Creator behind the creation. What stopped them from understanding? Why was Siti so adamant that her goddess of stone was real and worthy of her worship?

He paced the palace roof, his mind whirling with too many questions. God had blessed him with more abundance than he thought possible, yet some of the gifts weighed on him. Still, what better way to test the wisdom God had given than to use his wealth to explore the world? And how could he refuse the gifts of kings who offered their daughters in marriage?

Siti's accusations that he had broken God's laws grated, and he could not help but think that his mother would agree with her. But how was he to refuse these foreign kings seeking alliances? Though three hundred wives did seem excessive, the ambassadors of nations still poured into his kingdom from far and wide, bringing royal daughters and gold and silver and exotic animals and spices as gifts. All to hear the wisdom God had given him.

Suddenly the enormity of that gift caused an overwhelming burden to rest on him. He sank to his knees, his face to the stones of the roof. *You have given far more than I deserve, Adonai. I fear . . . I do not wish to take Your gift for granted. Let me use Your wisdom wisely.*

He waited, his forehead pressed to the smooth stones, hoping to hear the voice as he had that day in Gibeon, but only silence met his ear. He slowly rose, catching the curious gaze of his guards, dusted himself off, and looked heavenward again. The stars looked like silver refined seven times, pure, bright lights in the darkness.

Was this the real purpose of the wisdom God had given to him? To use it as light where there was darkness? Hadn't he tried to do just that in his attempts to convince Siti of Yahweh's power? Yet even his wisest argument had met with no success. He clenched his hands. The worst of it was that she goaded him, and his attempts to change her thinking seemed to make her more defiant to keep her beliefs exactly as they were.

What good was wisdom if it had no power to change the

most important thing in a person's life—their inner spirit, their heart?

He turned his gaze from the heavens to the city below him. His kingdom stretched from all the land west of the Euphrates River, from Tiphsah to Gaza, and he had peace on all sides. Judah and Israel, from Dan to Beersheba, lived in safety. And they were happy.

True, he taxed them and enforced laborers for his building projects, but he made sure they rotated the work, and he did all in his power to share his wealth with his people, making silver as common as the stones that crunched beneath his horses' hooves. Was it the silver that brought the people joy or the peace brought on by his alliances?

He took the steps to his rooms below and met Zabud in the halls.

"My lord king." Zabud quickly examined Solomon's gaze, then bowed low.

"Zabud, my friend, what are you still doing here at this hour? I expected you to be home with your wife and children." When was the last time he had visited his children? With so many wives and more children being born each month, he could barely keep count of them all.

Zabud rose and continued to search Solomon's gaze. "I was headed that way, my lord. But now that I have found you, I can see that there is something on your mind. Perhaps you wish to discuss it?"

His priest and friend knew him too well. Solomon determined to keep a better guard on his expressions and emotions. He studied his friend, thinking to send him on his way, then in a moment of spontaneity, he motioned Zabud to follow. They entered his quarters and Solomon left the guard posted outside. Servants brought wine and dates and cheeses, offering them on golden platters to both men.

Solomon waited while Zabud sipped from his cup, then leaned back, crossing his ankles. "Tell me, Zabud, why are the people of Israel happy?" He drank deeply of the rich wine and let it swirl on his tongue, tasting the varying flavors of the fermented grapes.

Zabud raised a brow and set his cup aside. "You ask a hard question, my friend. I suppose it is because there is at last peace in the land and you have made them prosperous."

"And yet, for all the work they do, all the silver they gain, and the rest they have in knowing peace, when they die they will leave it all behind for someone else to inherit. They can take nothing with them, so how is it they are happy while they live?" Solomon's mind turned this way and that, realizing that his reason for asking was not for the people but for himself.

"I suppose it is because they will die knowing they have lived a good life, one that was pleasing to Adonai." Zabud clasped his hands together, and Solomon could see his brow scrunch, a telltale sign that the question had left even the priest without an answer.

"So the people are happy because they love Adonai." He set his own cup aside and waved the servant away when he tried to refill it. "Yet I love Adonai and am not happy, Zabud. How is it that my wisdom keeps me from knowing the simple happiness of my people?" To admit his unhappiness surprised even him, for until this moment, he had not realized how much Siti's refusal to accept Adonai as her God, as Naamah had, bothered him. And every foreign wife with her foreign god filled his heart with guilt.

"I wish I could answer that, my friend," Zabud said. "I would need to understand the reason for the king's unhappiness. For God has given you everything a man could want. One would think that wisdom and riches alone would bring joy to a man's heart."

"And yet I am filled with guilt, for I know in my heart I have broken God's laws. I have married foreign women. I have amassed many horses and chariots from Egypt. And though my wisdom has not left me, it also accuses me of disobedience, despite the fact that I still worship Adonai alone. Am I to give up these things in order to find that simple pleasure my people seem to enjoy?" He paused and ran a finger along the rim of his cup. "But I know that I cannot give these things up, for if I were to return the gifts, there would no longer be peace and my people would no longer praise me in the streets."

"It is hard to be king." Zabud looked deeply into Solomon's eyes. "Perhaps your wisdom will give you a way to stop accepting the gifts. Be content with the kingdom as it is. Contentment can bring great joy." He smiled, but Solomon did not return the gesture.

"Contentment. Now that is a condition I have not known since I asked God for wisdom. For though His gift is great, it is a heavy burden. No man can carry the wisdom of God within his spirit without also carrying the realization that he is a mere man trying to hold the wealth of knowledge of the Almighty. It is a staggering weight." He had never shared such thoughts with anyone until this moment. But he knew that this was his battle—the never-ending desire to understand more. And by testing and seeking he did understand, and the more he knew the more his mind wanted to forget what he'd learned. "I think perhaps sometimes a person can be too intelligent for their own good, for all men end up in the same place. Perhaps it is better to be a fool."

"But a foolish king is worse than a wise one, would you not say so, my lord? For how could you carry out your duties or judge this great people as you do? Don't forget what great things you have been able to do because of wisdom." Zabud nibbled at a piece of cheese.

Solomon leaned forward and rested his elbows on his knees. "You speak truth." He sat in silence a moment, wishing however briefly that he could get out of his own skin, but in a heartbeat he knew that he had been taking wisdom for granted. "There is much good I can still do with this wisdom. Proverbs to be spoken, poems and writings to put to parchment for the next generation. Perhaps when I leave this world the writings will follow after me and not leave me forgotten to future peoples. If they can learn from my errors, then my life will have been worth something." Even if he never could convince Siti or his other wives to see Adonai as the only true God, perhaps their children would listen to a father's words. "Thank you, my friend. As always you have given me much to ponder."

Solomon stood and Zabud did the same, taking his unspoken cue to leave Solomon to himself. He bid farewell and left, while Solomon called for parchment and ink to record what he could not get out of his head or heart.

THIRTY-FOUR

Solomon stood on the temple mount and looked at the grand structure that finally stood completed to the exact specifications that God had given to his father. Seven years to bring it all together. Three floors of stone, cedar, and gold. Countless carvings and numerous bronze articles to use in the sacrifices, and the priestly items meant to be kept in the holy place. Only one thing remained during this seventh month on the Day of Atonement—to bring the ark to rest in the Holy of Holies as God had prescribed and offer sacrifices for the sins of the thousands of people gathered for the feasts of the Lord.

A sense of humility filled him at the enormity of the fast that was about to begin for him and his people. Would his foreign wives honor Adonai and participate in Yom Kippur and then Sukkot, the Feast of Tabernacles, to follow? Would they even understand the meaning of the forgiveness of sins?

He walked down the hill toward his waiting chariots. Pride had once swelled in him at the grand accomplishment. The work on this and his own palace, which was still in progress, and Siti's palace—not to mention trying to keep his other wives happy in a crowded harem—had distracted his mind from the sobering questions he had pondered most of his life. But to finish exactly at the moment God had assigned all Israel to repent of their sins had shaken all sense of pride and accomplishment. This structure had come about because God had intended and allowed it. Solomon had merely followed in obedience.

Surely God would take that obedience into account, wouldn't He? Hadn't God spoken to him during the middle of this great project?

As for this temple you are building, if you follow My decrees, observe My laws, and keep all My commands and obey them, I will fulfill through you the promise I gave to David your father. And I will live among the Israelites and will not abandon My people Israel.

Surely he had obeyed the exact specifications to create this grand structure. He glanced back up the hill where the temple stood like a gleaming light—a symbol of salvation for the nations. He released a sigh. And at last it was almost complete.

He turned to continue his descent, his guards following yet allowing him space. The Egyptian gilded chariot and matching mares stood waiting, the beasts pawing the earth in almost regal splendor. God had indeed blessed him.

If you follow My decrees . . . The thought intruded like an unwanted guest. He had done as God asked.

But the thought of the three hundred additional wives of royal birth who had entered Israel since his talk with Zabud that day years ago, when his friend had suggested he stop accepting the gifts of nations, mocked him. How was he supposed to refuse such gifts? He had looked into the matter from every angle and discovered it was simply impossible. How could he accept the gifts of the first three hundred countries or tribes, however small those kingdoms, and refuse those yet to come?

"My lord king." Benaiah approached and bent one knee, a welcome distraction to his occasional guilt.

Solomon motioned him to stand. "Walk with me, Benaiah. Tell me what you know." Benaiah had been protecting his family since the days of his father's kingship, and though he had aged, Solomon had no doubts of his ability to command the troops.

"The elders of Israel, all the heads of tribes and chiefs in Israel, have arrived in Jerusalem, my lord. The priests are ready to bring the ark to the temple tomorrow on Yom Kippur." He glanced Solomon's way as the two approached Solomon's chariot.

Solomon climbed to his seat behind his driver and motioned for Benaiah to join him. His commander acquiesced and Solomon gave the order to return to his father's palace.

"I want you to inform the elders and all of the people to gather at the tabernacle my father built and follow the priests to the temple mount at dawn," Solomon said. "They already know the fast begins tonight at sundown, but I want the trumpets to sound throughout the city to remind the people, to call them to begin the fast."

"Consider it done, my lord." Benaiah inclined his head and dismounted as the chariot came to rest in the palace compound. Solomon allowed a servant to assist him and guards flanked him as he climbed the steps and entered the palace.

So at last the ark of God would rest in the place he had built for it. Already he could hear the lowing of cattle and bleating of sheep from the fields outside the city. Tomorrow the priests would count them after carrying the ark to the Most Holy Place, where they would put it beneath the wings of the cherubim. Then they would sacrifice 22,000 cattle and 120,000 sheep and goats on God's altar to atone for the sins of every man, woman, and child in Jerusalem. They would dedicate this palatial structure on the grandest scale Solomon could offer. It was the best he could do for his God, who was worthy of that and so much more.

—⁓—

The following day, Solomon arose before dawn and dressed simply, not in his regal splendor but as one of his people. A simple circle of gold on his head set him apart, and of course the guards would not leave his side, but he had sensed throughout a night of fitful sleep that he needed Adonai's forgiveness as much as the people he ruled did. Perhaps more.

They arrived at the tabernacle before the crowds, and Solomon removed his sandals and walked behind the priests, his heart humbled with each step toward the temple mount. Crowds quickly appeared in the streets, walking in groups or two by two a good distance from the ark carried on poles by the priests.

He glanced about him for a brief moment, noting his mother and Tirzah walking with Naamah, her children, and Abishag. From another direction, on the outskirts of Jerusalem, he saw some of his many wives enter the area surrounding the mount, the place where foreigners were allowed. He looked toward Siti's palace, hoping. Would she set Bastet aside to worship with his people?

He continued on, following the priests as far as he and the rest of the people were allowed, and waited as they entered the Holy Place. Silence had descended as though it was darkest night, not early morn. He bowed his head, praying, waiting. Would God accept the priests? Had they done everything according to His law? He had warned them over and over not to make the mistake his father had made when they'd tried to carry the ark on a cart instead of the prescribed poles.

Time moved slowly, and he sank to his knees in the dirt outside the temple structure. He would not move to the outer court until the priests had safely returned from placing the ark between the cherubim in the inner sanctuary. *Please, Adonai, let them be acceptable in Your sight.*

The sound of the people kneeling disturbed the silence but a little. Solomon put his face to the earth, praying, when at last he heard the sounds of moving feet coming toward him. He looked up to see the priests withdraw from the inner sanctuary. Relief spread through him, and he slowly stood. Zadok and Zabud and many other priests emerged, but before they were fully down the steps about to begin their service of sacrifice, a cloud descended, filling the temple so fully the priests were unable to complete their work.

Solomon stood, mounted the steps to the outer court, and turned toward the people, then faced the temple once more. He lifted his hands heavenward and spoke. "The Lord has said that He would dwell in a dark cloud. I have indeed built a magnificent temple for You, a place for You to dwell forever."

He waited a moment, longing to hear some type of affirmation in his soul, but realized in a heartbeat that the cloud's presence was acceptance in itself. God was pleased with the work. Joy filled him as he sensed Adonai's pleasure. *Thank You.* Emotion overtook him. He blinked and swallowed twice.

He turned to face the people once more and blessed them. "Praise be to the Lord, the God of Israel, who with His own hand has fulfilled what He promised with His own mouth to my father David. For He said, 'Since the day I brought My people Israel out of Egypt, I have not chosen a city in any tribe of Israel to have a temple built so that My Name might be there, but I have chosen David to rule My people Israel.'

"My father David had it in his heart to build a temple for the Name of the Lord, the God of Israel. But the Lord said to my father David, 'You did well to have it in your heart to build a temple for My Name. Nevertheless, you are not the one to build the temple, but your son, your own flesh and blood—he is the one who will build the temple for My Name.'

"The Lord has kept the promise He made: I have succeeded David my father and now I sit on the throne of Israel, just as the Lord promised, and I have built the temple for the Name of the Lord, the God of Israel. I have provided a place there for the ark, in which is the covenant of the Lord that He made with our ancestors when He brought them out of Egypt."

Solomon turned again and stood before the altar of the Lord, his gaze resting on the cloud as he remembered the voice of God he had been privileged to hear, then raised his hands once more toward heaven. His prayer rang out across the compound and spread to the people surrounding him, but his heart was no longer focused on the people or his wives or advisors or guards or even the priests. He saw only Adonai, his Creator, and he knew that for all of this work, God did not reside in a temple made with human hands. He was not like Bastet or Chemosh or Molech or any other god his wives worshiped. The people needed to know Adonai and to pray toward this temple to Adonai alone. For only He forgave sins. Solomon silently prayed that God would forgive his as well.

When at last his prayer ended, the cloud lifted enough for the priests to offer the sacrifices of Yom Kippur along with fellowship offerings to the Lord in dedication of the temple. By late afternoon, Solomon also saw to it that the middle part of the courtyard in front of the temple of the Lord was consecrated, and there he offered burnt offerings, grain offerings, and the fat of the fellowship offerings, because the bronze altar that stood before the Lord was too small to hold them all.

By nightfall the people returned to their lodgings and Solomon to his father's house, but the Feast of Tabernacles, Sukkot, continued until the people had celebrated before the Lord for fourteen days. At last Solomon sent the people home. As they went, they blessed the king. And there was great joy in Israel.

CHAPTER

THIRTY-FIVE

The litter carried Siti through the East Gate and up the grand avenue that lined the way to Solomon's gleaming new palace. It stood like a gem between his father's older living quarters and the temple, which outshone both residences on the mount where it stood beyond Solomon's walls.

Bathsheba still reigned as queen mother, and she resided in the home of her husband along with Naamah, Abishag, and many of Solomon's other wives and concubines.

Siti stared through the slit in her curtained pavilion, awestruck at how much work her husband had accomplished in so short a time. But he had thrown himself into one extravagance after another until she feared it was her initial encouragement that had opened the door to his reckless testing of all things good or evil.

Had she pushed him too far? Asked too many questions?

Her team of Edomite servants stopped in the courtyard that was once King David's home and lowered the litter, then helped her alight. She met Akila on the steps, and her maid walked one step behind her as she entered what used to be Solomon's audience chambers, now used by lower judges and secretaries to handle Solomon's enormous business affairs.

She continued past scribes and recorders and men with bent heads in heated discussions, toward the halls that led to Bathsheba's chambers. Siti had often invited her mother-in-law to visit her own place of residence, but Bathsheba had quietly and gently refused. Siti sensed the reason had to do with the many images to Bastet she had put in prominent places. Though Bathsheba was kind to her, she had never accepted her foreign ways. To her credit, she never accepted the foreign ways of any of Solomon's wives and concubines.

A guard greeted them with a polite nod, and moments later Tirzah bowed to her. "Come, Siti. How long it has been since your last visit." She led her to a plush couch and quickly placed cool wine in a goblet of pure gold before her.

Bathsheba emerged from her chambers moments later, still in the process of knotting the belt of her robe. "Siti." She smiled as she walked toward her.

Siti stood and took Bathsheba's outstretched hands but did not miss the dark circles beneath the queen's eyes. "Did I wake you? I can come another time if you are not well." Bathsheba had always seemed the essence of health to Siti. To see her looking so tired, haggard even, was deeply troubling.

"No, no, my dear girl. I was merely resting." She motioned her back to the couch and sat near her in her favorite chair. "I fear I am not quite as young as I used to be."

She studied her mother-in-law. "But you are well?" In the black land where she came from, they prepared for death all of their days. But here in this place where so much frantic building activity commenced, where Solomon continually acquired exotic wealth—not only horses but apes and peacocks, silver, ivory, and gold of Ophir, which surpassed any gold she had ever seen—death seemed far from anyone's thoughts. Solomon had already built a tomb for his father, and his mother would one day reside there, but he seemed to take no thought to building his own tomb. Not like the pharaohs in her land did. Perhaps he thought he would never die.

"I am well," Bathsheba said, drawing Siti's mind back to her. "I grow more weary of late, but I am only tired. No illness has come upon me." She accepted a cup of cold water from her maid and drank. "So tell me, Siti, how have you been?"

Siti glanced at the liquid in the golden goblet—one of Solomon's gifts, no doubt—and sought the right words. "I am well, thank you." She glanced at Bathsheba. "But I have come because . . ."

The queen waited and her smile warmed Siti.

"I must confess to you that I fear I have caused Solomon to lose sight of the things he once thought important." She released a slow breath. "This is harder to say than I thought."

"You blame yourself for Solomon's frantic living." By the queen's look, Siti knew she understood.

"I fear . . . that is, in the beginning, I tested him. I was angry with him for not allowing me the freedom to worship my goddess in this place." Siti waved a hand over the room. "Even in the privacy of my rooms. So I challenged him, and then I made it my goal to see if he was really as immune to the laws he was breaking as he claimed."

Bathsheba's gaze remained steady, but Siti wondered what thoughts moved behind her troubled eyes.

"I didn't expect him to go so far—" Her voice caught, and she could not finish the thought.

"You did not expect him to test the gifts God has given to him." Bathsheba's voice held a hint of sorrow, and when Siti met her mother-in-law's gaze, she saw much knowing in her smile. "My dear Siti, you are not to blame for my son's choices. He has always been inquisitive, even as a child. But when our God granted him wisdom, I knew he would test its limits. He would not be who he is if he hadn't. But I fear he pushed his wisdom so far that he forgot the one who granted the gift."

"Has he stopped worshiping your god then?" She felt as though the air had somehow left her lungs at the thought.

"No." She took another sip from the goblet, then set it on a low table beside her. "No. I don't think he would go that far. But he has gone too far in some areas. His excess has surpassed anything I could have imagined." She sighed, and the weight of her comment was like a grand obelisk between them.

"What can I do?" Siti had not seen Solomon in months, and she wasn't sure she could just walk into his new palace, his new audience chamber, as she had years before and coax him to spend time with her. "Does he visit Naamah or Abishag any longer?" Shame heated her face, though she knew from her experience in a king's harem since her birth that this was the way of things. At least she could live her life in peace, surrounded by familiar things and people from her homeland. But she missed the one thing she had longed for more than the familiar. She missed the love she once thought Solomon would give her. And Bastet had yet to grant her a child.

"When he visits me," Bathsheba said softly, as though she, too, rarely saw her son, "he visits some of his wives as well. I do not think he stays long." Her smile was sad. "I am sorry you are forced to share his time. I was privileged to have much of my husband's affection, but our beginning came from far different circumstances. Sometimes suffering brings people together in a way prosperity never can."

Siti saw the slightest glimpse into her mother-in-law's past by the shadowed look that passed over her face. Solomon had told her some of his parents' history, and court gossip had filled in other details, but Bathsheba had never shared much with her. Perhaps because she was a foreigner. But perhaps more because she did not ask.

"I do not wish to see the king punished by his god because of something I caused." The thought had troubled her for weeks, months even, though this was the first time she had voiced her fear. "What might your god do to him for the foreign gods we have brought to your land? What might your god do to him for disobeying the laws given to kings?" She paused, clasped both hands more tightly around the goblet. "Please, my queen, tell me how I can undo the hurt I have caused." Though Bathsheba denied there was any wrongdoing on her part, her heart said otherwise. She was guilty. Her own arrogance had fed her questioning of his. She had to make things right.

Bathsheba stood and walked to her window, her back to Siti, who waited, begging Bastet to grant her wisdom. And in a blind moment of fear that such a prayer might offend Yahweh in King David's house, she even said a silent prayer to him for forgiveness.

Bathsheba turned and perched on the edge of her seat.

"Siti." She extended a hand and Siti took it, startled by how cold Bathsheba's fingers felt. "You must stop fretting over what is done. If God allows you to speak to my son, to tell him you were wrong, to tell him whatever you feel is best, then so be it. But my son will continue to be driven by the beast that wisdom has brought him. I fear . . ." She looked away for a moment as though trying to regain her self-control. "I fear that he worships the gift over the giver. And he sees himself as too wise to do wrong, for he believes his wisdom will stop him. Someday he will find he is wrong. But neither you nor I can tell him so."

She squeezed her mother-in-law's hand in a gesture of gratitude, but her heart felt heavy with the realization that Bathsheba carried a far greater burden than she. "You fear deeply for him," Siti said. "You fear he will be lost in his pride." For wasn't that what drove him?

But later, as her litter bearers took her home again, without her taking the time to attempt to find Solomon, she wondered if it wasn't pride that drove her as well. If she had not been so self-assured that she would be proved right, she might have bowed to Solomon's wishes and set Bastet aside. Was Bastet not as Solomon said, an object of stone and jewels made with human hands?

The thought made her insides quake with such a sense of disloyalty that she could barely stand straight once the litter stopped at the steps to her palatial home. Home. Where Bastet's grand figures stood on either side of the doors, much like Solomon's lions stood beside his throne.

Both were cats, images to remind them of power. So why were hers so wrong? And why had Solomon not been by to visit since Bastet had taken her rightful place?

She lay awake too long that night, and though she knew she would not be at her best, she decided she must see the king before the day was out. She needed to understand. And she needed to appease her guilt.

But a knock on her door too soon before dawn put an abrupt stop to her plans.

Akila rushed into the room. "My lady," she said, her voice still fighting the sleep that had eluded Siti. "There is news."

"Tell me." Though she knew by her maid's look it was not good.

"The queen . . ." Tears filled her eyes, and Siti's breath hitched as she sensed her next words.

"Has taken ill?" she interrupted.

Akila shook her head. "Far worse than ill, my princess. They say she has passed into the underworld." Her wide eyes showed more white than their normal deep brown. "How will she pass the tests of Osiris? She knows nothing of the gods or the things to say to enter eternity."

Siti shuddered, knowing it was true. Bathsheba would not have spoken with her of her gods even if Siti had tried to explain them to her. Solomon's response to them had told her that much. "Their god is different than ours, Akila. They have another path to travel than we do," she said. Didn't they? Suddenly she could make no sense out of any of it. She sank onto the edge of her bed, her limbs weighted and useless. "But how can she be gone? I just spoke with her yesterday. She tried to comfort me. She told me she was not ill, just tired." But hadn't she seen it in her eyes? She was weary beyond normal weariness. "Surely there will be a funeral." She was speaking just to hear words now.

Akila nodded. "The king will send word when the time comes."

She stared at her maid and wondered. Would Solomon allow his foreign wives to attend the burial of his beloved mother? Would he be thinking clearly at all?

She stood, suddenly filled with too much energy. "We will not wait. We will go to King David's palace and do what we can." She hurried to gather her clothes after Akila tied a strip of blue linen around her head with the ends hanging down her back—a symbol of mourning among her people. "Have the servants burn incense to their god in the queen's honor as well." It was the least she could do.

—⁓—

The cry of mourners greeted her long before the old king's palace came into view, despite their speed. She had commandeered a chariot for Akila and herself rather than the slower, more leisurely litter. Though Ra's bright rays had yet to return to the land of the living, people lined the streets, clothes torn, ashes on their heads. Bitter weeping grew louder the closer they came, and her heart raced with each clomp of the horses' hooves.

Her Egyptian chariot driver stopped at the back entrance, as close as they could get to the queen's rooms, and she fairly ran up the steps and into the brightly lit halls. Servants scurried here and there, and women's voices buzzed like the high-pitched thrum of bees. She made her way past the rooms that housed Solomon's wives and concubines, not stopping until she came to Bathsheba's door. She paused, though the guard barely paid her notice.

She peered into the room, saw Naamah and Abishag and

Tirzah huddled together in one corner of the sitting room while servants stood with basins and ointments near the queen's bedchamber. Suddenly she felt like an outsider in this place, for though Naamah was an Ammonite, she embraced Israel's god. Abishag was Hebrew and had held the faith of her people all her life.

Siti glanced at Akila, who nodded encouragement. She was Solomon's wife, after all, and one who ranked high among his many women. She belonged here, she told herself, though her heart slowed in uncertainty as she stepped over the threshold. She walked, head high, toward Tirzah and the other two favorites of Solomon and Bathsheba.

Tirzah rushed forward and took her hand. "Siti. How good of you to come."

Emotion filled her as she glimpsed the tears in the old servant's eyes. She pulled her into a warm embrace. Siti had never considered herself so above such women that she could not show kindness. Had she been born to a different family, it could be she who stood in Tirzah's place. "I am so sorry for your loss," she said when Tirzah pulled back and tugged her closer to the huddled group.

Siti glanced at Naamah first, then Abishag, and her heart stirred for them. "What do you know? I just spoke with her yesterday. How can this be?"

Naamah lifted her chin, and for a brief moment she sensed the old jealousy that the woman had exhibited when Siti first moved to Jerusalem as Solomon's bride. She couldn't blame her, really. Not when she had been his only wife for those first few years.

"She has not been well." It was Abishag who spoke, easing the tension between them. "It is not like the sickness King

David suffered. But I could tell she had grown weary, as if life had become too much to bear." She looked beyond her, and Siti turned at the sound of footsteps.

Solomon approached, his dark eyes swollen from weeping, his gaze distant, as one who dreams.

She stepped aside and allowed him to approach them, longing to take his hand, to comfort him. But she waited. Naamah deserved to be the first to comfort him, if he would allow it.

Naamah moved to close the gap between them. "My lord." She knelt before him and clasped his hand in hers.

He looked down, and it seemed he knew he should speak, but no words came.

Naamah kissed his ring and stood. She touched his face, brushed the hair from his eyes. "Please, my lord, come and sit. Let us get you something to drink, to soothe you."

He looked at her as though seeing her for the first time. "Soothe me?" A hardened look swept through his brooding eyes, like the flame of buried anger. "My mother is dead. There is nothing that can soothe that." He looked at each of them, his gaze resting on Tirzah.

"Oh, my boy," Tirzah said, coming toward him, her arms outstretched.

His dark eyes softened, the hardness crumbling. He pulled his old nurse into his arms and wept.

Despite Solomon's greater height and strength, it was Tirzah, bent and aging woman that she was, who led Solomon to a couch and coaxed him to sit. She sat beside him, and he rested his head on her shoulder, an action Siti had never seen from him. Not like that. She had never seen her husband grieve.

"What will I do without her, Tirzah?" Solomon's voice cracked, and she wished there were not so many servants milling about to hear the sorrow, the weakness of their king.

"You will rule Israel as you always have, my son," Tirzah said, her voice strong, though it carried a slight tremble. "And you will do the things you know she would want you to do. Obey the Lord and walk in His ways, as your father David did." She spoke other words, softer now, that Siti couldn't hear.

She glanced at her rivals, but they were caught up in watching Solomon, tears drawing lines down their cheeks. "Is there anything we can do?" Siti asked them when at last Solomon straightened, tore his robe, and took ashes from a pot a servant brought to him and poured them over his head.

"As the king has done, we will do," Abishag said, glancing Siti's way. She and Naamah walked closer to the king, sat on the floor, and followed his example.

Siti stared, trying to make sense of this custom, but decided now was not the time to show her foreign ways. She walked toward them, grateful she had thought to pull a Hebrew robe over her narrow shift, grabbed its collar and ripped it as she had seen the others do, and then sat among them farthest from Solomon.

He did not look her way, nor at anything in particular for the longest time, until she thought her feet would go numb from her cramped kneeling. But despite the quiet among them and the wailing in the other parts of the palace, she found something sacred in this moment. A son who grieves his mother so profoundly is a son who loved her well.

Siti wondered if he would grieve for her, for she was certain beyond all doubt that he did not love her as he had loved Bathsheba. If his mother had feared the direction of his choices while she lived, what would become of him with her gone?

———✺———

Hours later, Solomon stood dressed once more in royal finery at the head of the largest crowd Siti had ever seen. Gone was the grieving boy Tirzah had held in her arms. Returned was the king whose tears and bitter cries the people of Israel expected to see when they reached King David's tomb. It was the nature of royalty, which she knew far too well.

Bathsheba's body was not mummified as bodies were in her country, but rather lay on a gilded bier, lifted above the heads of the mourners, and carried before Solomon.

She followed, dressed in the garments of the Hebrews to honor her mother-in-law, though she did not stand as close to Solomon as Naamah and Abishag and their children did. Tirzah wept quietly beside the king, a great privilege for her that Siti was grateful to witness. Perhaps his old nurse would fill the role his mother had carried, as Siti often turned to Akila for comfort. But something inside her did not think so.

The heavy doors of King David's tomb squealed as they were pried open, and the crowd silenced as Solomon, tears still dampening his beard, turned to face them.

"Many among you once thought my mother an adulteress and a woman unfaithful to our God, to Yahweh. But I am here to remind you that not one of us who walks the earth walks it in complete integrity. There is no one righteous before our God, not even one. And though my mother stumbled and my father sinned against her, our great God granted them both grace and mercy. And in His kindness, He set me upon my father's throne, the secondborn son of my mother, who devoted her life to teaching me to observe all of Yahweh's commandments." He paused as though the words were too difficult to say, and Siti saw his Adam's apple move.

He looked over the crowd. "I charge you, by the grace of the I Am, our mighty God, to remember my mother with kindness. To preserve her memory for the good she has done. And when you pray for me, for yourselves, do not forget that our God is a forgiving God. My mother knew that better than I. Better than any of us. May we learn from her life and know it too."

He turned and nodded to the men who still held the bier aloft. Silence fell as the men carried the body of the queen into the tomb. But in the silence, Siti's heart still beat to the tune of Solomon's eulogy. His words were nothing like the words of the priests of her people. He did not say all the right prayers to guide his mother to a place of rest. It was as if he already expected her to be there, without the gods to guide her.

She struggled to understand. When he turned once more to dismiss the crowd, his gaze caught hers, and she could not keep the questions from her eyes. If only he could make her see. He had tried, she knew, but she could not grasp this strange thinking. There should be far more rituals involved, far more rites invoked. His mother did not even take her jewels with her into the tomb.

Solomon said something to Tirzah, then approached Naamah and Abishag. His children wrapped their arms about him, some of them already grown men and women, others barely reaching his knee.

Siti stood watching, alone in her beliefs. Alone in her confusion, wishing she had someone besides her maid to hold her close and love her too.

THIRTY-SIX

Solomon walked alone, followed by a contingent of guards, from his royal palace to the temple grounds. Three days had seemed like an eternity, and the walls of his home had grown oppressive, closing him in. His heart ached with grief too deep to bear as he nearly stumbled up the incline and had to shoo his servant away when the man raced to his side. He wasn't an infant who needed to be caught when he fell.

Sometimes a man fell to his knees of his own accord.

Sometimes he had stumbled out of sheer drunkenness, truth be told, but he was not filled with wine now. He had thought to drown his sorrow in strong drink, but wisdom told him that nothing could numb the pain of his loss.

Oh Adonai, how do I live without her? Such a foolish question it seemed for a man grown. It was not like she saw him daily or advised him on how to rule the kingdom. The truth hit squarely in his gut that he had neglected her more than he should have in recent days. Even recent years.

Ever since the temple's building project had consumed him, he had thrown himself into his work. And Siti's accusations of his disobedience to Adonai had provoked an almost fevered spirit in him to test his wisdom, to find meaning in life with one extravagance after another. Yet his wisdom had always won out, and he had proven to himself that whether rich or poor, it was always better to be wise than a fool. Happiness had often eluded him in his quest, and if he admitted the reason, he would have concluded that despair often accompanies great knowledge. But that had not stopped his desire to know, to be, to discover, to taste and see and wonder.

And the busyness had kept him from pondering Siti's questions. But it had also kept him from visiting his mother as often as he once had. The sting of that realization now felt like a heavy weight bearing down on him.

How did a man deal with such grief? If only he had been a better son. If only he had asked after her, visited her, brought her to live in his palace. But she would not have left his father's house, no matter how much he might have coaxed.

He reached the outer court where the altar and basin sat waiting for the evening sacrifice. Soon the priests would begin the nightly ritual and offer bulls and lambs on God's altar. He wished in that moment that he could go in and sit before the Lord as his father David had once done at the tabernacle, but the closest he could get was to enter a side room or the entryway, for no one but the priests and Levites could enter the temple sanctuary.

He climbed the steps to the doors and went as far as he was allowed, then knelt on the smooth floor, listening to the silence of the room. In the distance he heard the voices of priests and Levites, but they were muffled enough for him to block them out.

O Adonai, give attention to Your servant's prayer and his plea for mercy, Lord my God. Hear the cry and the prayer that Your servant is praying in Your presence this day. May Your eyes be open toward this temple night and day, this place of which You said, "My Name shall be there," so that You will hear the prayer Your servant prays toward this place. Hear the supplication of Your servant and of Your people Israel when they pray toward this place. Hear from heaven, Your dwelling place, and when You hear, forgive.

He had prayed that prayer on the day of the temple's dedication, but now . . . now it carried a personal edge. *Please forgive me for failing her.* How much he missed her! The weight of guilt did not lessen with the prayer, and he wondered if a sacrifice was expected. But the guilt he felt—was it actually anger at the Most High for taking her from him so soon? Or at himself for failing to be what he thought a son should be?

He rose slowly, head bowed. The cloud that had appeared at the dedication did not reside there now, though Solomon sensed that God's name still remained among them. But Siti had been right in her questions, and he should have listened to her and been more obedient to his God.

There is no one who does not sin. He knew that too well, and his heart told him that every excuse he had given to his wife was simply justification to pursue his own desires. Had not wisdom taught him anything? Was he to be bound to the longings of human flesh even with such a God-given gift?

He turned and went back the way he had come. There was some solace in coming to this place where he did feel somewhat closer to Adonai. But it wasn't until he took up his stylus and parchment and wrote his thoughts about his mother that he found greater relief. The walls of the palace no longer closed in on him.

However, though some of the weight lifted, his grief remained.

———m———

"More ambassadors are entering Jerusalem, my lord," Zabud said the next day after Solomon's fairly sleepless night. "They are here to pay their respects to your mother and have brought gifts to you to console you."

Solomon looked briefly at his priest, his friend, from across a table where they sat on his private balcony breaking the morning fast, then glanced beyond him. Zabud often stopped in early to check on him, especially this past week. Would he ever feel normal again?

"Did you hear me, my lord?" Zabud plucked a grape from a golden platter and popped it into his mouth, spitting the seeds in a small golden bowl.

Solomon took up his cup and sipped the tea, now cooled. "What kinds of gifts?" He cared not who visited, though that should have been his first question. He was in no mood to entertain ambassadors from foreign lands. Not yet. Maybe not ever again. Would that he could have crawled into Sheol after his mother.

What foolish thought was this? He had a kingdom to run and wives and children to keep him fully occupied, not to mention the building, expansion, and protection of the great land his father had left to him.

"More royal princesses are among those riding with the

contingencies from some of the more distant countries, and a few are from countries with which we are already allied. Hiram's Tyre is among them."

The mention of his father's friend caused Solomon to meet Zabud's gaze. "Hiram is a good man."

"As are many of the ambassadors waiting for an audience with you, my lord. They bring gold and silver and precious stones, of course, but the prizes they hope you will accept are the daughters of the kings who sent them." Zabud lifted his cup and drank, a deep sigh following.

Solomon stood and moved from the balcony to his chambers. Zabud rose and followed at a slight distance. "Why do they continue to offer me royal brides when I have already married a half sister or cousin in the same kingdom? They are trying to ruin me." *Like Siti.* "They want to see me reject my God and worship theirs. It is exactly the kind of thing Siti questioned and pushed for—not only to worship her Bastet but to allow her to do so in my father's own house!" He paced until his legs grew weary, and he sank onto a couch, his heart aching more deeply than it had before his friend's visit.

"My lord, you are a great king. The greatest in the world. You have it within your power to refuse the daughters of these kings, and that would not change their vassal state. They could not possibly come up against Israel's might and win." Zabud sat on the edge of a chair opposite Solomon.

Solomon stared at him, running the comment through his mind. To refuse them could spark anger, and anger could spark war. And while he had no doubt his men would fight under Benaiah's leadership, he had no heart for war. God had promised his kingdom peace. Did that mean he was just supposed to expect God to protect them while going on to provoke foreign nations who came to him? Or was that peace given in part because Solomon did all in his power to make it so?

"God would protect us, my lord," Zabud said, as if reading Solomon's thoughts. "He told your father yours would be a kingdom of peace."

"But does that remove all obligation from me to pursue that peace? Wisdom tells me no. Wisdom tells me that I must also play the part of peacemaker." He looked away, fighting a sense of growing anger. "But I am not ready, Zabud. Not for ambassadors, nor more wives of royal birth. And I have no need of wealth. Send them home." He stood again, restless, and walked back to the balcony to retrieve his cup. He snapped at a servant, "Have fresh tea made and make sure it remains hot."

The servant nodded. "Yes, my lord." He hurried from the room.

Zabud followed Solomon to the balcony again, where both men stood at the railing and looked toward the temple. Below them a stream of animals wound its way from the road leading to Jerusalem, laden with gifts and led by men wearing the colors of foreign lands. Camels with curtained pavilions obviously carried the princesses Zabud had mentioned. The line of men and animals spread beyond the temple out of Solomon's view.

"They have come a great distance, my lord." Zabud hesitated a moment, and Solomon glanced at him. "I am not saying you must accept their gifts, but perhaps allow them to refresh themselves here and welcome them, accept their condolences."

Solomon ran a hand through his hair, not caring how disheveled he looked. He walked back into his chambers and stopped at the threshold to his private sleeping quarters. His back to Zabud, he spoke softly. "You know, Zabud, I have no other desire than to sleep, to wish the world away. A man should be allowed time to grieve, even a man such as I." He faced his friend, searching his expression for some wisdom, some answer.

"Take your rest for the morning, my lord. I will command your servants to find accommodations for the visitors and have your cooks prepare meals for them, and if you still do not wish to join them tonight at the banquet, I will offer your apologies. The least we can do is give them three days to rest before sending them away, would you not agree?"

Solomon's mind whirled, his heart pulling him toward the quiet room, longing to shut out the world. But duty told him a king didn't act this way. Wisdom warred with longing until he wanted to toss the mantle of kingship away. But at last he met his friend's gaze and nodded. "Your plan is wise. And I will do my best to meet with them before three days have passed."

"Very good, my lord." Zabud bowed and left him.

Solomon crawled into his bed, trying to stop his mind from churning, wondering if he would have the courage to send the emissaries home without accepting a single gift.

THIRTY-SEVEN

A week passed, and Siti spent little time outside of her bedchamber. She felt listless, lifeless, and wished she held Solomon's drive for projects. She could remake the rooms in her palace, call in new designers to rearrange or recreate new tapestries and pottery. Perhaps a trip home would help, if Solomon would allow it. To see the Nile again, to gaze upon her mother and father one last time.

She petted Abdukar, whose once young, soft fur hardly rippled when she stroked him. He had thinned, and his fur had grown coarse in these past years. She would lose him soon. She looked at her faithful furry friend, Bathsheba's loss too close to her heart. Abdukar would be buried with the same dignity Lapis had been. But she could not do so here. He should be buried in Bastet's temple at Bubastis. The thought spurred her to finally move from her couch. She called Akila to join her.

"I want to go home," she said, stiffening at her maid's raised brow. "I wouldn't stay, of course. But I want to see my parents one more time before they take the path Bathsheba took." She looked down at her aging cat, then met Akila's gaze. "And I want to secure safe passage for Abdukar when his time comes. I just need to get Solomon to allow it."

"That could be difficult, my lady. They say he has shut himself up in his palace and won't even attend court since the last ambassador left. He is still buried in his grief." Akila moved around the room to straighten things Siti had tossed about in her boredom.

"True. But that should make him understand my request all the more." She stood. "Gather my finest clothes. I am going to see if he will allow me into those rooms." Her gaze glanced off Akila's skeptical one. "If nothing else, perhaps I can comfort him."

—⁂—

Gaining entrance to Solomon's palace was far easier than Siti expected, though she was not sure why she thought it would be so difficult. She was a king's wife. Surely that allowed her some privilege. But when she stood before the doors to his private chambers and saw the lion's-head carvings, so different from her Bastet yet so similar, she felt the old questions rise in her again. But she could not ask them now. Not after he had suffered such a loss.

The guard knocked and spoke with a servant inside Solomon's rooms. The door shut again. She waited, fearing he would deny her visit. But sometime later, after she thought to turn around and return home, the door opened and Solomon himself greeted her.

He extended his hand and she took it, but once the door closed behind them, his arms came around her so fast it took her breath. He held her in silence, as though he were clinging to something he dared not lose.

"Siti," he whispered against her ear. "I am glad you came."

He drew her into his expansive sitting room, and in the next few hours he fed her sweet fruits and wine, spoke of his mother, and told her stories of his youth that he had never spoken of before, filling in with greater detail the time when they were all forced to flee Jerusalem to escape his brother Absalom.

"Your kingdom suffered much in the years of your youth," she said when that story ended.

"Much of it due to the hatred of the previous king's kin, some of it the consequences of my father's sin." He looked beyond her. "I am sure one day I will suffer for my sins in a way my father did not."

"What sins, my lord?" She came and knelt beside him, but he pulled her up next to him instead.

"Was it not you who accused me of breaking the laws of my God?" His brow lifted in curious thought. "You know what sins, Siti. And many more since, I am sure. No man is completely pure in heart."

"Then how can they pass through the underworld? For if they cannot pass the test of a pure heart, they will be lost forever." The question came before she could stop it. She had not planned to speak of such things today. But by his look, he did not seem offended.

"Clean hands and a pure heart come from knowing when we have failed our God's standards and repenting. As my father repented when he took my mother, who at the time was married to another man." He took her hand and squeezed it. "Repentance brings a pure heart, Siti."

"So it does not matter if one knows the right things to

say to the gods as we pass through the underworld?" But she already knew what he would say.

"Nothing we can say or do aside from 'forgive me' will give us safe passage with our Maker." He stroked her hair, and she loved the way he sifted the strands from her face. He leaned close until she felt his breath, his lips brushing hers. "Can we not speak of loss just now? I am weary of tears." He kissed her then, gently, fully, as he had in the early days of their marriage.

She wrapped her arms around him and let him lift her into his. Their love was better than wine, and she gave herself to him with all her heart.

———✦———

Surprisingly, Siti stayed with Solomon for the next three days, as though she were a new bride and this was their wedding week. And she sensed, though she dared not believe it, that life had quickened at last within her. She did not think she had ever loved any person more than she did Solomon in those moments.

She said nothing of her suspicions, of course, because there was no way to prove such a thing for months to come. But as their time together came to its natural end, as all things do, and Solomon set to return to court, she finally found the courage to speak the words she had come to ask in the first place.

"My lord." She took his hand and gazed up at him, her smile soft, warm. "I would like to take a trip—with you, if you will have it—to visit my homeland, to see my parents once more." She kissed him lightly, then stepped back to watch his expression.

He stroked her cheek, his gaze kind. "You are homesick, my love? After such a time as this?" He glanced around the room, then searched her face with his intense gaze.

"Israel will never be like Egypt, my lord. And to be completely honest, I want to prepare a place for Abdukar when he passes, if you will allow it. He should be enshrined in Bastet's temple in Bubastis." She squeezed his hand, intertwining their fingers.

"Abdukar still lives, does he not?"

She nodded. "Yes, but he is not long for this world."

His brows drew down, a look she had seen often these past few days. "I am sorry to hear it. But does this mean you will take Abdukar with you and wait until he passes? You could be gone years, my love."

She had not considered that, nor how long she might stay. "I will bury him here then. I will simply buy the things I need for my servants to mummify his body when the time comes. But please, let me visit my family one last time." She hated to beg, but she knew that once she left these rooms, she would not be back for a long time. Solomon had too many other obligations, too many wives, too many foreign dignitaries coming from all corners of the world, too many building projects in Megiddo and Gezer and the Millo, and a fleet of ships the likes of which she had never seen. Not to mention his other palace in the forest of Lebanon, which she hoped he might take her to see one day.

He cupped her cheeks and looked intently into her eyes, but she did not flinch. "You will accompany my men when they make the next purchase of horses and chariots from Thebes. You may stay six months but no longer. The next group of men will bring you back."

Her heart felt lighter at his words, and she threw her arms about his neck, kissing him soundly. "Thank you, my lord! Six months will be plenty of time." She tilted her head. "But you will not join me at the first?"

He shook his head. "I cannot get away just now. Perhaps I will join the men who bring you back." He kissed her forehead, and she knew their conversation was at an end. "Give your parents my greetings."

"I will," she promised, smiling. She turned toward the door, for she recognized a dismissal when she saw one, and walked to the hall. Akila would return to gather her things when Solomon left for court. In the meantime, she hurried along the corridors to her waiting litter. She was going home.

Grace Note

The Teacher felt the wind in his face as the chariot took him through the streets, over the hills, into the gardens and parks and all of the places he had built for the sheer pleasure of doing so. *Pleasure*. In his wisdom, he knew happiness had to be found in wealth, in work, in all of the things a man seeks in his short life under the sun.

When had pleasure become displeasing?

The chariot came to a halt before the great city of Gezer. He gazed on the work his men had accomplished here. The knowledge that he had gained this great asset should have satisfied. Yet what good was a city, even fully rebuilt, when one day it would be captured again and someone would destroy all that he had done?

Disquiet threatened as it often did during his years of seeking to understand this life. Even wine and singers and beautiful concubines did nothing to bring meaning into his aimless heart. Surely God could give him some sense of worth. Couldn't He? Was there to be no joy in doing the work God had given him?

Must life be so endlessly repetitive and his pursuits so futile? *Because both the fool and the wise end up in the same place*. This too was meaningless.

CHAPTER
THIRTY-EIGHT

The air in the audience chamber where Nicaula ascended her throne bore a sticky feel, despite the scent of the pleasing frankincense burning in the sconces. The summer rains would be upon them soon, yet she already felt sweat trickle beneath the weight of the golden crown as she took her seat. Slaves lifted heavy palm fronds to cool the air—a welcome respite. She smoothed her elaborate gown and matching gold and purple robe, then took the scepter from her vizier, who waited patiently to sit on her right.

Najib was a comely man, one she had considered a near equal, one who could make a mother of her—if the law allowed it. How was it that her next in line for the throne could marry and bear children while she, Sheba's queen, must remain barren and unloved? She ignored the ache to her middle that such thoughts evoked and nodded, unsmiling, in Najib's direction.

"Did you rest well, Najib?" she asked as the buzz of her

299

courtiers' voices filled the chamber. He normally did not speak to her until she spoke first to him. It was custom. And they always followed custom.

"Yes, my queen." His mouth twitched into a half smile. A striped turban adorned his dark hair, and a blue robe with golden threads cloaked a trim body. The robe gave status to his role as her underling and heir apparent—at least until such time as she chose a child to follow in her stead. "Have you given any thought to the candidates brought to you a fortnight ago?"

The question was one he asked almost daily now, since Nicaula had commissioned him to search for another young female she could adopt. Ten years was long enough to grieve, at least as far as her advisors were concerned.

She met Najib's gaze but could not hold it. "No. I have not had time to meet the candidates." The truth was she had no heart to tear an infant from her mother. And the unwanted children who roamed the halls of the temples to their gods either were too old or had been handpicked to be priestesses. Her healthy fear of angering the gods kept her from choosing one from the temple grounds.

"You really must consider someone soon, my queen. The advisors are growing restless." Najib spoke truth, for she had seen the looks of impatience, yet still she put them off, claiming it was her right to do so.

"What? I should think you would be glad to be the one to rule after me if no one is chosen." She mocked him with her tone, but she knew by his look that even he did not wish to go against the ruling council who oversaw the goings and comings of Sheba's monarchs.

"At the rate you are waiting to choose, my queen, should

anything happen to you—may the gods forbid it—I myself
will be in my grave before this child is old enough to handle
matters on her own." He stroked a narrow beard that was
not truly a beard. His chin looked like that of a goat more
than a man, but it was his preference, so she said nothing.

"I will choose soon," she said, feeling suddenly cross over
it all. Besides, she still entertained a crazy notion of bearing
a child for the sake of love. It went against all of Sheba's
protocol, but hadn't such things been written of in their
poetry and sung in their songs? Why was their monarch the
only one who looked with longing on the idea of love yet
was denied its very pleasures?

This question was only one of many that plagued her in
the quiet moments of the night, or when she stood on the lat-
ticed balcony of her rooms and stared up at the lush mountains and waterfalls in the distance, wondering how such
beauty had come into being. Were the gods of her people, the
sun and moon and creatures of the earth, to be worshiped
for such magnificence? When she gazed at the heavens and
pondered, she felt only confusion. For despite the legends of
Astar, the sun goddess, and Sin, god of the moon, she saw
them more as heavenly beings than the powerful creators of
good and evil they were claimed to be.

A commotion at the end of the audience chamber drew
her attention away from her troublesome thoughts. Hadi,
her lead war general, approached the throne. She extended
the scepter. He touched its tip and bowed low.

"What news do you bring to me, Hadi?"

He rose up on one knee but did not look up. "I have news
from the north," he said.

"You may rise and speak."

He did so and nodded. "The king of Israel has sent a fleet of ships to the narrow passage of the Red Sea, near our ports. He has sent servants into our lands on the western shore to search for gold and baboons and spices and more." He paused, and she knew he held back more than he was telling her.

"Why would he do such a thing? Why not simply send to me and request these things? We have hunters and miners who search for gold and jewels and those who grow and cultivate the precious oils. For a price, he can have all he wants. Surely this king of peace I have heard of is not looking to start war with our own peaceful kingdom?" She narrowed her gaze at him, her mind churning. Why would King Solomon not send ambassadors to meet her? If he wanted an alliance, he certainly knew how to get such a thing, if the rumors were true.

"I do not know, my queen. Obviously either King Solomon thinks these lands fall under his rule—perhaps one of his other alliances has misled him—or he does not realize how vast a kingdom you command." Hadi dipped his head, and when he met her gaze again, she saw a look of determination there. "If you let me, my queen, I will take men and meet his ships and confront his captain. If need be, I will travel to Israel myself and speak to the king on your behalf."

"We have ambassadors for that, Hadi. I am not looking to start a war by sending my general." She stroked the scepter with one finger, the questions racing again through her mind. Solomon, supposedly the wisest of kings, should know the size of her kingdom. No, this was more than that. He was attempting to provoke something from her. But what?

Hadi cleared his throat and she blinked, realizing her distraction. "We did not know until now that King Solomon had built a fleet of ships to gather the spices and gold and animals he craves. I fear, my queen, that he will take what is ours and use it in trade with distant northern lands, replacing our camel caravans. Ships move much faster than camels, for the route is safer, almost uncontested."

She considered his words. There was no possible reason that Solomon would ignore her sovereignty. He had to know the boundaries of their lands, which spread from the south of Arabia to its tip, across the narrow channel of the Red Sea, and west, encompassing African lands. "Tell me what else you know about this king."

She had heard the rumors, of course. Solomon had built up Jerusalem and its surrounding cities with enormous buildings and palaces and stables for his chariots and horses. One of his wives, from Egypt, had a palace of her own, while others lived in opulent buildings fit for the princesses they were. But the most prominent rumor, the one she had pondered on her bed in the night, was of his wisdom. They said he was the only one who understood the riddles of the world, the riddles of the human heart. If he was truly so wise, why would he seek to incite her kingdom?

"You know, of course, my queen," Hadi said, standing stiffly at attention, "that it is said King Solomon is the wisest of men, that he understands the riddles of the gods."

"Of the gods too?" Would the exaggerations of his wonders never cease?

Hadi nodded. "He is also the most ambitious of kings in all the east." He met her gaze beneath a shock of dark hair showing below his bronze helmet.

"No one understands the gods or their ways, Hadi." She

challenged him with a look, but at the same time, her heart beat faster.

"Yes, my queen. But people have come from far and near to hear him speak about plant life, from the cedar of Lebanon to the hyssop that grows out of walls. They say he also teaches about animals and birds, reptiles and fish. They say his wisdom exceeds any man or woman in all the east and that it is his god who has given him this treasure."

She looked briefly at her court, then met Hadi's gaze once more. "You have become quite smitten with what these people say." She stared him down, waiting for him to admit that his sources were simple gossips spinning a wild tale. She wanted him to tell her that her heart was wrong, that the longing to hear this man was foolish. But her commander did not flinch. She sat straighter and lifted one sculpted brow.

"I would not lie to you, my queen." If he was affronted by her words, he did not show it.

She glanced at Najib, but he simply shrugged. The rumors surely had reached him as they had her, but neither of them had spoken of this king in more than amusing terms. There had been no need to until now. Now that his ships were invading their ports.

"Well, it seems that King Solomon has made one foolish choice," she said, sitting straighter. "His ships have entered the waters of our land without seeking my approval. Perhaps this king thinks a kingdom ruled by a woman is of little consequence?"

Hadi stood still a moment, as though not sure he should respond, but at last slowly shook his head. "My queen, I doubt that he has come in contact with any kingdom such as ours. His alliances with foreign kings have included marriage to many princesses . . . if the rumors are true." He paused and she waved him on. "Though he is said to have married more women than is prudent—"

"A mark of a fool for certain." She smiled, convinced she had made her point well enough.

Najib laughed softly and Hadi's lips curved upward. They respected her enough to know her feelings about any man who saw a woman as someone to adorn an arm or fill a bed or beget children—despite her hidden desire for one man's exclusive love. She was surely the foolish one to want something she could not have. But she would never say so.

"Yes, my queen, but the truth remains. Foolish or wise, Solomon has determined to take a risk and sent his ships to rest near our ports on the west side of the sea, and his men are scouring those lands even as we speak."

She studied Hadi, gauging his mood, her mind whirling. She had never been faced with such a situation. They were a peaceful people. No one had ever attempted to take what they sold so willingly. What motivated this foreign king to pursue even more than he'd been given? For the rumors also told of his great wealth, to the point that she could not fathom such a thing. Silver as common as stones? Impossible! Yet the questions continued. How? Why?

"What would you have us do, my queen?" Hadi looked to her, but he glanced briefly at Najib as though one person alone could not handle this problem. Or perhaps one woman alone.

"I have no intention of going to war with this man, Hadi. Sheba is a kingdom of peace, and I intend to keep it that way."

Hadi nodded. "Perhaps we can send the ambassadors

then, to explain his violation and garner a trade agreement. I could take a select number of soldiers to make our point." His eyes glistened, and she wondered if he was anxious to fight such a powerful man, which could only end up with Hadi at the end of a stake.

She shuddered and looked at him as the voices of courtiers droned beyond her. Najib tapped one foot—an annoying habit—and she caught the motion in her peripheral vision. She gave him a withering glance. He stopped.

She stroked her chin with one long finger and looked from one man to the other. What she wouldn't give for some wisdom now, to know how to approach this extravagant king and garner the trade agreement Hadi suggested. She sensed Solomon would not be easily persuaded. He would want a wife from among their people to seal their contract, and she had no desire to add to his ever-increasing harem.

Hadi shifted his weight from one foot to the other, but otherwise he showed no impatience with her silent pondering.

"Which god does he serve?" she asked at last. "If his god is so powerful, perhaps we can appease him to gain some of this wisdom for ourselves."

"They rarely use his name, my queen, but in my travels I have heard an Israelite or two quote their call to prayer, their Shema, which says, 'Sh'ma, Yisra'el! Adonai Eloheinu, Adonai echad.'"

Nicaula did not know why, but she shivered as the words fell from Hadi's lips. The buzz of voices around the throne room silenced, as though they were all held under a deep spell simply by hearing this call to worship and prayer to Solomon's god. Though their languages differed slightly, she understood the meaning. *Hear, Israel, Adonai our God, Adonai is one.*

Her whole being felt a sudden, joyous peace she couldn't explain. Hadn't she grown up worshiping sun and moon and beasts and stars? Yet she had never felt such peace in doing so.

"It is time I met this king," she said, surprising herself and wondering at her own sanity as she listened to the gasps throughout the room.

"Meet him, my queen?" Hadi's look told her he, too, thought her mad. "Surely a trip from our ambassadors would suffice."

Of course he would expect her to take his suggestion. What queen had ever traveled from this land to another country? What queen had ever left her rule to an underling? None. And her suggestion was ludicrous even to her own ears.

"We will send a servant with Solomon's ships to announce our coming arrival, and our ambassadors may join me," she said, refusing to back down despite her own sudden misgivings. "But I will travel to him. Arrange a caravan of camels. We will need to gather many gifts."

If Solomon were to join in an agreement, he would need appeasing, despite what he already possessed or had possibly already taken from her lands. She would give him those rare spices that he seemed anxious to claim, and more—gold and jewels and . . . her questions. Surely the wisest man in all the earth would enjoy sparring with an equal. And no doubt he had never met an equal of her caliber, for this was the era of kings, not queens. The anomaly of her existence as a ruling monarch should intrigue him. Perhaps in return, he would answer the questions that even her priests found vexing.

Hadi cleared his throat in the palpable silence. She put

her excitement on hold. "Speak. For it seems you will not leave until you do."

Her commander's ears reddened. He was not one most people spoke down to, but she found herself suddenly irritated with his obvious objections. "The journey is long, my queen. It will take many months, and certain sections of the highway can be perilous where bandits hide in the crevices of the rocks."

"Then I expect we will need an army of protection to form a wall around my retinue and my gifts." She crossed her arms, the scepter tight against her chest as she stood and drew closer to him. He did not move, as she had not given him leave. "I am going to Jerusalem, Commander. Whether the journey takes months or years, I am going. I expect you can handle the preparations for all I will need?"

He gave a slight bow. "Of course."

"Good. We will leave in one month, not a day more." She dismissed him then and glanced at Najib. "I expect you can handle the kingdom in my absence."

He nodded.

She left the room, knowing a month was not nearly enough time to prepare all they would need. Her servants would do what they must to make it work. And the kingdom would be in an uproar at her parting. But something in her would not shrink back, as though an unseen force beckoned her. Was this why Solomon had sent his ships to her ports? To draw her to him like some flighty princess begging for favors?

Solomon was in for disappointment and surprise if he expected that from her.

CHAPTER

THIRTY-NINE

The courtyard buzzed with life even before the sun made its debut in the eastern sky. Nicaula accepted the help of a servant to settle into the curtained pavilion positioned on the camel's back. The contraption resembled the one carried on poles by a litter of slaves, but its position over the hump of this gangly creature was not nearly as comfortable. The beast made her stomach lurch with the slightest movement. She squeezed her legs tight to the camel's sides and held on to the horn of the saddle, forcing herself to look straight ahead and not down. The ground, even from the camel's sitting position, seemed far, and when her servant climbed in front of her to guide the animal and bid it rise, she felt her head spin.

Her grip turned her knuckles white, and she was glad for the curtain that hid her from the watching men below. Najib would find concern in her weakness, and she could not worry him—especially when she had left him without an heir. She would address the decision of her heir upon her return, she promised herself. Perhaps Solomon would be able to advise her on the best way to solve this dilemma that seemed to constrict her heart.

She straightened, placed one tentative hand on her middle, still gripping the saddle with the other, and peered through the slit in the curtain. The other camels were rising on command, and soon it seemed as though the beasts had overrun her entire courtyard and the area beyond the gates.

The camels moved forward into a definite rhythm, and as the sun rose higher in the sky, she felt the sway keeping time with her pulse and grew used to the pace. She had no choice but to do so, for the trek to Jerusalem was not like a simple visit to the Red Sea or even a short barge ride to the other side of her kingdom. No, they had months of travel ahead of them, and she told herself to get used to the discomforts and think ahead to what awaited in Jerusalem.

Weeks passed in unending sameness, with the only change being the view from the camel's lofty height and the different faces she glimpsed as they passed through various cities. Her retinue took over the barren landscape outside the towns, while the camel drivers carrying their wares for sale camped closer to the cities' gates in order to trade with the merchants at dawn.

The sun dipped, suspended at its odd angle as it always was when night approached, and the lead camel came to a stop and lowered itself on knobby knees. Her driver followed the rest of those ahead of them in their typical straight line and helped her gain her footing on the unmoving earth. She'd grown used to this pattern, but by day's end she longed for her tent and her cushions and sweet wine and cheese and a place to lay her head. It took time for her servants to raise the tents and put everything to rights, so she called Fadia, her maid, to her side and walked with her toward the shores of the Red Sea.

"Fadia, I grow weary of sitting every day with nothing to do. No cases to judge, no work whatsoever." No queen did the tasks of a simple servant.

"How taxing it must be for you, my lady," she said, keeping one step behind Nicaula. "If you wish, and if it is not too disagreeable to you, I could show you how to work the bone needles and stitch patterns while you ride." Her voice dropped in pitch on the last few words.

Nicaula stopped and looked at her maid.

Fadia's cheeks flushed in the glow of nearing dusk. "Forgive me, my lady. I only thought to help."

Nicaula studied this woman who had spent more time at her side than her own mother and yet in all her childhood years had never once offered to teach her such a thing. Her mother, of course, would have never allowed it. Princesses could learn to draw and paint and create intricate mosaics and even play musical instruments and write poetry, as most of her people could read and write in their native tongue. But princesses and especially queens did not spin or weave or work with flax or wool—or worse, with goat's or camel's hair. Even intricate needlework, artistic though it may be, was left to the artisans and the peasants.

"Your offer is not one you would have made in Sheba." She looked into her maid's plain face, but Fadia would not meet her gaze.

"No, it is not, my lady." She clasped her hands and kept

her head bowed, for despite their closeness, her servants rarely spoke freely with her—a tradition long-standing in her realm and one she sometimes despised. How she longed for a companion of her rank! But in Sheba's borders, sovereigns were above all others.

"We have many restrictions. But of course, you know this." She turned to continue walking and Fadia followed, as Nicaula knew she would.

"Yes, my lady. I know it. But these seem to be circumstances that warrant change, and I thought . . ." She paused.

Nicaula glanced back at her. "You thought well, Fadia. I would like to learn this skill of which you speak. I feel as though my hands have become imprinted with the saddle's horn, and though I look now and then through the curtains, the landscape changes little. I find myself counting the movement of the sun across the sky, and even it moves faster than we do." She did not care that she was complaining.

She looked behind at the guards who followed them—another custom she'd lived with every day of her life. They were as much a part of her existence as Fadia, though they did not come so close. On this trip, she knew they wished she would stay near the confines of the camp. Most of the time she did so, just to ease their anxious minds and to escape Hadi's concerned lectures—as though he were king and she his underling! Sometimes he came close to insubordination, but she allowed it simply for someone to talk to who honestly cared for her well-being. Even queens who are loved by their people are still alone and often misunderstood at the end of the day.

"Would you like me to begin showing you tonight, once the tents are raised?" Fadia's tone had taken on an air of excitement, and Nicaula wondered how often she, too, had longed for someone with whom to share her skills or the things that brought her joy.

They stood now on the shores of the Red Sea, listening to the rhythmic lapping of water against the sands. She glimpsed her guards flanking them at a slight distance on either side.

She glanced at Fadia. "I would like that," she said, satisfied with the smile that suddenly wreathed her maid's face. "After we dine." She turned to look out at the water then, while Fadia simply stood behind and waited.

Nicaula gazed up at the display of colors spread like fingers across the darkening sky. Soon stars would fill the landscape, and the place where the earth and sky kissed would be so black the two would be indistinguishable. A perfect time and place to share such beauty with a beloved.

A stirring in her heart awakened her senses. How different life would be if she found someone to love as a man loves a woman. If her lot had fallen in places that allowed her such a thing. Why had she been so chosen? Why was she, a queen of such a vast kingdom, denied the most basic of pleasures?

Her heart ached as she looked down at the crab that scurried past near her toes. She stepped back a pace and watched it bury itself in the sand. If she could hide her intentions as easily as the tiny animal hid its body, perhaps she could come away different after this visit with Solomon. Would his wisdom fill the longing for purpose she craved?

Yet his wisdom, no matter how great, could not undo the traditions of her people, the histories long past that had set these rules in place. Rules that allowed Nicaula her own sort of wisdom to guide her people but also kept her prisoner within the confines of her realm, her safely guarded world.

Until now. The thought came unbidden, and yet . . . hadn't she embarked on a journey of change, upsetting the status quo of all that her people understood and had abided by for centuries?

She glanced heavenward once more, caught the last splashes of color dripping from the heavens to the waters below. The sun god had taken his journey to a place she could not go, and soon the moon would rise to guide them. But somehow even her gods did not bring her the direction or comfort they once did. Even they seemed to sense the change stirring within her.

Jerusalem could not come soon enough.

FORTY

Solomon tapped one finger aimlessly along the golden mane of the lion head that graced the arms of his throne. The audience chamber carried a noisy buzz of male voices—his courtiers, his scribes, minor judges, and endless servants. Standard-bearers stood at attention near the antechambers, and guards held drawn swords at the doors to his throne room.

He listened in silence as two men approached, asking him to judge between them. Twin brothers who could not seem to agree on which of them should get the bigger portion of their father's land.

"You are telling me, then," Solomon said, after he had heard enough and his patience had worn thin, "that no one is able to tell which one of you came first from your mother's womb? There is no midwife, no mother, no older sister or grandmother who has this information?"

One twin looked at the other, but the expressions on their

faces held nothing but animosity for each other. They shook their heads almost as one. "No, my lord. Our mother died years ago, as have all of the women who were near at the time of our birth. We have no sisters."

Solomon stared hard at them, but neither squirmed beneath his scrutiny. Odd. Perhaps his wisdom was failing him, but he was finding it harder to read a man's thoughts by his expression.

"Have you a younger brother?" he asked after a lengthy pause.

This time both men looked at the tiles beneath their feet. "Yes. There is a younger brother who is seven years behind us."

"Good. Then the land shall go to him and neither one of you shall receive the double portion. Let the youngest brother receive what could have gone to one of you had you not fought so hard to get your own way." He waved a hand in dismissal, unwilling to hear their protests. Both he and his father had not been the firstborn, yet God had elevated them above their brothers. If older brothers thought they stood a chance with him, they had better come with greater humility and a compromising heart.

He looked at his recorder, Jehoshaphat. "How many more cases are on the list for today?"

Jehoshaphat glanced down at his scroll, where he had been given the names of Israelites and foreign dignitaries who all waited in the outer court or antechambers for an audience with the king. An audience that Solomon was in no mood to give today. "There are at least twenty yet waiting to be heard, my lord king. One in particular has come with the captain of your ships from the land of Sheba. If you see no one else, I believe you might want to hear what this man has to say."

Solomon lifted his chin, his gaze narrowed. His fleet of ships had been one of the biggest accomplishments of his realm thus far, one in which he took great pride. He had sent them to various distant lands in search of exotic animals for his zoo and spices for his vast dining needs. The most recent trip had been to Sheba, where he had hoped to secure some of the rare spices and animals he had heard of from foreign ministers.

"Who is this man who traveled with my captain on my ships? One of Sheba's ambassadors?" He knew the land of Sheba was far from Israel and ruled over by a woman, if the tales were true. But why send someone to see him? Perhaps he had unknowingly violated some right they felt belonged to their land.

"I believe the man is a simple servant in the queen's court, my lord. He does not dress in the manner of a royal ambassador." Jehoshaphat scratched his bearded chin with the end of his stylus, then quickly stopped, his gaze barely touching Solomon's.

"Send him in. I will speak to him but no one else. I am weary of struggles today." He glanced away as his recorder turned to a servant to give the orders.

The buzz in the room increased at the news that the king would see only one more person today. So be it. He was tired of the mantle and crown, and he needed time away to think. To walk among the lilies or fields near his palace. How he wished to escape the guards and disguise himself as a normal peasant, to see and hear what his people really thought of him. But he was not sure he actually wanted to know such a thing. And it would not be safe. His guards would never allow it.

His chest lifted in a sigh as he waited for the courtroom to clear of the extraneous people, and the man of Sheba was escorted to the steps below his throne. He bowed low until Solomon extended the scepter and told him to rise.

"Speak and tell me why a servant of Sheba's lands has come into my ports on my ships."

The dark, thick-boned man wore the simple white tunic of peasantry, yet the quality of the material spoke of wealth. His robe of dark rust reminded Solomon of a deeper shade of poppy. He kept his head slightly bowed in respect but his shoulders straight in a posture of authority. This servant was used to dealing with kings, or at the very least his queen.

"My lord King Solomon, may you live forever." He dipped his head once more, his words carrying an accent Solomon had not heard before but found pleasing to the ear. "I have come ahead of my queen to inform you that she is on her way to Jerusalem even as we speak. She would allow no ambassador to speak with you but wanted to come to meet with you herself."

Solomon lifted a brow. At times foreign kings visited his court, but more often they sent their ambassadors, at least at first. This distant queen suddenly intrigued him. "Tell me, good man, why did she think it necessary to make such a long journey? And if she wanted to make the trip, why not seek passage on one of my ships? My men would have happily made room for her retinue."

"Our queen made the decision to come by camel caravan after she heard that your ships, my lord, had entered our waters and that your men were searching our lands for animals and spices, commodities that our people use in trade or sell for profit. She felt it necessary to visit you to see the purpose for the king's ships seeking to take from us what she would have willingly sold or given to him."

"Ah, I see." So his captain had gone too far in searching for animals and spices without seeking the queen's right to do so. No doubt she was coming in anger or at least in an attempt to seek a trade agreement. The humorous thought that she was coming to put him in his place crossed his mind, but he did not smile. "When she arrives, I will be pleased to meet with her," he said, his gaze fixed on the man.

"My queen will be glad to hear it. She has heard of the wisdom of King Solomon and intends to ask him many questions." The man bent one knee, then took a step back. "She should arrive within about four months, if all goes well."

So this queen was an intelligent person, coming a great distance to satisfy her curiosity. And most likely in need of a promise from him to no longer invade her lands. "Thank you," Solomon said. "You may go."

He must speak to his captain of this invasion of lands. The man knew better than to violate the sovereignty of other kingdoms. Solomon had made it a point to be at peace with his neighbors, his many concubines a testament to that fact.

He stood before the man had completely exited his chamber and descended the steps of his throne. He glanced back at the golden lions and caught sight of the spot where a throne used to sit, one he had brought in for his mother's use. The memory caused an ache in his middle. He turned away, walked through his private side chamber, and took the steps to the ground floor where his chariot waited. Guards moved at his nod and he climbed aboard. He said nothing as they drove slowly forward toward his palace.

As he sat in his chambers later that evening, nothing felt right, and he wished for the place that as a child he'd called home.

CHAPTER

FORTY-ONE

FOUR MONTHS LATER

Nicaula glimpsed the gleaming walls of Jerusalem long before the camel's gait slowed in the trek upward. The city was set high on a hill that made a defensible fortress. Walls lined every side with gates along various points, obviously meant to accommodate certain types of travelers.

Their camels drew along the Kidron Valley to the east of the Gihon spring. Her driver had informed her that they would enter through the Water Gate, check in at the armory, and then enter Solomon's city to the north. The southern part of Jerusalem, she was told in her talks with Hadi, had belonged to King David's rule.

She parted the curtains with one hand as they rode past the smaller capital that had once belonged to the famous David, whose kingdom stretched much farther than this singular city. It was said that David was the one who had conquered his enemies and lengthened the borders of Israel from the north near Syria to the Negev wilderness in the south.

As her camel crossed the narrow brook to approach the Water Gate, she could see that Solomon had built his city to be more than twice that of his father's. How much more, then, the vastness of his kingdom?

"With so many foreign wives, my lady," Hadi had said the night before they entered Israelite territory, "Solomon's kingdom stretches even beyond that of King David's. No enemy remains, for he has married the daughters of all opposing kings."

He chuckled at the thought, and Nicaula smiled in response, despite her earlier consideration that such a practice made Solomon a fool. She thought the whole thing completely ludicrous. How could a man build palaces, let alone rooms, for so many women? Hundreds, they said. She shook her head. She longed for one man to love, and Solomon had his pick of a different woman every day.

"I suppose he never grows bored," she said, suddenly struck with the awkward feeling that she would be the only monarch to approach this king without an alliance of marriage to offer. She had no daughters to give to seal a trade agreement or to convince this king to stay far from Sheba's shores.

"No, I suppose he does not," Hadi said, before she bid him good night.

She pondered long on the matter as she lay in her tent that final evening before they would enter Jerusalem's walls. Pray Solomon would accept her offerings—her gifts of spices and jewels and gold—as enough, for she could think of nothing else to give. Surely the frankincense and myrrh alone would entice him, for they were the richest and rarest of spices, and she had made sure that Solomon would receive the best of the crop.

But as she arose the next morning to Fadia's ministrations and her last ride on that insufferable beast—at least for many months—she worried. Would it be enough? And would King Solomon not only answer her questions and sign their trade agreement but also find her a worthy equal? She suddenly wanted that more than anything else that had brought her on this journey.

They passed through the Water Gate without trouble, and once her guards announced her presence at the armory, King Solomon's attendants sent word to the palace. Solomon's own guards led them to a grand building to the right of the palace where he received his guests. Opulent rooms spread before them, and she found herself whisked away to one draped in curtains of deep reds, with gold interlays lining everything from floor to ceiling. Wood carvings were also overlaid with gold, and she had to close her eyes against the glare of the light coming through the many windows and sparkling off the precious metal. Rich white carpets covered intricately tiled floors, while couches dyed in more of the deep reds had been placed in various sections of the large room.

She entered, weary and wary, and was met by one of Solomon's maids, who quickly offered her a seat and removed her dusty sandals. "I need more than a foot washing," she said, wishing now that the Gihon had been large enough to bathe in and that she'd found a way to do so. "My whole body is dusty from travel, and I need to change into better robes before I meet the king."

The maid nodded but did not meet her gaze. "Begging your pardon, my queen. If you will allow me to wash your feet, then they will be clean for you to walk about the room while I have the servants draw you a bath. The king would have you settle yourself and take your rest until this evening. Then you will join him at a banquet in your honor."

Her honor? How quickly had word traveled that he would know of her coming to prepare for a banquet so soon? But she did not ask. She would find out presently.

She extended her feet for the maid to wash and nearly melted into the chair as the girl also rubbed the ache from her toes and heels and arches. She applied a salty scrub to Nicaula's skin that she said came from the Dead Sea. Solomon spared no expense on his guests. But what did he expect in return?

The maid left after guiding her to the place where servants would fill a large bath with heated water. The room was already steaming from a fire set under heated wet stones near the high windows. Nicaula walked out, waiting until all was ready.

"Have you ever seen anything so amazing, simply for houseguests?" Fadia approached, her hands empty—an unusual sight. But here she was Nicaula's only attendant, not her servant in the way Solomon's maids were. Where Fadia would have been the one to wash her feet, Solomon's servants did the task for both of them.

"It is astounding, my lady," Fadia said, taking the seat offered her. "My rooms are larger than two of our houses back home." She fidgeted as she said it, but Nicaula knew she meant no censure of their homeland.

"It's all right, Fadia. I know that our kingdom is small in comparison. We may have land and wealth in what we can grow and the gold we can mine, but our people are not as wealthy as Solomon's people." She touched the threads on the tassel of a curtain. "We do not weave gold into our tapestries." Only her robes had such design, not her furnishings. But she kept her awe to herself. What kind of man had she come to see?

Suddenly she wondered at the wisdom of her visit. She felt small in comparison to what she had already seen, and this was only the beginning. Would she measure up to Solomon's women? Would she have the ability to converse on par with men her equal, or would the king look down on her simply because she was female?

These questions added to the many others she had entertained all her life. She could not help but consider that perhaps there were no solid answers.

FORTY-TWO

Solomon sat at a table of cedar overlaid with gold, the cushion beneath him also woven with fine gold. The stylus and parchment were spread before him, and birds chirped in the windows that opened on either side of this paneled room where he spent hours, sometimes long into the night, putting his thoughts to record.

He could have enlisted the help of a scribe or recorder but had long ago decided that there were some things that were better written than spoken. He'd grown weary of speaking with his officers and visitors and wives and concubines and their servants who constantly approached him with requests. His children were growing up like olive plants about him, and he barely knew some of their names.

He blew on the ink of the words he had just written, then ran a hand over the back of his neck. When had life become so trying? Did he not enjoy the work? The wealth? The wisdom? He had spent years building the temple, his palace, Siti's palace, and the Millo, and fortifying the cities he had gained. His servants had built a fleet of ships, and his men traveled to and from foreign countries to buy and sell chariots and horses and sell them in turn to other foreign kings. He had gold more plentiful than any kingdom before him and silver so plentiful even the common people thought it worth little.

He was a good king. Wasn't he?

He looked down at the words spread before him.

I, the Teacher, was king over Israel in Jerusalem. I applied my mind to study and to explore by wisdom all that is done under the heavens. What a heavy burden God has laid on mankind! I have seen all the things that are done under the sun; all of them are meaningless, a chasing after the wind.

What is crooked cannot be straightened; what is lacking cannot be counted.

I said to myself, "Look, I have increased in wisdom more than anyone who has ruled over Jerusalem before me; I have experienced much of wisdom and knowledge." Then I applied myself to the understanding of wisdom, and also of madness and folly, but I learned that this, too, is a chasing after the wind.

For with much wisdom comes much sorrow; the more knowledge, the more grief.

Did he truly feel so morose?

The sounds of servants moving through his house accompanied the voices of his officers outside his open windows. Birdsong started and stopped in the trees in the surrounding gardens. Perhaps a walk in the gardens would clear his mind.

He stood, letting the chair scrape across the wood floor. A servant appeared from a side room and offered him his royal robe, which he normally discarded in this place. He allowed the man to attend him, then moved from his private writing chamber to his favorite of many gardens that graced his palace. A soft breeze sifted the hair from his face, and he blinked at the sunlight streaming through a minimum of clouds.

Zabud approached from a stone-laden walkway. "My lord, at last I have found you."

Solomon peered at his friend and narrowed his gaze. "Am I so hard to find?"

Zabud touched a hand to his friend and slightly bowed. "Forgive me, my lord, but sometimes you seem to disappear from public view, and with so many projects and places for you to visit, the search can be a challenge."

"My guards always know where I am, Zabud. You flatter me to think I can escape them." How often had he wished that? Since his childhood when Benaiah had protected his father—and now Benaiah and his sons still did the same for him. Not to mention the many guards who protected his wives and children. Or the thousands of men who managed his household, his food supply for so many people, including foreign visitors, and his forced labor—the number was staggering, even for him. And yet among so many people, he could not escape the people, the work, himself.

"What is it you seek, Zabud?" He was suddenly in no mood for a conversation that reminded him of all he had left his private quarters to put behind him.

"I have news. I believe you will find it pleasing, my lord." Zabud smiled, and Solomon sensed the man was enjoying this game they played far too often.

"Tell me quickly then, so I might enjoy this pleasure."

"The queen of Sheba has arrived and is even now in the

guest rooms you have provided for her. The banquet is ready for her tonight." Zabud waved a hand in the direction of the banquet hall, smiling.

Solomon gave him a steady look. "Everything went smoothly at her arrival?" Somehow knowing this woman had traveled so long and so far to see him had caused him to want to prove his worth to her. Strange, since he did not know her or anyone from her lands save the messenger she sent.

"There has been nothing reported that has not gone exactly as you requested, my lord." Zabud clasped his hands behind his back. "The banquet hall is gleaming and the aromas coming from the cooking rooms carry throughout the audience hall. She will be delighted with the feast. I am sure of it."

"No one can be sure of how another will react, Zabud. Especially a woman of rank. But I am glad she has arrived safely and that my servants are treating her well." Solomon turned a corner in the path to head back to his palace, and Zabud caught up with him.

"Might I help prepare your wardrobe, my lord?"

His head attendant had already picked out every item he thought Solomon should wear for this event, but Solomon sensed nervous tension in Zabud's desire to do what his servants normally did.

"You may." Solomon moved forward and Zabud drew back a step. Suddenly Solomon was not sure he wanted his friend's attention, for his heart beat with its own anxiety. What would this woman be like? And why had she truly come?

—⁂—

Solomon stood motionless, staring at the door to his private writing chamber. Somehow the words he had penned earlier that day seemed wrong, too devastating and meaningless. And yet . . . he could not shake the melancholy that had played at the corners of his mind for the past few years. Even the promise of this visiting queen could not take away his underlying anxiety. What purpose was there in answering her questions, in appeasing her nation? He had placated too many nations, garnered more wealth than any king in any land, but it could not go with him to the grave. What purpose was there to his life?

He turned at the sound of his servants and the guards who waited at his door. They would expect him at this banquet. For months he had planned to appear, and it was the right thing to do. But suddenly he was not so sure he wanted to face what lay before him. Perhaps meeting this queen would be one huge disappointment.

The guards flanked him as he strode through the wide halls of his palace and to the waiting gilded chariot. He hopped up and sat behind the driver, who led the pair of perfectly matched steeds through Jerusalem's streets to the visitation hall, where his banquets for foreign dignitaries were held. Most kings would have hosted such gatherings at their palaces, but Solomon had quickly wearied of a houseful of strangers in addition to the many wives and children who were housed in his women's quarters. A separate hall worked to his liking, but tonight he could not perceive why he struggled to regain his earlier anticipation.

Perhaps God was warning him to be cautious of this foreign queen. Or perhaps he was simply weary of the needs of too many women. How many requests had come through his secretaries just today? One hundred and twenty, if his memory served him well. And at least a dozen of his sons and a handful of daughters had requested an audience with him, most with complaints or desires for something he could surely provide.

Did no one care to visit for the sheer pleasure of his company? But he had lost that feeling when he lost his mother, if the truth were known. Perhaps Abishag enjoyed his presence without demanding anything of him, but few others came without reason. And surely none of his children enjoyed time with him for time's sake.

When had he begun to feel old? How had he missed so much of his children's childhoods? Images of his building projects flashed in his mind's eye, and he knew the blame could not fall completely on them. He had busied his life with one major project after another and fulfilled one pleasure after another without satisfaction.

The chariot stopped at the visitation hall and he descended, led by his flag bearers, trumpeters, and standard-bearers, with guards before and behind. The hall stood ablaze in color and light, and the scents of roasted meat wafted to him. Whether he liked this queen or not, at least the food was never without pleasure. And there was always escape in wine.

He waited at the entrance for the trumpets and attendants to announce his presence, then strode to his place at the head of the main table with royal grace. It was what he knew. He had grown into his role through his mother's grooming and God's wisdom, and he would play his part whether he enjoyed it or not.

One glance across the room and he caught sight of the

queen from Sheba. His heart skipped a beat. Her dark beauty shone amid the blazing candles like pure onyx in the gold of Ophir. He stared for an unseemly moment before suddenly realizing that kings did not stare. Yet he could not seem to pull away.

Who was this woman who had invaded his lands and suddenly also his thoughts, his emotions, his heart? He would seek her out after the meal. Or soon. He would give her what she came to find. Whatever she wanted, he would give all to see that radiant smile aimed at him.

Perhaps life was not so meaningless after all.

FORTY-THREE

Weeks later, Solomon stood in the early morn at the door to the rooms he had provided Nicaula, his nerves taut and his heart beating fast. He flexed his hands as he waited. Guards stood watch at a distance because he had insisted on visiting the queen without fanfare.

The door opened on the second knock, as though his first had not caught the attention of those inside. Could the queen still be sleeping? But one step into the room told him otherwise as the servant, fully dressed, fell to her knees and a gasp came from Nicaula.

Solomon let his shoulders relax as he moved farther into the sitting area. "I am sorry, Nicaula, to interrupt you so early like this. Trust me when I say that it is not my practice to intrude on the private quarters of my guests." He stopped across from where she stood. A table of flatbreads and cheeses and dates lay spread behind the queen, with fresh goat's milk sweating in their golden goblets.

"I'm afraid you have caught me just out of bed. I have not

yet eaten, for I was admiring your city from the window." She motioned with her arm to the table. "I am happy to share if you have not eaten."

He glanced from the table to her and smiled. "This must seem most strange, and while I would enjoy your company and stay to break the fast with you, I only stopped by to ask you to dress in your finest clothing and please be ready to accompany me. I want to take you to the temple for the morning sacrifice—as far as the law will allow you to see it."

He studied her reaction, saw the spark of interest light her dark eyes. He had longed for this moment since her first questions to him about life and truth and gods and what purpose men and women held on the earth.

"So how soon do you wish me to be ready for this trip to the temple?" Nicaula's voice returned his thoughts to her words.

"As soon as you are able. I will send a litter for you, for it is a long walk from here. Perhaps within an hour?"

"I will be waiting," she said, setting his heart alight.

"When we get there, I will tell you about the time my God spoke to me." He tilted his head, assessing her. "I look forward to sharing our God with you."

The scent of roasting meat assaulted Nicaula the closer they drew to the temple. Solomon had ordered an ornate litter to carry her, while he rode ahead on a white mule. Though she had seen his storehouses of chariots in a neighboring city and his stables of horses at Megiddo a few weeks before—something that he seemed delighted to show her—he did not use either mode of transportation when approaching his god. She found this intriguing but not surprising. He had admitted, after all, that anything to do with Egypt was frowned upon or even forbidden by his god, so it made sense that the king would ride the royal mule uphill from his palace to this grand temple, where he would worship.

She peered out from the curtain of fine linen threaded with golden strands to see the golden and white stone structure standing taller than any place in Jerusalem. One could glimpse the pinnacle from any distance in any direction. The beauty of the gleaming stone and golden doors and bronze pillars and altar caused her heart to beat fast within her.

The Canaanite slaves who bore her came to a stop outside the wall surrounding the temple. One of the servants reached for her hand, helped her descend, and waited until she nodded that all was well. She blinked at the sun, now past dawn, and squinted to see Solomon some distance ahead, handing the reins of his mule to a servant. He turned and smiled when he saw her. They met and stopped a few paces from each other.

"I am afraid I cannot take you beyond the wall, but you can stand in the gate and see the courtyard. The temple itself can be accessed only by our priests now that it has been dedicated to the Lord and He has put His name there." He bent to remove his sandals, an act that surprised her, and she quickly did the same. Barefoot, they walked to the low gate in the wall and stood.

Before her an altar so high it needed stairs to reach the top blocked the full sight of the golden doors. A priest stood at the altar's edge with a torch, and as her gaze lingered on him, he lit the wood beneath the animal's parts. Smoke rose upward toward the north, blackening the sky.

She shivered, turning her gaze to take in the scene before her. A bronze basin stood on the backs of twelve bronze oxen to the left of the altar. Several bronze carts filled with water were alongside the grand gold, stone, and cedar temple. But the most stunning to her eyes were the two bronze pillars, three times taller than any man, standing sentinel on either side of the temple's golden entrance.

"I understand why only priests may enter your temple. It is the same in my country, though during the festivals men may enter to cohabit with the priestesses. Children born of their unions belong to the temple, though some of the temple's children come from the poorest among us who cannot afford to feed the many mouths in their growing families." To say so reminded her of her own empty house with nothing but servants and a disturbing lack of children's laughter. "But why must we stay outside the courtyard? Surely if I were not here, at least you, the king, could enter?"

Solomon met her gaze, his dark eyes probing in that inquisitive way he had. "Our priests are not women," he said softly, "though the daughters and wives of the priests may share in the offerings given to them. The poor cannot leave their children to grow up in the temple to become priests. One must be born of the line of Aaron to enter the priesthood." He paused, and she sensed that he was deciding how much to tell her.

"Israelites may enter the court to place our hands on the sacrifices we bring, to lay our guilt on the animal that will bear our sin. We may come here to pray toward the inner sanctuary where the glory of God dwells, but we may not enter His presence. Even the priest may enter the holiest of holies only once a year lest he die."

She heard the little gasp escape her lips before she could stop it. "Whatever for? Why would a priest die simply for entering a room?" Solomon had described the building to her on their trip to Megiddo, so she understood the layout behind those golden doors. She was simply not allowed to see them.

"Our God made specific rules for how He is to be worshiped. Some of Aaron's own sons died for offering strange fire on God's altar—not this altar, but the one Moses our ancestor built in the wilderness of Judah many years before I was born. This altar is a replica, though larger, of the tabernacle of that time. Part of the tabernacle still resides at Gibeon. But my father brought the Ark of the Covenant to Jerusalem years ago, and it rests now behind the veil in the holiest place. The high priest enters that place once a year on Yom Kippur, our Day of Atonement, the day when the nation repents of its sins."

He looked away from her to watch the smoke rise higher. More priests climbed the steps, carrying the bodies of sheep and bulls and goats. The whole thing moved like a well-ordered procession. Behind them trumpets blew, and singers stood along the sides of the building playing various instruments and singing songs praising Solomon's god.

Solomon closed his eyes and she did the same, listening. How hauntingly beautiful the sound, though Solomon had to interpret the words, for her Hebrew was not as strong as it could be. The words, so simple yet so profound, caused an ache within her. Over and over they sang, "His love endures forever." Did Solomon's god love the foreigner too?

Her knees grew weak as she stood there, too overcome with emotion to say a word in response to the sight before her. Solomon seemed to suddenly sense her wavering, for he caught her elbow, steadying her.

"I'm sorry," she said softly, afraid to disturb the music. "It is so beautiful that it makes me want to weep, and I am not a woman accustomed to tears."

"Our God has that effect on us all, Nicaula." His grip tightened, and he moved them to a bench just outside the wall and sat beside her. "He is a consuming fire, and yet His mercy is new every morning. He is a great dread to those who hate Him, who refuse to obey His commands, but He shows great kindness to thousands and to generations upon generations of those who fear and love Him. We owe Him everything. We owe Him our worship. It is the spirit within you that recognizes this fact and makes your knees weak."

She stared at him. She had never admitted weakness of any sort to any man, but this was Solomon, a man her equal, at least in the fact that they both ruled their own lands. He was one who understood her need to hold tight to her emotions, and yet here he sat telling her that even he felt prone to weakness, compelled to weep in the presence of his god.

"I do not know what to say or how to respond to your god, to this." She waved a hand over the area behind them. "It is beyond my comprehension and so completely different from the worship practices of my people."

"Do those practices bring you peace and fulfillment and a sense of rightness when your worship has finished?"

How probing his questions! Even more so than hers.

She slowly shook her head. "No." To admit such a thing felt treasonous, but it was the truth. "All my life I have wondered why was I born. Why am I here? What happens to us after this life? Are the moon and the sun really controlling our lives? Does it help at all to pray to them? I have asked them, and now I am here and feel as though your Yahweh has split open my inner thoughts and pierced my heart with his flames. I am undone by this city, your buildings, your wealth, your god . . . you." She said the last barely above a whisper. "Everything I heard in my country about your achievements and wisdom is true. I didn't believe what was said until I arrived here and saw it with my own eyes. In fact, I had not heard the half of it! Your wisdom and prosperity are far beyond what I was told. How happy your people must be! What a privilege for your officials to stand here day after day, listening to your wisdom. Praise the Lord your God, who delights in you and has placed you on the throne of Israel. Because of the Lord's eternal love for Israel, he has made you king so you can rule with justice and righteousness."

He took her hand and rubbed his thumb over her palm. "You are too kind, Queen Nicaula, and you ask many wise questions. I can answer them, but first I think it wise for you to return to your rooms or my gardens and pray to my God for these answers you seek. He has pierced your heart for a reason. Let Him finish His work and fill your mind with His truth. I will send my scribe to have some of the law read to you this afternoon. Then later we will talk again." He kissed her fingers and placed her hand in her lap, pulling back a pace from her.

His humility and the loss of his nearness left her empty,

but the music behind them made her hungry, thirsty, longing for understanding. She wanted to know this god of Solomon's. She nearly laughed at the thought. She really wanted to know this god Solomon spoke so much about. She wanted Solomon to tell her what it was like to hear his god speak.

But she knew by his look that Solomon would say no more about his experiences or his knowledge of this god until she had made her own peace with him.

―⁓―

Hours later as Nicaula sat alone in the guest suite of rooms, a scribe appeared at her door, scroll in hand. He bowed low, and she allowed him to sit at a table to spread the scroll and read the words by the sunlight streaming through the window.

She sat opposite him, feeling as though she were a young student again in her mother's palace, tutored by various men and women in the fine arts of leadership and poise and all things related to ruling a kingdom. She had learned of her peoples' gods in great detail and why certain festivals and sacrifices were made each year. But as the scribe read the words of Solomon's god, she felt her heart stir in a way it never had before. Nothing in her tutelage had prepared her for the overwhelming sense of dread that filled her as he read of the blessings and curses Israel would suffer, as nations around them had suffered, if they did not obey these words.

Was her nation standing on the brink of destruction for lack of such obedience? Was she?

She shuddered at the thought as he spoke of sin and atonement and ransom for disobedience. Her mind whirled with more questions than she had brought with her on this long journey as she at last bid the scribe farewell.

The sun had begun its descent as she allowed Fadia to dress her for dinner that evening. She assumed she would dine in the banquet hall with her retinue and Solomon's other guests, but when a summons to attend a banquet in King Solomon's private quarters came through one of his trusted guards, she felt her heart quicken and her anticipation grow with each step toward those rooms.

Solomon greeted her once his guard Benaiah allowed her entrance, and she blinked hard at the royal simplicity surrounding her. Where everything about his palace, the temple, his judgment hall, and his many chambers shouted wealth and extravagance, here the royal carvings remained but the intricate tapestries and mosaics and ornamented statues were missing.

"You came." His comment caught her off guard, and she saw him nod to her attendants to follow his servant to an adjoining room.

"You asked me to." She wondered why he had chosen to meet with her so privately.

He smiled, offering his hand. She took it, aware of the differences in their skin, though her richer mix of ebony and cinnamon seemed to shine next to his swarthy good looks. Her heart beat faster at his touch, and she felt her color heighten at this familiarity. He seated her on an exquisite couch. A low table piled high with food sat before them. He took a similar couch opposite her and stretched his legs in front of him, crossing his ankles.

"Yes, but you do have the right to refuse. Just because you are my guest . . ." He paused. "You are a queen, Nicaula.

I cannot expect you to come at my command as I would a servant."

She studied him. "Why did you invite me here?" She motioned to his rooms. "We could have spoken as easily in the banquet hall." Assuming he would have positioned her near him. New guests arrived daily, and they also demanded his attention. She could not keep him to herself for her entire stay, and in truth, she feared that she would outwear her welcome and the time would soon come for her to leave.

"I wanted the privacy," he said simply. "I deduced that you would have questions for me now that you have listened to my scribe read our laws to you." He plucked a date from a golden tray. "So, now that you have heard of our God and what He requires, what more can I say to help you understand?" He ate the morsel and spit the pit into a golden bowl.

She looked at him, at the casual way he sat so comfortably before her as though they were longtime friends. Her heart quickened again at the look he gave her, for though she sensed it held respect, she also saw interest in his gaze. Interest no man had ever paid to her and she found quite intriguing.

"I find sin and atonement concepts difficult to comprehend. Your god is so exacting, so . . . perfect . . . and it is as though he expects men and women to be perfect as well. If they break his laws . . ." She looked away, ashamed to admit that some of those laws had brought conviction to her own heart. How could one possibly not covet? She coveted the life she longed for—to live with a husband and children, not relegated to the role of virgin queen all her days, never knowing love.

"You find that you have broken those laws," he said softly, as if he could read her thoughts. "As have all men. And women. Our God gave the law to our ancestor Moses to show us what it would take for us to return to the place we were created to be in, the place of perfection, of Eden."

"What is Eden?" She had heard tales of this fabled place of beginnings.

"The name of the garden where Adonai Elohim created the first man and woman. But when they broke His law, everything changed. The first sin destroyed His perfect creation, and it has never been the same since. So God provided sacrifices, as you saw today at the temple, to atone for those sins so that we could be forgiven. But it is an ongoing process that waits for a time when sin will be fully atoned for. That time is not yet."

"How do you know these things? How can the blood of an animal remove the guilt of one who covets?" She could not imagine she would ever stop longing for what she could not have. No animal dying in her place could change how she felt on the inside.

Solomon accepted a goblet from a servant and she did the same. He pointed to the food, and she allowed the servant to fill a small plate with lamb and fish and bread and an assortment of vegetables. He sipped his wine, studying her a moment. Neither of them tasted the food.

"We place our hands on the animal before it is sacrificed and ask our God to forgive our sins. We confess them. If we have wronged someone, we make restitution. Then the priest spills the animal's blood, which acts as a covering for that sin we have confessed. We accept the forgiveness and then try not to continue to commit the same sin over again." He smiled slightly. "Of course, by the next year we will have committed an entirely new set of sins."

"In other words, what I covet today might be forgiven, but tomorrow I might covet something else. Must I wait an entire year to be forgiven then?" The process was starting to make sense, but at the same time it seemed overwhelmingly impossible to keep such laws.

"Yes and no." He touched the bread on his plate but still did not eat. "We are allowed to bring sin offerings to the temple whenever we are convicted of sin. But more important, God has given us prayer. We can pray toward the temple anytime, no matter where we are. It is the prayer of a humble heart that God hears. He tests the hearts and minds of His people. He does not care about our sacrifices. He cares about our hearts."

"Now you have most thoroughly confused me." She laughed, and he joined in. "Why do you bother with the temple and sacrifices if a simple prayer will suffice?" Who was this god who heard and answered prayer? Did he hear the prayers of a foreigner who did not know him?

"May I tell you a story?" His probing gaze caused a strange stirring within her.

"Yes." She leaned forward. She loved a good tale.

"There are two, actually." He picked up his plate and they began to eat. "The first king of Israel," he said after a long pause that made her wish to hurry his words, "was a jealous man named Saul. My father married into his family and later took over, by God's design, as king. Saul would not have lost the kingdom if he had obeyed the Lord, but he offered a sacrifice without waiting for the prophet Samuel to do so for him. Saul, as king, was not a prophet or priest. Even the highest office of king cannot simply do as he pleases in Israel under God's law. So because of his disobedient act, God tore the kingdom from him and gave it to my father."

"How unfortunate for Saul, but a blessing for your father. Still, could he not have been forgiven? Could Saul not have prayed, as you say, offered the proper sacrifice, and been restored as king?" Why on earth would a king not have done so if that were what his god required? The question burned in her as she waited for Solomon to answer.

"Saul's heart was not right," Solomon said, meeting her gaze. "He was more concerned with what the people thought of him than what our God thought of him. He did not repent of his actions or pray to be restored. He continued to make things worse as time went on. He grew jealous of my father and tried to kill him, until my father had to flee for his life. He ran from Saul for over ten years."

She covered her mouth, stifling a startled sound. "How horrible!" She could not imagine having to look over her shoulder every moment for who might want to kill her.

"Saul also consulted a medium instead of praying to the Lord. That is why the Lord allowed him to die in battle and gave the kingdom at last to my father." Solomon sipped his wine and set the goblet on the table.

"So sacrifice alone is not enough." She looked into his handsome face, wondering what sins Solomon had committed that he had to atone for, but the thought quickly passed as she again recalled her constant coveting of what she could not have.

"No," he said, his tone wistful. "And prayer does not always give us the answers we seek. Though God may forgive, He does not stop the consequences of our actions."

"I sense the second story about to be told."

He smiled. "The second is simply that my father was a good king, the best of kings, but even he had his weaknesses. He was grieving the loss of a beloved wife and let his grief rob him of his ability to do his work. He fell into sin with the woman who became my mother. My father had her husband killed when he discovered she was carrying a child."

She pointed at him, a question in her eyes.

"Not me. A brother before me who died seven days after his birth. My father had lived with the guilt of his sin for many months until a prophet confronted him, and he repented and prayed and fasted, begging God to let my brother live. But God had told him the son born to them would die, and he did."

Tears filled her eyes as she recalled Azra, the daughter she had adopted years before, who had died at only five years old. "How hard that must have been for both of your parents."

Solomon nodded. "It was. But when my brother died, my father rose, washed, went to the place where the ark rested, and worshiped. He knew he could not bring my brother back. He would go to him, but my brother would not return to them. Months later, God blessed them with me and chose me to reign after my father."

"So prayer brought forgiveness but did not stop the consequences. Would a sacrifice have made a difference then?"

Solomon shook his head. "Sacrifices alone do not please our God. But a broken and contrite heart He will not despise. He forgave my father and promised to make his name great, and He kept that promise despite my father's sins. My father died knowing he was right with our God."

She nodded. "And he expected to join your brother who

had died before him. To be with your god? My people—I— could not imagine spending our afterlife with the sun or moon."

Solomon laughed again. "Nor could I. But the sun and moon are created heavenly bodies. They are not beings and they are not gods."

"I think we will have to talk more of this." She did not want to admit it, but the conversation had her questioning not only the history of her people but whether to trust this impossible, powerful god of Solomon's.

"And I will tell you then what it was like to hear Him speak to me." He pushed the food aside and stood. "But before you go, come walk with me." He extended his hand and pulled her up, placing her hand on his forearm. They stepped out of his rooms and into a large adjoining garden-like courtyard.

Her heart betrayed her yet again as she smelled his spikenard and felt the touch of her hand on his arm. How close he was, and how much a man! What kind of child would come of a union between them? But of course, they could not marry. Why was everything so utterly impossible?

"What do you covet, Nicaula?" he asked, jolting her out of her thoughts. She was not in the mood to talk of her sins to him, and she thought their discussion of his god had passed.

"Why do you ask me this?" She could not keep the hint of irritation from her voice.

Stars glittered overhead, and the leaves moved like whispers in the trees above. Perfumed flowers left their scent on the breeze, and she found even the night beauty of the place enchanting.

"I want to know why the queen of Sheba has traveled for months to visit me and has finally admitted to me that she covets something she cannot have. I know that as king I can have anything my heart desires as long as I do not break the laws of my God. Yet you are queen of a vast realm but cannot have the thing you most desire? What is it you desire, Nicaula? Is it something forbidden or something not available to you in your country? How can I help you to achieve it?" He stopped at a bench, and they sat facing each other.

She could not look at him. "It is too personal a longing," she said at last. "And no, you cannot help me achieve it." Though he could. If she could have asked him. If there had been a way for them to marry.

Yet . . . she could ask him to simply give her a child outside of marriage.

But he had just told her what his parents had suffered for adultery. She shivered. On the other hand, she was not married, so would it still be considered adultery in his god's eyes? The questions haunted her, but she knew that she, a queen, could not simply give herself to a foreign king without legal benefit. It was impossible.

He studied her for the space of too many breaths. "You want to marry." His voice was a mere whisper, his breath near her ear. "Tell me I am wrong."

She shifted away from him. He leaned back. Silence fell between them. How much should she trust him? She had not shared this desire with anyone in her kingdom.

He took her hand in his. Her pulse jumped. He trailed a line from her thumb up her arm, causing shivers to work through her. Was this how he wooed those many women he had married?

She jerked away. "You are not wrong." She stood. "And there is nothing to be done about it."

He stood as well and faced her. "There are always solutions to problems. There is always a way."

"Not always."

He cupped her face, leaned forward, and placed the slightest kiss on her cheek. "Yes, always."

He walked her back to her rooms, leaving her shaken.

CHAPTER

FORTY-FOUR

Nicaula found sleep that night nearly impossible. She paced the guest rooms while Fadia and the servants slept nearby. She had no desire to keep anyone awake, for her heart was too full to share with another. Stepping onto the balcony, she looked up at the orb of the moon. The clouds had descended, first blocking the moon, then shifting and allowing her a perfect view. How often had she stood gazing at this heavenly body and silently praying for wisdom? But none had ever come.

Her people would wonder what had happened to her if she returned with new beliefs. Some in her council might even suggest her unfit to rule over them. Could she convince them that Solomon's God was true and that years of ancient history among their people, their worship of sun and moon and stars, was not? Did she believe this enough to change her thinking?

She shivered, stepped inside to get her cloak, and slipped through the courtyard door that led to the gardens. Guest rooms rimmed the perimeter. Hers was only one of many in Solomon's vast guest palace, though the opulence did not move her quite as much as it had now that she had seen Solomon's private quarters. She sensed that the extravagance he displayed was to impress the foreign dignitaries, but she wondered if deep down he disdained it. He was a wise man if he did not allow the wealth he owned to rule him or make him long for more.

What did Solomon long for? She had not thought to ask him such a question when it was he who had probed her own longings. And was a child, a family, really the one thing she wanted most? Or was she missing something more, something deeper?

She glanced heavenward again. *Show me the truth*. It was a simple prayer not aimed at the moon. In her heart, she sensed that she meant it for Solomon's God, but she was not sure where to look to pray. Toward the temple? Should she turn and face the place where Solomon had said his God had put His name?

She moved farther into the garden until she could see a place in the wall that was not obscured by the trees. The tallest point of the temple glowed in the moonlight, and she knelt in the dirt, facing its direction. Bowing before a deity was not new to her. Even queens sought the priests' guidance and prayed for the blessings of the gods. How could she rule without their knowledge? Yet now . . .

Are You real? Will You guide me if I trust You? Do You hear the prayers of foreign rulers? I am not of Your people, nor can I be, for I must return to my own, yet I want to know You. I want my people to know You. I want the child I choose to follow after me to know You.

She stopped, listening to the stirrings of her heart. No words were spoken. She heard no voice. Had Solomon's God spoken to him in a voice that others could hear? But she sensed peace, affirmation. And suddenly she knew. This God—she could trust Him. She could believe the words of the law and stop trusting in objects in the sky that had no voice.

But how would she know His voice? How would she hear Him speak to her to tell her how to rule? To tell her how to relinquish the great desire of her heart?

She slowly stood, brushed the dirt from her robe. *I don't know how to follow You.*

The image of the scroll the scribe had read to her surfaced in her mind's eye. She could ask Solomon for a copy of the law to take with her. He would not deny her. She would learn to follow his God by the words written.

Her heart felt light, and she twirled in the moonlight like a young girl. "I will trust You," she said, her prayer taking flight. She knew it in a heartbeat, and with the knowing she realized that most of her questions were answered. She came from the Creator, her purpose was to rule Sheba by leading the people to follow His ways, and when she passed into the netherworld, she would see Him. She would not be abandoned to a place she could not understand. She would belong to the one who had made her.

She walked back to her rooms and slipped into the darkened interior. The bed beckoned her, and she curled under the covers.

But the morning brought more questions, and though the peace remained, the desire for more still lingered.

Nicaula did not see Solomon that morning, which suited her, as she still pondered the new faith she had embraced the night before. Fadia met her after the morning repast, helped her don a simple gown, and applied a spot of kohl and ochre to her face.

"Have you ever thought about the things our people believe?" She looked at Fadia through the bronze mirror as her maid twirled her hair in a set of ringlets that would rest beneath a thin veil and a golden crown.

"Believe, my queen? I'm not sure what you mean." Fadia took care to lay the veil exactly in the middle of her head.

"Faith in the gods. Do you ever question the process of the priesthood, the festivals, whether the sun and moon are truly gods?" She turned to face her maid, saw her dark cheeks flush in the morning light. "Do not fear, Fadia. I do not ask you to speak treason."

"Forgive me, my queen. It is the gods I fear most, and I do not wish to speak a word against them." She looked at her feet, and Nicaula wondered in that moment just how hard it would be to convince her people to trust a God they could not see.

"But what if the sun and moon are merely objects made by a greater God, a Creator? Wouldn't it be more right to fear Him than them?" She studied her maid's posture. She held the crown in her hands but would not meet Nicaula's gaze.

"You speak of Solomon's god. You have asked many things of him, questions you have raised all your life." She looked up then and offered Nicaula an understanding nod.

"Yes. I have spoken to Solomon and had his scribe read the words of the law to me." She looked beyond her maid a moment, not entirely sure she should trust her. But hadn't she trusted Fadia all her life? If not her, then who in her kingdom would welcome such news, such a change of heart from their queen? "I believe them, Fadia. I decided last night to trust the God of Solomon. I want to know Him, His teachings. I'm going to ask Solomon to make me a copy of the law to be read to our people." She'd said more than she'd intended, but she watched Fadia, holding her breath, hoping her maid would find the announcement pleasing.

Fadia slowly nodded. "I have heard much talk of Israel's god from the servants. They say his temple is not to be rivaled, but that no image inhabits it."

"Their God has no image. He is a Spirit whose presence inhabits the temple. He hears the people's prayers—even those of the foreigner." The thought had grown with the rising sun, and she knew deep within her it was true. *Will You help me choose a child to succeed me?* She wanted to please Him, though she still could not deny the desire to have a child of her own.

"So what will you do with the priests and the temples once we return? You know there will be those who oppose a new faith." Fadia placed the crown on Nicaula's head, and she knew her maid spoke truth.

"I will introduce things slowly. I will choose a child and teach the law first to her, and in time I will have it read to our people. Surely a God as great as Solomon's can convince the hearts of our people to believe in Him." She looked at her maid. "Do you believe in Him?" It was such a personal question she almost regretted asking it. "Do not be afraid to disagree with me, Fadia. I know I probably should not be asking." But she wanted to know.

"I am learning things that amaze me," she said. "I want

to know him. I want to believe in him, but I think it will take time."

Nicaula nodded, knowing by her maid's look that she feared offending the gods of their people, feared how their people might look upon her. And why not? They had always thought they knew the truth. But she had never seen the sun or moon perform a miracle or give her peace. She had never thought a bright round light could probe the hearts of men and women. Perhaps these thoughts alone had made her ready to hear Solomon speak.

The only question her newfound faith in Solomon's God and Solomon's wisdom could not answer was what to do with this longing for her own child. But was Solomon right? Was it possible to have what she longed for—to find a way?

Perhaps in their next meeting, she would ask him what solution he would give to her dilemma. If he was so wise, as she had seen, then how could she marry and remain in control of her kingdom? Or how could she have a child and not marry at all without offending his God?

Her mind whirled with possibilities, but she discarded them all. No answer would come to her, not even when she silently prayed. Perhaps a sacrifice was needed? But she sensed this was not like going to her priests to read omens. Solomon's God had given him wisdom. Let him dispense some of that wisdom to help answer her dilemma.

CHAPTER

FORTY-FIVE

Solomon sat at the back of one of his Egyptian chariots as his driver took him to his Palace of the Forest of Lebanon between Jerusalem and Jericho. He breathed deeply of the crisp morning air, his gaze taking in the fields and trees brimming with color and the various cities set along the path between the palaces.

Building had become his passion since the construction of the temple, his palace in Jerusalem, and Siti's palace nearby. But as he devoted resources to fortifying cities throughout his kingdom, his many wives had also required places to live and to display his power and wealth—thus his need to build another palace.

To honor his parents, however, and because most of his wives were foreigners and worshiped foreign gods, he had built the palace outside of Jerusalem and named it after the many cedars of Lebanon used in its building. He reasoned his need to keep distance between those who followed Adonai and those who did not. He could not bring himself to allow his foreign wives to live so near the temple. No. It was a temptation to want them near, but he feared the voice, the sound of God's warning ever in his ear.

The drive to the palace was one that took a good part of the morning with all of his retinue before and behind, but he needed time to think, time to deal with the questions Nicaula had posed to him. Time to decide how he could give her the one thing she coveted but refused to accept from him.

He could marry her. He was one of the few who stood as her equal, and if she would have him, he could give her a life she craved. But as that thought rolled over in his mind, he quickly discarded it. He could not place her in his harem as if she was like any princess from a foreign land. She had a kingdom to rule and must soon return to it. Marriage was impossible, for as a result she would give up her kingdom to his and Sheba would become part of Israel. Nicaula and her people would never abide such a thing.

The chariot drew closer to the hill that overlooked his sprawling palace where hundreds of his wives and concubines and their children resided. They would expect him to spend at least a week with them, and he would do it if not for the fear that Nicaula would depart Jerusalem before he could return. He would stay a few days, perhaps.

Of course, his officials would warn him of any attempt by her retinue to leave, and he could order his men to stall their departure until he returned. He couldn't neglect his entire family during her stay. And it felt inappropriate to invite Nicaula to meet all of his wives. Especially when he knew she wanted to marry one man and he had hundreds of women to satisfy his every desire.

He shook his head at the irony. Why would a kingdom

demand that their monarch remain a virgin? Adoption could be the only way to pass down the kingdom and keep it in a familial line. The idea struck him as absurd. But Sheba was not his to rule, and he had no intention of asking Nicaula to give it up.

Was it marriage she wanted most though? Or would a child suffice? He could give her a child. But not without marriage or some type of legal agreement. He would not become an adulterer and suffer the consequences that had plagued his father. And he could not make her a concubine.

The chariot pulled through the gates and into the courtyard of his Lebanon palace, and he could already see the faces of his wives and children looking down from the many windows. They would descend on him in a heartbeat, and still he had no solution to the queen's dilemma.

Perhaps the distraction of his family would suffice and an answer would rise from his time away. Surely the wisest man in the entire world could solve the desire of one woman's heart.

The Palace of the Forest of Lebanon stood three stories high, wider and longer than the temple Solomon had made for the Name of the Lord. But, he reasoned, he had followed God's exact specifications when building the temple, whereas God had not given him direction in any other building project. And Solomon needed the room in this extra palace to house his growing family.

"It is only fitting for a king," he had said when Zabud had questioned his decision to add this second palace. "Where else would you have me put the kings' daughters who are now my wives?"

Zabud rubbed his chin, glancing past Solomon as though uncertain in his response.

"Come now, my friend, you have never hesitated to speak your mind with me. I know you are longing to do so now, so speak." Solomon gave him a pointed look.

"I only wonder . . ." Zabud paused, glanced at him. "The palace already houses six hundred wives and their children, and yet I know you entertain the thought of more. This place is large enough for twice as many, and I fear . . . *Are* you planning to continue to accept the women of foreign nations here?"

Solomon walked about the roof of the palace now as the words of his friend played in his thoughts. The women who lived here were Ammonites, Moabites, Edomites, Sidonians, and Hittites. A niggling sense of guilt pricked his heart as he walked the length of the tallest roof, his guards keeping a necessary distance. *You must not marry them, because they will turn your hearts to their gods.*

But he had not allowed that to happen. Was this decree from the Lord not the very reason he had built the palace outside of Jerusalem, far from the temple?

A memory wafted to him of when he and Naamah were children and he had explained to her that Molech was not a true god. And she had believed him. If the mother of his heir could come from Ammon, what harm was there in keeping the peace through marriage alliances with these other lands as well?

"Father?"

He turned, startled at the interruption to his thoughts. Two of his older daughters, Taphath and Basemath, had climbed the stairs and found his hideaway. But then, he had never been good at evading his wives and children.

He turned to face them and smiled. "What can I do for you, my beautiful daughters?" He lifted a hand, touched their faces.

Taphath tilted her head into the palm of his hand, as she used to do as a young child. But one look at these daughters told him they were no longer children.

"We want you to seek husbands for us," Basemath said, lifting her chin. The girls were as opposite as the bright and pale colors of the sky at sunset, yet perhaps that was why they enjoyed each other's company as they did, for none among his children seemed as inseparable as they.

"Yes," Taphath said, taking a step away from Solomon. "We do not want to wilt like poor fruit on the vine."

"And there are some who find us attractive." Basemath offered her father a mischievous smile.

"No man has the right to come anywhere near you without my permission." Solomon felt his ire growing but held it in check lest he ruin this moment. Basemath had always toyed with the feelings of others, and Solomon had given her the unfortunate ability to weave her words around his heart.

"They have not come near, Father," Taphath said, casting a frown in her sister's direction. "But they are among your governors who are in charge of providing for the king's household. Such men seem worthy of marriage to a king's daughter, do you not think so?"

"You have seen these governors how?" He would need to have a discussion with his advisors and leaders about their interaction with his children. Had his men gone against his will to actually speak with his royal household?

"Do not worry, Father," Basemath said, coming close and slipping her arm through his. "Ahimaaz of Naphtali has no idea that I watch from afar when he rides the lead horse with multiple carts carrying the daily supplies. I only hate it when his month is fulfilled and I must wait an entire year to glimpse him again!"

He glanced down at her pretty, pouting mouth and laughed. "My child. You hold a desire for a man you have not met based solely on how he looks on a horse?"

Her cheeks darkened to a bright pink hue. "Taphath is no better!" She backed away from him, and he knew he had embarrassed her despite her bold countenance. "She is in love with Ben-abinadab of Naphoth-dor. He comes four months before Ahimaaz."

Solomon moved away from his daughters, assessing them. Would he ever understand the thinking of a woman? Yet these girls were just children, barely old enough to know their own minds.

Clearly not. The truth stood that if indeed he allowed their choice, his daughters would marry men they had simply seen through an open window.

"Please, Father, at least consider our requests. Did you not choose these men because they were trustworthy? Surely you would not have picked them to be your governors if they were not men of worth, men of valor." Basemath crossed her arms and met his gaze with one of challenge. Whatever was he supposed to say to such wily words?

"What have your mothers to say of this? Do they even know you have accosted me here? You know they should be the ones to speak of this to me." He couldn't keep the hint of irritation from his tone even though he admired his daughters' audacity. "And tell me—why would you wish to marry men of Israel when your mothers are foreigners?"

"You are of Israel, Father," Taphath said softly, erasing his ire. "Which makes us part of Israel too. You do not employ foreign men to lead your people, and we want to marry leaders in your kingdom. Like you."

What happened to his sense of wisdom when he spent time with his daughters? Or his wives, for that matter? They had an uncanny ability to win him over regardless of his better judgment. The niggling of his earlier memory of God's warning tickled his ears. *This is why He warned against such marriages. I am much too swayed by them.*

No he wasn't. They might get their way in some matters, but he had never once allowed them to worship their gods in his presence nor worshiped those gods with them. Siti's face came to mind, but he blinked away the image of Bastet and how her entire palace seemed like a shrine to the Egyptian goddess. That she had promised to raise their son to know his God above hers appeased him little. He had far less control of the way his foreign wives raised his children than he cared to admit.

"You are persuasive, both of you," Solomon said, looking from one daughter to the other. "I will give you this much. I will think on it, and I will speak with both men to seek their minds on the matter. Perhaps they are already wed or have an agreement with another. You cannot know about a person simply by observing them."

"You can learn things by asking about them." Basemath's smile resembled a smirk.

Solomon folded his arms over his chest. "And it seems my daughters have done just that."

They both slowly nodded.

"Ben-abinadab is not betrothed, and when he commands

his men, he speaks quietly, with authority. His men respect him, and he is kind to his horse." It was Taphath's turn to blush as she described the man she had never spoken to, only observed these past few years. How long had his daughters been of age and he had not noticed?

He held up a hand. "You need not convince me. I will speak to your mothers and to these men. If I find them acceptable, I will send word." He would promise to tell his daughters his answer himself, but he knew he could not keep such a promise. As it stood, he knew he must set his course to return to Jerusalem at dawn, despite only three days here.

"Thank you, Father!" Taphath came close and clutched his arm, resting her head on his shoulder. "But could we not return with you to Jerusalem to hear the news sooner? We long to visit the city again."

He stood there feeling the weight of indecision, sensing the grasp of his wisdom slipping away. At last he sighed and shook his head. "No. Another time I would consider it, but now is not that time." He could not tell them that Nicaula's face had not left his thoughts in spite of his pacing and his daughters' distraction. He would address their desires after he had considered the best solution to Nicaula's. He could not let this extraordinary queen leave his kingdom with even one longing unanswered.

"Soon," he said, unsuccessfully trying to push aside Nicaula's last conversation with him. "I will send word to you soon." He kissed each of their foreheads, dismissed them to return to their mothers, and resumed his conflicted pacing.

FORTY-SIX

Two weeks passed before Nicaula saw Solomon alone again. Dignitaries from foreign lands—including Hiram, king of Tyre, an old friend of King David's, she was told—seemed as drawn to Jerusalem as she. Solomon, always the obliging king, made sure his servants saw to their comfort. They ate at his elaborate table spread with stall-fed cattle, pasture-fed cattle, sheep, goats, deer, gazelles, roebucks, and all sorts of choice fowl, not to mention the vegetables, spiced olive oil, desserts, and wine in abundance. Every time she sat in the banquet hall, placed among the kings who were his visitors, she could not help but marvel. Hundreds upon hundreds of men and women filled this place. The hall itself was larger than her audience chamber back home.

Also surprising was Solomon's treatment of her as his equal, despite her title of queen. He recognized her rule, and not once did he suggest that she was merely on par with his queenly wives. It pleased her to know that she was respected here.

She spoke to one of the visiting kings sitting to her right—from Ammon, if memory served her well. He was an old man, a vassal of Solomon's, for King David had conquered his land years ago.

"King Shobi," she said, glancing at him as the servant refilled their golden wine goblets, "tell me, how long have you known King Solomon?"

Shobi turned and looked at her with a gentle smile. "I am not really a king, my queen." His humility astounded her, for he wore the simple crown of a monarch. "My brother was once king of Ammon, but he lost the kingdom to Solomon's father. My brother made some very foolish decisions."

She nodded, though she had not heard the tale. "So you have taken his place?" This man now had her interest, and she wondered what type of alliance he had with Solomon.

"My kingdom is no longer a sovereign kingdom. We are Israel's vassals, but the blow of that loss has softened since Solomon wed my daughter Naamah. She was his first wife and bore his heir, my grandson Rehoboam. So though we are less than we once were, we are acknowledged well in Solomon's eyes. Naamah has embraced Israel and their God. Her mother was an Israelite." He picked at the food on his plate. "But I'm sure that is more than you cared to know. Tell me, what causes a great queen such as yourself to travel so far to this place?"

It was her turn to study her plate. So his daughter was Solomon's wife, her son his heir. So many thoughts filled her at this news. Naamah must hold great power in his life, and yet in the time Nicaula had been here, she had heard nothing of her. She knew Solomon had many children and his heir apparent was in training at court among Solomon's advisors, but that gossip had come to her in pieces from Fadia.

She avoided Shobi's question with one of her own. "Your wife was an Israelite?"

He smiled and sipped from his cup. "You use the same tactics I've seen in Solomon, answering a question with a question. A wise way to avoid giving one the answers they seek." He gave her a knowing look.

"I was simply interested in your wife." She willed her face not to flush, grateful that the ebony hues of her skin helped hide the blush of lighter-skinned peoples. "How did you meet her? Why would an Ammonite marry an Israelite?"

He shrugged. "She was a slave in my father's house. When my brother was deposed and I was set in his place, I freed her and married her. I learned to believe in Elohim because of her."

"So Solomon's God accepts foreigners." As she had felt. As she had hoped.

He nodded. "Yes. If they repent and believe and accept His ways."

She sat in silence a moment, pondering his words. "Then I guess you have learned the answer as to why I would travel so far to see King Solomon," she said, meeting his gaze. "I had heard of his wisdom and of his God. I wanted to know both."

The conversation continued around her after that, but she was lost in thought, considering this new truth. This God was the God not only of Israel but of all who would have Him. Israel might be His chosen race, but others could be grafted in, like a gardener might graft one branch into another. Her people could carry on this faith in her land and be part of Israel, of their God, even away from Jerusalem.

Her heart felt lighter with the thought.

— ᴍ —

Nicaula left her rooms the following dawn to walk among Solomon's vast gardens. She would meet with Hadi in a few hours to plan their return trip to Sheba, and the thought saddened her, for she had yet to resolve the second greatest dilemma of her life—what to do with the desires of her heart. Would Elohim be happy with her going against the protocol of her people just because of her longing for love?

She glanced heavenward, silently praying for wisdom, but at the same time realizing with certainty that she would return to Sheba, choose a child, adopt her, and go on with her life. She would spend her days teaching her people of Solomon's God, the true God. Her God. That realization overshadowed everything, even the longing for love.

"You enjoy walking in this place."

She startled at Solomon's voice, for in all of the time she had spent in his visitors' quarters, he had come to her door only once. She had never seen him walk these gardens.

"And you do not." She turned slowly to face him, head high, fearing that he would see her heart pounding in her chest. His presence had a way of setting her emotions to flight.

He stepped closer. "That is not true. I love this place." He waved his hand to encompass the gardens before reaching for hers. "It is just that I have my own gardens closer at hand, and unfortunately, time consumes me with obligations that do not include visits here."

"But you are here now." She tilted her head, searching his gaze, feeling the strength of his hand in hers. Should she pull away? Why had he come?

"Yes." He smiled, though it held less confidence than she normally saw when he stood before his courtiers and counselors and servants and the hundreds of people who sought him daily. "I heard you are thinking of leaving."

She lifted a brow. "My servants must learn to keep their tongues from wagging."

"Were you not going to tell me?" His tone sounded almost petulant.

"Of course. I was simply planning my course for our return. We cannot overstay our welcome." She squeezed his hand, and he intertwined their fingers. She did not stop him.

"You could never overstay your welcome." He searched her face. "I have thought much on your desire, and I must admit, you pose a great dilemma."

"My desire?" She had not expected him to consider it again after their brief talk weeks before.

"To marry." His look held its own desire, and she felt a strange flutter in her middle.

"I told you before, that is impossible."

"I have thought about it from many angles." He stroked his beard and walked with her along the garden path. "If you marry, it must be to someone of your rank, which means you must marry a king. But if you did so, you would be joining your kingdom with his, and he would become the ruler of all. You would end up a queen like my wives are queens, not the leader of your people."

"Exactly why I cannot marry, unless I choose to marry an underling." She had thought of that, but those closest to her already had at least one wife. It was not as simple as she was making it sound.

"You cannot marry beneath you."

"And I cannot marry my equal."

He stopped, facing her. "You could if that man was willing to marry you and then let you go."

She stared at him. "What purpose would there be then in marriage? We would live in separate lands and never see each other." She wanted love. Not long-distance connection.

"Marriage could give you a child to take with you. The child would become your heir." He grasped her other hand, holding her hostage with his gentle grip and probing look.

"The child would also belong to his father. I could lose him to the other kingdom." She couldn't bear the thought. "It would be better to adopt a child from my people, as I did years ago."

"So you already have a child."

"She died when she was five." She looked at her feet.

Silence followed that remark. "I'm sorry," he said at last. "I did not know."

"I did not tell you."

He coaxed her gaze upward. "You have been unable to choose another child since."

She nodded, hating the sting of tears. He brushed them away with his thumb.

"I had her brought to the palace as an infant. She had the best of care, but when she took sick, there was nothing anyone could do. My advisors want me to choose another—in fact, it is all they talk about these days—but I have not been able to do so." She pulled one hand from his and tucked a loose strand of hair under the sheer veil beneath her crown. "I was actually praying to your God for wisdom. I had hoped to ask you what I should do, but I see I did not even need to."

He smiled, taking her hand again. "Come sit with me." He turned her and guided her to a bench not far from where they stood. Birds twittered above them, and the scent of lilacs permeated the air. She sat, adjusting her skirt, and he joined her. They were close. Too close for the attraction she felt for him. This was not wise. She would not give herself to him, and she could not marry him. But the sheer power of his presence held her in her seat.

"I want to tell you something." He paused, waiting for her full attention.

"I'm listening."

He nodded. "I have loved many women."

She did not flinch, for hadn't she known it from the start? "You have married often."

"Yes. I married Naamah in my youth before the throne was secure in my hands. I married Abishag to keep my brothers from trying to take her and lay claim to my throne. I married Siti to gain the city of Gezer from her father. The others have been gifts from foreign kings seeking to keep peace with me, to make alliances."

"How many wives do you have now?" Did he love them in the way she imagined love? But how could he? How could any king—any man, for that matter—truly love a woman when he shared himself with others?

He glanced beyond her. "I have not counted of late. Close to seven hundred, I'm told." He looked back at her. "I have loved a few of them in the way my father loved my mother. The others I love in different ways."

"But you call all of it love? How can your heart be so divided? Surely a woman wants undivided love." It was a bold thing to say to him, but she was not his vassal or his wife. She was simply a guest who could leave when she pleased. She could say what she wanted—a privilege of royalty she appreciated, especially since other privileges were by custom denied her.

"A woman probably does indeed want a husband who is all her own. It was our God's design from the beginning." His look was shadowed, and she wondered what thoughts went through his intelligent mind.

"Yet you do not keep your God's design?" Sometimes she found Solomon completely wise and astoundingly bright, but this attitude toward his God confused her. Did he think himself above the very laws he'd had read to her?

"Kings are sometimes forced to make decisions that are not their first choice. Surely you know this." He touched her arm. "I was given a kingdom of peace. Marriage seems the wisest way to keep that peace. Besides, our God gave the laws to kings not to marry many wives lest they turn his heart away from Him. He spoke audibly to me in a dream and offered me whatever I wished. He granted that wish and so much more. I will not betray Him by turning away from Him, when He has granted me all of this." He lifted his arm in a wide arc to encompass his kingdom.

Nicaula studied him, believing him, for he was incredibly convincing.

"But," he said, shattering her sudden trust in him, "I also have a confession."

She waited, holding his gaze. The scent of the garden flowers wrapped around them like warm perfume, and she felt bathed in the Creator's love. Such beauty He had made for them. She basked in the kiss of the sun on her cheek, but at the same time she leaned closer, longing for Solomon to share his heart.

"When I marry a woman, she joins my family. She is not free to return to her father. It is part of the agreement when we sign the treaty."

"A king's wives are a show of his wealth." It was a custom in other lands. But not in Sheba.

"And a bit of his pride," he admitted, his face flushing. "It would be like ripping me apart to let any of them leave or to turn my back on them. Once they are mine, they stay in my kingdom. Besides, for another man to claim one of my wives would be tantamount to treason."

"This is not new, Solomon. Every kingdom knows that a king's wife becomes his property. She belongs to him." She puzzled over why he chose to tell her something she already knew. "I don't see how this helps my dilemma. I think it is best that I let God have my desires and return home to adopt a child of my people to raise as heir to the kingdom. But I do appreciate all you have taught me. In fact, I would like to ask you for a copy of the scroll of the law to take with me so that I can teach God's laws to my people."

He stared at her for so long that she wondered if he had heard her.

"If that is all right with you," she added when he did not speak.

He shook himself. "The scroll? Yes, of course." He stood and paced in front of her, making her suddenly nervous. She wondered what she had said or done to bring about his agitation.

"I fear you do not understand what I am saying to you, Nicaula." He stopped in front of her and knelt.

"No, I fear I do not." Her heart picked up its pace again at the intensity in his gaze.

"I have never met someone like you, Nicaula. Every wife in my kingdom is good in her own way, but no one has your knowledge or understanding . . ."

"Or holds a rank equal to yours."

He nodded. "You have read my thoughts."

She sensed a question in his eyes. "What are you asking me, Solomon?"

"I am saying that I am willing to go against everything any king in any kingdom has done because I want to give you the thing you most desire." She saw his Adam's apple move as he swallowed. He took her hand again. "I want to marry you and give you a child."

"We've been over this. It's not possible."

"It is if we sign an agreement that we will be man and wife, but then, once you conceive and the child is safely born, I will let you go back to your kingdom. You will rule from Sheba and I will remain in Jerusalem. We will be bound by a child of our love, nothing more. I will not seek your kingdom and you will not seek mine. But I would give you the honor of my name and the freedom to remain Queen of the South. And as you asked months ago, I will keep my ships from your lands and only gain spices from you through trade and pay you a fair price for them."

She could not speak as she processed just how much he was offering her. Marriage. A child. A trade agreement. And the freedom to return to rule her kingdom without him?

"How do I know you will keep this agreement? Let us say

I took your offer and conceived. If I bear that child here, he or she would belong to Jerusalem, and I would not be guaranteed that I could return with him or her."

Was it respect or frustration she saw in his gaze? "The documents we sign would not stop you. They would guarantee you safe passage home."

She wanted to believe him, for her heart had been drawn to him from the beginning, almost as much as she had been drawn to his God.

"Why?" she said at last, for it was the only word she could pull from her jumbled mind.

"Why would I do this?"

She nodded, realizing all of a sudden how humble he looked kneeling before her, as if she was his monarch and he her subject. It made no sense.

"I want you to know what it is like to be loved." He said it as though love was something only he understood or could give. He leaned closer. "And I have come to realize that I love you, Nicaula. If you were a princess, I would seek an alliance with your father. But I can only come to you as my equal, a monarch like myself, and offer you myself. If you will have me."

He loved her? She found the concept intriguing and confusing, and she knew she could debate the meaning of love with him for weeks. But something in his manner stayed her words. And the flutter in her heart betrayed her own longings. She had respected Solomon from the moment she met him. She had looked on him with awe as she saw the way his God had blessed him. And in the secret part of her, she had imagined such a moment as this. She just did not expect it to actually take place.

Is this how You answer prayer? Or am I dreaming?

"I don't know what to say," she said at last. "I am honored and bewildered and not certain at all if this is wisdom or folly, even from the wisest man on earth."

He smiled at that and slowly stood. "But you will think on it?" He seemed anxious to be off, and she realized she needed to meet with Hadi. How the time had flown!

"I will think on it."

He turned to walk her back toward her rooms. "I will make sure you receive the scroll."

FORTY-SEVEN

Nicaula watched Solomon leave the gardens after depositing her in the guest rooms she had occupied for almost three months. After another four-month camel ride, it would be nearly a year before she returned to her kingdom. She could not possibly accept Solomon's suggestion. It would keep her away for at least another year, and traveling home with an infant could be risky.

No. It would be best to return soon and do as she had planned from the start. The thought left her feeling morose. Why could she not have the thing she longed for most? But it was foolish to keep asking the impossible.

A knock on her door pulled her attention from the window where Solomon had long since disappeared from sight. A servant ushered Hadi into the room, and she sat opposite him on the couch. She would miss all of this when she was forced to ride a camel home again. The very thought made her want to stay, but unrest would arise in her kingdom if she did not soon return.

"My queen." Hadi bowed low before sitting where she had pointed. "You wish to discuss the return trip?"

She nodded. "Yes. With all of the gifts Solomon has provided, do we have enough camels to carry everything? Are they secured enough to be hidden from thieves? Is there a quicker way to make the journey?" The last came out unexpectedly, for she was already weary of the thought of travel.

"King Solomon has provided extra camels to carry the gifts, my queen. He offered to send guards to return with us for added safety, but I think we can do well enough on our own. Unless, of course, you want me to accept his offer?" Hadi lifted a dark brow and tilted his chin in question.

She knew her general could keep her safe without Solomon's added guards. But Hadi would not refuse the king without her permission.

"If you think we are safe alone, I will trust you to kindly refuse Solomon's offer." And should she refuse his offer to her? But that was another matter entirely. "How long do you think we can stay without jeopardizing my rule? I know we will have been gone nearly a year, but . . ." She paused. Dare she ask such a question without being willing to give Hadi a reason?

He waited, watching her.

"I wondered if it would hurt matters if we stayed longer."

"Than a year? That is, a year including our travel?" She knew he had heard her correctly, but the idea clearly startled him.

"Yes. I am thinking of staying another month or two, perhaps three." If she wed Solomon and conceived quickly, she could return once the first few months of the birth sickness had passed. She did not relish traveling with an unsettled stomach.

"May I ask why?" He stroked his sparse beard, his look

confused. "We have seen Solomon's lands and heard his wisdom. Is there a reason to stay of which I'm unaware?"

She saw a hint of discouragement in his eyes, and she realized he missed his family. It was unfair to ask her guards and servants to stay away from home so long. Yet if she was to have a family of her own, was there any other way?

"I am not ready to answer your question," she said, meeting Hadi's gaze. "I do not ask this frivolously, Hadi. If we stay, it will be to satisfy a personal desire and strengthen our kingdom."

He stared at her for the briefest moment, then studied the rug beneath his feet. He was dressed as he always was in his military garb and looked uncomfortable in such plush surroundings. He shifted his position, and she knew he wanted to press her for answers.

"I will tell you this much," she said, hoping she did not regret her words. She glanced about the room, making sure they were alone. "But I must have your absolute promise of silence, for my decision is not yet made."

He nodded and placed a hand over his heart. "You have my promise." He, too, looked about them.

"Solomon has asked to marry me, to give me a child for an heir, and to secure a trade agreement with us—a promise not to invade our lands for his gain but to purchase whatever he requires from us." She released a breath, not realizing until that moment how hard the words would be to say to one of her people.

Hadi's eyes widened. "I see." He said nothing more for a lengthy pause. "And you would have his guarantee that the child would rule our lands, that you would remain our sovereign?"

She nodded, touched by his wisdom and concern for their people. "I would be breaking the customs we have set for monarchs," she said, searching his face for some reaction.

He did not look at her but studied something beyond her. "You would marry a man you could never see again?" He did look at her then, his intense gaze surprising her. "I do not know how hard it is to be in your place, my queen. But I know that I love my wife and I want to be with her often. If you do this, you give up any real chance at marital love."

"But our people want to keep me a virgin queen, Hadi. At least this way I could bear my own child." But could she? What if she was barren and never conceived? She could end up living in Jerusalem for months, maybe years.

"I cannot tell you what to do." He clasped his hands, looking submissive.

"But you can tell me if the people will accept me if I do this." She wanted him to assure her, to give his approval.

"There will be some who will accept it in time. There will be others who will feel betrayed. You risk many things if you accept the king's offer."

"And I risk a life of loneliness if I don't."

They stared at each other, saying nothing. At last she stood. "Speak of this to no one," she repeated. "I may decide it is folly. I may accept. I do not know." Was that a pleading quality in her tone? How she wished Solomon's God would give her wisdom in this!

Hadi stood and stepped slightly closer but kept a respectable distance. "I will support whatever you decide to do, my queen. And I will do all in my power to convince the people to support you."

She read the sincerity in his eyes. If he had been available and closer to her equal, she might have married him years ago. But she would not take him from a wife he loved.

"Thank you, Hadi. Your devotion is more than I deserve."

"It is the least you deserve."

She did not agree, but she walked him to the door and thanked him again just the same.

———————

She slept fitfully that night and the next and the next. She did not see Solomon again during those three days, as she had chosen to stay in seclusion. Why oh why was life so hard? If it had been hers to choose, she would have led a different life. She would have chosen the family of her birth, met and married a commoner, worked, borne him children . . . The thoughts, the anguish, would not cease.

Marriage to Solomon . . . Even his suggestion had to have taken great humility on his part, for to love her and let her go—the idea was completely unheard of and bordered on ridiculous. If he did such a thing, he could lose respect among his peers. His foreign wives could grow restless and demand things he did not wish to give. Some might send messages to their fathers to beg help in gaining more rights from Solomon, for none of them would have such privileges as she. Never mind that they did not hold the position she held. Marriage changed a person's status. Everyone in every kingdom knew it.

Why was she torturing herself with the impossible? But oh, to have a child—Solomon's child! Her mind whirled with thoughts of such pleasure.

The dark of night had invaded the sky as she paced by candlelight. Fadia had come to her twice asking to help, worry in her expression. But she could help her no more than Hadi could. This was a decision she must make alone.

She knelt beside the couch, her knees warmed by the soft wool rug, and buried her head against the cushions. *O Adonai Elohim, God of Solomon, I am but a child in my knowledge of You. I do not have wisdom to refute or accept Solomon's request. I do not know whether this would please You or dishonor You. But I want to honor You. Please, give me wisdom as You once gave to Solomon.*

She lifted her head at the sound of a soft knock on her door. No one visited so late into the night, and her servants were abed. She rose slowly and walked to the entry. A guard stood outside, but he had apparently allowed the knock. Curious, she pulled the latch and opened the door.

"Solomon." She felt suddenly weak at the sight of him. He looked as haggard as she.

He stepped into the room and shut the door, not asking permission to enter. And then, in a moment she did not expect, he took her in his arms and bent his head low, his lips brushing hers. "Say yes," he whispered against her ear. "I cannot bear for you to go without knowing . . . without granting your every wish." His touch trailed from her ear to her jaw, then he leaned in again and kissed her until she nearly melted against him.

"Solomon." Her words were breathy, her heart pounding like an unsteady drum. "I can't."

"Yes, you can. You can marry me quietly and then leave if you must, but please, Nicaula, don't say no. Let me show you my love." He sifted his fingers through her unbound hair, and she suddenly realized that she was in her nightclothes. He should not be here. This was not the way he had said it would be. She could not just give herself to him here, now.

She pushed against his chest, forcing him back a pace. "Solomon, please. Do not force your will on me. I have been thinking and praying of nothing else these three days. You must give me more time."

"There is a time for everything, Nicaula, and this is the time for love."

How convincing he sounded. How much she wanted to believe him. And suddenly she knew she could not deny him. Not when he stood there offering her everything she had ever longed for. He could give her the dignity of marriage and a child of love. And if she said no, might she lose that precious trade agreement her people expected? She could not have him bringing his ships into their ports and taking their spices without price. He had the power to do so, for they were not a warring people or as vast a kingdom.

She stared at him, searching his dark eyes, trying to read truth and motive in his expression. But all she saw was a man's desire for a woman, something she had witnessed but never experienced herself.

"Yes," she said after a lengthy pause. "I will marry you, and we will wait until I conceive a child, but then I must return to my people. Do you agree to my terms?"

He laughed, a pleasing sound, his smile gentle. "A bargain I cannot deny you for the simple pleasure of having you." He lifted a hand as if to pull her close, but she backed away.

"Not until then." Though she desperately wanted him to kiss her once more. "If you stay now, I will be tempted to do more than your God would find pleasing."

He sobered then, and she knew her words had hit their

mark. He would not displease Adonai Elohim. "At week's end then. We will plan a small ceremony at my palace, and you will stay with me until you conceive. Then you will wait three months before you travel home."

She nodded. "We will have a scribe ready the agreement, including the trade agreement, before the ceremony." If she was going to go against protocol, this would appease.

"Exactly as I promised." He smiled again. "Though not exactly, for I would keep you with me until I could bless the child on my knee."

She hadn't thought of that, or of the other birthing customs in the law of his God that she was as yet unaware of. But she would put them into practice at home. For though she hated the thought of leaving him, she was Sheba's queen first. And suddenly she realized she missed that role almost as much as she longed to marry Solomon.

He left smiling, but she still doubted.

FORTY-EIGHT

Solomon turned at the sound of his guard's voice announcing Zabud's presence. He allowed the visit and motioned to a couch for his friend to sit opposite him. "You have news for me?"

"Plans for the ceremony at week's end are going as you requested, my lord. I'm afraid keeping it quiet is not quite as easy, however."

Solomon lifted a brow. "Which wife is spreading the news?" Hadn't he known that his servants would talk and his wives would soon know?

"I do not know which wife, my lord, but news has spread all the way to the palace of Lebanon, and two of your daughters are asking to attend the occasion." Zabud's expression held a mixture of concern and chagrin.

"Taphath and Basemath." Of course they would want to come to Jerusalem. Hadn't they just pestered him to allow them to marry? And here he was taking another wife.

"Yes. But you knew this already."

"I suspected. They want to wed two of my district governors. They accosted me when I visited the palace of Lebanon
nearly three weeks ago." Solomon stroked his bearded chin.
Even then he had barely listened to the girls, his thoughts
continually taking him back to Nicaula.

"Will you allow them to come?" Zabud drew his thoughts
back to the question he preferred to avoid answering.

"I see no purpose in it," he said, leaning into the couch. "If
I allow these daughters to come, more daughters will want
to, then their mothers, then the wives here in Jerusalem. My
purpose for a private ceremony will be broken."

"I will send word then. You will consider their requests
to you though—soon?" Zabud folded his hands in his lap,
but his gaze did not waver from Solomon's.

Solomon released a sigh. Indulging his passions was
both exhilarating and draining. Coupled with building
projects and running his kingdom, it left little time to tend
to the needs of his family. He relied on servants to handle
their requests. He should never have visited the palace of
Lebanon while Nicaula remained in Jerusalem. There was
a time for everything, and this was a time to celebrate her
visit, not focus on the women who would still be there
tomorrow.

The thought left him the slightest bit morose. He had no
guarantee that he wouldn't lose one of his wives or children.
Nor did he have a guarantee of a long life, especially if he
did not obey God's commands. But he had, hadn't he? He
had honored his parents and their memory, and he did not
worship the gods his wives worshiped. Long life was not
what he had asked of God, but God had promised it to him
if he would obey.

But would God grant the same to his family? The thought of loss brought him upright and he stood, suddenly agitated.

"What is it, my lord? Did I say something to displease you?"

His friend's concern caused him to turn. "No, no." He paused. "Life is confusing, my friend. You are used to my musings by now." Solomon offered him a half smile

Zabud nodded. "Very much so, my lord. And you will have plenty of time to think about your children at a later time. In fact, if you would like, I will have their mothers and your close advisors work out the details, speak to these governors, and see if an arrangement is pleasing to you—after you have had time with your new bride." He stood as Solomon had and bowed low.

"Very good." Solomon bid him rise. "Do as you have said." He turned toward the window as Zabud left the room. Was he doing the right thing marrying Nicaula? To let her go back to her people—how could he do it? What had possessed him to think to do such a thing? That he loved her he had no doubt. But to sacrifice for love—that was a concept he had never put into action. Marriage had always been for his convenience, to promote his kingdom, to satisfy his desires.

Wasn't that exactly what he was doing now? Marrying to satisfy his lust for Sheba's queen? Or did he truly love her?

Words to the love poetry he had written with Naamah and Abishag and Siti floated through his thoughts.

How beautiful you are, my darling! Oh, how beautiful! Your eyes behind your veil are doves. Your hair is like a flock of goats descending from the hills of Gilead. Your teeth are like a flock of sheep just shorn, coming up from the washing. Each has its twin; not one of them is alone. Your lips are like a scarlet ribbon; your mouth is lovely. Your temples behind your veil are like the halves of a pomegranate. Your neck is like the tower of David, built with courses of stone; on it hang a thousand shields, all of them shields of warriors.

Was it only Nicaula's beauty that beckoned him? But no. She was intelligent, and none of his wives rivaled her. She questioned him but she also made him question. She was perfect in so many ways.

He glanced through the open window upon the hills in the distance, a view he turned to often when his thoughts grew troubling. And those thoughts had led him to this place, this realization that Nicaula was the one woman he would cherish above all others. He did love her. And he would give up his kingdom to have her if that was what it took. Though allowing her to leave him after only a few months would be far harder than giving up a mere kingdom.

But wisdom told him pride sacrificed itself for love. He hoped this kind of love was worth the risk.

FORTY-NINE

You are truly going to marry King Solomon?" Fadia's question two days later, after another sleepless night, sounded most jarring in the light of early dawn. Nicaula yawned, knowing she had spoken the words—or mumbled them in her exhausted state—but struggled to understand the shock on her servant's face.

"I said so, didn't I?" She rubbed a hand over her eyes. She had told Fadia days ago, yet her maid continued to question her. Had she truly agreed to marry the man? Memories of his knock, his kiss that still left her shaken, the desire in his eyes . . . How could she have refused him? But she had refused persuasive men for far lesser requests in times past. Was her desire for love so strong that she had no power to keep her head? This city was stealing her ability to be strong in her own right. She was awed by its beauty, awed by Solomon's power.

Perhaps too awed.

She glanced toward the window that overlooked the gardens. This trip had afforded her one thing for which she would remain forever grateful—a sense of peace in coming to understand Solomon's God. All her questions Solomon had answered. All of the things she had debated over the years—the role of their priests, the power of their deities, why they were here, who she was—seemed small now in comparison to the Creator she had come to see as real, the one she still longed to know about in greater depth.

"But how can you marry him?"

Fadia's nagging question interrupted her musings. She felt like a drunkard from so little sleep these past few nights. Was that what had caused her to give in so easily? But there was an attraction between them. Even she could not deny it.

"He asked me, Fadia. I said yes. We can marry as equals because we are. I do not have a father to arrange such a thing or to ask permission of. That's how I can marry him." Fadia's question annoyed her more than she thought it should. Why did it trouble her?

"But . . ." Fadia looked away, and Nicaula knew she would not speak again unless prompted.

"But what?" She was too tired to stop herself. If her maid could give her good cause, could talk her out of doing something foolish, was it not wise to listen?

"This is not a marriage, my queen. It is simply a man wanting a woman, and whether it is legal or not, you will be simply one of his loves. You will never have time to know him beyond these few months. What benefit is this to you?" She placed her hands on her hips as though she were Nicaula's mother instead of her servant.

But Nicaula did not reprimand her. Instead she forced her weak legs to stand and walked to the window. She looked out on the gardens awash in the pure pinks of dawn. This place was enchanting, beguiling, like its king, and she suddenly wondered why she had not seen it before.

"I came seeking wisdom, Fadia. I wanted to hear Solomon speak, to see if he was as knowledgeable as they claimed."

"And you did." Fadia stepped closer, placed a hand on her shoulder. The touch comforted as it had in her youth. "But what more can Solomon truly give you? There is no guarantee the two of you will conceive an heir. Many women take years to bear, and you know as well as I that you cannot leave your kingdom for years."

Nicaula rested a hand on the windowsill. Fadia was right. Of course she was. Solomon wanted her as he wanted all of his women, but despite his sacrifice of giving her up to her kingdom, it wasn't enough. She could not be a distant wife or a concubine. Men would lose respect for her—especially those in her kingdom. And if she bore Solomon a son, Rehoboam could think him a rival for Solomon's throne. That could bring war to their borders.

She cupped the sides of her head, unable to stop a headache from throbbing against her temples.

"Are you all right, my queen?" Fadia took her arm and led her to the couch, lifting her legs so she could lie prone. She then called for water and more pillows and hurried to pull the blinds to darken the room.

"Thank you, Fadia," she whispered when all was quiet once more. "I fear the strain of these decisions has taken a toll."

"Completely understandable, my lady." Fadia placed a pillow beneath her feet and covered her with a thin blanket. "Rest for a while. I will make sure no one disturbs you."

Nicaula closed her eyes, wishing rest was possible.

The next day her headache had fled, and she felt almost normal again. Hadi returned to her chambers, and they sent the servants, all but her own guards, from the guest rooms.

"How can I help you, my queen?" Hadi lowered his head in a bow.

"I am in a predicament," she said, twisting the belt of her robe. Even now, despite the decision she had made in the night, she did not feel at peace.

"I will do whatever you wish," he said.

"I wish I knew what that was." She looked toward the door, then back at him. "I have agreed to marry Solomon at week's end. It will buy us the trade agreement we seek and perhaps give me an heir."

He shifted from foot to foot and clasped his hands.

"I don't know if I can go through with it."

He studied her, something he rarely did. "You fear losing the trade agreement or the child?"

"I have no guarantee of a child, and I cannot stay here long enough to beget one. But if I go now and refuse him, he could refuse to sign the agreement and we could face the burden of his ships on our shores." This troubled her more now than it first did, and she wondered how she could so easily have put aside the wealth of their lands for the sake of a man she knew but a little.

"We can defend our shores, my queen."

"Solomon has many ships and more troops than we do."

He looked at her for a lengthy breath. "You do not wish to marry him but you said yes?"

"He is persuasive."

Again, he simply looked at her until she nearly squirmed. "You love him."

"I do not."

He smiled but quickly hid it. "You are at the very least attracted to him."

She nodded. That she could not deny.

"If marriage to him changes nothing but gives us this agreement we came to seek, is there harm in it? You could wed him and leave at the end of the wedding week."

"I agreed to wait until there is a child and then stay three more months."

Hadi shook his head. "That is not wise, my queen. The kingdom cannot have you away so long." He paced the room.

She sat and stared at him, praying God would give him wisdom to give her, for she was not receiving it on her own. Surely there was wisdom in counselors—even if there was only one counselor she trusted here with her.

"If you marry him and leave and have not conceived, then it is not the will of Solomon's god for you to bear his child. We would have our trade agreement, and you can return home, adopt a child, and reign as you have been. No one need know of the marriage if it is done in secret."

"Solomon had suggested we keep it quiet." She let Hadi's words roll around in her thoughts. "I would not be guaranteed an heir."

"Life carries no guarantees, my lady. Even a child born to you may not live."

Thoughts of Azra filled her mind.

"The trade agreement will ensure peace. Solomon will get something he wants from you and you will get something you want from him."

"I will feel like a pawn, like any other wife he owns."

"No other wife has the bargaining power you have. No other wife will return to rule a kingdom."

She sank back into the cushions. A trade agreement for love? Why not just purchase the agreement with the spices they had already given him? She should have insisted on it from the beginning, if she had not been so enamored with his wealth and his wisdom. But he had gifted her with much in return, so how could she possibly request such a thing when there was little but herself she could give him?

A sigh worked through her. "You are right, Hadi. We cannot stay. And I must marry him to secure our wealth and safety." Not that she thought Solomon would turn against her people, but she did not know him well. All monarchs could grow angry and spiteful at times. Even she had known such feelings.

"Perhaps his god will look kindly on you, my lady. A week is sometimes time enough." His smile told her he knew of what he spoke. But she could not imagine why Solomon's God would favor her when everything within her said she was being foolish for the sake of attraction.

FIFTY

The week flew past in a blur, but the closer the day came to their quiet ceremony, the more Nicaula questioned her own judgment. Solomon did not return to seek her out. In fact, the only time she saw him was in the banquet hall, where she sat at a different table with other dignitaries. Now and then she caught him looking her way, but his expression remained passive except for the twinkle in his eyes.

Her heart waged war within her during those days, and she could not understand why. She had been so thrilled with Solomon, with someone to confide in who faced similar trials and asked difficult riddles in response to her own. She had never met anyone like him. Why then did she feel jittery, like a bird longing to take flight?

Fadia joined her one afternoon as they walked with guards surrounding them through Jerusalem's streets. They would be leaving soon, and she wanted a taste of this city once more. Perhaps if she toured closer to King David's part of the city, she would find some sort of peace with her decision.

"I think I am making a mistake," she said without looking at her maid, knowing Fadia would hear as she kept close to her side. "I don't know how to fix it."

They wove their way through the narrow streets, avoiding the crowded market square. She glanced at their guards, grateful for their presence, though she knew no harm would come to her here. Solomon would have hung anyone who harmed a visiting foreign ambassador or king. If his people did not know her by now with her royal garb and dark skin, they would today, as she made sure to dress as a queen lest anyone think her approachable. She wanted nothing to do with strangers, only the city itself with its limestone houses and beautiful gardens.

"I wish I could give you some good advice," Fadia said, stepping closer. Nicaula looked at her maid, saw her pinched mouth and the concern in her gaze. "Is there no way to get the king to give you the trade agreement without the marriage? Can you not offer him something else?"

She shook her head. "What else? I am the only prize he favors, Fadia. To marry the virgin queen of Sheba—even with all of his wealth—he would have something no other man on earth would have. Our people would no longer allow me to remain their queen." The realization suddenly hit her full force.

All along she had imagined that she could be different than the queens who had ruled before her. She had told herself that no one need know of this marriage, and if a child came of it, she would keep him or her secret and claim to adopt the child later. Of course, if it was a boy, the line of virgin queens would be in jeopardy.

"I cannot do this." She stopped midstride and faced Fadia.

"We must return to the guest rooms and summon Hadi at once." She started walking back the way they had come, all desire for one last look at the city gone.

—⁓—

Hands clasped behind his back, Hadi stared at Nicaula as she paced.

"I was wrong. Despite my attraction to Solomon, I cannot do this to our people. I cannot go against every tradition and law of Sheba's queens, not even for love."

"But what of the trade agreement?" His words were quiet, but she heard them loud in her ears.

She stopped to face him. "I will go to the ceremony and we will sign the agreement. We will dine together, and his priest can say whatever is said at his weddings, but then you must sneak in and take me away. Have the caravan ready outside the city, and we will leave before Solomon is aware of it."

Hadi looked at her as though she had lost her mind. "He has guards, my queen. They would follow us."

"I will slip some herbs into his drink. He will sleep. His guards can be bribed." She did not question whether Solomon's God would approve of such a plan. She only knew that she could not give herself to him for one night and never see him again. No, it was far better to remain as she was, adopt a child, and live her life apart from this, from him.

"You are not thinking clearly, my queen. What if he destroys the agreement when he discovers your ruse? You would not have fulfilled your part of the bargain. He would hold it against us—against our kingdom." Hadi's dark brows nearly met above his wide nose. His thick arms strained the garment he wore, but he stood as he was, unmoving.

Nicaula sank onto one of the couches, defeated. She would either lose her peace or lose her kingdom. She could not protect her people from an invasion of the wealth of their lands if she did not do this, and she had no heir to rule in her place once they discovered she was no longer fit to be their queen.

She glanced at Hadi. In two days her life would change completely, and she had no power to stop it. Even if she tried to run, she would put everyone with her at risk of Solomon's censure and possible retaliation. But would he really harm her kingdom or her if he loved her as he said he did?

She closed her eyes. "You are right again as usual, Hadi. Nonetheless, prepare the camels for the journey home. We leave in two days."

FIFTY-ONE

The morning of her wedding dawned too quickly. She allowed Solomon's maids to treat her to special baths and ointments and cosmetics until her skin fairly glowed. She was used to such treatments, of course, but never with the anticipation of what awaited her this night. Her initial fears had subsided, and she had convinced herself that she would either talk Solomon out of consummating their union or keep the secret from her people. She saw no other way to protect her lands.

She faced the fact that she had still not decided which one of these two options she wanted more, for her heart betrayed her at every turn. Solomon had been to visit her the night before, and this time when he kissed her, she was not sure she could ever leave him. She found her tongue too loose, and she definitely said more than she should have.

"I'm leaving for Sheba the day after tomorrow," she'd said after his breathy kiss nearly pulled all strength from her.

He backed away a step, looking her up and down. "That

was not our agreement." She could see in his eyes that he knew she spoke truth. He was not happy.

"Not originally, no." She crossed her arms over her chest, protecting her heart. "But I cannot stay away from my people any longer. I came for a trade agreement and to hear your wisdom—"

"And to test me with difficult questions."

She smiled. "That too."

"So you have gotten all that you came for, and now you will leave me." There was hurt in his tone.

"I have not yet secured our trade agreement." She looked at him, watching, waiting.

"You would like this agreement without the marriage. So you no longer desire love?" He took a step closer.

She felt his breath against her cheek. "I did not say that."

"You did not have to. I can see it in your eyes." He stroked his beard a moment, then touched her forehead. "What are you afraid of, Nicaula?"

She looked at him, felt his fingers slowly cupping her cheek, saw the intimate longing in his dark, probing eyes. Her limbs turned to liquid, useless to prevent his soft caress. "I am afraid of losing my kingdom for the price of securing fair trade. I have nothing to give you that you do not already have. You—me—we are in a dilemma I cannot sort out, and I know that when I return, if the truth is exposed that I am no longer their virgin queen, I will lose my crown."

She spoke the words honestly, without flinching, all the while losing herself to the way his arms came around her and he held her against his beating heart. They stood there for many moments, neither of them speaking.

"I will sign the trade agreement," he said at last. "You do not have to marry me."

She leaned back, searching his face. "You mean it."

"I would not say so if I didn't."

"What gain is there to you then?" He would give her all she asked with nothing in return?

"The knowledge that I helped you achieve your desire. If this is your desire, then that is what I will give." His smile was sad. "But I will admit, I wish the dilemma was not so hard for you. I would give you the love of family. And if I am perfectly honest, I would keep you with me to rule at my side." He tucked a strand of hair behind her ear. "I fear I am in love with you, Nicaula. But sometimes love is not enough. Sometimes one must let go of those they love."

"You would do that for me?" No one had ever done something so sacrificial for her, and she had a hard time believing him.

"Yes." He intertwined his hand with hers. "If that is what you want."

The memory of that conversation surfaced now as she waited for the evening ceremony. In the end, she could not refuse him because she could not deny her own desire. It was unseemly for her to accept all from him and offer nothing in return. She could not ask him to give to her freely.

The wedding would take place in only a few hours. She told herself she was ready.

—⟶⟵—

The small audience hall in Solomon's palace could not compare to the one in his judgment hall, where he dispensed wisdom and tried cases. It was more like an antechamber or a small banquet room, where a canopy had been raised in the center and a few of his servants stood as attendants. A priest in the garb of white tunic and breastplate of jewels stood before a table where the marriage papers and the trade agreement lay side by side. A small bowl of soft clay sat between them.

Solomon lifted his hand, removed his signet ring, dipped it into the clay, and placed his seal on the trade agreement. Nicaula followed his pattern and did the same. They looked at each other a moment.

"There is no need to continue, Nicaula," Solomon said as a servant rolled the parchment and more seals were placed along the folds. The trade agreement was secure. He had seen to it first. She did not have to sign the marriage papers.

"I will listen to the words read," she said softly, turning to face the priest. The marriage agreement secured her right to rule and ensured that any child she might bear would remain hers alone. Solomon relinquished all parental and marital rights to her.

As the last words were said, she felt a stirring in her middle. She felt ill at the farce this marriage would be. She sounded like a selfish child, demanding that all rights remain hers, giving him nothing but her body for one night. She placed a hand to her stomach and faced Solomon once more.

"This is not right." She spoke softly, though she knew the priest could hear.

"It is completely right. It is my gift to you." He took her hand and squeezed her cold fingers. He leaned close. "I want you, Nicaula. And this does not have to be the end. I can travel to visit your kingdom, and perhaps one day you can again visit mine."

"You know that is not likely to ever happen."

"We do not know the future."

He took his ring again and affixed his seal to the parchment. All they needed was her signet ring to do the same and they would be man and wife. At least in the eyes of his God, for no one else but the priest and a few servants witnessed this.

He held one of her hands, then reached for the other and gently pulled the ring from her finger. Their gazes held as he dipped the ring into the clay and pressed the seal next to his.

He handed the ring to a servant, who quickly wiped all traces of the clay from it and handed it back to Solomon. He placed it once more on her finger. Her heart pounded at his touch. He had given her so much, and in his giving he had wooed her and won her with nary a protest on her part. She had allowed him to seal their marriage. She had not curled her fingers tightly against his intent. She had watched every step and said nothing.

"So it is done," the priest said, jarring her from her thoughts. "In the sight of Almighty God, may your union be blessed, and your children after you."

He left them then, and the servants and guards fell into their usual places as Solomon escorted her down a long hall to his private chambers. Her palm grew moist beneath his warm hand, and she felt a sense of disbelief mingle with a heightened awareness of him. His spikenard wafted to her, a pleasing aroma, and as they entered his rooms, leaving the guards and servants behind, he ushered her to his couch and sat at her side.

His kiss tasted sweet, like the finest dates she had enjoyed at his banquets. "You are most beautiful, Nicaula."

He kissed her again before she could respond, and his hands slowly removed her crown and veil. "How delightful is your love, my sister, my bride! How much more pleasing is your love than wine, and the fragrance of your perfume more than any spice." He pulled the jeweled combs from her dark hair. "Your lips drop sweetness as the honeycomb, my bride. Milk and honey are under your tongue. The fragrance of your garments is like the fragrance of Lebanon."

She recognized the cadence of poetry in his words, songs sung and words spoken at weddings from Egypt to Israel.

"Dark am I, yet lovely," she said, joining him with a few of the words she could recall. "Dark like the tents of Kedar, like the tent curtains of Solomon."

"You are a garden locked up, my sister, my bride. You are a spring enclosed, a sealed fountain. Your plants are an orchard of pomegranates with choice fruits, with henna and nard and saffron, with calamus and cinnamon, with every kind of incense tree, with myrrh and aloes and all the finest spices." He lifted her in his arms, his words spent with kisses, and carried her to his bed, which was dripping in the scents of some of the very spices he had named. Spices that had come from her lands.

Spices that covered all the doubts she had left.

FIFTY-TWO

Nicaula awakened to Solomon's bare arm stretched across her, the two of them tangled in the finest linen bedsheets she had ever known. "You must send me your best artisans and bundles of flax. I simply must have a bed as soft as this."

He leaned up on one elbow, smiling down at her. "I think I can grant this one small request." He traced her face with his fingers and bent to kiss her again. "But can you grant me mine?"

It was her turn to shift and rise up to face him. "Anything," she said too quickly. "I will give you whatever is within my power to do."

By his look she suddenly realized how foolish her words were, for she had gone to great lengths to keep what she had. Now after one night with this king she was willing to risk everything? But of course, what was written and sealed could not be changed with a rash comment.

"Stay." His face held such earnest desire that she wanted to give in to him. But Hadi would be waiting with the caravan near the armory, and they would leave Jerusalem behind in only a few hours' time.

"I can't."

"You said anything." His possessive touch was impossible to resist.

"I was not thinking straight."

"Nevertheless, you gave your word." He pulled her close, and she did not want to leave.

"For how long? My men are waiting and ready to leave."

"They will wait willingly." He looked at her as though he knew more than he ought to about her own retinue.

"What have you done?" She sensed she had somehow lost the power to do as she pleased. Had she missed something in the reading of the marriage ketubah?

He kissed her thoroughly, making her long for him again.

"Tell me." She tried her best to be insistent. She could not let him break their agreement.

"I simply warned your general that you might need a few extra days." He stroked her hair. "Were you really going to run off before the end of our wedding week?"

"You knew it was my plan." Her stomach growled as the sun peeked through the bed curtains.

He laughed at the sound. "You are hungry. Come."

He led her to a table servants had spread with dates and cheeses of many varieties from cattle, goats, and sheep. They dipped bread in sauces made with dates and nuts, and he fed her as though she were a child. Her heart yearned for him, longed to give him exactly what he asked—to stay not only for a few days but for weeks, months, years. She wished in that moment to never leave his side.

"For a few more days," she said when he placed the last date on her tongue. "I will finish the wedding week, but then I cannot stay." She couldn't. She must make sure he did not persuade her again.

By the look in his eyes, she knew he had won a victory that she suspected he always intended to win, one that would give him what he had wanted all along. Her.

She only wished she could have let him keep her.

Each one of those seven days at Solomon's side was as though she had stepped into a dream. They did not leave his rooms except to walk among the gardens at sunset, and she had not known how many ways he could show his love for her. Words came from his lips as though he had spent months crafting them, and at night he sang to her, wooing her with love far stronger than any of the heady spices that burned from incense holders in his rooms.

By week's end he tried once more to get her to stay. "One more week," he said in that same enchanting tone. When she refused too many times, his look grew petulant, then sad. He did not grow angry, though he did try as many ways to entice her as he had when he'd proven his devotion to her, to all that she was.

"I cannot. This time you cannot change my mind, Solomon. I will lose my kingdom." The chance remained that it was already lost by her heedless actions.

"I will miss you," he said at last, walking with her to the door of his chambers. They had dressed in royal garb, a king and queen ready to travel from his palace to his armory, where her large retinue waited.

"And I, you." She took his hand and kissed his fingers to show she meant it.

She faced him then, before the door opened upon the world and they returned to separate lives. She blinked back unexpected tears as she searched his handsome face. "Love is far different than I expected. You shared more of your heart with me than I had thought possible, than I thought you would. I am honored by your trust."

"I have never before married a woman my equal, nor trusted one to keep my words close to her heart."

They had talked of many things during their week together, of hopes and dreams, of riddles even he struggled to understand. He had confided that sometimes he thought of life's futility. At first his statement had surprised her, but then she realized that though he had heard his God speak, it was not the same as walking with a friend day by day. In the quiet, when God was silent, doubts could plague any man.

"Your words are safe with me," she promised, leaning close to kiss him one last time.

He held her as though he would not release her, but at last they parted and opened the door, walking in silence through the corridors toward his waiting carriage that would take them the rest of the way.

He took her hand and helped her up, then joined her of his own accord. His driver headed out slowly, and she thought Solomon would speak to her again, beg her one last time to stay. But he waved instead to the crowds, and she did the same. They were a king and a queen of separate nations, pleasing the people they served.

It was time she returned to her lands to do just that.

FIFTY-THREE

Solomon stood in his chariot until Nicaula's caravan could no longer be seen, disappearing through the city gate. He could return to his palace and watch from the rooftop until the last camel made it through the Kidron Valley and onto the King's Highway headed south, but he could not bring himself to watch her fade from view so completely.

He turned at last and headed to the judgment hall. To work. To forget. There was a time for everything, and this was not the time to mourn, though his heart told him otherwise. What had he done?

He entered the hall behind his standard-bearers and took the steps to his gilded throne. His secretary brought a case of a labor dispute before him, then another of brothers who could not agree on whether to forgive a neighbor's debt. Men lined the hall, waiting for a turn to speak with him, and he heard each complaint through a mild sense of disillusionment. What did any of this matter now without Nicaula?

Ambassadors from foreign lands approached with more

wishes for peace agreements, princesses waiting to be accepted into his harem. His head spun as though he had indulged in too much drink.

Zabud appeared from his right, and Solomon turned and motioned him closer. "Tell me you have a perfect excuse to allow me to escape this madness."

Zabud smiled. "Perhaps an excuse, though it may not be perfect. You asked me to handle the situation with your daughters and your governors, and the governors are here requesting an audience with you. That is, if you are up to questioning them regarding marriage to your daughters."

"It is better than discussing marriage to twenty more princesses." He ignored the nagging thought at the back of his mind that he was likely going to offend these visiting nations by slipping away before entertaining their requests. "Lead me to them." He stood abruptly, dismissing the waiting men for the rest of the day, and followed Zabud to an anteroom where two of his governors, Ben-abinadab and Ahimaaz, waited. They bowed at his entrance.

He took a seat on a smaller throne and bid them rise. "Thank you for coming," he said, looking each man up and down. He rarely met with his governors, only their superior commander, Azariah. Once the initial men had been picked from each district, that was the last of his contact with them except in a general meeting of all leaders. "I will assume by your presence that you are aware of why you have been summoned."

Each man nodded. "Yes, my lord," they said in turn.

"It seems," Solomon continued, stroking the arm of the throne, "that my daughters find you pleasing. Of course, I have seen to it that you are acceptable men to wed them." He watched their expressions. It was a father's duty to protect his daughters, unlike his own father had done with his half sister Tamar, though David had been duped in that sad situation. Still, Solomon reasoned, hadn't God given him wisdom to discern? Was not now a perfect time to use that wisdom?

"Are each of you willing to enter the royal family, to stay true to only one wife, my daughter, and to serve me faithfully the rest of your days?" He leaned into the chair and looked first at Ben-abinadab.

"Yes, my lord. I would find it a great honor to marry your daughter Taphath. She would remain my only wife as long as I live, and nothing could cause me to ever be unfaithful to your kingdom, to you." He bowed again, and Ahimaaz said similar words.

"Good," Solomon said at last. "We will have the agreements drawn and you will be notified when the weddings are to take place." He would let the girls' mothers make the arrangements, as he knew he would hear no end of complaints if he allowed servants to handle such things.

The men soon left him alone with his guards and Zabud. He looked at his friend. "This is the first time." He glanced beyond Zabud and could not get Nicaula's face from his mind.

"The first time, my lord?" Though Zabud surely knew of what he spoke, he sensed his friend's prodding. Was it so obvious that he was feeling lost and morose this day?

"They are the first daughters to wed. I have daughters old enough to marry, and yet nations still bring me their king's daughters to enter my harem. What am I to do with all of them, Zabud? What does it matter anymore?" He heard the petulant tone in his voice and realized in an instant that he wanted to hide in his rooms and weep. But he held the emotion in check.

"You already have seven hundred wives, my lord, and nearly one hundred concubines." Zabud paced before him, but Solomon paid his actions no mind.

"So why not simply accept more? I will never get Nicaula to return. Perhaps I will find someone new to challenge me as she did." Though saying such a ludicrous thing out loud nearly made him laugh.

"It is your decision, of course," Zabud said slowly, stopping to face Solomon. "But Adonai, blessed be He, would likely say you already have too many."

It was an audacious thing to say to a king, and Solomon stared at his friend, advisor, and priest. Was he right? Had Solomon offended Adonai with his many wives? His wisdom had not stopped him from each decision to marry, and he had not worshiped their gods, but neither had he heard God speak again on the matter since he had dedicated the temple.

As for you, if you walk before Me faithfully with integrity of heart and uprightness, as David your father did, and do all I command and observe My decrees and laws, I will establish your royal throne over Israel forever, as I promised David your father when I said, "You shall never fail to have a successor on the throne of Israel."

But if you or your descendants turn away from Me and do not observe the commands and decrees I have given you and go off to serve other gods and worship them, then I will cut off Israel from the land I have given them and will reject this temple I have consecrated for My Name.

"I have not worshiped their gods, Zabud. Wisdom tells

me that this was the main reason our God told kings not to marry foreign wives."

"Or many women at all. As you just commanded your governors to stay true to your daughters, our God would wish the same for their king, my lord. You know this." Zabud clasped his hands in a gesture of entreaty.

Solomon felt the heat of anger rise within him but again held his emotions in check. *You do know it*. But he ignored his annoying conscience.

"That will be all, Zabud. I will think on your words." He rose and descended the steps, then left the room without a single glance back at his friend. He needed time to breathe, to think, to do what he had told himself he did not need—to mourn. It *was* the time to mourn Nicaula's loss.

As he entered his chambers and sent everyone from the room, he stood at the window looking toward the distant hills, a silent tear slipping down his cheek. He would never get over her. In that moment, he realized that he had made the worst decision of his life in marrying her. Marrying her and letting her go.

A year passed and Solomon heard nothing from Nicaula—no word of a child. Had she conceived and given birth but thought it unnecessary to tell him the news? Or had she been as so many women and not conceived in their short time together? She would be completely free of him in such a case. Or if she had died in childbirth, surely he would have heard.

In time he did hear from his ships' captains that Nicaula had a son named Menelik, and it was said that she had been teaching her people the ways of Adonai. So their time together had not been wasted after all. Was Menelik his son?

Pride and despair in not knowing for certain mingled equally in his heart, and despite Zabud's continual advice to the contrary, Solomon indulged his passions with zeal. After his daughters wed, he accepted two hundred more concubines. His workmen could not build rooms for them quickly enough, and the Palace in the Forest of Lebanon grew.

But despite his search for a woman as pleasing as Nicaula, he did not meet one who matched her in spirit, in intelligence. And none were his equal, for no other land boasted a queen as its sole ruler, nor would such a queen want to give her lands to him. He knew because he had spent years and much wealth sending men to seek such a woman.

Solomon sat behind his chariot driver and felt the wind in his face as the man led his retinue to inspect each of his building projects. Spring had brought the almond trees to bud, and flowers dotted the fields in a colorful rainbow display. Nicaula would have loved the sight.

He caught a glimpse of the new construction to a shrine he had allowed some of his wives to build. How could he deny them when they pleaded continuously for a place to worship Chemosh, Molech, Ashtoreth, and more? The guilt he had felt at first no longer plagued him, as he told himself they were worshiping what they knew while he remained true to Adonai. He saw no danger in indulging them as he had Siti those many years ago.

If only they had all been as Naamah, Abishag, and Nicaula and accepted Adonai as the only God. But he had known of the risk when he loved many women. If the truth were known, he wasn't sure he cared anymore.

The chariot passed by the high place east of Jerusalem and moved in a circle back toward his city, where the temple shone like a living thing from this distance. His own palace held much less glory in comparison to the amount of gold he had poured into making the Lord's temple the centerpiece of Jerusalem. As it should be.

It did not matter that he was allowing these other shrines, for they could never outshine the Lord's glory nor Solomon's own devotion to his God. No matter what the future held, even in his lingering grief over Nicaula, one thing would never change. His love for Adonai. Of that he was very sure.

Postlude

The Teacher lifted a shaky hand from the scroll in the small room where he penned his thoughts, crafted his poetry, created his songs and proverbs and books. So many books about the many things wisdom had taught him.

Wisdom. The very gift he had been granted now mocked him as he laid the pen aside and sifted a hand through his graying hair.

Meaningless. The word stared up at him, carrying the weight of his life in that one thought. How had he allowed the great gift of wisdom to become more important than the one who had given it? How proud he had been! How certain that his wisdom would keep him from falling, from disobeying, from worshiping any other than the true God.

All the wisdom in the world had not kept him from becoming the greatest of fools.

Your kingdom will be torn from the hand of your son, God had told him after his heart had grown cold. He'd felt remorse then, which had lifted only slightly when Menelik came to visit and he could teach Nicaula's son the ways of

Adonai. But the young man's visit left a hole bigger than Nicaula's loss the moment he'd left Jerusalem.

Remember your Creator in the days of your youth, before the days of trouble come and the years approach when you will say, "I find no pleasure in them."

Those years had come the moment Menelik left and had increased when God spoke the third and last time to him. Rehoboam would not rule a kingdom as large as his. The glory and splendor of the wisest king on earth was soon to end, and his heart could beat with only one word.

Meaningless.

He stared at the pages, blotted with his final words of wisdom for his sons, should they care to read them. He had always been the Teacher. He had loved that role more than being a king. If only that role had satisfied him.

Not even the books that lined these shelves brought the joy they once did. *Of making many books there is no end, and much study wearies the body.*

How was it possible that he could have lost his first love of Adonai and fallen so far? Was temptation so subtle that even wisdom could not win over it? How then did a man remain righteous as his father was said to have been? His father had sinned grievously, yet Adonai had forgiven him.

Life would not be meaningless if he could have lived as his father. If he had obeyed as God commanded. If he had heeded his own wisdom.

No. God's wisdom. Not his. He had squandered the gift.

The thought caused him to rise and move from the seat that had grown tiresome, and he walked with effort through the halls of his palace. His servants still obeyed his word, but he sensed that everyone knew life had shifted dramatically. For the first time in his reign, he had lost his peaceful kingdom. All because he had given in to his foreign wives and worshiped what was forbidden.

Because of his grief in losing what he had once willingly sacrificed.

Meaningless. Even sacrifice. Even love.

He stepped into the courtyard garden and listened to the birds sing the song of eventide in the trees. Perhaps love was not meaningless, he reasoned, recalling Menelik's visit and the beauty of his mother's love. And God had a purpose in all things, whether he understood it or not. Fearing God mattered most. This was the conclusion he should have learned long ago.

The Teacher knelt slowly in the dirt, tears filling his aging eyes, and lifted his gaze heavenward. *Forgive me.* Then he bowed low, heart humbled, and worshiped.

Note to the Reader

King Solomon, in my opinion, was a man of vast mystery, a complicated and sometimes tormented soul. While this series of ebooks-turned-print is about the women Solomon loved, we cannot know the women without understanding the man who loved them.

Scripture gives very little information about these four women who graced Solomon's life. We know that Naamah was likely his first wife and mother of his heir. We also know that she was from the country of Ammon. Beyond that, little is known.

Abishag has more page time in Scripture due to her relationship to King David and the drama of Adonijah's desire to marry her after David's death. As for her eventual marriage to Solomon, this is speculation, though at the very least she likely remained part of his harem. Her relationship to Solomon was a crucial part of his rule, and Adonijah's request was treasonous, as I portrayed in the story.

Siti is the fictional name of Solomon's Egyptian wife. We

know almost nothing of her except that she was given a palace of her own and that Solomon gained the city of Gezer in marrying her. Her mention and Solomon's infatuation with Egyptian horses and chariots helped me understand his character—especially since God had warned kings not to do exactly what Solomon did.

The queen of Sheba is the only one of these women whom Scripture speaks of in both the Old and New Testaments. Her mystery and the tale of her visit to Solomon have been spoken of in legends from Ethiopia to Arabia. There is debate as to the area where she ruled, so I chose to combine the two regions under her leadership, as they're near each other, at least on the maps I could find. Whether she and Solomon had a son named Menelik is a tale straight from Ethiopia. If you read the ebook *The Queen of Sheba*, you will see that I do not ascribe this son to Solomon, though we cannot know for certain.

In the end, this story of Solomon's many loves is really a story of Solomon and his relationship to his God. The wisest man who walked the Old Testament paths and rode in royal splendor throughout a vast kingdom still fell away from truth, from obedience to all God had asked of him. He let passion rule him and learned to trust the gift instead of the giver. How easily we do the same! Ecclesiastes is equally a poignant, sad, and hopeful book, because at the end of all things, when we face our lives and can only look back, we will see the places where we succeeded and where we failed.

Solomon was missing the understanding of the future grace that would come in the person of Israel's Messiah and spent many pages writing words of despair. But in the end, he came to realize that even amid our failures, life isn't meaningless but can have great purpose if we fear God and keep His Word. May we learn to do just that.

In His Grace,
Jill Eileen Smith

Acknowledgments

As with every book I write, there would be no book without the help of so many fine people to lend their expertise along the way. So a huge thank-you again goes to Lonnie Hull DuPont, editor, animal lover, and friend. Thank you for catching the things I get wrong and for cheering me along the way. The laughter and cat stories we've shared are wonderful memories.

Jessica English—I will always love your editorial style. Thanks for fixing my mistakes and making it a pleasure to edit.

Michele Misiak, Karen Steele, Gayle Raymer, and the team at Revell—thank you for all you do. You make the work a joy!

Wendy Lawton—thank you for being there for me, both as an agent and as a friend. You are always the encourager and I appreciate you.

Jill Stengl—thank you for looking at this series from the very beginning and making me believe I could actually accomplish the work. You are a true friend.

To my dear friends—what would a book be without you

to do life with along the way? My life is richer for having known you all.

Randy—the things we've faced in this life together have made me love you more each day. Forty years and counting, yet not one day would I take for granted. I love you always.

To my beloved children and granddaughter. I love each one of you—and I always will.

Thank you, Adonai Eloheynu, O Lord our God, for who You are. For showing us through Solomon's writings that life is not meaningless but has great purpose in You.

Jill Eileen Smith is the bestselling, award-winning author of the Wives of King David, the Wives of the Patriarchs, the Daughters of the Promised Land, and the Loves of King Solomon series. Her research has taken her from the Bible to Israel, and she particularly enjoys learning how women lived in Old Testament times.

When she isn't writing, she loves to spend time with her family and friends, read stories that take her away, ride her bike to the park, snag date nights with her hubby, try out new restaurants, or play with her lovable, "helpful" cat, Tiger. Jill lives with her family in southeast Michigan.

Contact Jill through email (jill@jilleileensmith.com), her website (www.jilleileensmith.com), Facebook (www.facebook.com/jilleileensmith), Twitter (www.twitter.com/JillEileenSmith), Instagram (www.instagram.com/jilleileensmith/), or Pinterest (www.pinterest.com/JillEileenSmith/).

Meet

Jill Eileen Smith

at **www.JillEileenSmith.com** to learn interesting facts and read her blog!

Connect with her on

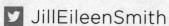 Jill Eileen Smith

JillEileenSmith

ONLY GOD CAN HEAL OUR HEARTS

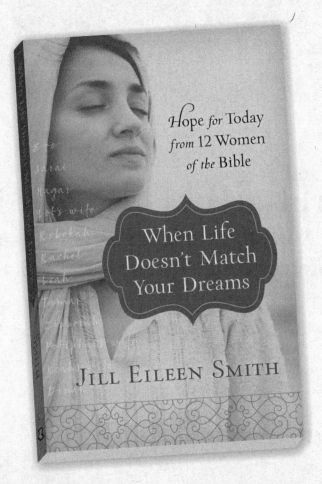

Hope *for* Today *from* 12 Women *of the* Bible

When Life Doesn't Match Your Dreams

JILL EILEEN SMITH

Bestselling author Jill Eileen Smith connects the hardships of twelve Old Testament women with our lives today to show readers that only God, not time, can heal our hearts' broken desires and dreams.

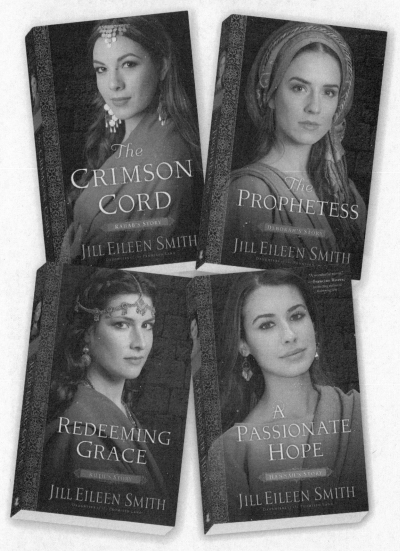

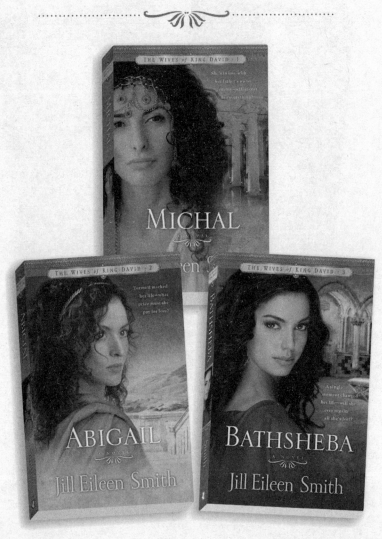

JILL EILEEN SMITH
Brings the Bible to Life

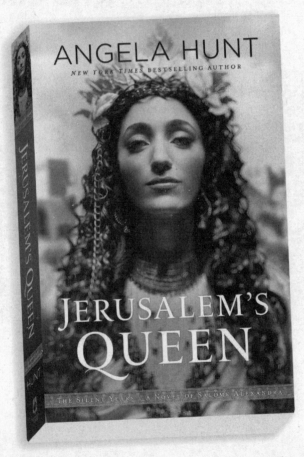